FILE UNDER FATHERS

Geraldine Wall

Books in this series:

In memory of my father, James, with gratitude and love.

4

'The web of our life is a mingled yarn, good and ill together.'

All's Well That Ends Well by William Shakespeare
Act 4 scene iii

1

'No,' Anna said, 'no, I won't do it. I can't believe you're even asking me.'

Ted made smoothing motions with his hands, moving them from side to side like a blind person feeling for something to grab in the darkness. 'It's not what you think – *he's* not what you think.' Sweat was breaking out on his upper lip under his moustache making the bristles send out tiny flashes like something metallic in a microwave under the harsh fluorescent light of his office. He took a half-step towards Anna and then, noting her fierce expression, rapidly took a half-step back.

Anna stood facing him with her arms folded and legs braced as though she was the one who was to be placed in danger, not the girl. Unknown to Ted (how could he know?) images were whirling in her brain that were the stuff of nightmares. But these were memories not dreams, memories of the crunch of a knee in her back, a fist cracking on her head.

'Good God, Anna, you're shaking. Sit down.' He steered her towards the comfortable Important Client chair and half pushed her into it. 'Do you want some water?'

She breathed deeply and the patchy red mist cleared from her vision and her heartbeat slowed. 'No thanks, Ted. I'm ok.' She looked up at his alarmed face. 'Just don't ask me to find the daughter of a murderer who is coming up for parole.'

Relieved that she was more her normal self, Ted leaned his cushiony backside against his desk and scratched at his chin. 'Put like that,' he said, blinking at the carpet, 'put like that, I can see what you're thinking but this is no ordinary murderer.'

'Define "ordinary murderer",' Anna instructed icily.

In the tense pause that followed they both turned their heads and stared out of the window at the top storey of the library just visible on the skyline, its golden funnel gleaming bravely in the weak February sun, a dry-dock ship dreaming of oceans. Since she had come to work for Harts Heir Hunters over five years ago Anna had done her share of the ordinary bread-and-butter cases, the ones which paid the overheads on the smartly renovated offices of Harts that edged the canal bank of the city centre and had once held freight bound for London, Bristol, and all points north. But along with the probate work and Treasury List there were less mundane cases and Ted had sometimes turned to her to take them. Flattery and cajolery had been dropped long ago in the light of her cynical gaze when presented with another 'interesting' case so now he just gave her the facts and waited. Usually she did accept, sometimes she didn't. There were, after all, other, more experienced genealogists than herself working for the company.

'And don't give it to anyone else, either, Ted,' she warned, breaking the silence. 'This is high-risk and it could explode the reputation of Harts if it blows up on you.'

'Mm,' said Ted. He glanced at his watch and moved back behind his desk. 'Maybe have a think, eh? We'll talk again. I didn't get a chance to, um. I have to go now.' He was looking anxiously round the office, his forehead creased like a bloodhound scenting an escaped rabbit.

Anna stood up and moved to the door. 'If you're looking for your green sports bag,' she said, 'Josie's got it in Reception. You left it in the loo apparently.' Ted loved his sports bag. Anna suspected that just holding it made him feel taut and toned. She empathised with him. She had once felt the same about holding climbing gear but that had very quickly worn off given real slippery rocks and impossible overhangs to say nothing of shamefully trembling legs.

'So why didn't she bring it up?' Ted demanded, back to his usual ebullience.

Anna shrugged and closed the door behind her before walking slowly down the corridor to the general office where her own desk was. She had not wanted Ted to see it but she was still shaken by the images that had assaulted her when he had announced the assignment. She thought she had laid them to rest months ago or, at least, the power of them to rock her. Surely he was mad to take on this case? Was he really so unaware of the potential for violence? How could a murderer not be a violent person? But then, of course, she remembered Briony. That had been manslaughter by any court's definition and only that huge miscarriage of justice in the Chicago courts had labelled it murder.

But in this case, Robert Johnson's, there was no doubt. He had been sentenced to life imprisonment for murdering his mother's boyfriend with a kitchen knife when he was nineteen years old. There had been twelve stab wounds. He had pleaded guilty. Now Ted wanted Anna to find the daughter he had last seen as a baby who would now be roughly the same age as he had been when he threw away his freedom. Fat chance.

Briony. Anna sighed as she wove her way through the desks towards her own. Two images thrust themselves into her head almost simultaneously - Briony screaming abuse at her through the filthy glass of the visitors' room of Cook County Jail in Chicago, her hair in rats tails, her skin gleaming grey with sweat and lack of sunlight, and Briony as she had seen her a week ago when she met her with Kimi to celebrate her thirtieth birthday in an upmarket French restaurant in Brindley Place. Now Briony's expensively cut and styled blonde hair hung in a perfect curve around her sharp bones and eyes the colour of shadows in icebergs. That night she was wearing, Anna had noted with envy, a heavy silk oyster-coloured suit which didn't wrinkle like Anna's only silk shirt did but instead clung and skimmed in all the right places. She had tiny pearls in her ears and a fine gold chain round her neck and looked every inch what she now was, a highly-paid criminal lawyer doing very, very well.

Briony had clearly bullied Kimi into scrubbing up for that meal. It wasn't that Kimi was less attractive than Briony, in fact she was, in her own way, quite striking - it was that she was totally uninterested in her appearance. When Anna visited them at the farm Kimi would inevitably be in jeans and a shapeless top reeking of horses. For work at the family firm she kept three identical black suits hanging in a wardrobe (one to wear, one to have cleaned and one spare she had told Anna triumphantly) next to five white cotton blouses together with two pairs of low-heeled black shoes. That way she didn't have to think about it, especially since her house-keeper, Linda, did the ferrying to the dry cleaners, the laundering of the white shirts and the daily polishing of the black shoes. In any case, anyone meeting Kimi for the first time would notice nothing about her appearance except the extraordinary eruption of coils of hair surging from her scalp like Medusa's snakes. She even had the glare to go with the hair-do. When provoked Kimi would be quite capable of turning strong men to stone - Anna had seen her do it.

Anna sat at her desk and eyed the pile of 'to do' notes on it. It was nearly home time so she could just mop up a few little admin jobs that might make the pile less daunting. As she sorted through the papers, not risking looking at her emails which would give her another stack of things to do, she wondered what Ted was up to even contemplating taking on the case of Robert Johnson. Had it got to do with a substantial fee, it usually had, but who would pay him? Surely a convict wouldn't have any money, would he? But then, Anna remembered an item on the radio news about how some prisoners were now making fortunes out of drugs droned in to them and other scams that they could operate through their phones. But Ted wouldn't do it for just the money – it was too high risk as she had pointed out. There must be something else. A horrible possibility jumped up in her mind. Ted belonged to various establishment clubs and organisations in Birmingham – he was the ultimate clubbable man. Someone, a prominent and influential someone, must have either called in a favour or promised a favour.

'You're just playing at working,' Suzy said, pulling a chair up to Anna's desk. 'There's only ten minutes to go before school's out so stop that and tell me what Ted wanted.'

Anna smiled at her and leaned back in her chair gratefully. Suzy appeared dizzy and superficial with her posh accent, 50's make-up and three-inch spike heels but Anna knew from many personal experiences how kind she was, and how smart. 'Promise not to tell?' Suzy, wide-eyed, crossed her heart with a scarlet index finger. 'He wants me to work for a convicted murderer – find his daughter for him, can you believe?'

Suzy considered this. 'What do you know about him – the murderer, I mean?'

'Nothing, I didn't give him a chance to tell me. Why?'

'People kill other people for a lot of different reasons, don't they? Sometimes there's no reason at all which is the most frightening, I think. But it may be worth hearing Ted out.'

'I never expected you to say that,' Anna said.

'Oh well, you know. I had an uncle whom I adored as a child and he killed someone.'

'Really? Why?'

Suzy bent forward and put one elbow on the desk resting her head on her hand so she could speak quietly. 'Uncle Ollie didn't get on with people much, well, grown-ups – children loved him – but he did really care about his animals. He had a little sanctuary in his garden for strays and injured wild-life, you know, as well as his own pet mutt, a kind of mixed-up terrier called Charlie that he adored. It used to sleep next to him in bed and had a bowl of milky tea when he had his. The sort of thing people might disapprove of nowadays but the dog was healthy and happy. Quite a character. They were inseparable.'

'Oh, he had a place like Safe 'n' Sound?' Anna thought of her dad's partner, Diane, who was probably at this moment bustling around the animal refuge with a wheelbarrow full of something disgusting.

'Sort of, but on a much smaller scale. There weren't so many places like that then. This was over twenty years ago.'

'So what happened?'

Suzy sighed and Anna realised how unusual it was to see the immaculate brows wrinkle and the lips painted with eighteen-hour colour droop. 'When Uncle Ollie was out one evening picking up an owl chick someone had found, a burglar broke in and as well as stealing anything he could find to sell, he, well – I won't go into details but he, er, silenced Charlie and not cleanly but viciously, if you know what I mean. I suppose he wanted to stop him barking.'

'Ugh,' Anna shuddered.

'Uncle Ollie came back just as the man was leaving in his van and recognised him and assumed he had come to post a flyer through the door because he was an odd job man. But when he walked in to the house - ' Anna nodded, meaning you can spare me the scene. Suzy took a deep breath. 'He just went to the hall cupboard and took out the rifle that had been his dad's, loaded it, shot poor Charlie and then went to the man's house and shot him right in the face when he opened his front door.'

'Oh, God.'

'Of course he was convicted of murder because it wasn't self-defence, it was definitely pre-meditated and courts look upon vigilante actions like that very sternly, don't they?'

'But he must be out now?'

'No, he died in prison – nothing violent, he got cancer, but my dad said he really just lost the will to live once Charlie had gone.'

'I'm so sorry, Suzy, that's awful.' They looked at each other soberly. 'Maybe you're right, I should give Ted a chance to tell me about Robert Johnson. I suppose it pushed my buttons and I reacted emotionally.'

Suzy got up and slid the chair back to its place. 'Understandable given what happened to you,' she said, 'but on a brighter note there's a sale on at Mango. What about tomorrow lunchtime?'

'Go on then, but I'm not buying anything.'

George was supposed to be cooking, Anna remembered as she drove home, but would probably have forgotten to shop because he was getting out the latest issue of his poetry magazine and would be fussing and muttering in his shed among piles of printed pages. Never mind, if he needed stuff it would be good for her to walk down to the High Street even in this murky winter drizzle. There were still at least six pounds to shed from Christmas - the same six pounds which had effortlessly seen off her New Year's resolution in January.

She parked her car behind her father's Peugeot and Faye's ancient Micra in the drive blocking them both in. Sometimes Anna thought that the words 'Move your car!' were the only ones her daughter ever uttered, or rather yelled, at her mother and grandfather these days. She looked up at the front of the house to the bedroom window of her own room. In a few days Faye would have moved out of her double room and Ellis, who was crammed into a compact den at the back, was practically camping on the landing waiting to get into it. Faye was, to put it mildly, not happy about this prospect and an unhappy Faye was not restful.

In the kitchen Anna was surprised by the sight of George despondently chopping up turnips and carrots and a very good smell of simmering chunks of beef flavoured with herbs and onions coming from the hob. 'Alright, Dad?' she asked experimentally, dropping her work bag on the old dining chair which was no longer safe to sit on but which she couldn't bear to throw away and had tucked in a corner.

'Copier's on the blink,' he said grumpily. 'I've phoned them to come out but they can't do it until Friday.'

'How many copies did you get done before it packed up?' Anna put the kettle on and pulled a mug from the dresser. 'Do you want one?'

'Not just yet, love, thanks. Only fifty.' He picked up the chopping board with its tottering mound of diced vegetables and swiped them into the big pan. When he turned back to Anna, his reading glasses perched on the end of his nose were opaque rectangles from the steam.

'You should get a new one,' Anna said, rummaging for the biscuit tin which she had this time hidden behind the mixing bowls, 'how much are they?'

'Too much, but Ashok might be on the trail of one that his son's company is getting rid of because they're upgrading.'

Anna dipped a ginger biscuit in her tea. 'Good – that sounds promising. Is he coming to the poetry evening on Friday? I haven't seen him for ages.' Anna couldn't remember a time when Ashok had not been part of their lives; he was her dad's closest friend and fellow poet, the nearest thing she had to an uncle. She thought of what Suzy had told her about her own uncle and felt sad for her. 'You could get those fifty magazines ready for the post though,' she said, cradling her mug and thinking that she should make the effort to go upstairs and get changed. 'It would be a start.'

'Yes, he's coming on Friday. That's just what I was hoping to do,' George said, brightening, 'could you just keep an eye on this?'

'Of course I can,' Anna said, settling back and pulling the biscuit tin towards her.

George paused at the back door before going out to his writing shed and pulled on his woolly jacket. 'Faye's upstairs,' he said, 'with a bin bag.'

Anna leaped from the chair and ran up in time to see Faye bundling linens from the airing cupboard into a large black bag. 'Whoa there!' she shouted, 'What are you doing?'

Faye turned a flushed face towards her mother. She must have been home from work for a little while as she was wearing jeans and a hoodie. Anna wondered what else she had pilfered. Strands of her tangle of chestnut hair were sticking to her face with the effort of her task. 'You never use these!' she pleaded, 'I have literally never seen these on your bed.' She was packing Anna's favourite denim-striped duvet set.

'That's because you never go into my room. You can't have these, Faye, I love this set.'

'Ugh. So mean.' Faye tried another tack. 'You can't expect Jack and me to sleep on the mattress. Is that what you want?'

'Take your own sheets – you'll be in the same bed at the flat.'

'But these are nicer. Please, Mum, please. You would be giving us a flat-warming present so this way you won't have to buy anything.'

Anna had read that Britain was short of negotiators for Brexit. They had not met Faye. 'No. Put them back.'

'You never use this either,' Faye said, conceding the duvet set but not ready to give up entirely and pointing to a neatly folded white quilted bedspread in its own see-through bag. It was Anna's treasure. She had found it at the church jumble sale wrapped in an old curtain and suspected that the astute women who organised the event had not realised such an exquisite thing was there. A little ashamed of herself she had paid and started to run off with her prize and then gone back and put £5 in their collection box which was still nowhere near its value. It was a thing of beauty. The bag to keep it clean after she had laundered it, which she had bought from the pound shop, had cost more than the bundle.

'Don't ever even think about taking that,' Anna said very firmly. 'That is mine. I mean it, Faye.'

'Other people's mothers - ' Faye began, and then, glancing at her watch and grabbing the bulging bin bag, pushed past Anna on her way down the stairs. 'I'm not in for dinner – tell Pops – move your car!' and she was gone.

Anna did the switch and ran back up the stairs. Before folding the now crumpled linens and putting them back in the cupboard she did a quick check to see what else was missing but couldn't remember what was in the wash. She had mixed feelings about Faye moving out to her first flat and one of those feelings was the worry that Jack, who was a gentle and kind young man, didn't know what he was letting himself in for.

As she changed out of her work clothes Anna contemplated her bedroom, the glowing yellow of the walls and the freshness of the white woodwork and furniture, the splash of colour from cut flowers that were her winter indulgence. It had been over two years now since she had decorated it and she still loved it. In the spring when she put away the winter-weight duvet she would take out that pristine white bedspread and she imagined how the sun and the shadows from the creeper along the eaves would dapple it in changing patterns as the breeze stirred the vines.

A familiar smell stung her into action. She pulled a jumper over her head and ran down the stairs to rescue the stew.

Over dinner she decided she would talk to her dad and Ellis about the job Ted wanted her to take on. Ellis was fourteen now and often had useful things to say and her dad had been her most reliable sounding board all her life. She had taken in what Suzy had said, but it was easy to make connections between people which were actually meaningless. Yes, Uncle Ollie who had murdered someone had not been a violent person, quite the contrary. Robert Johnson had also murdered, possibly with provocation, but that didn't mean that he was a safe man to put in touch with a possibly vulnerable young woman.

'Mike's dad and mum are going to let us practice our gig round there,' Ellis was saying through a mouthful of dumpling. 'They're going to be out somewhere for a couple of hours.' Not for the first time, Anna blessed them silently.

'That's great but don't forget the neighbours,' Anna said looking round for the dog. 'Will you take Bobble over with you?'

'Yeah, Mike's mum said he could have the bone from their lamb leg. He's zonked from the park in the front room.' He forked up another mound of stew. 'No, it's fine about the music, we'll be in the basement. It's really cool.'

Neither Anna nor her father asked what they would be playing because they had asked before and found the answer incomprehensible. Grime, was it? Or something fusion? It made Anna feel old and guilty – she should be up with these things. Ellis' dad would have at least made the effort. All they knew was that it was very loud. 'Have you found another base guitar?' she asked instead, trying to be interested and wishing it was spring when the tennis club would be back in full swing for Ellis to work off his energy.

'Only Henry and he's a bit of a dabster. You know, not totally serious.' George grinned appreciatively at his grandson. The love of words seemed to have been passed down. Ellis had outgrown the pleasure of using sophisticated adult words and now collected anything arcane or quirky, preferably both.

Anna pushed away her empty plate and twisted round to take a satsuma from the fruit bowl on the sideboard. She began to gently tear the skin away, a task that she found almost as pleasurable as eating the segments. 'Do you both mind if I just run something by you from work for a minute?'

'Throw me one of those, would you?' George said.

'Is there any crumble left, Mum?'

'I can't remember – have a look in the fridge. There may be a dollop of cream.'

Once they were settled she told them about Robert Johnson and Ted's assignment and they talked it over for a few minutes until it became a general discussion on which creatures kill their own species and which don't. But just talking about it a little made Anna realise that Suzy had been right – she needed to find out a great deal more and maybe even meet this man before she could dismiss the idea of a search for his daughter. For one thing, why didn't he know where she was? If the girl's mother had removed her from him and then tried to destroy all traces so she couldn't be found, as may be the case, wouldn't that in itself sound a very loud warning klaxon?

As the others got up from the table, now talking about Langur monkeys, she started to clear away the dishes and stack them by the sink. She and her father took turns to cook the evening meal and the other one cleared up the kitchen. Ellis had to unload the dishwasher before he went to bed, put everything away and see to his own breakfast dishes since they all left at different times. Faye was supposed to straighten the living room and push a vacuum round downstairs once a week but her absence, when she finally moved out, would not make a noticeable difference, Anna thought.

When the dishes and pans were rinsed and stacked and the dishwasher was whooshing, Anna poured herself a glass of wine and padded into the sitting room with her phone. Bobble was stretched along the old three-seater sofa, his head on one arm and his tail on the other like an ancient fur coat. Hearing someone come in, he half opened one eye and politely executed a sleepy thump with it. 'Get off the sofa, Bobble,' she said automatically which prompted a huge yawn and another tail thump before he was asleep again. She sank into one of the arm chairs and texted, 'Hey, are you busy?'

'Call me in half an hour,' Steve texted back. 'We can chat then. Love you.'

'xx,' Anna texted back and then thought for a second and added another x.

2

As she hurried from Harts' car park along the canal bank and up the brick steps to the plate glass doors, Anna wished she had not decided to dress to intimidate. The rain was now coming down in curtains turning the blue brick of the canal edging stones to shining black and the surface of the water to popping like a fizzy drink. The canal boat residents in the Gas Street Basin further down were sensibly nowhere to be seen but cosy spirals of smoke came from some chimney pipes. A soaked cat streaked by on the tow-path below looking furious.

'Soon as, he says,' Josie, the receptionist, greeted her from behind her pale oak surround. 'He's got to go out in half an hour so you'd better be quick.' Anna ran up the green glass stairs and into the women's loo. She stuck her head under the hand drier, brushing furiously to get the hair to lie flat or at least all go in the same direction, tugged down her skirt and hurried out to Ted's office, her feet squelching in the ridiculous smart shoes she'd put on. But when she tapped on the door and he called her in, she found he was in a genial relaxed mood, or appeared to be. Ted owned Harts, had started it from scratch twenty-five years ago and was, mostly, a fair boss, but never to be taken at face value except when his haemorrhoids were playing up when his behaviour became Wagnerian.

'Ah, Anna. Come in, come in. How's things? Kids ok?'

'Yes, thanks, Ted. Faye's moving out.'

'Mm. Sit down, no, you can have the big chair.' Ted stayed behind his desk which meant he had observed Anna's business-like attire and was squaring up with a statement of his own authority. In fact, Anna was not flattered by being put in the Important Client chair as it was built for a much bigger person and she felt foolish that her legs didn't quite reach the floor. If she sat back they would stick straight out like a child. She had no doubt that Ted had noticed all this and had pretended to flatter her while actually putting her at a disadvantage. She edged forward so that her feet touched the floor and straightened her back. 'Now then, shall I fill you in, or would you like to ask questions?'

He had definitely thought this conversation through as he didn't usually present his employees with such considerate options. 'Go ahead,' she said, 'I'm listening.'

Ted spread his stretched fingers on the top of his desk making sausage wigwams of his hands. 'Ok. To pick up where I left off before, Robert Johnson is no ordinary murderer in the sense that he has never been violent apart from that one act. He's been in prison now for nearly twenty years and has not had one single reprimand for anything - he's never even raised his voice no matter how provoked.'

Anna thought, but didn't say, that that could mean anything, including that he was a psychopath. Harold Shipman wasn't a shouty person.

'That's why he's now in an open prison,' Ted went on, 'and he has never taken advantage of that.' Seeing that Anna was still unimpressed, Ted went on, 'He's even taking an Open University course in something. He got A levels before the tragic event - '

'When he stabbed a man to death in a frenzied attack,' Anna put in.

'Well, yes. But sticking to this course is pretty admirable, don't you agree?'

Anna didn't want to agree. Having academic qualifications was no guarantee of moral integrity in her opinion, in fact, she'd known several people with doctorates whom she wouldn't trust as far as she could throw them.

Ted shifted in his seat, shuffled the papers on his desk without actually tidying them, and played his big card. 'Don't you want to know why he killed his mother's boyfriend?' he asked, and when Anna said nothing went on, 'The bully had been knocking his mother about for years and she would leave but he would find her and promise it would never happen again and all that.'

'Mm,' said Anna, who had expected something of this kind.

'It was mostly black eyes, pulled hair, choking, that sort of thing, you know.'

'Just the usual domestic terrorism, then,' Anna said evenly.

Ted glanced at her uneasily. 'But Robert came home one day to find him about to attack her with a broken bottle and he just grabbed a kitchen knife out of the drawer and went for him – just to stop him, really. It's a common reason for young men to kill, you know, that either their fathers or some other blokes are violent to their mums.'

'Yes, I'm aware of that,' Anna said quietly. 'If that's the case, and there was history of the partner's violence towards his mother, why was Robert convicted of murder and not manslaughter?' The more heat she felt in her emotions, the calmer she must try to be, this was no time to let the rage she was experiencing rise up to fog her brain.

Ted looked sober and despite herself she responded to his unusual expression by considering taking what he would say seriously, although she still wondered was he playing at sincerity or was he genuine? 'Remember, Anna, this was twenty years ago, although I don't know for a fact that it would be different now. Two things: Robert himself was not the subject of the attack and the prosecutor made a case that he could have dealt with the event differently – called the police, for instance.'

Anna snorted. Who would believe that the police would respond fast enough to prevent an imminent glassing? 'What was the other thing?'

'Robert is black. The other man was white.'

'Ah.'

'Also, Robert was taller and stronger. The prosecutor said that he could have used his strength to pull the man away.'

'But he was very young,' Anna said, trying to be fair, 'and may not have had the confidence he could do that.'

'Yes. The defence pointed out that Robert was not into contact sports, in fact, sport of any kind, and was therefore unused to exercising his muscle power. He had never been in a fight in his life - he and his friends were interested in science and computer games, that sort of thing. In other words, he looked big and strong but he didn't act or possibly feel big and strong.'

Ted was silent and Anna thought about what she now knew. On the one hand it was entirely possible that Robert had been convicted partly because of his race. Statistics certainly show that in the UK conviction rates for the same offence are biased against minorities. His physical bulk could have made the verdict be murder, not manslaughter, as the jury was presented with visible proof of it by seeing him in the dock.

On the other hand, there had not just been one or two stab wounds, there had been twelve. It's perfectly possible that someone can go along calmly under circumstances where they are not stressed and then have it in them to lose control violently given sufficient provocation. Provocation could come from a daughter who meets her father for the first time and is angry about quite a lot of things. She took a deep breath. 'Can I meet him, Ted, before I come to a decision?'

'I can arrange that,' Ted said, looking more cheerful.

'And I would appreciate your answering another question, please.' Ted sighed almost inaudibly. 'Why are you taking this on? This case, I mean. I can see very clear reasons why you shouldn't so why are you?'

'I know you're not going to drop this, but if I tell you I don't want it going any further, Anna, ok?' Anna nodded. 'The Governor of the prison is a friend, well, a long-time acquaintance, if you like, and she feels strongly that he is a good person and deserves to have the opportunity to at least meet his daughter. Do you know that over the years he has made a card for her on each of her birthdays and written a letter to her every single month – they're all in a box just in case one day he gets to meet her?'

If Ted thought this would sway Anna he was wrong. Sentimentality over people we have harmed can easily look like love and commitment when in fact it's mere narcissism.

'And how long has the Governor known Robert?'

Ted looked shifty. 'Um, she's been in the Midlands for about, er, five years? Robert was moved back here to get ready for his parole since he comes from this area and that's when she met him. I don't know her that well, of course.' He re-considered, obviously thinking that this might undermine his efforts on Robert's behalf. 'Well, I do know her enough to trust her instincts but I'm not, you know, familiar with her.'

Anna managed to conceal her amusement at this classic Freudian slip. Unknown to Ted his affairs, or at least some of them, were an open secret in the main office largely because he used the plain back of any scrap of paper he had to hand to write notes to the researchers. He seemed unaware that this legendary tight-fistedness over stationery was revealing far too much. Just last week Jonathon had received a note asking him to make a phone call, the reverse side of which was a print-out of a reservation for a double room at a Wolverhampton hotel in Ted's name. Just to follow up Jonathon had casually asked Ted on the morning of the reservation whether he was off anywhere nice when he had popped into his office and noticed him getting his coat and briefcase together. Ted had replied that he was practicing on the indoor golf range at his club and then going home. QED.

'Ok, Ted,' she said, sliding off the edge of the chair as gracefully as she could, 'just let me know when you've arranged the visit and we'll take it from there.'

'You won't regret it,' Ted said, beaming.

She let herself out and walked down the corridor passing her own open-plan office and on a few steps to Steve's room on the right. She could see through the corridor window that the light was subdued as usual except for the luminous screens which were banked up on the far wall. He was alone so she tapped briefly on the door and went in, shutting it gently behind her.

'Hi,' she said.

Steve turned in his chair and smiled at her. Even now, even after all this time, his smile punched her heart so that it lost its rhythm. 'Ok?' he said. 'How did it go?'

'I said I would see him, meet him – Robert Johnson.'

'I'm not surprised, I thought you would.'

'Ted's given me some background stuff on him but it could mean anything or nothing and I just want to get a sense of what kind of a man he is.' It was so hard not to go to him, lean her cheek against his, slip her arm round his shoulders. The familiar scent of warm cotton and wool mixed with the unique musk of his body made her put her hands behind her back as if to guard herself against temptation.

'Anna, thanks for - ' the door opened and Josie burst in, ' - the data. Just what was needed.'

'My pleasure,' Anna said, smiling and turning to go. She knew how he had planned to end that sentence.

It was Friday night, poetry night, and Anna was looking forward to the weekend. It had been a boring and frustrating day at work – one of those days when it seems like no-one you phone answers and where websites crash just when you had got to the section you needed. The only really useful thing she had accomplished was to go through a hundred and thirteen emails and delete half and answer the most urgent of the rest.

She was making a toad-in-the-hole. Bobble had cantered into the kitchen as soon as she opened the fridge door to get out the sausages and was now woofing and slobbering. She held them up high and dodged round him into the hall.

'Ellis, have you taken Bobble out for a walk yet?' she called up the stairs.

'Coming.'

Fortunately, Bobble had calmed down as his puppy years were more or less over but the dog was enormous. George had taken it upon himself to go down to the covered market in the Bull Ring at the end of Saturday trading each week to pick up bargain cuts of meat for the animal which he then cooked and froze. Bobble ate anything so the meat was supplemented by scraps left over from family meals and as an after-dinner treat Bobble would lick the plates in the dishwasher if the machine door was left down. Ellis liked taking him out now – the size of the beast improved his street cred in the park – and Bobble was lazy enough not to want miles of exercise. Every time she saw the dog Diane muttered, 'Sorry, dear,' to Anna since it had been at Safe 'n' Sound that Bobble, then a cute, hairy puppy, and Ellis had met and bonded.

Ellis appeared with the lead in his hand. Bobble, in a quandary, looked first at the sausages Anna held up high (since he could reach the counter tops) and then at Ellis, then back at the sausages. 'Walkies!' Ellis called, slapping his thigh and shaking the lead, and that decided things.

'Put him in the garden when you get back, will you?' Anna asked, 'So we can eat in peace.'

She was beating the batter when George came in from his shed to wash his hands. 'Well, the repair man's been,' he said, 'and it lives to print another issue.'

'Good.'

George took a beer from the fridge and sat down at the big oak table. There was no need to use a coaster, the surface of the wood bore the marks of twenty-odd years of cooking, homework, games, DIY projects and now, dog scratches. What the antique dealers called approvingly, 'age'. 'Is Steve coming with Alice?'

'I think so. He may not stay for the poetry though because Alice gets exhausted by the end of a school week so he may need to take her home. Faye said she'll be here for dinner but thankfully without Jack or we wouldn't have enough chairs.'

'I'll lay the table in a minute and get Alice's cushions stacked.'

'Thanks, Dad.' Anna poured the batter over the half-cooked sausages and carefully placed the big roasting tin back in the oven. She pulled open the fridge and got out carrots and broccoli.

'Are you doing baked potatoes with that?'

'Yes, they're in.'

George drained the last of his beer and scratched at his stubbly chin. 'Did you come to a decision then? About the convict chap?'

Anna stopped slicing the carrots. 'No, not really.' She told her father what Ted had told her. 'I've asked to go and see him but I'm worried because my instincts about whether he's safe may not be reliable.'

'How old's the daughter?'

'Twenty. The same age as Faye. Not a child, but still - '

'So, wait a minute,' George said, 'that means that she was a tiny baby when he was sentenced or not even born?'

'I know. I didn't ask Ted about that because I want Robert to tell me himself. I want to see how he talks about her.' And she needed to know why the mother didn't want him to have anything to do with her.

'You're a pretty good judge of character, Annie,' George said, getting up, 'I wouldn't worry too much.' He went out to the passageway between kitchen and garden and came back with two smiley-face cushions spattered with stains which he put on a dining chair. 'There's a new subscriber to the mag, an artist professionally but a cracking poet. Will you read some of hers later?'

Anna had just opened her mouth to reply when the door to the hall burst open and Ellis, Bobble and Faye appeared, shouting and barking. It had been like this for days and Anna was sick of it. 'Take the dog into the garden, Ellis, and both of you just stop shouting, for goodness sake.'

Faye slumped on to a kitchen chair and crossed her arms. 'I don't see why he has to have my room at all. What if I want to come home?'

'You can't leave Jack to pay the rent on his own if you decide you don't like it, Faye. We've talked about this. You've signed a six-month lease so you're not going to need your bedroom. Ellis is too big for his room now – don't be selfish about it.' Anna checked that the water was boiling and scooped the carrots in, glancing at the wall clock.

'What if I want to stay over sometimes, not move back in, just, you know, visit?' She put her chin into her cupped hands and beamed sweetly at Anna. 'I might miss you all, I might miss my mum and my pops.' Anna sliced the broccoli carefully to stop herself saying something she might regret.

'Well, in that case you can sleep in Ellis' old room.'

'It stinks.'

'It does not stink,' Ellis said, coming back in. 'I'm going to have to open the windows and get a fumigator in your room to make it habitable for Bobble, let alone me, with all the chemicals you need to make yourself look human.'

'And what about if Alice wants to come and have a sleepover with me? That room of his is far too small,' Faye continued, reading her phone and texting with her thumbs.

Anna turned down the flame under the vegetables to simmer and put out water glasses and a jug. George had exited the scene. She sat down at the table and looked at her daughter. 'Faye,' she said, 'can I ask you something? I mean, something serious?'

'Go on, then,' Faye said, immediately putting down the phone and dropping the wheedling. Ellis went to the fridge and got out his apple juice.

Anna cut to the essence. 'If you found out that your biological dad, who you've never met, was a convicted murderer and wanted to see you, would you want to see him?'

'Yes!' said Ellis. 'That would be a real *coup de foudre*.'

'Why are you such a relic, Ell, she wasn't asking you.' Faye turned back to her mother. 'How old is this daughter?'

'Your age. That's why I want to know what you think.'

Faye considered this, rubbing her nose with her forefinger exactly as he own father used to do. 'I would want to, I'd be too curious not to,' she said, 'but I'd want it to be on my terms.'

'How do you mean?'

'Is he still locked up?'

'In an open prison, but yes, he'll be out in a few weeks I think.'

'Ok. I wouldn't want him to know where I live or have my phone number or anything like that – I wouldn't want him to be able to find me if I didn't like him or trust him – but I would want to see him as long as he's under guard. Yes, I would.' Anna wondered if Robert's daughter would feel the same. It would have so much to do with what sort of young woman she was and how well-supported by her family and, well, so many other things.

'Right. Thanks for that.'

Faye jumped up from her chair at the sound of the front door closing. 'Lisha!' she called, 'in here, Sweetie-pie!'

'Hi Steve,' Ellis said, grinning at the man as he came in bringing a puff of cold air. 'It's Alice's favourite. Turds en croute.'

Steve smiled at them all and bent down to undo Alice's pink wool coat but she pushed at his hands. 'I'm not a baby, Steve, I can do it.' He made a surrender gesture and took off his own coat placing it on the old chair. Alice struggled with the throat button until Faye scooped her up and undid it for her. 'Your hair smells nice,' Alice said, nuzzling into it, 'it smells of clean.' They adored each other mutely until Faye kissed the little girl's nose and put her down. Faye had not yet told Alice that she was moving out and would be around far less than she was now. That was a tempest brewing.

Anna pulled a bottle from the rack and waved it at Steve, who nodded. She got the glasses and unscrewed the cap. 'You've had your hair cut,' she smiled at Alice. 'It looks good.' She poured the wine and handed a glass to Steve, setting her own next to her place on the table.

'No, it doesn't,' Alice said, glaring at her. 'Steve made me. I hate it.'

'It was in your eyes, darling,' Steve said gently.

'I want my hair like Faye,' Alice persisted.

Steve sighed. Faye had long, thick, heavy hair with a natural curl like her father's but Alice's was like a dandelion clock, fine and thin, silver blonde and dead straight. 'My hair's just ordinary,' said Faye, unexpectedly coming to the rescue, 'yours is like, er, moonbeams.' Ellis snorted his apple juice down his nose.

'Ok,' Anna said quickly, 'it's about ready. Call Pops, will you, Ell? But don't let Bobble in.'

Steve plopped Alice down on her cushions and came round to the cooker. 'Can I help?' He got the hot plates from the warming drawer and then lifted the toad-in-the-hole from the oven as Anna drained the vegetables. 'Do you want me to serve?'

'Thanks. There's baked potatoes, too.'

It was so ordinary, just like any family settling down round the table for an evening meal. A stranger popping in on this scene would find the commonplace routine of three generations cooking and eating and chatting pleasant but unremarkable. Because a stranger wouldn't know. Anna passed the pan of broccoli and carrots to Steve so he could put a spoonful on each plate as he served the food. She leaned back against the sink and looked at them.

George, just in from the shed, now rubbing his hands from the cold blast outside, was peering eagerly at the food steaming on the side, his squirrel eyes black and bright in the weather-beaten flesh between dishevelled hair and the roughly trimmed beard that Ellis now called 'thrummy'. He had brought Anna up alone after her mother had walked out on them when Anna was just a toddler. Who, looking at him trundling round the supermarket with his plastic shopper and his list, a little stooped, a little scruffy, would guess what a fine and original poet he was and how many people of all ages he had encouraged to find the same joy and release in writing as he did to say nothing about what a great dad and grandfather he was.

Alice was now holding her knife and fork upright like spears, her pale skin and silver hair belying her warlike nature - who would know that she had almost died, had been in intensive care for over eighteen months after the car accident which killed her parents?

Then Faye and Ellis, so different in their personalities but both bearing that rich auburn hair that their father had bequeathed to them. Ellis was so much like him that sometimes Anna's breath caught and she had to turn away. He was already as tall as Faye and much taller than herself but with Harry's skinny, long-limbed frame. Unlike Faye, Ellis had his dad's green gold eyes fringed with dark lashes. But Harry was gone and had, in fact, been absent for years before he died.

Who, observing this scene, would guess that Steve was not their father and her husband, had no children of his own and was instead Alice's uncle who had taken on her guardianship with tender stoicism, losing his marriage in the process? (That he had become her lover was still a source of wonder for her.)

But, of course, that's the same for everyone, she thought. The ordinary young man you pass on the street could be a refugee whose family had been lost in a bomb strike far away - the woman on the check-out till could be the sole carer for a mother descending into dementia. We move among each other so anonymously but each has a story. What was that saying – we should be kind when we meet someone because most people are carrying a heavy load? After all, Robert Johnson was not part of a banal family dinner, was he? For him an evening like this may seem to be an impossible dream.

Steve had put her food on the table and turned to see why she had not joined them. 'Hey, when the cook doesn't want to eat we're all in trouble!' Anna sat down next to him thinking that right now her own load wasn't feeling that heavy at all.

3

Kara unlocked the back door and paused, listening to the silence in the house and trying to decide what kind of silence it was. Tense? Sulky? Dangerous? But it was an empty silence, the kind that she longed for, so she slipped her shoes off before she stepped in, tucking them into the old drawstring sports shoe bag from school days that hung on a hook just inside the back door. She would have liked tea but couldn't face wiping the polished granite surface down to remove any splashes and then rubbing with a dry towel and then having to worry that the tea-bag had dripped somewhere. Easier to get her mug and fill it with cold water. She took the tea-towel from the rack and dried the drops that had spotted the stainless steel sink, folded it and returned it to its place and then, feeling a small tide of joy rise, made her way up the stairs to her own room, her shoe bag in one hand and her cup of cold water in the other.

It only took a few minutes to strip off her uniform, hang it up and slip into her joggers and hoodie. She pulled off the scrunchie that bound her hair into a fountain and shook it loose while she got into the first of her sites. She'd been thinking about Tassie all day waiting for the moment when she could check on her. She could have looked at break-time but it was better like this, it made coming home more interesting to wait until she was in her own room.

It would be really dangerous, it must be, to find your way in a country where you didn't even speak the language. Had Tassie learned some words, some helpful phrases? Probably. Definitely. What would happen if she was ill? There was Ben, of course, travelling with her but Kara remembered him from school and thought he would be useless in a crisis. In fact, she knew he would be useless. She remembered that time in the playground when he and his mates had been playing some boy game and he had accidentally on purpose stumbled into Izzy knocking her over so she cut her lip on a piece of glass. He had just stood there gawping while the blood streamed out and it had been Kara who had run as fast as she could to the office to get Mrs Watson, the first-aid lady.

Today's blog photo was of Tassie posing against some mountains, snow-covered at their peaks, with rainbow-coloured hot-air balloons passing by high up behind. You could tell how clean the air was from the sharpness of the light; everything was crystal clear, blue and white and golden brown. Tassie was in the usual shorts and shirt and laughing, always laughing, her blonde hair blowing across her sunglasses. The photo was captioned 'Atlas Mountains!' There was always an exclamation mark on the captions as though she was excited by everything. As well she might be, Kara thought enviously. It seemed almost unbelievable that at this very moment her old school friend was in such an exotic place when Kara was here, sitting on the only bed she'd ever known in the narrow room she had woken up to almost every day of her life. She could ask Jackie where the Atlas Mountains were, or Helena, she seemed to know loads of things. She could look them up now but she liked to have an excuse to talk to Helena.

Remembering seeing Helena that afternoon, Kara jumped up to rummage in her work bag. It was always a good day if Helena was in her room when Kara had to sort it out. It meant they could have a bit of a chat while Kara straightened the bed and dusted down the surfaces. Helena Stansfield was the talk of the home. As the girls got together for their lunch break they would often chat about her. What was such a glamorous woman doing there? She was younger than the others, they knew that because Renata had seen her birth date on something, in fact she was only just over sixty and seemed to be ok health-wise. True, she went away a lot on little holidays, or said she did, but who would want to live in such a place if they didn't have to? Not that Church View was horrible, it was quite cosy and friendly and people seemed happy there mostly (except those that would grumble about anywhere), but still, it wasn't posh and it wasn't at all the sort of place you'd expect Helena to choose.

Helena had asked Kara a lot of questions about herself over the three months she'd been there so Kara hoped she didn't mind when she got asked questions back. She didn't seem to, although when she didn't want to answer she had a way of turning the question away without it feeling rude. Helena had run a model agency in Birmingham when she stopped being a model herself and one day when she was sitting at her dressing table she had pulled Kara gently to her to sit beside her on the little bench. She had made Kara look in the mirror so there were the two faces next to each other and had explained how pleasant faces are regular, in fact, the average of proportions of all faces, but how really beautiful faces had some quirkiness, some memorable and unique and pleasing feature. That was what made supermodels different from clothes' catalogue models. Helena had said that Kara was a little too short to be a model but that her face had that thing that made it beautiful. 'Your face has good regular bone structure and your mouth is well-shaped, but your eyes,' Helena had said, 'are stunning.' This was news to Kara who had been called 'cat-face' and 'weirdo' by the kids at school until they grew older and dropped the name-calling out of boredom. She had never been called beautiful even by her mother, well, especially by her mother.

Kara drew out of a plastic bag the deep red silk-velvet top which Helena had given her that morning. It was cut slim in the arms and had a deep cowl neck with a fitted, ruched waist. Helena had made her slip her uniform off and try it on and she was right, it fitted perfectly – it made her look like a proper woman. It was the most gorgeous thing Kara had ever worn. Helena had been almost as pleased as she was and had said, excitingly, 'Plenty more where that came from,' which meant from her wardrobe as they were the same size. Tassie would laugh at her wearing the clothes of a granny, if Helena was a granny, but Kara thought Helena was the most stylish person she had ever known of any age. Anyway, think of Helen Mirren and Meryl Streep and even Judi Dench, they didn't go round in sloppy cardies and shapeless skirts, did they? Unless they were acting, obviously.

Her phone jingled with the irritating football chant Gerry had put on which she kept because he might be offended if she changed it. Gerry had texted, 'Pik u up 7 – b redy,' with a winking emoji. She held the red velvet to her face inhaling Helena's fragrance that made her think of lying in the sun in a garden full of flowers and then hung it carefully in the wardrobe. She sighed and pulled open the drawer of her bedside cabinet to get out her razor. She knew what Gerry was expecting.

The pub wasn't too crowded so she went and sat with Lauren and Shell while Gerry went up to the bar where his mates were. Shell and Maz were getting married in a few weeks and there was a lot to talk about. It was fun to look at dresses and veils and think about what Maz should be made to wear which he wouldn't throw a fit about. The look would be formal but he had refused to wear any kind of uniform so it might come down to tails and a top hat which was classy but then there was the problem of Maz's stumpy legs.

'Don't get me wrong,' Shell said, 'I actually love his legs, they remind me of toddlers, you know how cute and chubby their legs are? But those tail-coats aren't kind, are they, to people Maz's shape? He could end up looking like a real penguin.'

'Would he wear a kilt, then?' They all stared at where Maz was leaning against the bar and forgetting to suck in his paunch and grinned slyly at each other. 'Maybe not, eh?'

'How's your wrinklies?' Lauren asked Kara, sipping her drink through a straw as she always did, 'I don't know how you can stand it.'

She and Lauren had done an NVQ Level 2 in Childcare at school but by the time Kara could apply after her mum's illness there hadn't been any jobs so she had changed direction and gone for the vacancy at the retirement home rather than not work anywhere. She had meant it to be just a stop-gap but months and then a couple of years had gone by and she was still there.

'I don't mind it,' Kara said defensively, 'they can be fun. They've had lives, you know, and some of them are sweet.' She had not told them about Helena yet and wasn't sure why not. She felt protective towards the mystery lady, as she thought of her, and was growing fonder of her, too, and didn't want them to probe and keep on at her.

'Yeah, but, you know -' Lauren said, making a face, 'potty stuff?'

'There's not much of that,' Kara said, 'only a few of them can't always manage, and they didn't ask to be that way, did they? I mean, they're still people. I don't see the difference. You're cleaning up poop all day, aren't you?'

Shell, who loved her job at the beauty salon, could see she was getting upset and as Gerry approached them changed the subject. 'Hey Gerry, you'd wear a kilt, wouldn't you? Tell Maz he's got to.' Gerry laughed and pointed at their empty glasses but Kara put her hand over hers so he asked what the others were drinking and went back to the bar.

Lauren's eyes followed him. 'I can see your Gerry in a kilt,' she said, and there was something in her voice that tightened the atmosphere, 'No problem.' Kara studied Gerry who was now teasing Maz and telling him to show them his legs. She kept forgetting that he was good-looking, that he could be an object of desire. There were too many other things cluttering up how she felt about him like how he didn't always brush his teeth and, well, other things.

Shell intervened by thrusting an open magazine at them. 'This is it,' she said, 'not this exact one obviously, it's over ten thousand, but this style.' They all leaned forward to see and sighed.

The pub was getting crowded now and the noise from the bar louder. In two corners there were large screens with games going on but no local team was playing so people only glanced at them when the roar went up that meant a goal had been scored. Kara thought about Tassie up in the mountains seeing snow-covered peaks out of her window as she fell asleep. She would be asleep now, probably, because it would be later there and in any case they couldn't drink alcohol, could they?

They had been inseparable in the Junior School, her and Tassie, teachers used to joke about it. But in Charfield Academy something had happened and Kara had never really understood it. Obviously, they were in different classes for GCSE subjects because Tassie was really bright and Kara plodded. 'Kara's a bit of a plodder,' her mum always told people and she made it sound just a little bit like plonker so that her dad would smile. But the split had happened before that, in Year 9. Tassie always seemed to be dashing off somewhere or had piano lessons she had to go to and then the worst thing, the thing Kara would never forget that had finished their friendship, was that she had not been invited to Tassie's thirteenth birthday. Tassie had put loads of photos up on Instagram so Kara knew who was there and she had cried for days and that was the end. 'No point in crying,' her mother had said, 'stuck up madam. Who does she think she is?' So after that Kara kept away from her and Tassie was moved to a different form so they hardly saw each other but every time they passed in the corridor Kara felt her heart clench a little with the loss of her.

When Tassie was planning her year of travelling after A Levels, she was asking for donations from everyone, anyone. It had something to do with a charity so Kara had sent her Christmas money and that had bought her the right to follow Tassie on her blog. She felt no bitterness towards her, she was just puzzled about what had happened and what she had done wrong. And she missed her.

Shell had been a new arrival at the Academy at the beginning of Year 10 but she and Kara had immediately got on well and when she confided eventually how hurt she was by Tassie's rejection of her Shell had been great. 'There's nothing wrong with you, you're really nice and kind,' she had said putting her arm through Kara's at the end of school, 'it's just what happens sometimes.'

'Oh look,' said Lauren, digging Kara in the ribs so the sight and din of the pub rushed back, 'your dad's home.' Kara focussed on the scene at the bar and there he was, an arm round Gerry as always, grinning and shouting with the lads. She ought to go and say hi to him really since he'd been away for three days driving up to Aberdeen or somewhere but she'd just wait a bit because Shell was on to which hairstyle she wanted and Kara had some ideas about that.

Both Diane and Joan turned up even though it was now bitterly cold and there were snow flurries icing the trees and grass. Ashok was already there with George admiring the ancient but heroic copier which had done its duty by them once again. The shed's halogen heater kept the place cosy and George had a small collection of lamps from charity shops which he put on when he was not alone at the big desk so there was a welcoming glow when Anna and the two older women joined them.

Joan pulled a plastic tub out of her carrier bag and plonked it on the desk. 'I haven't bothered with plates,' she said, 'I expect the mice will be grateful for crumbs, anyway. Carrot cake.'

Anna stood up. 'I'll pop in and get a knife. Does anyone want anything?' She pulled her jacket round her and ran the few yards to the back door. She was pleased that Joan had come because her poetry was always interesting and sometimes moving but also because she was worried about her. They had met years ago on the case where she had to find Briony so she could claim her inheritance after her mother's premature death. Joan was Briony's mother's next door neighbour in Northfield and had become a friend and confidante to Anna through the ups and downs that had followed. By rights she should have been the natural partner for George, not the bluff and earthy Diane, but the attraction of one person to another is usually unfathomable.

Settling herself back in the shed in the old car seat that leaned against one wall, she shot a sideways glance at Joan. She looked thinner, there was no doubt about it. Her cheeks had new shadows in between the wrinkles. She had never been fat, in fact, she had always been trim and energetic and had a small frame like Anna herself although *she* had never been described as 'trim' – far from it. But there's slim and there's thin, Anna thought, and Joan looked thin. She glanced at her again. Wasn't her skin paler than usual, too?

'What?' Joan asked, looking up from her poems, 'What do you keep looking at me for?'

'Just thinking about starting on the carrot cake,' Anna lied.

Joan got her phone out of her bag. 'George, would you do me a favour? I was telling my poetry group about that poem you wrote for Anna's mother – you know, you read it at her funeral. It was so lovely. They want me to video you reading it, but only if you want to.'

'Sorry, Joan, that one's a bit personal.'

'Ok, what about the one about universal love – I can't remember the title.'

'Seeing Me Seeing You?'

'Yes, that one. We want to edit readings together and play them on a loop at the interval at our International Poetry Day meeting.'

'Can we do it at the end?' he said. Joan nodded.

Ashok shifted in his deck chair and reached in his bag for a chocolate orange. 'Gotta have our vitamins first, my dears,' he said, 'gotta get your five a day.' He tapped the foil and opened the loose segments to pass round to everyone. Was George sad, Anna wondered, that Faye and Ellis never came to these sessions any more, not since Harry had died? There used to be young people here and not just them but their friends which he had enjoyed, but he never said anything. She made a mental note to have a quiet word with Jack and see if he would come one Friday now that he and Faye seemed to be serious about each other. He was so quiet it was difficult to find out what his interests were. Faye worked with him at Mecklin's toy factory in the design department and described him as 'a creative genius,' but that could mean anything.

'Boy,' said Diane dryly, 'Carrots and oranges. We are healthy, aren't we?' She picked some shreds of hay out of her cardigan and said to George, 'Don't give me anything soppy to read, dear, I'll just bawl my eyes out,' and sure enough she was already tearing up. Anna made a questioning face at her father and he mouthed, 'Puppy died.' This sort of thing was bound to happen given that Safe 'n' Sound never turned any animal away and despite the best of care for some of them the rescue had come too late. Diane never got hardened to it although Anna had observed that when people whom she knew died Diane was much more phlegmatic.

'I've got a cheery one I've written,' Joan said, 'if that's ok, George. When you're ready.'

And so the weekly hour of forgetting the world outside began and Anna slid into that relaxed state of listening to others and reading aloud herself that was almost like meditation, a kind of spiritual comfort zone that she had known almost all her life. The poems were usually original ones which had come to George in various ways. Sometimes established poets sent him their collections to critique or to review in his magazine or sometimes a new writer would send just one poem, carefully printed and folded, or even hand-written and decorated, to test the waters and hope for kindness. George had the knack of being both honest and appreciative in his responses and the fact that he had taken the writer seriously was often enough of an encouragement. As she listened she let her eyes roam over the now-faded graffiti that Faye and her grandfather had spray-painted all over the shed to baptise it years ago.

When they stopped for a cake-break and the others were swapping ideas about another training class that might take Bobble (unlike the ones he'd already been ejected from) Anna leaned over to Joan. 'Are you all right?'

Joan was a tidy eater and swallowed before she answered. 'What?'

'I thought you looked a bit peaky.'

'No.'

'You're lying,' Anna whispered, 'I can always tell. What's the matter?'

Joan hesitated and then whispered back. 'I'm not ill, I'm worried. I can't tell you now.'

'Can I come round after work on Monday?'

Joan reached out and squeezed her hand. 'I'll have the kettle on.'

By ten o'clock the house was quiet since Ellis was at Mike's and Faye was with Jack and their friends. George was squashed to one end of the sofa and asleep in front of the evening news with Bobble's head on his lap. Anna texted Steve and waited for a reply.

When it came she pulled on her warm parka and stuffed her keys and phone into the side pocket. Then, feeling both foolish and excited, she turned the little carved Ethiopian guinea fowl on the bottom shelf of the dresser round so that its red beak faced backwards. It was a signal to her dad that she was going to be out for a while. He would know where she would be.

She opened the front door carefully, pulled up her hood against the frigid air and clicked it softly shut behind her letting the Yale lock catch. Each pebble of the gravel drive had its own cap of snow and the car windows had slippages of white folded in on themselves like whipped cream. She stopped for a moment and looked up at the sky. Just at that minute a rag of grey cloud cleared the moon's face and there it was, set against its deep blue infinity, forever watching. Was Robert Johnson looking at it, too, she wondered. Did open prisons have windows in the cells?

She walked quickly down the road away from the park and towards Steve's house only fifty yards away. By the time she turned in at the gate she was almost running but she saw the front room curtain drop as he came to let her in.

Four days later Anna was trundling along the middle lane on the M5 on her way to visit Robert Johnson but she wasn't thinking about him, she was thinking about Joan. When she had popped in on the way home from work on Monday, Joan had initially been evasive pretending that there really had been nothing wrong and all was fine.

'Oh come on,' Anna had said, taking her tea into the living room behind Joan and sitting down on the sofa. 'I know there's something.' She was always comfortable on Joan's furniture for the simple reason that it fitted her. When Joan had bought her little house after the tragic and unexplained death of her husband and son Howard thirty years ago she had ordered a new sofa and chairs to suit herself because Ollie had been away at university and only visited briefly. They were still in good condition. Anna could sit back on Joan's sofa and put her feet on the rug.

'I like your hair longer,' Joan said, sipping, 'it's very fashionable. It brings out your bone structure. Has anyone ever told you, you look a bit exotic, a bit Persian? I can see you reclining on a divan and nibbling a pomegranate by a fountain while gorgeous men read love poems.'

'As if, and don't change the subject – I am, on this occasion only, immune to flattery.'

Joan sighed. 'I wish I hadn't said anything.'

'You haven't said anything. Spill.'

Joan uncrossed her legs and jiggled her feet. She was wearing her usual navy trousers and a roll-necked jumper Anna knew she had knitted herself. She always dressed unobtrusively but neatly and kept her white hair cropped short, in fact, her appearance was like her house – well-kept but not showy. Anna knew that in Joan's garden the roses would have been pruned and her bulbs planted, the tender plants would have been mulched and there would be, even now, seeds growing in labelled yoghurt pots in her little greenhouse. Joan was all about order and taking care, except for her poetry that revealed the depth and passion of her inner life, full of vibrant memories and an acute, sometimes painful, sensitivity to everything she encountered.

'It's only money,' Joan said nervously.

Anna knew from her own experience that there was no such flippant phrase as 'only money' if you didn't have enough of it. 'Go on,' she said.

'Well, I have my state pension, of course,' Joan said, staring into her living flame gas fire, 'and a little work pension. Walter's life insurance got used to buy this house because we were in a Forestry Commission place before – we'd never owned our own. And I've been ok with that. I can manage if I'm careful and even have a week away each year at my poetry retreat. I had to be frugal when the boys were little and Walter wasn't earning much and the habit stuck. There's a Cash ISA that Ollie puts something in twice a year for my birthday and Christmas so that covers car expenses and gives me a little cushion for emergencies, not that the interest is anything now.'

'And?' Anna prompted when Joan stopped.

'This is so boring.'

'What's happened?'

So Joan had told her that three separate roofers had advised that she now needed a new roof since it was leaking into the loft and causing damp patches on the bedroom ceilings. It would cost thousands which she didn't have. She absolutely refused to ask her son Oliver, who was a successful civil rights lawyer in New York and who, Anna suspected, would gladly have stumped up. The bank wouldn't loan her the money since she didn't have the slack in her income to pay it back. A local roofer had offered to let her pay in instalments but where would that money come from? She was thinking of seeing if the supermarket would give her some shifts even if it meant night work stacking shelves.

'You're sixty nine!' Anna had protested.

'Soon that will be the retirement age for most people,' Joan had replied. 'There are plenty of people my age still working. I'm fit enough. I'm just worried they won't hire me.'

Anna negotiated off the motorway and on to a roundabout that would take her into the Worcestershire countryside. Joan had a point, she thought, because she looked so slight and frail although she wasn't. So much for all the media chat about wealthy pensioners – there may be far more of those than ever before but there were still many who weren't.

The prison was well sign-posted and Anna had no difficulty finding it. This would be the third prison she had visited but the other two had been quite different from each other for all that both were Victorian closed jails. This one would, presumably, be different again. Her Visiting Order was approved by the gate and she was waved through to the visitors' car park. Getting out of the car and stretching, she looked around and saw that this facility was very modern.

She was parked between two rectangular red-brick blocks each one three stories high with an asphalt yard between. To the left she could see a row of greenhouses and some sheds and to the right, behind a security fence, was another car-park, perhaps for the staff. Some hundred yards away was a row of tall conifers looking like soldiers standing in a line and more farm buildings, this time made of breeze block. Perhaps in the summer this scene would be softened by foliage but just now it was a bleak outlook. She turned to look around and there was very little human habitation in sight although the A road she had used wasn't far away. As she stood taking it all in a minibus appeared and disgorged a small group of men who chatted with each other as they made for the nearest block – not new arrivals, clearly, maybe they'd been out at work?

The prison staff were friendly enough, checking her details and pointing out the tea and coffee machine. She had remembered to make sure she had a pound coin for a locker to put her stuff in. She went into the visitors' toilet and checked her appearance in the mirror. She had decided to wear her single-breasted moss green wool jacket and fairly smart black trousers with low heeled boots so that she looked, she hoped, professional but not official. Under the jacket was the cream wool sweater that Steve had bought her last Christmas which felt warm and reassuring the second she put it on. No jewellery except for gold studs and just a smidge of lipstick. Only an idiot would visit a prison made up to the nines.

She was led down a corridor and then shown into a small room with a round table in the centre and two chairs softened by royal blue padding on their seats and backs. 'He'll be down in a minute,' the officer said, and walked away. Anna looked round. Three more chairs had been placed against the wall and there was an institutional-style clock on the wall. In two of the ceiling corners were cameras. On the table, which was about three feet in diameter, was a notice on laminated card which read: 'Visitors and Detainees, please be aware that you are being observed and can be heard at all times.' At this point Anna realised that the room had no door and only a small window high up. She had thought of open prisons as being rather cosy institutions, a bit like an old grange or manor house and maybe some of them were, what did she know? Maybe the officers were more concerned about the behaviour of the visitors than the offenders?

The officer re-appeared. 'This is Robert Johnson,' he said to Anna, and then, to someone out of sight, 'Your visitor's in here.'

In one second she took in an avalanche of data, ready as she was to critically assess every aspect of the man. Yes, he was tall but not particularly muscular – more wiry and sinewy in his forearms and his neck than bulked up from work-outs and weight training. He was wearing a dark T shirt and jeans which could well be standard issue or could be his own. His face, which he had kept turned slightly away from her until he was seated, was deeply lined for a man who must be under forty - it was as though his head was much older than his body and he reminded her of something, something she had seen in a gallery, perhaps? When he settled, linking his fingers loosely on the table, and raised his eyes to hers she remembered what it was, a woodcut of a fisherman she had seen in an exhibition of West African art at the British Library. It was his eyes that were so distinctive, she decided, because they were the colour of black tea and sloped up at the outer corners as if he had some oriental heritage. Already his eyelids had dropped back down making his expression hard to read. Nevertheless his quick glance at Anna had taken in a great deal, too, she felt.

'Hello, Mr Johnson,' she said, trying to put a smile into her voice, 'I'm Anna Ames from Harts. Thank you for seeing me.'

He looked uncertain and then held out his hand. 'Thank you for coming.' She had not expected to shake his hand but took it as to not do so would be rude but a small part of her resented his taking the initiative. Was he a controlling person? His hand was warm and the pressure light and he immediately withdrew it and placed it back with its companion on the table. The offering of the hand had overwhelmed her impression of his voice so she made a mental note to listen carefully when he spoke not only to his words but to his tone. She had come, after all, to hear him talk. She decided to start with an unchallenging question.

'This looks like a very new facility,' she said, 'have you been here long?'

He glanced up at her briefly then and she wondered if he was relieved to answer such a straightforward query. 'Three months. I was at North Sea Camp before in Lincolnshire – that's a Cat D open prison, as well, but they often transfer you closer to home when you're coming up for parole.' His voice had a slight upwards Midlands' cadence but was pitched low and at the end of this short speech he cleared his throat as though to speak at all was not something he did much. Three months, thought Anna, so Ted had deceived her about how well his friend, the Governor, knew him.

'My line manager told me that you're studying with the Open University.'

'Yes.' Again, she had the impression that the nudges and hints, the meta-language of normal conversation was lost on him. He had answered her question literally, monosyllabically, whereas it had been intended as an invitation for him to talk.

'What is your interest? What are you studying?' she tried again.

'Astronomy,' he replied unexpectedly, 'I'm learning about the stars.' For the first time the anxiety in his face diminished a little and when she nodded and smiled to get him to say more, he took the hint. 'It was when I was transferred to North Sea Camp,' he said, 'from the closed prisons I'd been in before. You look out east at the sky over the sea there and the stars are amazing when there's no cloud.' He paused. 'I'd not seen them before because there's too much light in Birmingham at night. Then for a long time I didn't see the sky at all.' He stopped again, seeming surprised to have said so much, but then looked eagerly at her. 'I didn't know it could be like that – I didn't know what the proper sky at night looked like but it's always there, it's like a sea above you.' He abruptly fell silent and looked down as though he had broken some rule.

'I know what you mean,' Anna said, despite herself, 'I live in Birmingham and you can only ever see the brightest stars but we used to watch them for hours when we went on holiday to Cornwall.' He smiled, his eyes still downcast, and she wondered if he felt he had made an ally of her already.

She steadied herself. 'Robert, I'd like you to talk to me about your daughter.'

'I only knew her for one week,' he said, so softly she barely heard him. 'The night she was born in the Women's Hospital - she was so tiny. I couldn't believe that a person could be that small.

They gave her to me to hold and she was so soft, so warm, so light. Nothing like it.' Anna was silent remembering holding her own babies and he was right – there is nothing like it. But she was not here to be emotional and sharing.

'Why didn't you see her after the first week?' she asked, wondering if even then there had been trouble between the young parents.

When he spoke again, Robert's tone was flat. 'Two days after she was born I registered her – I was so proud to put my name on the birth certificate, and my mum was over the moon. But a few days later I went home after visiting hours and he was there, someone had told him where we were living, and he was raving, off his head on something, and when he saw me he smashed a bottle to go at her and I stabbed him to stop him and he died.' In the silence that followed this Anna could hear the electronic tock of the clock on the wall. 'The police came and after that I was always locked up. I never saw her again.'

'Didn't her mother visit you in prison?'

'Vicki. No.'

'Never?'

'No. I wrote but she never replied.'

'Do you know why?'

He shrugged as if to say he didn't know why or, maybe, to say it was obvious why she wouldn't want anything to do with him, why their daughter should not be contaminated by knowing him.

'So now you're almost ready to be freed you want to see her?'

Robert's head, which had sunk low, jerked up. 'No!' he almost shouted. 'No, I don't want to see her! I don't want her to see me!'

Anna was startled. 'But I thought that was the point of hiring us, Harts, I thought you wanted to meet her and get to know her?'

'No, not at all. What good would it do her to know what I am? I don't know what her mother has said but I don't think she's told her about me. I think she was too shamed.'

This was so unexpected that Anna had to take a moment to digest it. She stood up and walked up and down behind her chair. Ted must not have known that Robert didn't want to meet his daughter or he would have told her right away to reassure her – they had both made the assumption that he wanted her traced to get back in touch with her – to have some sort of relationship. 'Then what do you want?' she asked.

Robert rubbed his forearms as though they were cold. He looked at Anna earnestly. 'I want you to find her so that you can tell me how she is. I want you to tell me about her, if she's working, if she's married, if she's happy,' his voice softened, 'what she looks like. I know it may be too hard because Vicki may have changed her name and Kara's.'

Anna sat down again. 'Why didn't you do this before?' she said.

'I had no money to pay you until a year ago when my mum died and left me her house,' he replied simply, 'and then something else happened.'

'Go on.'

'My best mate at school was Dave. He's stood by me through all this. He sends me a Christmas card and, if he can, he visits – it depends where I am. I only ever got visits from him and my mum when she was alive. When I wrote to him and told him I'd been moved here he came and he said he'd seen Vicki with some bloke in the Bull Ring shopping. So, she didn't move away, did she? It seemed to make finding Kara more possible. Do you know what I mean?'

Anna gave him a half smile. She needed time to think through all the things that she had learned and to process her own emotions. She reached into her bag and brought out a pad and ballpoint pen. 'If we do go ahead,' she said, 'I'll need Vicki's name when you knew her and her date of birth if you can remember and maybe her old address. Oh, and Kara's date of birth, too.'

Robert was clearly expecting to be asked for these details and didn't hesitate to give them to her from memory. 'Vicki's mixed race, too,' he said, 'like me. My mum was Irish. I'm not sure but I think her mum came from Jamaica, Vicki's.'

'What about your dad?'

'Died when I was ten. I don't know where he came from but it could have been one of the Caribbean islands, he didn't speak like a Brummie. I wish I'd asked mum more about him but it's too late now.'

'You're not alone, most people don't ask.' Anna had all she needed, more, in fact, but she couldn't resist asking, 'What was your mum like?'

Robert's face relaxed. 'She was a good woman. Mary Ryan. She came over from County Mayo to work in the Birds Custard Factory and met my dad. She was always talking about Ireland. She'd do anything for anyone, but when my dad died it was hard for her on her own – not just for money – she was lonely, and that's when he moved in on her. It wasn't her fault that he turned out to be a rotten apple.'

'You must miss her.'

'I got permission to see her in hospital, the Queen Elizabeth, just before she died. She could hardly talk but she said something to me before she went.' Anna watched him. 'She said, "Sorry, son." But it wasn't her fault, it was his and all these years she's been blaming herself.' As would I, Anna thought, seeing a son's life destroyed by the man I had brought into the home. True, it was his fault, the vicious abuser, but unless his mother was a very tough woman it would have been impossible for her not to see her own role in the tragedy.

She stood up again and buttoned her coat. 'Thank you for explaining,' she said, 'I've got a clearer picture now, I think. I'll write to you in a day or so when I've had a chance to talk to my manager.'

'But will you do it?'

'I can't promise just yet. It's an unusual situation and I just need to think things through.' He seemed to deflate in front of her and it took all her resolve not to agree to help him then and there. 'I won't keep you waiting, Robert, and if we can't do it, we'll suggest someone else.'

So she left him sitting in the featureless room and made her way out through security to her car. Driving home she tried to interrogate her conflicting feelings and impressions but every conclusion, whether positive or negative, came with a question mark. She could easily believe that the young man that Robert had been, exhilarated by becoming a father and in full protective mode from holding his vulnerable baby, would encounter the unexpected scene at home with an explosion of action to save his mother. Anna pondered the extraordinary randomness of events which propel lives in their various directions like un-moored craft caught in currents they are powerless to avoid. If he had not just held his daughter in his arms or if his mother's tormentor had not found her, Robert's life would have been quite different. As it was, a minute of violence had defined the next twenty years and possibly more.

She had been most surprised by his not wanting to meet his daughter. She could see how Ted could have misunderstood this, thinking that his desire for the daughter, Kara, to be found meant that he wanted to have some kind of relationship with her – most people meant that. His shocked reaction to this assumption had seemed genuine and was understandable but could it be trusted? If Kara was found wouldn't he then quickly change his mind and want her in his life?

Then Anna remembered what Faye had said about this situation – that she would want to meet him but on her own terms. Even if Harts did take on the job and find Kara, that didn't mean that she would be automatically in danger. If he did decide he wanted to see her, she could still call all the shots and withhold any personal information from him. So much depended on what kind of woman Kara, or whatever she was now called, was.

Anna drove on through the gloom of a late afternoon in February threading between lines of traffic on automatic until she was tired of thinking about it all and switched the car stereo to a baroque ensemble and let that waft her home.

5

Kara's shift was coming to an end and she was tired. The overcast sky and the few people who could be seen from the front lounge hurrying down the hill into town reminded her how cold it was outside and what a bitter walk home she would have. What was there waiting for her, anyway? Even if Tassie had blogged again, she was finding that each episode of fun and adventure made Kara feel even more discouraged and lonely when she switched the screen off.

She drew the curtains, checked that the room was tidy and went out into the short corridor to Helena's room and tapped on the door. 'It's only me,' she said, 'Do you want anything before I leave?'

Helena opened the door and smiled at her. Her silver hair, cut to an elegant shoulder-length bob, framed a face bright with intelligence and warmth and Kara readily smiled back. 'Do you have time for a cup of tea?' she asked, and Kara slipped gratefully inside. There was always a hint of fragrance in Helena's room, not scent, not perfume, nothing as heavy as that but definitely a fragrance. 'I'm pleased you've dropped by,' Helena went on, as though Kara was a friend, not very junior staff, 'I'd just put the kettle on. Biscuit?' She got a tin out from her cupboard and eased off the lid, peering inside like a child. 'Ooh. There are some chocolate ones left! '

Kara smiled and sank down into the little upholstered club chair tucked hospitably near the largest radiator ready for any visitor. It was so comforting to be here, especially now that it was dark and dreary outside. Helena remembered how she liked her tea and put two biscuits on a little china plate for her and set the mug and the plate on a round table beside the chair. 'Now,' she said, 'tell me what you've been up to.'

What had she been up to, Kara wondered, that might interest Helena? Not last night's sweaty tussle with Gerry, not her daily fix of virtual adventure via Tassie. 'My friend Shell, Michelle, is getting married soon and we've narrowed it down to two hairstyles.'

'Tell me.' And Helena really did seem interested.

'Um, well, she's got shoulder length hair but it's not very thick. She wants it up in a kind of windswept look, you know, with little fake roses in the curls but I don't think she's got enough body for that.'

'Mm. What was the other one?' Helena asked, nibbling her biscuit.

'Scraped back really close to her head and then a false bun on the back.'

Helena considered this. 'What's her shape of head like? Is it large, I mean compared to her body, or small?'

'Small, I suppose, she's quite well-covered.'

'In that case, how about the first style but with extensions? They would really bulk up the look and I would worry that the second idea could be too severe. That scraped back look is very unforgiving whereas curls look romantic and you can position them strategically, can't you?'

Kara nodded thoughtfully but really she didn't care so much as usual what Shell did with her hair at this moment. She was luxuriating in the cosy room, the tea and biscuits, the way Helena made her feel. 'That's a great idea, I'll tell her. What about you, are you off anywhere?'

Helena put down her tea and leaped up from the chair to grab her tablet. Kara noticed that she didn't even touch the arms of the chair when she got up and she never sighed when she sat down. She was slender and agile and elegant and it was unfathomable why she would want to be here with old people who really needed care and attention, who could no longer manage properly in their own houses. Helena sat down again, opened the tablet and showed it to Kara. 'Look, what do you think?'

There was a picture of a large white hotel perched up high with gardens dropping down full of rose arches. Kara pressed the right arrow and bedrooms appeared with massive king-sized beds and huge windows and shining bathrooms. She kept pressing past the restaurant and bar and a harbour full of little yachts and fishing boats jumped up, the sun shining brilliantly, the sky deep blue. 'It looks lovely,' she said. 'It must be abroad?'

'No,' Helena laughed, 'so you have to imagine it without the sun and without the flowers!'

'When are you going?'

'This weekend. I've booked a taxi to the station and then they'll meet me at the other end. It's in Devon.'

Kara had not wanted to click on the tariff tab but guessed that even in winter it would be pricey. 'You're going with friends?' she asked, feeling a little chill of loneliness under her heart.

Helena took the tablet back and shut it down. 'No, the hotel will send a car to meet me, that's what I meant.' She smiled gently at Kara. 'Have you ever been to Devon?'

'No,' said Kara. 'I've never been anywhere. Well, except Birmingham sometimes and Worcester with my mates.'

'You don't go on holiday with your parents?'

There had been a time, Kara suddenly remembered, when they had gone somewhere. She was very little and it wasn't the seaside. They had gone on an aeroplane which had been amazing because you could look down on the ground so far away and see what birds must see. She had pressed her face to the window and not taken it away until they landed. Her mum and dad were all loved up and couldn't stop touching each other and they had stayed at a place with a little swimming pool, well, a paddling pool for her, and there was a kind woman who looked after her and the other kids all day and played games with them. Where was that? 'I did once,' she said, 'but I don't know where it was.' She felt stung by the pity that she seemed to see in Helena's face. 'My mum and dad work hard but the pay isn't great,' she said defensively, 'and mum likes the house nice so they spend on that.'

'Money spent on improving property is never wasted,' Helena said, but Kara knew she was just being kind and, even though it was Helena, she resented it.

'Why do you go away so much?' she asked, wanting to put Helena on the spot but instantly feeling ashamed of herself.

She thought Helena wouldn't answer and worried that she had gone too far, after all, she was not a friend, she was just staff and Helena was now looking into her mug with such a solemn expression that it scared her a little but then she said quietly, 'I'm looking for somewhere, that's all. I'll know when I've found it.'

So that was it. Maybe Church View was just a rest-stop between selling her own house and buying another? It made sense although it didn't seem to be the cheapest option but renting a flat and having to furnish it and take a lease and all that might be expensive, too, and less flexible. Devon sounded like a lovely place to retire to. Kara had seen it on Countryfile and thought it was like something from story books. Helena would spend the weekend going round looking at properties but she would want to be comfortable while she did it. 'I hope you don't mind me asking, I was being nosy.'

Helena beamed at her. 'Of course not. I was being nosy about you, anyway!'

'It's nice in here,' Kara said, 'but I'd better go. Thank you for the tea and biscuits.'

'You're very welcome, wrap up warm for the walk home, won't you?'

It was a raw cold but at least now Kara had something to think about and began a fantasy about what kind of house Helena would buy and whether, maybe, impossibly, she would invite Kara to visit.

At home her dad was sprawled on the leather sofa in front of the tv so she said 'Hi' to him and went up to her room. She decided not to look for a blog from Tassie, it was too lowering, and in any case she was seeing Shell at her house in an hour and could put Helena's suggestion about the hairstyle to her. After all, Helena had been a model and run an agency, it wasn't surprising that she had useful tips.

'Kara?' her dad called up the stairs.

She opened the door. 'What?'

'Your mum says to get the sheets off your bed and into the wash.'

'Ok.'

'I'm off out.'

'Ok.'

She heard the door bang shut and dashed to the bathroom to have a quick wash and clean her teeth before getting into her comfy leggings and top. She would text Shell and see if she wanted her to bring anything from the Subway although she usually didn't because her mum or her dad cooked dinner for them all. Kara pulled off her scrunchie, brushed her hair and then wound it back on. She thought of Helena's cosy room and the tea and biscuits. She didn't want Helena to leave when she found her new house but, of course, she would – she was like an exotic hibiscus or something among the dowdiness at Church View. She pulled off the duvet and shook it free of its cover and then took off the sheet and the pillowcases ready to put them on to wash before she went out. Maybe not a sandwich, it was too cold for that, maybe a chicken burger for a treat.

It was already ten o'clock and Anna knew she should start making a move to go home and get ready for work tomorrow but being on the sofa with Steve was too hard to give up. It had taken weeks, months even, to get used to the different physicality of him. Harry had been long and lean and at first Steve's slightly smaller, more muscular body had felt strange to her touch however much she wanted it. His hair was thick and spiky, like an animal's pelt, whereas Harry's had been silky and had sprung around her fingers. He touched her differently, sometimes even awkwardly, because he, too, was getting used to a new lover. It didn't help that they had to behave like teenagers making out while the parents were away at Steve's but Anna felt embarrassed to confront Faye and the adolescent Ellis with the reality of their love-making. Steve thought it would be no big deal to them but Anna wasn't so sure. George, with no discussion needed, had suggested the Ethiopian guinea fowl signal so, 'I know where you are if I have to call you.' It was an unresolved issue and, after all, there was no hurry but it would be so good to wake up together in the morning, share those lovely warm sleepy moments before the day has properly begun, have breakfast together.

They had been talking about her visit to Robert and Steve thought she should go ahead and try to trace Kara. After all, there was now no danger to the girl even if Robert did turn out to be an unstable parent because she may never know him and if she did, she could manage that safely with a little advice along the lines Faye had suggested, couldn't she? Anna had admitted to Steve that she had liked him a little, felt sorry for him, but that she distrusted that reaction and wondered if it had been engineered.

'You're over-thinking it, maybe,' Steve said, kissing the top of her head as she lay curled against him. 'It could be just as it appears – any guy could lose it under those circumstances and especially a kid of nineteen.'

'Mm.' It was cosy there on the sofa and Anna's eyes were beginning to close. Steve had stopped kissing her and she suspected he was dozing, too. The small sounds from the street wove in amongst the Mozart piece which Steve had on his docked phone. An empty bottle and two glasses rested on the coffee table. Anna hated the thought of having to go outside even if it was only a few yards.

She burrowed deeper into the hollow of Steve's shoulder and wondered if it might be possible to stay after all.

'Stop it!' Alice shouted, 'Go to your own house!'

Both of them sat up straight and stared at her groggily. The little girl was standing in the open doorway with her arms folded and a furious expression on her face. Steve said, 'That's rude, Alice, don't talk to Anna like that.'

'You woke me up,' Alice said to Anna. 'I heard you laughing.' Anna couldn't remember laughing but was too busy struggling between guilt, resentment and amusement. The resentment could win if she let it. After all, Alice was only six.

She stood up. 'I was just leaving, anyway,' she said to Steve. 'It's been a long day.'

'Why are you here, anyway?' Alice demanded. 'You're always here. This isn't your house.'

'Alice,' Steve began, 'this is not acceptable behaviour. Anna is our friend and she can come here whenever she wants - '

Alice ignored this and glared at Anna. 'He's my Steve, he's not your Steve,' she said firmly and in the next moment was stamping up the stairs.

'Darling, I'm so sorry,' Steve said, 'I know she loves you really, I don't know what's got into her.'

Anna smiled at him and hugged him round the waist. 'Not just my two to worry about, then?' she said. 'It's ok, Steve, I understand, I really do. It was a shock for her to see me here and she never has been one to hold back, has she?'

'Do you think I should have a talk with her?'

'Oh, let's leave it for now,' Anna said, shrugging into her coat and zipping it up. 'We can plan a bit of strategy when we're not so tired. I'll let myself out so you can go and tuck her in.'

The cold air outside woke Anna up and she found its freshness surprisingly bracing. She strode down the road, head up to look at the sky thinking of Robert, but only one or two of the very brightest stars, maybe Arcturus and Polaris were visible. She imagined him watching the night sky at North Sea Camp, gazing and gazing with his head back until his neck ached at the brilliant crystals thrown across the blackness under which he stood and how he would gradually learn to see patterns in that scattered treasure and name planets and constellations and how that would re-connect him with the grandeur of the world.

Since Faye's car was so small, Anna and Steve were enlisted to carry stuff across to the new flat on the Coventry side of Birmingham on Saturday morning. Alice insisted on going in Steve's Yeti as if to guard him, Anna thought, but Ellis came with her. He was, of course, being very, very helpful knowing that once this move was over he would have the big double room all to himself. Mike was coming in the afternoon and they would set up all the techie stuff and cover the walls with posters.

'And move your old bed in there for now,' Anna added. 'We'll see if we can find a bigger one for you in a while. I'll show you how it takes apart when we get back.'

'Can I have Bobble? I could make a sort of nest for him in the corner – he'd love it.'

Anna negotiated out of their street carefully very aware that she could see nothing through the rear view mirror heaped as the car was with Faye's stuff. 'He wouldn't like the loud music, Ell, it would drive him mad.'

'I could use earphones – it would be nice to have him there when I'm actually going to sleep.'

'You could give it a try but don't let him on your bed or he'll never get off it and you'll be the one in the nest.'

Jack was already at the flat with his parents so Anna introduced herself and the others and they all gazed around. There were three rooms – a living room with a small kitchen area at one end, a bedroom and a bathroom. It was above a computer shop and had been passed on from a school friend of Jack's who was now off to London having finished his degree. After four years of housing students it was not looking particularly fresh, Anna noted.

'It's filthy,' Jack's mum said, 'the bath is green with mildew.'

'I think it's great,' Ellis said anxiously. 'I'm really jealous.'

'Come back in one month,' Faye said, 'and you won't recognise it! We have plans, don't we, Jack?' They high-fived each other like kids.

'Do you want us to help you unpack the stuff?' Anna asked, hoping the offer would be refused, 'Or shall we take you to the pizza place up the road for lunch and then leave you to it?'

Alice had fallen silent as all this was going on and had stopped pretending to help carry things in. She stared at Faye now.

'Aren't you coming back?' she asked in a small voice. 'Aren't you coming home?' Anna and Steve looked at each other. Faye was supposed to have explained to Alice what was going on and reassured her that she would be back often to see her. She had clearly forgotten.

Faye went over to her and knelt down. 'Oh Lisha, Sweetie, I'll be coming back all the time. It's just that Jack and I want to live together here now because he's my boyfriend. You like Jack, don't you? You can come and play sometimes! It'll be fun. That would be great wouldn't it?'

Alice took a step back. 'I hate you,' she said quietly. 'I don't want to be your friend any more.' Steve put his arms out for her but she walked past him out of the flat and sat down on the top stair, leaning her downy head against the crusty wall. But Faye barely noticed because Jack was explaining to his dad how they were going to re-arrange the kitchen and getting it all wrong so she needed to sort that out. It was only natural, Anna thought, but she wished her daughter had been more sensitive.

All through the pizza lunch Faye chattered away but Alice didn't cheer up and Anna realised that this was the first time that she had seen the little girl be hurt rather than demanding or defiant. Alice having a tantrum because she couldn't get her way was one thing, a very common and annoying thing, but Alice in distress was quite another. Steve sat next to her and gave her the best bits of garlic bread and even Ellis tried to distract her with a napkin aeroplane but she wouldn't eat or talk. Eventually Anna mouthed at Steve, 'Do you think we should go?' and Steve nodded and asked for a box so Faye and Jack could finish the pizza for supper.

They said goodbye to Jack's parents, kissed and hugged Faye and returned to their cars with Alice holding Steve's hand, her chin on her little chest. Anna heard him suggest stopping for a cream cake which usually rallied her, but she saw the child shake her head. Oh dear. Ellis, on the other hand, was ecstatic and didn't stop talking about his plans for the bedroom all the way home.

As she drove Anna tried to remember what strategies they had tried with Faye when she had been upset as a child but couldn't think of any occasion when she couldn't be worked round either with an ice-cream or some retail therapy. But then, Faye had never lost someone she loved, not when she was a child. She was more than a friend or a big sister to Alice, she was, in some ways, more like the mother the girl had lost as a baby. They would need to handle this carefully and she would message Steve about it when she got home.

But it was Kimi who came up with an idea to help Alice. She and Anna were riding sedately along a muddy track that skirted a copse on the farm and Kimi had been in full flow about Briony for at least twenty minutes. Anna was so relieved that Kimi wasn't insisting she force herself and the poor horse to jump hedges (which terrified them both) or do endless circuits of the paddock to 'improve your seat' that she was happy to let her moan on. Kimi was ahead of her so Anna could let herself slump and not push her heels down as she should. Maisie, the horse, was much of the same mind as Anna and plodded along stoically only slipping on the mud when she momentarily dozed off.

'I just can't believe that anyone wouldn't be thrilled to have ringside seats at The Horse of the Year Show,' Kimi repeated. 'I thought it was the best surprise ever. It's not as though I hadn't booked a really good hotel, too. I wasn't expecting her to slum it but she can be so narrow in her interests, sometimes.'

Anna patted Maisie's mud-spattered neck, inhaled her gamey horse smell, and smiled. 'Perhaps she doesn't like surprises,' she said.

'No, that's the thing,' Kimi said, turning to look at Anna. 'Pull her head up and don't slouch. That's the thing – she specifically said she wanted a surprise. Apparently she meant a weekend in Rome or some such thing. Where's the fun in that? I don't want to trail round a city with thousands of other gawpers looking at old buildings.'

It was Sunday morning and Steve had reported, when she phoned to check, that Alice was still sunk in gloom even after a night's sleep. Anna had been reluctant to come on this ride but then, she almost always was. There had to be fleecy clouds scudding across a blue sky and temperatures in the 20's to say nothing of bluebells in the woods for her to actually look forward to a ride, but spending time with Kimi was the equivalent of downing a stiff drink and she usually felt better for it when it was over. Today it was bone-cold in that comatose, misty way that February brings but Maisie was considerably working up a sweat and was beginning to steam so at least Anna's upper half was not too chilled in her fleece and quilted jacket. It was her feet that were like lumps of ice in the rubber boots. They were actually aching. To take her mind off that she peered into the copse to their left hoping to spot muscular green shoots poking through the thatch of dead grass laced with brambles. Even though this was Kimi's private land, her farm, there were still plastic bottles and cans tossed into the thickets.

'We've got a bit of a problem on our hands,' Anna said. 'Alice is really upset about Faye leaving – I mean quiet upset.'

'Oh, that's the worst,' Kimi replied. 'Rhea used to have epic sulks that lasted for days when she was a kid.'

'How's she doing?' Anna asked. Kimi's daughter had developed schizophrenia when she was in her mid-teens and had needed residential care for years. She was now in a group home as a half-way stage to being independent. Her doctors had advised Kimi not to have her back on the farm just yet since she would be so isolated when Kimi was out all day at work and that isolation would not be good for her. Anna knew how deeply distressed Kimi was about Rhea and was surprised that she had mentioned her in such a casual way. It must be a good sign that Kimi herself was coming to terms with it.

'Not too bad. She had a bit of an episode last week when they all went out to the shopping mall but quite honestly those places drive me insane.' They clomped on a little further. 'But go on about Alice. Has Steve tried to distract her?'

'Yes. He took her to see The Jungle Book yesterday afternoon but she was still subdued when they came out and when he put her to bed and read to her he said she didn't even want him to kiss her goodnight – just turned away and huddled into her pillow.'

'Couldn't you ask Faye to pop over this afternoon – just to prove that she will be around sometimes? That she hasn't gone for good?'

'I could.' Anna doubted that Faye was in any mood to come back to visit so soon with all the frantic nest-building that was going on but she could ask.

Kimi, on her Morgan mare Beauty, or Beautiful Dreamer to give her the show name, speeded up to a fast trot to cross the big field next to the stable yard and Maisie followed suit as horses usually do so Anna dutifully gripped with her knees and rose up and down more or less in time to the jolting stride. They walked the horses into the yard and slid off. Anna's height was a bit of a handicap with unsaddling but Maisie, empathetic horse that she was, would lower her head so that Anna could grasp the bridle between her ears and pull it off. For the saddle she had developed a technique of her own. After pushing the metal stirrups up their leather straps and unfastening the girth from under Maisie's comfortable belly, she just tugged hard on the nearest flap and jumped back. The saddle slid off so she could, sometimes, catch it. After that it was brushing and hoof cleaning and so on which she enjoyed as much as the horse clearly did.

Kimi straightened up from where she was washing the mud off Beauty's elegant fetlocks. 'You could bring her here,' she said. 'Sometimes animals take kids' minds off their problems and there's Prinny to look at.' Prinny was Beauty's second foal, now one year old and a joy to watch prancing about.

'Do you know what,' said Anna, 'that may be a brilliant idea.'

'I'm full of them,' Kimi said, bending down again, 'like The Horse of the Year Show.'

6

Ted was delighted that Anna's meeting with Robert had gone satisfactorily and said he would not assign her any new cases so she could concentrate on this one. He didn't seem to be interested that Robert didn't want to meet his daughter and Anna knew now that the fee Harts was getting on conclusion of the search wasn't inflated so it must be that he wanted to impress his Governor friend with the efficiency of his company's employees. He had certainly smartened himself up in the last couple of weeks losing the awful moustache and buying much tighter trousers reminding her of Mr Pickwick in the original illustrations. She wondered if Mrs Ted was aware of her husband's distractions and if so, if she was grateful.

Anna settled down at her desk with a coffee from the new machine the staff had insisted on Ted putting in and prepared for a long day but she found Vicki and Kara in less than an hour. The Index of Marriages told her that Vicki Gates was now Vicki Brandon and the Electoral Register confirmed that Robert's friend Dave had been right, she hadn't moved far. She was in Bromsgrove, the market town only a few miles south of Birmingham's city limits on the far side of the sandstone ridge covered with pines known as The Lickies. On the Electoral Register she was listed with Graham Brandon and Kara Brandon living at 46 Elgar Crescent. So, she had not felt sufficiently intimidated by Robert Johnson to move far or to rename herself or Kara. Also, he could not have been part of a criminal network or she might have been afraid of those of his mates who were still free but in contact with him. Perhaps she had just put him out of her mind.

Since Kara was still living at home that meant she might either be a student or working, or she might even be unemployed. Finding this information would be more tricky. If Anna was to put her under some kind of surveillance then she would need to know where she spent her days and realising this made Anna aware for the first time that the job wasn't really tracing someone at all. It was private detective work. She wouldn't mention this distinction to Ted, who wouldn't be interested anyway unless she was asking for a rise, because she enjoyed a bit of sleuthing and there was no danger of anything blowing up in her face with this case unlike some of the previous ones.

She tried Kara Brandon on Facebook and was lucky again. The profile photograph was a typical girls' selfie of three friends, faces pressed together, tongues stuck out. It wasn't hard to see which one was Kara – she had her father's eyes that sloped upwards at the outer corner over high cheekbones. The few photographs Anna could access were not of much interest, more of the same, so she looked for Vicki but found nothing. Kara had not updated her profile since Charfield Academy days so Anna was no nearer to finding out where she worked, if she did.

It was still early, not even lunch time, and Anna didn't want to work on the reports from other cases she had to finish. She felt restless and needing action so she decided to go out to Bromsgrove and just look at the area, maybe even take a photo of the house. She downloaded a map of the town, checked that Elgar Crescent was on it and printed it off in case the satnav was being moody. On the way out of the building she would pop in on Steve and put Kimi's idea to him. They hadn't talked at length on Sunday because his parents were visiting from Derbyshire. Possibly, Anna hoped, they had cheered their grand-daughter up.

Seeing he was alone in front of his screens she went straight in and sat on the stool next to his swivel chair. 'Hey up,' she said. 'Good visit?'

'Yeah,' he smiled at her, 'it was. I thought my mum would work her granny magic on Alice and she did cheer up a bit while they were there, but once they'd gone it was back to the miseries. The worst thing is she won't talk to me or shout about it or anything. It's so unlike her.' Anna relayed Kimi's suggestion and Steve said he'd have a word with her and see if she liked the idea.

'Don't do that,' Anna said, 'she won't understand what it's like. Let's just take her to the farm next Saturday - make up some excuse. I think once she sees the horses, especially Prinny, she might really enjoy it. Kimi's got a donkey, too. It's the best friend of one of the horses.'

'Perhaps not mention best friends,' Steve said.

Anna drove south out of Birmingham on the A38 and was in Bromsgrove within an hour. She parked in the Asda car park and walked the short distance to the High Street over a small brook. The shopping streets were mostly pedestrianised and there were pubs and charity shops and a few clothing chain stores together with the usual chemists, opticians and card shops. As in her own High Street coffee shops were now more numerous than pubs although in the days when this had been a proper market town with cattle and sheep and so on for auction, there would have been at least a dozen of them. As it was she counted three in a short walk. In the centre was a statue of A. E. Housman and on two corners were Big Issue sellers. An unremarkable country town, Anna thought, pleasant enough and no doubt with its own traditions and high days, in fact she had a vague memory of she and Harry bringing the children out here to a fair once. She wondered if Vicki had found work here or whether she liked it enough to be willing to commute to Birmingham or Worcester.

She went back to the car, consulted her map and drove out of the car park and through the one-way system to the estate which contained Elgar Crescent. The maze of curved streets which made up the estate made her think that this must have once been a council estate but now she suspected that most of the properties were privately owned as the exterior décor varied so much from house to house. Mostly they were neatly kept and well-maintained and it wasn't hard to find Elgar Crescent so she stopped near to number 46 in a spot where she hoped she could observe without arousing suspicion. The house was red brick with brown-framed double glazing, each window having a small rose set in its centre, and was extremely neat, the front garden having been replaced by bitumen hard-standing marked out with indentations to look like crazy paving slabs. Wooden lapboard fences, also neat and new, bordered both sides of the property so appearances must matter to either Vicki or Graham that they were willing to pay for a matching fence to the one they were responsible for. There were no flowers or shrubs but it was winter and more than possible that they preferred hanging baskets and tubs rather than a garden needing maintenance. There must be two cars to need that much parking.

Beyond this Anna couldn't deduce anything apart from the fact that the family were probably not too hard-up and she was beginning to feel awkward as young mothers and grannies passed by with pushchairs on their way home from the shops. She had been pretending to talk on her phone which now seemed foolish so she snapped a photo and put it away.

As she drove off she thought about how she could find Kara's whereabouts when she was not at home and how then could she try to observe her. This might turn out to be the most difficult part of the job. Briefly, she considered going to the local secondary school and pretending to be someone connected to Kara to see if they knew where she was but that was, of course, absurd as there would be no way, quite rightly, that they would tell her even if they knew. She spent the next hour in a coffee shop on the High Street downing a late lunch and a cappuccino hoping that her luck would hold and Kara would walk in. She didn't.

But on the way back to the car park an incident happened. Anna had just given her change to a Big Issue seller who was standing on the High Street by the corner of a shop and the alleyway Anna needed to use so she turned the blind corner quite close to the wall and almost ran into a man who was coming in the opposite direction, also close to the wall. Normally people smile and apologise to each other and move on when this sort of thing happens but not this time. The man raised balled fists to Anna and swore at her so vehemently that drops of his spittle hit her face. His eyes were bulging so much that the pale irises looked like mussels wobbling in livid maroon flesh. It was so unexpected and hostile that Anna didn't have a chance to respond or protest before he had pushed past her and gone.

As she walked on an elderly shopper shrugged at her meaning, what can you do, people are crazy, and Anna managed a half-smile back but she was shaken. The town was so sleepy and ordinary, the morning almost boring (since she had not seen anyone enter or leave the house as she had been hoping), and then this. We all operate our normal lives from behind bubble-wrap, she thought, but then something sharp, sickening and dangerous rips that flimsy layer open and we realise how vulnerable we are. When she got into her car she sat for a moment until her hands stopped trembling. She wondered if people who had never had violence done to them would have the same reaction. Would she have been able to shrug it off before?

Kara was, in fact, at home that day because she had caught a cold and was huddled in bed with a box of tissues watching The X Factor on her laptop while Anna had been sitting outside the house wondering where she was. The worst of it was the sore throat which made swallowing painful and she had read on the lozenge box that she couldn't suck more than one every four hours. She texted Shell but it was a busy day at the salon so she couldn't talk. Lauren worked at Teeny Tots but they weren't allowed personal calls when they weren't on a break. By two o'clock, just as Anna was paying for her coffee and wrap and preparing to keep a look-out for her, Kara was feeling so sore and lonely that she phoned Gerry. She soon realised her mistake.

'You at home in bed?' Gerry said when she told him how rotten she felt. 'Nice. I'm only up Aston Fields – I'll get Tony to let me leave now, we're nearly done here. Unlock the back door and I'll come up as soon as I can.'

'Leave your boots on the paper by the door,' Kara said weakly, 'but I really do feel ill, Gerry.'

'I'll soon make you better, babe!'

She had met him at the pub, The Grapevine, because he was a mate of Shell's boyfriend, now fiancée, Maz, and they had made up a foursome to go to a club in Worcester. Nothing had ever been said but he had just assumed from then on they were an item and she had not felt able to question that. She supposed she was weak not to dump him but everyone else, certainly her dad, seemed to think he was a great guy and they were a good match. He was all right. He didn't treat her badly and, as far as she knew, didn't cheat on her but was that really enough? Did everyone's heart sink when their boyfriend announced he was about to turn up? It seemed weird. Maybe she was weird.

She did as he had asked and padded down in her bare feet to unlock the back door but then hesitated. She would have preferred to get dressed and see him in the living room but he knew she'd been in bed when she called and that might look a bit odd. In any case, by the time she had got back upstairs with a glass of water, she heard the back door close and he had already arrived.

He slipped into her room asking, 'Where's your mum?' He knew, of course, that her dad was off on another long-distance haul up north. He knew her dad's jobs better than she did.

'At work. I feel really rough, Gerry, my throat's on fire.'

He was on the bed now and pushing his hand down under the duvet. 'It's all right, I won't kiss you – I don't want to get it. Come on, you're all warm, move over and let me in.' So Kara obediently wiggled across the narrow bed while he stood up to unzip his jeans.

It was soon over and he stretched out on his back, tucking her under one damp armpit. 'Tony's a right laugh,' he said to the ceiling, 'he's got this lady in Droitwich he calls his exercise machine. He says it's the best exercise because you work up a cardio sweat but you don't put any strain on your joints. Ha!'

'You'd better not be late back,' Kara said, trying not to care about the acrid smell, 'you'll want to get something to eat.'

Gerry stroked her nose with his fore-finger and rolled out of bed. She watched him pull up his jeans and fasten his belt and then bend over to pull on his socks but a small spasm of distaste at the sight of the pale grey bulge of flesh over his pants made her wonder again if it was normal to feel this way. Should she finish with him? It was a tempting thought but just then he turned at the door and smiled at her and she knew she couldn't be so unkind.

The wintry afternoon was closing down into a chill fog as Anna mounted the step and turned the key in her own front door. The honey sweetness of Elvis' voice greeted her begging someone to love him tender accompanied by the wailing of two adolescent male voices. She dropped her coat in the hall and her bag on the kitchen chair and put the kettle on. On the big old table there was a slew of mail, mostly advertising, and a free paper which she might glance through later. She walked to the back window to see if a light was showing in her dad's shed but it was dark. She felt restless and irritated because now she had found Kara she wanted to meet her and couldn't figure out how to do it. Most of Harts' cases involved looking for beneficiaries of probate – people who had lost touch with, or, in some cases, never known the deceased but who would inherit. This job with Kara was quite different. Normally it wasn't a problem to contact a person but in her case it was strictly forbidden.

Was there any cake? Anna searched in the cupboard with the big plates where she'd hidden the tin and the weight of it felt promising. Sure enough, three of the weekend's cup-cakes had made it this far. She picked them out on to a plate and made three mugs of tea leaving the spoon in one to identify Mike's since he took sugar.

The boys were up in Ellis' new room and were gyrating around with their upper bodies only as though their feet were nailed to the carpet. They had quickly discovered that vinyl is not the same as electronic music and that if you leap about you end up with scratches in your precious records. Ashok had dug out an old turntable and they were using that but whining for a new one.

Anna knocked with her elbow and called out for them to open the door. Ellis got to it first and grinned at the sight of the tray. 'Thanks, Ma!'

The room looked awful. Now the big bed had gone together with the dressing-table and wardrobe, the blue carpet was two-tone – bright and faded. Well, three-tone, really, because it was also grubby in places. Ellis' single bed, itself hardly a thing of beauty, was rammed against one wall with the result that it couldn't easily be made so he had adapted by simply pulling the sheets up a few inches and his wardrobe, which had fitted snugly into the old room's alcove, had revealed itself to be a nasty orange colour with only the doors chipped white. Bobble was reclining like a hirsute duchess on a pile of blankets in a corner and must have been out for a run because all he could manage when Anna came in with the tray was a tongue-lolling leer. The place looked like a squat.

The boys sat on the floor while she perched on the end of the bed. There must be a spare chair or two somewhere in the house to bring up. 'Do you remember Dad and me painting your room and doing just the front of that wardrobe? It must have been at least seven years ago. We just couldn't be bothered pulling it out because you had it full of junk.'

'Are you referring to my prodigiously extensive collection of geological specimens?'

'And the rest.'

Mike swallowed the last of his cake and stared at Ellis. Elvis had lapsed into silence. 'What are you doing, you idiot?'

'I'm fletcherising my cupcake if you really want to know,' Ellis replied haughtily.

'What?'

'It was a theory at one time that it was good for you to chew your food so much that it liquefied,' said Anna, 'but I doubt it was intended for cupcakes – probably tough meat. Can I ask you both a question?'

'Go on, then,' said Ellis lifting the record off the turntable and slipping it reverentially into its sleeve.

'I've got a case where I have to find a way to get to know someone a bit without it looking suspicious. I've found out where she lives but not where she spends her days.' Bobble staggered to his feet and wandered over to the plates on the floor. 'I can't think how to make contact.' One of the curtain tracks had come detached from its bracket and the curtain was trailing, she noticed with annoyance. The boys were treating the room like a field den.

'Can't you knock on the door and pretend to be selling something?' asked Mike, flicking his long fringe out of his eyes and ruffling Bobble's head.

'I could but they'd just turn me away, wouldn't they – they wouldn't ask me in, and, anyway, I need a kind of on-going contact.'

'You just have to find out where she works,' said Ellis. 'Then, if it was, say, a shop, you could become a regular customer. You'll have to do a stake-out at the house and follow her to see where she goes.'

Anna absent-mindedly put her own plate down for the dog. Sometimes she thought it was the family that needed training. 'It's a bit weird, though, isn't it? I'd have to sit in the car and wait for hours, maybe, until she came out.'

'You'd have to take a wee-jug with you in case you were caught short,' said Ellis practically.

'Or park by a hedge and nip behind it,' said Mike.

'I think not. If you come up with any other bright ideas, let me know. I'm going down to make dinner. Can you stay, Mike?' She picked up the licked plates and put them on the tray with the mugs.

'Thanks, I'll text mum.'

After dinner she approached George with the problem but he was less enthusiastic about the idea of a stake-out. It could be seen as stalking, couldn't it? Imagine explaining to the police that she was only trying to find out confidential information about a young woman so as to pass it on secretly to her father who was a murderer.

'Mm.'

'Is there any chance that she's a professional? I mean, would she be on some kind of professional register?'

'She's too young. She'd have to be a student or at work – or unemployed.'

'Ok, then.' George clawed his fingers back and forth over his brindled chin doing a fair imitation of a dog with mange, Anna thought. 'Why not be straight-forward about it? Write to the young woman saying that her father would like to know how she is but is not going to bother her?'

'Apart from the fact that Robert has specifically told me not to, she was a new-born when he was locked up. We can't be sure that Vicki has told her about him.'

'How old was Kara when Vicki married Graham?'

'Three. She may not even remember a time when he wasn't there.'

George stood up and began to collect the pudding plates. 'Maybe explain to Ted that you've hit a brick wall? Let him work out how to go further, if at all?' He took the stack of crockery over to the sink and started to rinse them off, raising his voice over the noise of the water splashing. 'It's not really the kind of thing you're employed for, is it? He hasn't always been too conscientious about exposing you to risk. If you did follow her and you were picked up by the police he may not back you up and then your professional reputation would be compromised.'

'You may be right,' Anna sighed. 'I'll run it by Steve.'

'Good idea.' He slotted the plates into the dishwasher, glanced round the kitchen to check for stragglers and slammed the door shut. 'How's Alice doing?'

Anna stretched her legs under the table and scraped crumbs together into a little pile. 'Not well. She's still really down. I asked Faye to pop back and she said she would but she hasn't done and to be honest, I do understand. I mean, setting up your first independent home with your first serious boyfriend is a big thing. Maybe she'll come over next week.'

George leaned back against the sink, pondering this. 'She's had a lot of disappearances, hasn't she? Alice, I mean.'

'I don't think she remembers her parents – she was really only a baby.'

'No, but there may be some deep residual sense of loss. Those early years are so vital as you know yourself.' It was true, Anna had been aware of the void left by a missing mother for most of her life even when she was an adult and had stuffed it with substitute mothers until the real thing came along which turned out to be angst of a different kind. 'But there have been other losses, too, haven't there, since she came to live around here?'

For a second Anna didn't know what he meant and then she did. 'Harry. Yes, of course.'

'And Rosa. She formed a real bond with Rosa while she was here looking after Harry and then, later, she was here with me when I was recovering and Alice was often round.'

'Of course, she loves Rosa. I go to see her but I never think of taking Alice. When I was riding on Sunday Kimi suggested bringing her over to see the foal and the donkey and all that.'

'Yes, that could be a good distraction.'

George had now pottered over to the back door and Anna knew he was eager to get out to the shed. 'Thanks, Dad. I'll just pop down to Steve's and be back by nine. Ok?' George acknowledged this and turned to go out at which point she saw the dark band across the back of his cardigan where he had leaned against the wet sink. 'You will put a warm jacket on until the heater's got going out there, won't you?'

'Don't you start,' George muttered, 'I don't need two minders, thank you - Diane is more than sufficient.'

Anna stayed at the table for a little longer after the outside door had banged shut. George was right. Three years ago this table was crammed with chairs at dinner because Faye was here and Harry and sometimes Len and even Rosa, as well as Steve and Alice herself on occasion. Now when Alice came there was only Ellis and George and herself, the Steve-snatcher. No wonder she kept her lance sharpened and at the ready.

She picked her phone out of her pocket and called Rosa.

7

Later, while Steve sorted out Alice's lunch-box for the next day, Anna put her plan to him that this Saturday they would make a bit of a fuss of Alice by taking her first to visit Rosa on her canal boat in Selly Oak and then out for a burger and then into the country to Kimi's farm to see the animals and maybe, if it was not too cold or wet, have a ride on the donkey. Each part of this would be a surprise so the cumulative effect may lift her sad mood.

'Thanks, Anna. We can give it a go and hope for the best. I've never known her to be like this and I've tried everything. Her teachers say she's quiet there, too.' He snipped a little cluster of black grapes off the big bunch and tucked it down the side of the tub.

'Where is she now? It's a bit early for her to be in bed.'

Steve glanced at his watch. 'Her friend Mina's mum came and got her for an hour so the girls could try on bridesmaid dresses for Mina's auntie's wedding. She'll be back any minute.'

Anna got up. 'So I don't have to worry about her attacking me if I grab you?' she said, moving in on him. 'Step away from that lunch-box immediately and surrender to your fate!' She loved the way he laughed and flushed when she teased him, as though he had permission for once not to be serious and responsible and she loved the way she felt when his arms surrounded her and he covered her face and neck with kisses. But when the front door banged they sprang apart. No point in upsetting Alice.

'Sorry we're a bit late,' Mina's mum said breathlessly, 'there were hundreds of those little buttons that drive you mad. We'll have to plan an extra half hour for getting the girls ready.'

'Thanks for bringing her back,' Steve said.

'Oh no, I have to drop a couple more off, so I'll be on my way.' She nodded to Anna and dashed out of the kitchen.

'Hi Alice,' Anna said, smiling at her, 'Did you like your dress?' Alice stared at her.

'Did you?' Steve asked.

'It was all right,' Alice said to Steve. 'I'm tired. Will you come and read me a story?'

'Go up and clean your teeth, love, and I'll be up in two shakes of a lamb's tail.'

Alice glowered at Anna. 'You go home now,' she said, but when Steve began to protest Anna shook her head at him and smiled at Alice, picking up her coat and making for the door.

'I'll give you a call in an hour or so if you don't mind, Steve. There's a work problem I want to pick your brains about for five minutes.'

'Ok.'

As she walked up the road she thought about what George had said about Alice having lost the companionship of people she loved over the past couple of years and she knew how she felt. She loved Steve but she still missed Harry, her friend and husband for over a quarter of a century, and she thought she probably always would. It wasn't just the in-jokes and rapport they had shared and the rhythm of their days that ended talking quietly over the day in bed, usually about the children, it was the physical presence of him – the comforting smell of his hair and the easy touch of his hand.

At his funeral someone had offered to read the popular piece, 'Death is nothing at all.' It tries to say that it is as if the dead person is not gone but is only in the next room but that didn't feel true for Anna. For her, once Harry had died he had become as unavailable as a star in the sky. Yes, there were the memories, of course there were, but she missed the living, laughing, fleshly him even though that had diminished so much.

So, of course, Alice was frightened of her now – scared that Anna would take away Steve, the most precious person of them all – because while Harry and Rosa and Faye had gone, Anna was still there. In the child's mind perhaps Anna had somehow been causing all this loss. Who knew what was going through the little girl's head and what gave her bad dreams at night?

Around eight-thirty Anna paused the recorded documentary on conditions in British prisons she had been watching dutifully and decided she would save the rest for another time as to be further depressed must be counter-productive. She curled into the end of the sofa and called Steve.

'Ok? Is she asleep?'

'Yeah.' Steve sounded exhausted himself. 'All the hype over the dresses must have worn her out, thank goodness. I'm sorry she was rude to you.'

'No, I understand, don't worry.'

'So what was this work thing?'

Anna explained about Kara and what Ellis had suggested. 'Any ideas?'

'No, to be honest. But let me sleep on it.' Anna knew that Steve had access to classified information through the clandestine contract work he did for the National Crime Agency sanctioned, of course, by Ted who profited both directly by having Steve's skills at the researchers' beck and call and indirectly by a government fee he received. Probably Steve could find out where Kara worked but was so ethical that he would never do so – there was no point in asking him. 'Listen, though.'

'Yes, I'm here. What?'

'Don't do what Ellis suggested. Don't do a stake out – that's a really bad idea.'

'You sound tired, love. I'll let you go.'

'Ok. Goodnight Anna. Love you.'

The following morning at seven o'clock when it was still dark Anna, with her work clothes on and her work bag in her hand, eased open the front door. Ellis appeared on the stairs in his pyjamas with Bobble in tow needing to go out, took in the scene and raised an eyebrow at her. Anna put a finger to her lips and closed the door quietly behind her. The truth was that there was no other way.

There was very little traffic on the roads to Bromsgrove and even the major roundabout at the junction of the A38 and the M42 was quickly negotiated so Anna was back in Elgar Crescent well before 8.00. She drove slowly up and down looking for a good vantage point where she would not be too obvious and not finding one. It was an ordinary street with no hidden corners or partly concealed laybys so she parked in a different place from before about ten houses away from Kara's.

This time she had brought a clip-board with random sheets of paper and a pen and every now and then made a scribbled note which was, in fact, a shopping list for the weekend. It meant she could stare into space as though she was thinking when she was watching the front of the house keenly. If the police asked her what she was doing she was sunk. There was absolutely no reason she should be here. The only thing she could think of to say was that she wanted to check her records that a client still lived here but was too early to knock, but weak, very weak and quickly disproved.

It was that time of a winter morning when the street lights and a hesitant dawn have a half-hearted battle. When she had arrived it was definitely dark but now the lights looked decorative rather than useful and suddenly they went off. But at least the day was dry, so far, and Anna pondered what to do if Kara did not appear – she might be in college and not due in until the afternoon, or away for some reason – this brief stake-out was a long shot at best. If she did appear and moved off on foot then Anna would have to leave her car, she couldn't curb crawl alongside the woman, but then there would be the risk that she would be picked up by a car-share or get on a bus and be lost. Should she drive a short way and wait and then drive on again? That seemed just as likely to fail and might look even more suspicious. There were two cars at the front of the house, a chunky four-wheel drive and a little red Honda about five years old. That could be Kara's but it could equally well be Vicki's.

Just as Anna was mulling all this over the front door opened and a woman hurried out. She was wearing a dark coat with the hood up and tights with sturdy heeled shoes. Was this Vicki or Kara? Anna peered hard but couldn't see clearly. Was there something more mature about the woman's clothes? Vicki would only be in her late thirties, she wasn't old. Anna bit her lip and then, as the woman got into the car, decided that there was something about the length of the skirt and the style of the shoe that was possibly older rather than younger although they could simply be work related. It was just the vaguest feeling. The car disappeared down the street and Anna bit her nails.

She switched on the radio and felt increasingly uneasy. The pedestrian traffic down the street had increased and some people were frankly looking into the car at her. Would it be more suspicious to re-park or to stay where she was? If anyone tapped on the window and asked what she was doing could she bring herself to tell an outright lie and say she was making notes for the Council? It wouldn't be the first time she'd used lies of convenience to get what she wanted but that didn't justify it. For all she knew she was already being observed from a window or two and her registration number noted and perhaps even reported. Steve was right, this was a bad idea.

Then a movement at number 46 focussed her attention. The front door opened and someone female in a green parka with a faux fur trim was coming out. Anna switched off the radio and grabbed her bag throwing the clip-board on to the back seat. The woman set off quickly on foot down the street towards Anna who pulled on her gloves not glancing in the person's direction except for a quick look as she was almost level with the car. Yes, it was Kara. Anna let her go past and then got out, locked the car and set off thirty yards behind her.

It was a chilly morning and Kara walked fast with her head down and her hands thrust in her pockets so that Anna had to almost run to keep pace with her. At the end of Elgar Crescent she turned right down an A road and then after fifty yards crossed over to the other side. She had not used a crossing and Anna couldn't possibly just do the same, it would be too obvious she was in pursuit, so she walked on and when Kara turned left, Anna had to wait until the traffic had thinned before she could cross. When she got to the other side she took the same side road that Kara had and caught a glimpse of her disappearing. Anna hurried on but took note of the street name as it was possible that Kara would dodge about all over the place and then Anna would be lost. At the end of this road was a T junction with Old Road which dipped sharply downhill, Anna guessed towards the High Street, but there was no sign of Kara. The houses here were large Victorian villas for the most part, set back from the road with trees and tall shrubs in their front gardens. Anna ran now, sure that Kara had turned into one of the driveways, and she was going so fast that she almost missed her in her haste. Kara had stopped at the front door of a large house and was talking to another young woman. Anna leaned against the pillar gate-post breathing heavily, not daring to glance up the drive to see whether Kara had gone in.

'Are you ok?' It was the other girl.

'Fine, I'm fine,' Anna smiled, gasping. 'I've been power walking to try to lose weight but I need a breather.' These lies were far too easy for her.

'Yeah, this hill is a real work-out, but you see oldies steaming up and down all the time. They've got more energy than me!' The girl pulled up her hood and wiggled her fingers. 'Bye.'

Now she was gone Anna could read the sign set back from the road, 'Church View Retirement Home' and a phone number. She risked a good look up the drive and saw that Kara had definitely gone inside. Of course, the young woman could be visiting a relative, a grand-parent, maybe? Then she had a brain-wave. She took out her phone and dialled the number, edging away back up the hill.

'Church View.'

'Oh, hi, you don't know me but a young woman just turned into your drive and I think she dropped a five pound note. I was walking up the hill and found it. Would you mind asking?'

'Just a minute.' There was a pause and then she heard the woman call, 'Kara? Can you check if you dropped any money on the pavement outside just now?' After a moment of some subdued murmuring, the voice said to Anna, 'No, she's not dropped any, but she says thanks for checking – she's got to get the breakfasts out so she can't come to the phone.'

'Sorry to have bothered you.' Result, as Ellis would have said.

Back in the car she did an internet search for Church View, sucked up the information and started the car. She would only be a few minutes late into work with a bit of luck. What she would tell Steve and George about how she found Kara's workplace was a much trickier issue and by the time she had got to the busy roundabout she had decided to come clean with the truth if they asked. She was getting much too glib at lying.

Shell had narrowed it down to three hairstyles for her wedding – the usual shoulder length cut fluffed up which would require loads of hairspray, the scraped back look with false hair chignon, and Helena's idea, the romantic look with extensions and satin rosebuds. The girls felt that sufficient progress had been made to have a go at doing each one to get a rough idea. They were all in Shell's bedroom rummaging through the bag she had brought from work.

'Stop playing, Lol!' Shell cried, seeing that Lauren had found a length of hair and was making a moustache with it. 'Those are really expensive – don't mess about. They don't know I've got all this.'

Kara was laying out the objects from the bag in neat rows so she could see what was there. She had been looking forward to this evening all week - lazy hours with her girl-friends playing with hairstyles, gossiping, having a glass or two of red with no deadlines and nobody giving orders - but then Gerry had texted her and put a cloud over everything. He had said he would pick her up from

Shell's at 10.00 to go back to his place since his mum and dad would be out which meant she would now have to rush.

'Tell him you can't,' Shell said, brushing her hair back off her forehead and spraying as she did. 'You promised me first.' Kara bent over her sorting. She couldn't admit to Shell that Gerry made a stupid fuss if she turned him down and went on at her for hours and she couldn't face it. Maz did just what Shell told him and was grateful but Kara didn't seem to have the knack of getting her own way with Gerry and it made her feel foolish and weak.

'It'll be you two next,' said Lauren, and Kara didn't know whether she sounded envious or was mocking her.

'No,' she said, 'I'm not ready for that. I've got to sort my life out first.'

The chignon was judged to be too severe and made Shell's nose look big so by nine thirty they were labouring at concealing with clips a dozen extensions under Shell's meagre layers of hair.

Kara stood back to look at the effect and then darted forwards to make an adjustment. 'You'll have to trim those front ones and put the curling tong on your ends but I think that looks really pretty. Don't you, Lauren?'

'Can't we just shorten these a bit?' Lauren made snipping movements with the scissors.

'No,' Shell said, 'these are from stock, we can't do anything to them, I told you. I can get a better colour match than these, anyway.' She turned her head from side to side looking in the big dressing table mirror and hitching up hanks of hair to see what the shorter length would look like. 'I like this style – it makes me look like one of those princesses out of Game of Thrones. Can you just lift up the top bit, Kar?'

'My tail comb's gone rough, it'll snag.'

'There's a pin-tail one on the bed – use that,' Shell suggested, so Kara worked through the strands with the metal spike, lifting and separating and flicking. Shell stared at the result. 'You're good, you are,' she said. 'If I can get the extensions trimmed, would you do it for me, Kar? I mean on the day. I'd rather you did it than one of the girls from work.' Kara blushed with pleasure. This was exactly what she had hoped Shell would say.

'And it would save you a shedload of money,' Lauren put in.

So when Gerry said he was outside Kara gathered her stuff together and ran to meet him feeling excited about her new responsibility. He pushed the door of the van open for her, which was nice of him, so to reward him she leaned over and gave him a kiss. 'You stink of hair stuff!' he complained but he was in a good mood, laughing and grabbing at her knees.

Inside his house Gerry took her into the living room instead of his bedroom and pulled the curtains shut. Gerry's mother wasn't like Vicki and there were magazines on the floor and flattened cushions on the leather couch and even a used mug perched on the coffee table. Kara liked the clutter and kicked off her shoes without asking so that she could curl up in the matching chair. Gerry's mum was much older than Vicki because this was her second marriage and Gerry had been a bit of an afterthought, as she had put it to Kara. Privately Kara thought this was why he was so spoiled. They indulged him in a way her mum would have sneered at, never expecting him to help in the house, which his dad did willingly, or even contribute any of his wages to help out. Perhaps that was why he didn't take to being crossed, as he saw it.

He came in from the kitchen with a six-pack of lager and a bottle opener, a massive bag of crisps between his teeth. Kara laughed, relieved that they had not gone straight up to the bedroom. 'Shell's asked me to do her hair for the wedding,' she said.

'I've got a treat for you, baby,' he replied, 'come and sit over here with me.' His face was shining with a light sweat and he seemed excited.

'What is it? Have you won the lottery?'

'Wait till you see this. Tony gave it me.' He was slipping a DVD into the slot and Kara thought that if this was Best Championship Goals 2015-2016 or similar it would give her a chance to think how to prepare Shell's hair so it was in perfect condition for the big day because she overworked it and it needed proper conditioning. Gerry came back to the sofa and pulled her close. 'Take a look at this, babe, you won't ever have seen anything like it.'

But it was not football. After a few minutes Kara said in a small voice, 'I don't like this kind of thing, Gerry. Can you stop it, please.'

He was groaning at the forty-eight inch screen over the fireplace. 'Look at the tits on her, Kara, they're like fucking footballs. Oh no, look now - ' Kara pushed away from him and stood up. 'What? What? It's only a bit of fun, what's the matter with you, you tight mare?'

She began to pull her coat on. 'I don't like it Gerry. It upsets me - you know that. If you don't turn it off, I'm leaving.'

Gerry paused the frame. 'I've only got it for tonight – Mick's got it tomorrow. Come on, Kara, it'll get you going.' His hot, red face pleaded with her over the back of the sofa and rage rose up in her.

'It has got me going,' Kara said, anger flaring into her voice. 'I'm off if you care more for that disgusting stuff than you do for me.'

He turned back to the remote control and clicked 'play.' 'Shit shag anyway,' he muttered just loud enough for her to hear.

The words came out of her mouth as though they had been waiting to be said for too long and couldn't wait any more. 'Well, you'll be pleased we're over, then.'

Outside on the street the cold wind was clean and bracing. Instead of being upset or guilty she realised that she felt unburdened – she felt free. It was as though she could take a proper breath for the first time in months. Her phone tinkled and she put it on silent. As she strode through the quiet streets every now and then lifting her eyes to a clear, starlit sky, she almost laughed aloud with the joy of being free of him, of it. There would be others probably but for now she had her life back and the first thing she'd throw out when she got to her own room would be the razor.

But when she got home and turned in the hallway to go up the stairs as she always did, her dad called out from the living room. 'Kara? Come in here right now.' What had she done? Her heart thumping, Kara took a couple of steps into the room to observe in two seconds that her father was drunk. It didn't happen very often. Her parents rarely went out together but she remembered that they'd gone round to her dad's sister for dinner and that always put Vicki in a foul mood and that riled her dad. Her dad drank on the weekend but not like this – his face was purple and he was swaying as he stood up.

'Where's Mum?'

'In bed. She's just as pissed off with you as I am.'

'Why? I haven't done anything.'

'Gerry's rung. He says you've broken it off and you won't take his calls. Is that right?'

'Yes.' Kara stared at the simulated grain on the laminated floor desperately trying to come up with an explanation she could give her father. 'We're just not right for each other.'

He took a step towards her, spittle forming little balls on his wet lips. 'Oh, isn't he good enough for you, eh? He's earning, isn't he? He's not knocked you about, has he? You should count yourself lucky that a fit lad like him wants you. Oh, but he's not good enough for little Kara who's so bloody special!'

'Dad. Can we talk about it in the morning?

He took another step forward until he was so near that she could see the broken veins on the ridges of his cheeks and the open pores on the ball of his nose. 'Don't you call me Dad,' he spat, 'I'm not your dad, so there. Get on the phone to that boy and tell him you've changed your mind.' Then, as she stared at him in shock, his expression changed in front of her eyes from rage to a puzzled, wary look. 'I'm going to bed.'

Kara sank down on to the sofa. She heard her father's heavy steps go up the uncarpeted stairs and then across the landing. The bedroom door clicked shut. A huge hole seemed to have opened up inside her as though she had been hollowed out with a disembowelling knife. She sat very still for some time and then stood up, walked into the hall and turned out the lights before climbing the stairs so quietly that her feet seemed not to touch the treads.

8

There was rain in the offing on Saturday morning but they decided to go anyway and when they reached the parking spot for the canal tow-path it was still dry. Alice had not spoken at all on the short journey, sitting with her little legs stuck out from the back seat playing her game.

Steve zipped up her anorak against the cold, although she could certainly do it for herself, and the three of them slipped their way along the muddy track to Rosa's narrowboat. Anna wondered if Steve's gentle indulgence with Alice was helping or hindering. It was never a good idea to reward bad behaviour but it wasn't as though Alice was being simply naughty. Even so, Anna thought a little less cossetting might bring her back to normal. Obviously, she was not going to say this to Steve and when Alice saw that smoke was coming out of the battered steel chimney on the boat she looked animated for the first time in days.

The boat was a colourful sight on a dreary February morning with its traditional paintings of castles and roses in primary colours on the doors and even the bedraggled little Christmas tree on the roof complete with baubles, which Rosa hadn't yet packed away yet, gave it a jaunty look so when the large form of Rosa appeared in her purple cardigan smiling and waving they all hurried towards her.

In the galley Alice clung silently to Rosa burying her head in her woolly folds and for a second Anna was hurt but batted the feeling away. Alice loved most things about the boat, her favourite place being the fore-cabin where Rosa's bed was so, while Steve and Anna sipped their teas and ate the brownies they'd picked up on the way, Alice disappeared into it with Rosa. Steve smiled and cocked his head to one side hearing the child's voice and Rosa's soft replies. 'This was a good idea, Annie, she's cheered up already,' he said.

'What are they talking about?'

'I can't hear that – but she is talking.'

Telling Steve and George that she had followed Kara to her place of work had not been as difficult as she had thought as both merely shook their heads. 'I knew you would,' George said, 'but now what?' That problem had been exercising Anna a great deal. How could she manage to get to know Kara without arousing suspicion? What cover story could she use to get entry to Church View?

The cabin door opened and Rosa appeared bent almost double to get through and then Alice could be seen sitting cross-legged on the bunk with some coloured wool making a braid. Rosa's hair, usually stained exotically, was for once its own flaxen colour but to make up for it Rosa was wearing a wonderful long waistcoat under her cardigan made up of a rainbow of crocheted squares and a red tartan scarf. Anna pushed her mug towards her and mouthed 'thanks' but she didn't smile back. 'How's Dean, these days?' Anna asked, wondering if Rosa's criminally inclined brother was upsetting her.

'Gone off again,' Rosa said. 'I expect he'll be back when he needs something.'

'Does he keep in touch?'

'Sort of. Texts once in a while.' Rosa seemed to rally herself and looked more kindly at Anna. 'What have you been up to? Anything exciting at work these days?'

Steve huffed. 'It could have been very exciting.'

So Anna explained about Robert and Kara without using their names but as she talked she remembered that Rosa herself was, off and on, a carer for elderly people. She was a woman of many talents but, more than that, she had been ballast for Anna on several occasions when she had nearly been ship-wrecked by events. Rosa was a young woman, only in her twenties, but Anna often felt that she was the mother, the ideal mother, calm, serene and endlessly accepting and comforting, and Anna was the kid.

'So this home is in Bromsgrove?' Rosa asked when Anna stopped talking. 'There's a few there, retirement and nursing. I used to be moored up in the Tardebigge basin when I worked at one of them. I'd cycle in.'

'Oh,' Anna said as casually as she could, 'what was the name of it?' She couldn't tell Rosa the name of Kara's home, of course, but if it came up, that was a different thing.

'Fairmount,' Rosa said. 'So what are you going to do now?'

'Check with Ted would be a start,' Steve said, 'not to suggest something outrageous.'

'Oh, come on, you know he loves a *fait accompli* so he doesn't have to make a hard decision.' Anna traced a ring on the table top with a puddle of spilled tea. 'I've been thinking about how to get in, you know, get to know the daughter a bit, but I've not come up with anything yet.'

'Have you got DBS clearance?'

'Yes, I have. We often have to work with elderly people so we've all got them.'

'So is that some kind of clearance from the police like you have to have to work with children?' Steve asked and both women nodded. Alice called to Steve to look at what she had made so he got up carefully and they all turned and twisted so that he could get by to move up the narrow cabin.

'Didn't you used to be a librarian?' Rosa asked when she and Anna were settled again. 'Maybe you could volunteer to do something with that?'

Anna sat up. 'You're a genius, Rosa. I could offer to read to them – even take in a selection of short stories or poetry that they might like.'

'Or magazines. They love to be read to, especially if they can't do it themselves any more. Well, we all do, really, don't we?'

Alice came up to the little table and held out the rainbow braid she had made to Rosa. 'Tie it on me, Rosa,' she said, 'Please. On my wrist.'

Steve was smiling and Anna felt relieved and grateful to Rosa. 'It's lovely,' she said, 'clever girl!'

Alice turned her back to Anna and didn't reply.

When they were back in the car it was as though the visit hadn't happened and Alice returned to her tablet and her silence. Steve glanced at Anna sympathetically and it was true, she was feeling a little bruised, but there was still the visit to the farm.

Kimi was out in the stable-yard brushing down the hosed concrete and wearing only a short-sleeved T shirt and padded body-warmer on top of her ancient jodhpurs. Her hair was leaping about her head like a clutch of lambs' tails. It made Anna shiver to look at her. When she saw Steve's car turn into the yard she propped the brush against the wall and walked towards them pushing sweaty strands off her face.

'Hi.' She peered into the back of the car. 'Hey, Alice, nice to see you.' This was about as much of a concession as Kimi ever made in speaking to children so Anna hugged her, catching her breath on the stew of horsey smells. Alice had never been to Kimi's farm before so she was lead round and introduced to several horses' heads which stuck out from their stable half-doors. One dark bay bared its teeth and stretched its neck out to the little girl who leaped back frowning. The foal, it turned out, was in isolation with a cough. A light drizzle had begun to soak the air.

'So, here's our donkey, Big Ears,' Kimi said, throwing back a barn door to reveal a barred pen with the animal in it. The donkey, who'd been working on its hay bag, looked at Alice and Alice looked at the donkey and both looked away. 'I can pop a saddle on if you want a ride?' Alice took a step back and shook her head mutely and Anna could tell that Kimi was now at the end of her resources. What could you do with a person who didn't want to ride? Such a thing was beyond comprehension.

'Might there be a hot chocolate on the go?' Anna asked.

In the farm kitchen Alice sat at the big table on two cushions and cradled her mug glancing every now and then around her as though some other wild hairy creature was about to emerge. Kimi and Steve were discussing the possibility of a climbing trip so that she could see if she liked it and he was doing his best to persuade her to come on a club climb. 'Can't you just take me up?' she asked, 'I can't be doing with group things. I'll write out a disclaimer so you won't be liable if I fall off and kill myself.' Steve looked down at the table. 'Oh, bloody hell, sorry, Anna. Sorry, sorry.'

The kitchen door opened and in came Briony. Her cool gaze took in the scene. 'Excuse the pyjamas,' she said, 'I'm totally jet-lagged. Can't seem to wake up. Is there any coffee?'

'Have you just got back from somewhere?' Anna asked stupidly, glad of the interruption, 'Where have you been?'

Briony yawned and gathered the matching robe a little closer, leaning on the door post. 'Brasilia. Conference.' Neither Kimi nor Briony were verbose.

Steve nudged Anna's knee and nodded his head at Alice so Anna turned to look at her. Alice was staring at Briony with a dropped jaw and an expression of deep awe on her face. Briony's pyjamas and robe were delicately embroidered cream satin and the bare skin of her face, neck and arms, recently tanned from South American sun, glowed against the fabric. Added to this effect were her glacier blue eyes. Alice Meets a goddess, Anna thought, hoping that Briony would not spoil the effect with a tactless comment. But instead Briony folded her arms and faced Alice with interest. 'I know you, don't I?' They had met before at a barbeque but Alice had been much younger. The woman and the child appraised each other. Alice could almost be Briony in miniature and not only in looks.

'I'm Alice,' the child said, 'I'm six. I'm Steve's.'

Kimi placed a mug of coffee on the table and Briony glided over to get it. 'I'm Briony, I'm thirty and I'm Kimi's,' she said to the child. 'We're getting married soon.'

This was news to Anna, although hardly unexpected, and both she and Steve jumped up to hug the women and congratulate them. Alice, whose eyes had never left the vision that was Briony, put up her hand as though she was in school.

'What, sweetie?' Steve said, 'You can say whatever you want, you don't have to ask permission when you're not in class.' Kimi and Briony were now standing close together with their arms loosely around each other's waists smiling and Anna couldn't help thinking that it must be love as Kimi was still in her spattered and rank yard clothes.

'Please,' Alice said. They nodded and smiled at her to continue. 'Please can I be your bridesmaid? I've got a dress already with twenty-two buttons.'

Kimi and Briony glanced at each other before Kimi said, 'Of course. You'd be perfect for a flower girl, wouldn't she, Bri?' Alice went bright pink and actually clapped.

It was all going so well, Anna thought. Alice was clearly smitten with Briony and would have one wedding already under her belt before this one so she wouldn't be nervous, but at that point Briony herself ruined it. 'You'll be going to Anna's and Steve's wedding soon, as well, won't you?' Even Kimi crunched up her eyes and grimaced at Briony. 'What?'

'We haven't actually got plans - ' Steve began, but was halted by Alice who scrambled down from her chair and ran to Anna slapping at her and shouting, 'Go away! You can't have my Steve! I hate you!' Anna tried to hold her little hands away but it was Steve who picked her up, now incoherent with wailing, and took her outside.

'Whoops,' Briony said calmly, 'Good luck with that, Anna. I'm back to bed. See you.'

Kimi walked her out to the car and offered the best she could by way of consolation. 'Do you fancy a hack on Sunday afternoon?' she said, 'Blow away the cobwebs?'

'I'll phone you,' Anna replied, getting in to the front passenger seat, 'but thanks.'

Half a mile up the road Steve stopped the car in a lay-by. He turned round to look at his niece. 'Alice, I know you're upset and we're both sorry about that, but Anna is doing all she can to make you feel a bit happier. She's not taking me away from you, she would never do that, she just wants to be part of your life as well as mine. Can you say sorry for the mean things you just said?' Alice shook her head furiously. 'All right,' Steve said, turning back and putting the car in gear, 'We'll talk about it properly later so just have a think.'

He took Anna's hand with his free one. 'Are you ok?' Anna nodded and they drove on. She watched the brittle hedges soaked to a dark grey pass by and tried to imagine them frothing with green in the spring. They were nearly home when her phone pinged and she read the text from Rosa. *Alice says she wants to come and live with me. What's going on?*

'Drop me at mine,' she said to Steve, 'I've got some stuff I have to do.'

Kara hardly slept thinking of what her father had said. Did he mean it? Was it true? Or was he just upset that his plans to have Gerry as his son-in-law were derailed? He certainly seemed to like him better than he liked Kara, and, come to that, she suspected that Gerry wanted the relationship with her for the same reason – he and Graham had far more in common than she and he did. (Why was she now calling him Graham and not dad, in her mind?) She got up early, washed and pulled on a sweatshirt and jeans because she was going to confront Vicki and not let her get away before she knew the truth. Graham was not touchy-feely affectionate like some of her friends' dads, but Vicki was cool with her, too. She had thought this was just how it was, but if she was another man's child then he would be less interested in her, wouldn't he?

When she couldn't sleep she'd gone on to Tassie's blog which was a huge mistake. Now there was a backdrop of a gorgeous coastline with tree-covered hills and miles of posh hotels and yachts. It looked like the Caribbean. Tassie called it 'the turquoise coast of Turkey' as she posed on a stone wall, tanned and blonde, with her knees drawn up, pointing to things and naming them while Ben presumably, filmed her. When Tassie wiggled her fingers and then blew a kiss at the camera to sign off, Kara was too suddenly back in her narrow, gloomy room so she had crept back to bed to curl up and suck her thumb and think bleak thoughts.

Now she sat in the kitchen at the little square table with a mug of coffee and two rounds of toast. She had dropped crumbs on the floor, she realised, and there was a rash of them round the toaster, too, but she didn't care. How can you make toast without leaving crumbs round the toaster? Her buttery knife lay across her plate and she rebelliously nudged it on to the wood so a smear was left. Vicki usually got up early on Saturday even though it wasn't a work day as she liked to give the house a good clean before going out with her friends to the shops. Usually Kara got dragged into the housework, too, to do the 'water jobs' her mother disliked, like scrubbing out the bathroom. She picked at her nails, waiting, her heart beating hard, a tight knot pushing at her ribs.

Ten minutes later Vicki rushed in and went straight to the tap to fill the kettle but not fast enough for Kara to miss the closed expression on her face. He'd told her what he'd said and what he'd said was true. Kara stood up. 'So I'm not his daughter,' she said, her voice shaking, 'am I yours?'

Her mother pushed past her to get to the socket. 'Don't be so dramatic, of course you're mine.'

'But not his.'

At this Vicki turned and faced Kara, leaning on the worktop as the kettle began to roil with heat. Her face bare of make-up looked tired and tense and it was probable that she, too, had had a bad night. 'No. You're not his. You should be grateful – he's been like a dad to you, hasn't he?'

Kara had no answer for this. What were dads like to their daughters? It was true she had always had food and a house and clothes; he had helped her mum provide for them and once in a while they had done things together and had fun when she was little. Was that what being a dad was? 'I'm not saying I'm not grateful,' she managed at last, wilting a little under her mother's hostility.

'Well, then.'

'So who is he? My real dad – who is he?'

'You don't need to know.'

'I do. Of course I do! What happened – why haven't you ever told me?'

Vicki seemed to consider before she spoke and Kara could see she was struggling to decide how much to say but then it was as though she mentally gave up the effort and as she turned to pour the boiling water into her mug, she said, 'Because he's no good.'

Kara folded at the waist as though she had been punched and sat down. 'Tell me, Mum, tell me.'

But Vicki had closed off and only said, 'I need to get going sorting this place out, it's a tip. If you don't want to help you can get upstairs but before you do you can see to the mess you've made in here.' Kara stood up trembling. 'And be nice to Graham – he pays the bills round here, madam, your pittance doesn't make a dent. And you can apologise to Gerry, too, while you're at it, you silly girl.'

Kara opened the cupboard door and took out a dustpan and brush. She would not cry, she wouldn't give Vicki the satisfaction, because she had made up her mind what she would do. She knelt down and swept up the toast crumbs from the white-tiled kitchen floor, tipped them in the waste and then got the damp dishcloth and scooped the table-top and counter clean. When she had finished she went back upstairs, closed her bedroom door and searched for websites which might help her find her father. Within minutes it became clear she needed to know two things – a full name and a date of birth – neither of which her mother would tell her.

Vicki's older sister Elise lived in Birmingham but the two were estranged so Kara hardly knew her and she may never have known her real father. Vicki had always kept herself to herself except for her close friends but Kara realised these were all from her mother's time in Bromsgrove, none from Birmingham where Kara had been born and where Vicki had lived before. She heard the front door shut and looked out to see Vicki getting into her car. Graham's car had gone, too, so he had sloped off rather than face her.

As she walked downstairs Kara realised that her jaw was aching and that her teeth had been clenched for what seemed like hours. She opened her mouth wide and massaged the muscles on either cheek. She went into their tiny unused dining room and squeezed round the white padded chairs to the bureau where she knew her mother kept receipts for purchases and other official documents. As she removed each small stack of papers, she placed them face down on the dining table so that she could put them back in the same order. Near the bottom of the cupboard was a creased brown envelope with 'Certificates' hand-printed on it.

With trembling fingers Kara carefully unfolded each separate piece of paper. First, she found her nan's death certificate from 2006 and then, a year earlier, Vicki's dad's. Kara could barely remember them as Vicki had not wanted to be close and visits had been few. A hazy memory of thin old people with papery faces and brittle grey hair drinking tea from cups and saucers floated across Kara's mind but it might not have been them. The only thing that remained was a framed wedding photograph of them kept in the same drawer which showed her nan in a knee-length stiff pink dress and a little round hat with a veil and her grand-dad in a dark suit and a flop of fair hair. She paused and picked up the photo. Seeing them next to each other Kara realised how dark skinned her nan had been. She looked quite exotic next to her new husband who seemed very pale and English in comparison. She smiled at the names on the marriage certificate, Pearl and Alan. She wondered if they had been happy and how they had coped with their daughters' falling out and estrangement.

Next came Vicki's birth certificate and her marriage certificate for Graham Brandon. Kara looked at the date and realised that she had only been three when they tied the knot so they must have decided to act as if Graham was her father. That was around the time that they'd come out to this house so the neighbours wouldn't know any different.

There was only one more folded certificate in the envelope. Kara withdrew it slowly and picked it open as though it might explode. 'Certified Copy of an Entry of Birth,' it read, for 'Kara Gates, girl. Name of Mother: Victoria Gates.' Kara's eyes were blurring and she rubbed them impatiently. 'Name of Father: Robert Johnson.' Under the address column was written her nan and grand-dad's address where her mother must still have been living.

Robert Johnson. She knew his name. A deep gasping breath came as though she had swum a long way underwater and only just surfaced.

Kara quickly returned the papers to the drawer and ran upstairs to her laptop. There was no date of birth for him on the certificate but he probably was about the same age as her mother and they were definitely in Birmingham, maybe both in Nechells, so she could see what a simple trawl would find. How hard could it be?

When the genealogy websites sprang up she only recognised one so she clicked on that and found you had to subscribe but then she saw she could sign on for a week's free trial so she set up an account. Her fingers were shaking so much she kept hitting the wrong key. She entered his name and was asked for a time frame for his birth so she thought for a moment and gave a five-year window around the time of Vicki's birth in 1979 although it was hardly likely that he was younger since she was only eighteen when she'd had Kara who had so selfishly 'ruined her life' as she had told her daughter more than once.

There were fifteen men with Robert Johnson in their names in that time frame. Some had a different first name with Robert for the middle one, some had Robert as a first name, but all were listed as being registered in Warwickshire which included Birmingham with no further detail. Kara had no idea what to do next. She looked round the website and couldn't make head or tail of it. She entered her mother's information and found that with a date of birth there was only one option – the right one. She had to have her father's date of birth. Kara sat staring at the screen and biting her nails.

Over the next hour she searched Facebook and Google and was none the wiser. There were so many Robert Johnsons all over the world - musical ones, sporting ones, American ones, even Swedish ones – it seemed like the most common name a man could have.

It was no use trying to bully her mother into telling her even if she knew – in any case, Kara was too intimidated to do that. Vicki could be very stubborn and even vicious once she'd made up her mind. Could she be shamed into giving her the information? Kara tried to remember any techniques that had worked when she had wanted something from her but couldn't think of any.

She sighed, thinking about the long day ahead and the burden of this new, shattering knowledge. She felt sore and tearful but also as though she might explode. Shell was off for the weekend with Maz and Lauren was too snide to tell this sort of thing to but there was someone who she could tell – Helena. Helena was never shocked and always interested in anything Kara disclosed and she was not going anywhere this weekend so she would be there in her cosy room just reading or listening to music. It was a little unusual for staff to go in on their time off but not unheard of. Some of the girls would run errands for the residents or take in something if it was a birthday. Yes, she would go and talk to Helena.

She sat down at her dressing table mirror and started to brush her hair.

9

When Anna walked into the kitchen she found Ellis bent over the ironing board. 'Hi, what's going on?' she asked, as she pulled off her coat and slung her bag on the chair. She felt defeated. What could she do to allay Alice's fears and make a friend of her? Neither of them had said as much but it would be impossible for her and Steve to live together if Alice continued to be so hostile. Glimmerings of antipathy towards Anna had surfaced before but because Faye was around they were easy to ignore since Alice was so sunny with Faye. Anna walked over to the kettle, shook it, and switched it on.

'Look,' Ellis instructed, lifting up a crumpled white dress shirt, 'I got it from the Heart Foundation, isn't it wicked?' He was as thin as a rail and the almost the tallest one in the family at fourteen with a top knot of glossy auburn curls and those dark-fringed lion eyes from Harry.

Anna leaned back against the counter waiting for the kettle to boil. 'Where are you off to then? Dinner and dance at the Ritz, is it?'

'No, it's for the band. It demonstrates my sartorial *sang-froid.*'

Pouring the boiling water into the mug, Anna said, 'Do you talk like that at school?'

'Of course, why?' Ellis smoothed one sleeve along the board and picked up the snorting iron.

'Don't they give you a hard time?' She bashed the tea bag about and went for the milk.

'Of course the whifflers and the lumpen proletariat do.' He looked up and flashed a grin at Anna. 'They call us the posers.'

'Us?'

'The band – me and Mike and Bean and Dan. Henry's pushed off.'

'I can't see Mike getting himself gussied up in a dress shirt. You're not all wearing tails, are you?'

Ellis put the iron down on its end and regarded her. 'No, of course not. The whole point is that we each individually demonstrate that how we dress makes a statement about our self-concept but it's not just us. Everyone does.'

George wandered in from the shed looking frazzled and went over to the kettle to feel it. Anna pulled a mug off the shelf and handed it to him. 'I don't,' he said. 'I just wear what's comfortable.'

Ellis wagged a finger at him. 'Ah, no, you see, that's exactly the point. You have chosen every item of clothing you put on. Consciously or unconsciously you are stating aspects of your ideology. In your case you are presenting yourself as someone who wants to be thought of as a person who doesn't value appearance and who refuses to co-operate with a consumerist culture. You dress like someone who doesn't care how he dresses which is quite devious, really. You are projecting your values through your clothes just like everyone does.'

'Are there any biscuits?' George asked.

Anna looked round the room. 'I can't remember where I hid the tin.'

'Bottom shelf of the vegetable baskets,' Ellis said. 'It's the semiotics of fashion. That's why we're owning the perjorative label put on us – we're calling the band The Posers, because that's what everyone is, does.'

'I've never seen Mike in anything apart from his school uniform or a T shirt and jeans,' George said, pulling out the biscuit tin and putting it on the table. 'I hope there's some shortbread left.'

'And that's what he'll wear in the band. You're missing the point, Pops. The image he has chosen for himself is expressed through that. It's his pose, just like your old cardi is your pose and this dress shirt is my pose. Bean's wearing a frock to pose as someone unfettered by gender labelling.'

'Ok,' said George, ready to scurry out of the back door with a pocket full of shortbread fingers. 'Good for you, I think. Did you get the food shopping while you were out?'

'Yup. Put away. Have you checked your Twitter account?'

'Um, will do.' George looked guiltily at Anna. 'He's set one up for me.' Anna tipped her head in a non-committal way and he made a bolt for the shed.

'Are you cooking, Mum?'

Anna sat down at the table with her tea and shook the contents of the biscuit tin. There were only custard creams left so she picked one out. 'Mm. I'll start in a minute.' She was a little worried by the conversation with Ellis. There was a fine line between being self-confident enough to brush off ridicule, which she was pleased about, and being arrogant. She didn't like the way he had called other kids 'lumpen proletariat' even though he had grinned at himself. He was a good student, always at or near the top of his class, and she didn't want him turning into a show-off. For a few more moments he ironed silently being especially careful with the ruffles down the front and then he shook the shirt, put it on a hanger which he hooked on a cupboard knob and then unplugged the iron and put the board away. She expected him to go up to his room but instead he sat down at the table with her.

'Mum?'

'Mm.' Anna eyed the biscuit tin and picked out another custard cream as a delaying tactic since she didn't particularly like them.

'We've got a new band member.'

'Oh, right. What's he wearing then? A space-suit to signify that his country of choice is cloud cuckoo land?'

'Oh, ha ha. It's not a he, it's a she. Kirsty. She's going to be our vocalist.' There was something in his voice when he said her name that made Anna's finely tuned maternal antennae stiffen.

'Great,' she said cautiously.

'She's in my science group for physics, she's really clever and she asked me if she could join so we're giving her a trial.' He paused and stared hard at the pitted and scored table top. 'She's got amazing long blonde hair and she says I make her laugh.' He looked up at Anna, his mouth twisting up just like Harry's did when he was trying not to smile. 'She told me she listens to James Blunt but I said I'd forgive her if she promised never to do anything like that again.' He got up from the table and took the shirt hanger down and then stopped, remembering something. 'You'll never guess who I saw in the fruit and veg shop. Joan. She's working there now. She says she loves it.'

'Really? I must go round. She said she was thinking of getting a job.'

'Why?'

'Needs a new roof.'

'Oh, right. Give me a shout when dinner's ready unless you want some help?'

'It's ok,' Anna said, 'you go and practise posing and I'll get going before I empty the tin.' She listened to the thumps his feet made as he ran up the stairs and wondered if he was aware of how obvious the signifiers of infatuation were. He was clearly darted for the first time in his life. But before getting out the meat and vegetables she turned to the back door and walked the few steps outside to George's shed.

Inside there was a cosy fug from the halogen heater and a glow from George's desk lamp that highlighted his furrowed brow. He was bent over some papers, pen in hand, but looked up when she came in. 'You look a bit like a gnome in this light,' she said, slipping down into the old rocker, 'shouldn't you be stitching lieder hosen or something?'

George regarded her over his glasses. 'How rude. It wasn't a gnome, it was an elf. Besides,' he sat up and beamed at her, 'I am choosing grey hair and wrinkles to signify age and wisdom.'

'Ha!'

'How did it go with Alice today?'

Anna's heart was still sore. 'Mixed. She was thrilled to see Rosa, didn't like the animals at the farm and has fallen in love with Briony. Made them promise to let her be their flower girl.'

'They're getting married?' Anna nodded. 'Well, that should cheer her up.'

'It's just me, Dad. It's just me that's the problem. She thinks I'm going to take Steve away from her. He has spoken to her, he did in the car, but she won't have it.'

'Tricky.' George did not put down his pen or the papers. 'Can you give her a present, maybe? It sounds crude but children give great significance to gifts.' He glanced down. 'I'm very impressed with this submission, Annie, it's from an Iraqi student at the university – beautifully nuanced. I might ask her to our Friday evenings, with a friend, of course.'

Anna stood up. 'Good idea, Dad, I'll go and get started on the casserole.'

'Can you make sure the door catches as you go out? I've got to put a new lock on.'

Helena was not in her room but Kara tracked her down to the day room where she was reading a letter to Mrs Whitaker who was almost blind. She smiled at Kara in a questioning sort of way so Kara said, 'When you've got time, could I talk to you?'

'The door's not locked. Why don't you go in and make us both a tea and I'll be along in five minutes?'

Helena's room was neat and pleasant smelling as always and Kara wondered if she was anyone's nan, she would be a lovely one. As she waited for the little kettle to boil Kara tried to remember if Helena had visitors and couldn't think of any, but then, she went out a lot. She was one of the few residents who still had her own car so she would probably prefer to see friends and family away from Church View. Kara made the tea as Helena liked it and carefully put the china mugs on their coasters on the small polished table. She didn't have to wait long, in fact, it seemed too soon that Helena slipped in the door. She hadn't practised what she would say.

'That looks lovely,' Helena said. 'Would you like a biscuit or something?' Kara shook her head. They both picked up their mugs. 'Everything ok at home?'

'Not really.'

'I'm listening.'

Kara stared at the rim of bubbles round the milky tea in her mug not knowing where to start. 'I've had a shock,' she said, abruptly. 'I'm a bit wound up.'

'I can see that. Just take your time, I'm in no hurry.' Helena was sitting with her back to the light from the window and her silver hair was rimmed with brightness but her hands were steady as they held her drink in her lap. She waited.

'My dad says he's not my dad. Graham. He told me he's not my dad when he was angry about something on Friday night so I looked on my birth certificate and it's someone called Robert Johnson. I never knew.'

Helena put her mug down on the coffee table as though she now couldn't trust herself not to spill the tea. 'How do you feel about that?'

'I asked mum about it and she just said she hadn't told me because he was no good.'

They sat in silence, Kara's knee trembling until she moved her foot to relieve it, and then there was the sound of a trolley clattering down the corridor. 'What are you thinking?' Helena asked finally.

Kara's chin shot up. 'I don't care if he's no good. I have a right to know him and I'm going to find him but I can't because I don't know his date of birth. Mum won't tell me.'

'Ok. You're angry and upset. Are you sure you want to do that?'

A single tear rolled down her cheek. 'I am angry and upset,' she said, 'but there's something else that I've only just realised. I'm excited. They don't care much for me, but he might, my real dad.' She glanced quickly up at Helena's face but she saw it was troubled, not smiling. 'I know he might be dead or anywhere, I know that.'

'He might not be what you want, I was thinking,' Helena said quietly.

'But I've got to give him a chance haven't I? He knows I exist because his name is on the Certificate and it was only a couple of days after I was born so he must have registered me himself, mustn't he?'

'Maybe.'

'I have to try at least but I can't get anywhere without a date of birth and the websites are confusing, too. I need some help.'

But after they had talked about ways that the information might be found they could only come up with two options, both unlikely to be helpful. One, of course, was to press Vicki and see if she would tell Kara but the chance of that was remote as she would have nothing to gain from it and maybe it could bring a lot of hassle to herself and Graham if Robert was traced. The only other option was Elise, Vicki's estranged older sister.

'I don't know where she lives but I know where she works,' Kara said, 'unless she's moved. She's been on reception in a doctor's office in Birmingham for years. Mum took me there once when I was about nine because my nan had left some bits of jewellery for mum in her will and Elise wanted to pass them on to her. She was nice to me, she gave me a lolly.'

'But you were very young, can you remember the name of the practice?'

Kara smiled for the first time, it felt like, in years. 'I do remember because it had such a nice name, it was called Love Lane Medical Centre. We went there on the bus because Vicki didn't have her own car then.'

Helena got up and went to her desk. 'It could have changed its name but let's have a look.' As she tapped the keys Kara sat very still remembering the scene years ago.

Vicki had not even greeted her sister properly but had just said, 'I'm only here for the things mum left me. I can't stay,' and

Elise had smiled at Kara and given her the lolly. 'You're a little beauty, aren't you, sweetheart?' she'd said. Then she'd got a bag out from under the counter and passed it across to Vicki. 'I get off in half an hour,' she'd said, 'can't you just have a coffee with me?' but Vicki had grabbed the bag and pulled Kara roughly away.

Helena got up and gave Kara a piece of paper. 'It's still there - I found it,' she said. 'I've written down the phone number and the directions. Are you ok?'

'I've just remembered something,' Kara whispered. 'When we saw her she said I had his eyes. She said I had my dad's eyes but I thought she meant Graham. She did know him.'

Anna wasn't at all sure it was the right decision but she now felt she had to come clean with Ted. She thought about what could be fudged and there wasn't much, but there were things that could be omitted and it would then be up to Ted to grill her. He would certainly notice any gaps in her account, he had the instincts of a gun dog, but he may decide not to pursue what he didn't want to be told.

He was waiting for her behind his desk, arms folded, with a genial smile pasted on to his face. Had he had his hair cut a little shorter round the back and sides? 'Anna - how are the kids?'

She decided not to pull up a chair and to keep it brief. 'Fine, thanks. Faye hasn't so much left home as taken it with her but - '

'I presume you've come to tell me you've found the girl? I knew I could count on you.'

'Yes, I have found her, Ted. She's living and working in Bromsgrove.'

'Good job. I'll send the man his bill.'

'Well, no, you can't, because he didn't just want to know where she is, he wants to know if she's ok.' She watched Ted's face, observing the calculation flicker behind his eyes. If the job continued then the fee would be larger. On the other hand, this really wasn't the sort of work they normally did and Ted would have hoped for a quick result and a grateful Governor friend.

'You can't go to her home so what's her job?'

'She's a care assistant in a retirement home and I do have an idea for how I could get closer to her but it would involve a little bit of deception.'

Ted rolled his lips round his teeth in the odd way he had. Then he looked out of the window and yes, he had had a sort of middle-aged hipster haircut. It looked awful. Finally he turned back to Anna. 'What had you in mind?' So she told him.

'It would only be one afternoon a week, I thought.'

Without hesitation he said, 'Too slow – you need to go every day for a couple of weeks. Tell them you're between jobs and want to do something useful before you move on and that your mum had been in a home like this one in Northumberland, or somewhere, and had enjoyed it when volunteers went in and read and you'd like to do the same for others. Giving something back, people say, don't they? You've chosen this home because you put a pin in a list. You chose Bromsgrove because it's a nice little country town and you like to get out of the city when you can.'

'Um,' Anna began.

'You can use my name for a reference, email only, and I'll tell Josie to put anyone asking about you straight through to me or take a message. I'll expect you in here as usual every morning. Anything else?'

'I'd like to update Robert on what I've found so far, I know he's desperate for information and I don't want to put it in a letter.'

'You could easily put it in a letter,' Ted said, 'but I've no objections to you going in your own time.' He picked up a manila envelope from his desk and offered it to Anna. 'Give that to Suzy, will you, she's waiting for it.' Anna took the hint and made for the door but as she opened it Ted said, 'And you'll notice I didn't ask how you found out where she worked so proceed with caution. I might not always be such a pushover.'

Suzy took the envelope with a grimace. 'I am so fed up with this case,' she moaned, 'it's so pedantic and Ted knows I'm a broad brush type girl.' She pushed back in her swivel seat. 'How goes it with you?' Anna noted with admiration how the dark blue of Suzy's silk blouse set off her fair hair perfectly and that her ear lobes bore what looked like not-so-tiny diamonds.

'Mixed. Are those earrings new? Are they diamonds?'

'Yes and yes. I'm back with Rob now he's earning and this is a small sign of his gratitude.'

'I thought he'd gone off in despair to find himself in Thailand when you dumped him?'

'He did, but then he met this guy who needed an English business partner in the artefact trade and hey presto, we're back on.' Suzy flicked her ear lobes saucily.

Anna smiled at her. 'Do you know, I sometimes think that your material girl credentials are not totally authentic. I suspect you're an old softie and you're very, very fond of him.'

'No, hard as nails, darling. Hi Steve.'

After a couple of minutes' chat Steve said to Anna, 'Have you got a minute?' and she followed him into his office. He didn't close the door and they both sat down near the screens that were always lit up. She hoped he didn't want to talk about Alice because she didn't have anything to offer and it bothered her to think about it.

'I've had an idea,' Steve said. 'How about us going away together, I mean, with Alice, so she can get to know you better? Only for a weekend.'

'She's known me since she was two,' Anna said.

'In the background, yes, but if it was just the three of us then, you know, she might see that we can be a unit.' Light from a screen was hitting his irises at an oblique angle and granulating the blue and grey into shards of quartz against his flushed cheeks. She realised for the first time how worried he was. Alice was a stubborn and, it had to be said, rather indulged little girl but Anna knew Steve wanted more than anything that they would set up home together. She wanted it herself but not at the price of continual warfare. Also, it had never really been discussed whose house they would live in and Anna didn't want to leave her own. If she was honest with herself it wasn't just Alice who was stalling.

'I don't know, Steve. Faye's only just left and she's raw from that, I think.'

'Ok. I won't push it.' Steve sat back and glanced at the hand-written notes he kept on his desk which Anna knew would be some form of To Do list. 'How did your meeting with Ted go?'

Anna stood up. 'Fine really. He gave me the green light so I'll phone the home and see if I can wangle my way in.'

'See you tonight, maybe?'

'Probably. I'll call you.'

On the way home that night Anna parked just off the High Street and walked round to their local greengrocers, now called Nowak's. Joan was bagging up some sweet potatoes for a young couple as she instructed, 'So then a spoonful of brown sugar mashed in with the butter and baked. Delicious, and so easy, and they're packed with complex carbs so a meal of that will keep you going for hours.' They smiled and paid and thanked her.

'Hey,' Anna said, 'Don't you have shops in Northfield? Play down your own end!'

'Hello, dear, give me a hug.' Joan looked round her at the colourful mounds of produce and winked. 'I saw it advertised online and I thought, well, I could bother you sometimes.'

'We'd all love it, you know that. But how are you finding the hours? I must say you're looking fit.' The worrying pallor had gone and Joan's beloved rosy cheeks were back and Anna thought she detected a little more roundness in the flesh as though she had been gently pumped up.

'It's made me realise how housebound I've been,' Joan whispered. 'I get to chat to people all day here so I'm never tired until I actually get home and put my feet up and that feels good, too. You know, being part of the working world and all that.' She pulled Anna closer, glanced towards the back of the shop and whispered, 'He's lovely, Piotr, the son, about your age and his dad, Jakub, works here, too. Can you see that little office? Don't look now – oh, you have.' But all Anna had seen was the top of a thickly sprouting grey head.

It was a little chilly in the shop but Joan was trussed up in two sweaters and a padded waistcoat with a Snoopy apron tied tightly over the lot and had completed the outfit with her gardening gloves with the fingers cut out. 'I was a bit worried about you when Ellis told me he'd seen you, but you've got bright eyes and a wet nose and you're definitely wagging your tail. Not too much for you?'

Joan hugged herself. 'They're so nice to me,' she said, 'I feel as though I'm part of the family. They bring me lunch when they get their own and they're always making delicious coffee.' Suddenly she focussed like a terrier scenting a rat. 'I forgot to tell you, don't tell your dad, the poetry group loved his video so much Diane and I have posted it on Youtube!'

'Is that a good idea?'

'We think it's a great idea. He's been published so many times in the small press world, this could take him through to the next level!'

At home Anna went straight upstairs to get changed into jeans and her favourite old sweater which Harry had always referred to as 'your dog blanket.' She looked at herself in the mirror and grimaced at how dull her winter skin was. Even with the heating on low it was so dank and dark outside that she was chilled. It had not been a bad day; Ted had been as amenable as he ever was, she had got a visit to Robert organised and, best of all, Church View had been open to the idea of her volunteering once they'd checked she had DBS clearance. So, it was all good but the Alice problem still nagged at her uselessly since she couldn't think of a remedy or even a plan. George had suggested a gift but that seemed like either bribery or rewarding and reinforcing Alice's irrational fears. She was just emptying the laundry basket to take a bundle down to the washer when Bobble starting barking wildly from Ellis' room. She ran to it and flung open the door.

Mike and Ellis were fighting each other, grunting and sweating, with Bobble bowing and barking and then leaping on Mike and it was not a game, even the huge dog was on the verge of getting seriously hysterical and taking a lump out of one of them. 'Stop it immediately!' she yelled. 'Get down, Bobble, come here!' The dog ran to her and then back again to the boys barking continuously like a sea-lion. 'What on earth's going on?'

The boys stopped and stood still with their heads bowed looking furious. Anna went to the dog and grabbed its collar. 'Nothing,' Ellis said.

'I've got to go,' Mike slipped past her as she struggled with the dog.

Anna turned to Ellis who was now sitting on the bed, his mouth in a hard line and his face white. 'What's going on?' She dragged Bobble over to his pile of blankets and told him to sit and for once he actually did, groaning as he settled and flattening his ears to show there were no hard feelings.

'Don't want to talk about it,' Ellis said.

'You and Mike haven't fought since you were kids,' Anna said, seating herself beside him, 'so what set this off?'

Ellis mumbled, 'He wants to come climbing with me and Steve and I said he couldn't.'

'Why?'

'He's always hanging around – I'm fed up with it. He's not even a good drummer.'

'He's your oldest friend,' Anna said, bemused, 'Why are you being so horrible?'

Ellis leaped up off the bed. 'You don't know what you're talking about!' he shouted, 'I'm not being horrible, he's being a bastard! I'm taking Bobble out and don't say anything else to me about that tosser, ok?' The commotion of six legs pounding down the stairs was followed by a brief pause and then the slam of the front door.

Anna sat for a few minutes on the bed after he had gone. Ok, he was a teenager and so was Mike but this fight was so uncharacteristic for them that she was concerned. Ellis had always been such an easy child to raise – sometimes she'd even worried that he was too helpful, too sweet, too forgiving, unlike his sister who was the opposite. Perhaps now Faye had left he felt free to move into her psychological space? Maybe the family dynamic, disrupted first by Harry's absence and now Faye's, was going through another metamorphosis. She bloody hoped not – it had been soothing to have a peaceful house for the last few weeks. Mr Ransome's words came back to her from the talk he had given at the last parents' evening. He had said that as parents they should be careful not to force friendships or reconciliations between peers as their own child knew his or her peers best and there may be a good reason for the falling out. But Mike? They had known Mike almost all his life and he was a great kid, sensible and good-natured.

It was no good raising this with Ellis now he had told her not to, she would have to respect that and maybe it would just blow over. She looked around the room which had got, if anything, shabbier since Ellis had moved in and decided that a good neutral subject would be a discussion on what he wanted to do with it. Make-over therapy.

She took out her phone and rang Faye. 'Hello darling, are you all right?' she said hopefully.

'Mm. Mum, you don't need all those chairs in the kitchen any more, do you?'

'Yes.'

'I knew you'd be like that. But there's some great ones at the Bargain Basement shop for only £20 each – you could get two of them for an early birthday present? The white ones.'

'I'm very well, thank you.'

'We're going to flick different coloured paint at them – primary colours – it will be so cool, but it would be cheaper to use your old kitchen ones.'

'Any chance of popping round to see Alice?'

'Super busy, Mum.'

Anna ended the call and stared out of the window at a sky now completely dark. Rain was tapping like fingernails on the glass and she got up and walked over to pull the curtains closed.

10

Kara sat nervously in the waiting room of Love Lane Medical Practice and chewed the skin round her thumbnail. She was wearing her new black jeggings, tan ankle boots and her best sweater, a boxy beige V neck, under her parka. It was getting hot so she took the parka off and folded it on the seat beside her. She knew that Elise had seen her because she had waved her fingers and then mouthed, 'Ten minutes,' because she was on duty until 3.30. Kara had taken extra trouble with her hair, spraying the palms of her hands with product and then threading them through so that when she brushed the hair back and trapped it with a band the flat hair shone and the loose hair was curly not frizzy, for once.

She hadn't told Elise what she wanted, she'd just said who she was and could they talk and Elise had immediately agreed and suggested today, which was Kara's early shift at work, so she had made it here in time on two buses.

Helena had had another idea to help Kara in her search and she was excited about it but wondering if she dared ask. If Elise could come up with Robert's date of birth, Helena had said, she should talk to Jackie who might be able to trace him more easily than she could. Kara didn't know Jackie Barker, the social worker who visited Church View, very well but she had worked with her from time to time and she seemed nice if a bit scatter-brained. Helena had said she was an amateur genealogist and loved tracing people.

'Hi darling,' said a breathy voice, 'I'm so sorry to have kept you waiting!'

Kara stood up. 'Hi.' She didn't know whether to put out her hand or not but Elise gathered her in her arms and was hugging and kissing her.

'I thought I'd never see you again,' Elise said, helping Kara on with her parka, 'I was so thrilled when you called! I would have recognised you anywhere, you're even more gorgeous than when you were a kid!' She was somehow sweeping her niece along while she chattered and it seemed only a few minutes before they were seated in a little café down the street from the Practice. Kara was pleased but a little overwhelmed. Only Shell at her most excited was ever this demonstrative and she wasn't used to it.

While Elise ordered and talked, Kara studied her. Yes, she could see a likeness to her mother but Vicki's face had fallen into severe lines as she had aged whereas Elise's eyes radiated a fan of wrinkles. Of the two sisters, Vicki was probably the more conventionally attractive because Elise had a lumpy nose and was a little overweight whereas Vicki went to the gym regularly and took care of herself. So far Elise had only spoken of herself and not asked any questions but when the drinks arrived with two pastries, Elise sat back and stopped the stream of words.

'Thanks for meeting me,' Kara said.

'Don't be silly – I told you, I'm really pleased to see you. So, how's Vicki?'

From her now serious tone, Kara realised that Elise must think there was something the matter with her sister which, of course, made sense. 'Oh, mum. She's fine, she's the same. Not best pleased with me, though. It's not about her – it's about my dad.'

A guarded look came into Elise's eyes. 'Do you mean Graham?'

'No, I mean my real dad. I mean Robert Johnson.'

Elise let out a long breath and regarded Kara cautiously. 'She's told you, then.'

Kara felt an uprush of emotion so strong that tears filled her eyes. 'No. He did - Graham. He'd been drinking and he was mad with me and it just came out – I don't think he meant it to.'

Elise stretched out her warm hands and took Kara's trembling ones. 'That's a bad way to find out. I'm sorry, darling. She should have told you long ago.'

'After that I found my birth certificate with his name on it.'

'That's right,' Elise said, gently massaging Kara's hands, 'Robert did register you while Vicki was still in hospital. I offered to go but he wanted to and he wanted to make sure his name was on the certificate – he was so thrilled to have you – it was like he'd fallen in love with you at first sight.'

'Really?' Now the tears fell and couldn't be stopped. She had a father who loved her, a father who wasn't just putting up with her but really loved her. She loosened her fingers from her aunt's grasp and fumbled in her bag for tissues. She would find him and nothing would stop her. Somewhere in some deep, shamed place in her heart, she had prepared herself that he had simply walked away because he didn't want a baby, didn't care for her at all, but now, knowing that he had loved her, it seemed like a fleshy rose bloomed instantly in her chest almost choking her. 'Then why don't I know him? What happened?' She sniffed and straightened her back.

'I can't tell you that. Vicki made me promise I would never tell you so I can't – it's her place to do that, anyway.'

The huge tenderness inside her made Kara's next question urgent - impossible not to ask. 'Elise, is he dead? Tell me if he's dead and there's no hope because I can't bear wanting to find him and not knowing that.'

Elise sat back in her chair looking as if she was going to burst into tears herself. 'I'm so sorry, Kara, so sorry you're going through this when you shouldn't have to, but, no, I don't know that he's dead. I don't think he is.'

'Thank you.' There was silence then as the two women recovered from the emotion of the moment like canoeists who have come through rapids and are resting on their oars. They both looked around and were surprised to find that the café was now full of kids in school uniform ordering chips and hot chocolate.

'Did you know him, then?' Kara asked quietly after a few moments.

'Yes, I did. We were in the same class at school.'

'Really?' It seemed incredible.

'We weren't friends particularly and he didn't start going out with Vick for a couple of years after he was in my form but I knew him, yes, I did.'

'What was he like?' Kara could hardly breathe, waiting as Elise pondered.

'Nice. A bit quiet. Good at maths which heaven knows I wasn't. Oh, wait a minute, I've remembered something – he had an unusual name, not Robert, another name, and the kids used to make fun of him over it and he'd go really dark red which of course made them laugh all the more because you don't often notice black people blushing.'

'He's black?'

'Mixed race but they always call that black at school, don't they, the kids? Light skinned though, like your mum – I take after Pearl more.'

Kara wanted to scramble over the table and pull more information from Elise's head by force. 'What else? What else do you remember?'

'I'm sorry, darling, I don't think I can say any more.'

'Mum said he was no good – that's why she didn't tell me about him.'

Elise looked serious. 'That's not true, Kara. Don't believe that.'

A light went on in Kara's brain. She had almost forgotten what she came here to ask. 'Auntie Elise, do you remember his birthday?' After all, if he and Vicki had been a serious item even if they weren't married then they would have celebrated birthdays with family, surely?

'Um, let me think.' She looked up at the ceiling and her lips moved but finally she said, 'No, I can't, sweetie, I'm sorry. I was busy with my own boyfriends and not interested much in Vicki's.'

'What time of year, maybe? Anything?' Without a date of birth Kara could go no further, Helena had been sure of that at least. She needed it to give to Jackie, assuming that a woman she barely knew would help her find him.

'I don't know if this is any help but I do remember that he was older than me. We did a statistics exercise in a maths class and we had to be ranked in birth order for it and he was definitely older.'

Kara was now biting her lip uncontrollably. 'I'm sorry, Auntie, I don't know your birth date although I should.'

Elise patted her hand. 'I'm sure Vicki never mentions me let alone suggests a nice birthday card, don't you worry about that. It's just after Christmas, of all the inconvenient things, it's December 27th, 1977.'

'So does that mean that Robert's would have been between September and December?'

'It must do, mustn't it? Sorry I can't be more precise.' She glanced at her watch and turned sideways to pick up her jacket and bag from the chair beside her. 'I have to go. I've got to get Connor's tea for him. Let me just put my number in your phone if you want me to.'

Kara stood up, too, handing over her phone eagerly. 'I won't forget your birthday this year,' she said warmly. 'I don't care what happened between you and mum, I want to be friends with you. Is that ok?' And again there was that warm, fragrant hug and a kiss on the cheek.

The two women parted on the street, Elise going off to retrieve her car and Kara making for the bus which would take her back into Birmingham city centre. She stood waiting at the stop with a gaggle of noisy school kids milling about, the boys laughing and punching each other and the girls shrieking and giggling. A wave of sadness came over her as she recalled the affection and comfort of Elise's hug and found she couldn't remember if Vicki had ever held her in her arms and kissed her. Surely she must have done? Was she really so unlovable that her own mother didn't want to touch her? She lifted her chin to stop any tears coming and thought instead about what she had learned about her father, hoping that it was enough.

This time Robert was there waiting for her and leaped to his feet when Anna was shown into the same little room. He was well-mannered enough to remember to shake her hand but couldn't bring himself to go through the usual small talk.

'You've found her? You've found Kara?'

It was all she had said in the email and she was sorry that it had been two days before the visit could happen so he must be desperate to know more. The least she could do now was tell him everything she had discovered so far quickly.

When she had finished and he had asked his questions, he sat back and stared at the wall behind her as though he was watching a film projected on it. 'I can't believe it,' he kept saying, 'I can't believe you've found her so quick. I thought it might be months, years. Vicki hasn't even changed Kara's name.'

'That certainly made it easier.' He looked different, Anna thought, and tried to work out what it was. The lethargy and downcast eyes had disappeared and even his speech was sharper and more fluent without the hesitation and pauses she had noticed before. He was coming back to life - perhaps that was it. He was now leaning forward and scanning her face.

'Don't tell her, though. Don't tell her about me.'

'No, I promised, I haven't forgotten and I do understand. You can't know at this stage whether she believes Graham Brandon is her father. I'll just try to get to know her a little over the two weeks so I can fill you in a bit more. Is that ok?'

'Yes! That's great.' He laughed and the sound had a note of hysteria in it. 'Could you get a photo for me? That would be incredible if you could. It would be amazing.'

'I don't know how things work in an open prison,' Anna said, 'but can you access Facebook?'

Robert looked as if he'd been told he'd won the lottery. 'Man!' he cried, 'Facebook!' He blinked rapidly and added, 'We have to get permission to message people and we can't set up our own account but we can go on to other people's. It's supervised all the time but I think they'd let me at least look at her profile picture. Is she on it?'

'Yes. It would be Kara Brandon, of course.'

'How would I know if it's the right one?' Robert said. 'There might be more than one.'

Anna smiled. 'Look at the eyes, she's got your eyes.' Robert gasped and Anna looked away to give him a moment while she pulled her notebook out of her bag. 'Do you mind if I do a bit of research into your dad's family while I'm getting to know Kara? It would be interesting to know where he came from, wouldn't it? It wouldn't cost you anything, I'd just like to do it if I can. We genealogists are pathologically inquisitive and that movement of people from the Caribbean to Birmingham is fascinating – we often trace people's family back there. So far, I haven't been offered a trip to follow up leads but I live in hopes! No, just joking, but would you like to know?'

This time Robert grinned properly and it made his face softer and lighter and she could see for a moment what a nice-looking young man he must have been. 'Just don't turn up any criminals,' he said, 'I want to be the only black sheep, you know, not one in a line!'

'So, your dad's name?' Her pen was poised.

Robert huffed. 'He had one of those crazy Caribbean names and he landed me with it, too! Lindo, he was called, Lindo Johnson and it's my second name. I was teased bad about it at school so I don't use it.'

'I think it's a great name,' Anna said, 'at least it's different, not like Anna or - '

'Robert.' He smiled down at his hands. 'My dad had a mate, someone from back home, called Florence. His mum wanted a daughter and when she got her sixth son she said she was going to use her favourite name, Florence, anyway, whether he liked it or not.

107

Huh! So when he came over here he changed it to Florenz and told everyone his dad was Italian and they all thought it was really cool.'

'You said you were ten when your dad died. Can you remember the date?'

'Yeah, no problem. Mum used to take me out to where his ashes are buried every year on the day and we'd leave daffodils in a jam jar.' So Robert gave her that and the date of his parents' wedding at the Birmingham Register Office and she put her notebook away and got up to leave.

Robert stood up, too, his hands in his pockets, looking down at the floor. 'You don't know what this means,' he said, 'what this means to me, that you've found her – my girl. It's given me a reason to live. I may never even speak to her but I can watch over her, you know? When I'm out, I mean. I can maybe walk past her sometimes, even?'

Anna sighed and looked at him. 'I'll do what I can to find out a little more.'

As she walked out of the prison to her car Anna wondered how Robert would cope if he knew for certain that Kara believed Graham to be her biological father. How could anyone cope with that? Anna put herself in his shoes and imagined seeing a daughter or son of hers and knowing she could never reveal herself. The last thing he would need after twenty years in jail would be restraint by a different, and perhaps more galling, leash.

But on the drive back home she shelved Robert's situation and thought of Ellis instead. Yesterday evening Mike's mum and dad had come round to talk about what was going on with the boys as they were now refusing to even speak to each other. They had sat around the kitchen table, knowing that Ellis was round at Steve's watching a match with him on his huge television and that Mike was swotting for a French test.

George set out the lemon drizzle cake he had made that afternoon and passed round plates. 'It's probably just a spat,' he said, 'they're both good-hearted boys so they should get over it.'

'I don't know.' Maggie pushed the cake around on her plate and then licked her fingers. 'Mike says he doesn't know what he's done wrong. He's very hurt.'

'I'm not sure I like the sound of this band, to be honest,' Anna said, 'calling itself The Posers. It all sounds a bit like so-called ironic one-up-man-ship to me. Maybe Ellis is going through a bit of a peacock phase.'

'But he's never been like that before, has he? Is this the dreaded puberty raising its ugly head?'

Anna smiled at John, who was going through this for the first, and only, time. 'Could be,' she said, 'Faye was all over the place between thirteen and fifteen but she's never been the most accommodating child.'

'So we have no idea what's caused this rift?' George asked.

'Ellis just walks off if I bring it up.'

'Ok, well, if any of us discovers anything, shall we let the others know?' John asked and they all nodded. 'Let's just keep supporting them, eh?'

'I'm sorry that Mike is hurt,' Anna said, breaking up her cake and getting ready to eat a piece, 'you know how much we think of him.'

'Well, let's at least do justice to your cake, George, you make a mean bit of patisserie. Are you wheeling out the campervan again this year?'

Later, after they had gone and the kitchen was tidied up, Anna and George went into the living room and turned on the evening news. There was some global leaders' summit that the press were frantically speculating about and neither of them was paying attention.

'I'll ask him to come and help me and Diane sort the van out at Safe 'n' Sound, he usually likes going there and it will give Bobble a run,' George said. 'We might be able to get a few days away in March when the light lasts longer. He enjoyed doing it last year – climbing up the step-ladder and sluicing it all down with great buckets of soapy water. It was covered with pigeon droppings - you know, they nest in the barn.'

'With Mike,' Anna remembered.

'Oh, yes. Hm.'

'Did you have a best friend when you were a kid?'

'There was a gang of us.' George was still looking at the tv screen but not seeing it. He ran a blunt hand through his hair and then rubbed at the bristles under his chin. 'There was me and Chips and Candlesticks and Ginger – no girls, of course.'

'What? Are you telling me you didn't have a nickname? What was it?'

George turned and grinned at her. 'Highly classified, this.'

'Ok. My lips are sealed.'

'Pinky.' Anna laughed so he went on, 'It was because one time when it was my mum's turn to use the copper boiler in the yard she'd accidentally put a red flannel shirt of my dad's in with the whites – underwear, you know, it was all white in those days, or grey more like – and boiled it. So all our undies came out pink. Had to wear them, we didn't have money to replace them, so I got called Pinky Drawers until they couldn't be bothered with two words.'

Anna stretched out and yawned. 'I'm sure you looked very cute in them. Why Candlesticks?'

'In those days kids like us seemed to always have coughs and colds and boils and that sort of thing. This lad had a permanently runny nose so there were always two stripes of green snot from his nose to his mouth, like tarnished candlesticks. Not many of us had hankies so it was the sleeve that caught it, but a kid like that got the name like the red-headed ones were always Ginger. Do you remember me taking you all to those Back-to-Back houses off Hurst Street that the National Trust have done up?'

'I do. Ellis was in infant school then and Faye was top juniors. Ellis thought it was very cool to have an outside loo in the yard!'

'Cool, it was freezing – that's why we had gazundas for when we were caught short in the night.'

'Faye did a project on it, didn't she, for school? It must still be somewhere. I remember her interviewing you.'

'All the big cities had thousands of them at one time but they were built as cheap housing in the eighteenth century so they were slums by the 1950's. They've done a good job on those few of them left but you just don't get what it was like when forty people were living around one yard sharing the loos and the copper and washing always strung across the yard. Going back made me realise how hard my mum had it bringing up even one child let alone the six or seven that were in some families. It was the cold and damp in the bedroom I remember most. I always put my clothes between the sheet and the blankets so they would be warm to put on in the morning. In the winter there was often ice on the inside of the glass, but, of course, we knew no different until dad got the printing job and we moved out and up – our very own terrace house with a proper bathroom – it was another world.'

Anna's thoughts strayed back to Mike and Ellis. 'So what did you get up to with your gang?'

'We spent all the time outside. No one would want to stay in those little rooms and the mothers would chuck us out after breakfast on holidays. We'd run about town, everywhere, down to the market to see what we could pick up or what was going on and play cricket and footie against the walls. We made a cracking go-kart out of scraps from the builder's yard once. She'd give me a piece of bread and margarine or lard, jam if we had it, wrapped in greaseproof and that was lunch. We were usually out all day.'

Anna stood up, yawning again. 'Who needs a living history museum when we've got you?' she said, bending to kiss the top of his head.

'Try not to worry too much. It'll sort itself out.'

''Night, Dad.'

11

Kara had woken early and there was still half an hour before she would need to set off for work. The atmosphere in the house was horrible with her mother hardly speaking to her even though she didn't know about the visit to Elise. Graham had barely said a word for days and Gerry's demanding texts had abruptly stopped so she guessed her so-called father had put him in the picture. It was a relief not to be at his beck and call anyway. She had thought about telling Shell but her friend's head was so full of exciting wedding plans that it seemed like too big a thing to share right now. She couldn't wait to get to work to talk to Helena about it and try to get hold of Jackie.

The great thing was that Elise had texted her last night because she knew the woman who was now the Principal's personal assistant at the school which she and Robert had gone to and her friend had looked up his details swearing her to confidentiality. The date was the thirteenth of October, 1977. Instantly, it was locked into Kara's memory.

To pass the time she clicked on to Tassie's blog which she'd neglected for a few days. Where was she now? Tassie could be vague about what town or even what country she was in. The point seemed to be posting pictures of herself looking tanned with very little on, Kara thought. She seemed to be in a harbour somewhere sunny with lots of white boats with blue awnings but then an image leaped up of her sandwiched between two men, all of them grinning like mad. One of them had an arm round Tassie's bare mid-riff. The message under it just said, 'Bye bye loser Ben, hello boys!!!****' Kara frowned. Surely Tassie wasn't stupid enough to take risks, especially if she was now travelling on her own? Maybe she'd just asked strangers to pose with her to rile Ben. If she'd still been friends with Tassie she would have emailed or texted her and told her to be careful. Glancing at the screen she noticed that it was time she was leaving and she leaped up and grabbed her bag, excitement rising up in her at what the day might bring.

At work everything was in full swing for breakfasts so Kara didn't have a chance to drop by the office until nearly ten o'clock after she'd tidied the rooms and made beds for those who needed help. She tapped on the glass half door and heard Mrs Bandhal tell her to come in.

'Hello, my dear,' she beamed to Kara with all her sparkling teeth on display, 'How can I help you?'

'I just wondered if Jackie, I'm sorry I don't know her last name, is in today?'

'One of your ladies or gentlemen is requesting Ms Barker's help?' Mrs Bandhal ran a tight ship at Church View and would want to know why any resident might want to talk to the social worker from Bromsgrove District Council.

Kara twisted her hands nervously. 'No, Mrs B, it's me. I just want to ask her something. Nothing to do with work but it won't take a minute.'

Mrs Bandhal smiled generously and waved a cashmere clad arm in reassurance. 'No problem, dear, you're a good worker and the residents like you. If you need to talk to Jackie just take the time you need to do it.' She took her glasses off her head and popped them on to the bridge of her nose gazing at the rota on the wall. 'She's in at 2.00 to see Mrs Simpson but you might want to catch her before her appointment because she'll be off again straight after that.'

'Thanks.' Kara withdrew and hurried down the corridor towards Helena's room but when she knocked there was no reply and as she gently opened the door she saw the place was empty.

From then on the day dragged and the routine tasks seemed more tedious than usual. At twelve thirty the lunch had to be got out and some people needed help with their food and there was still no sign of Helena so she must be gone for the day. After helping the kitchen staff clear away and making sure that the residents in the lounge had cups of tea if they wanted them, Kara saw that it was almost ten to two. She almost ran down the corridor to the office but there was no sign of Jackie, only the secretary was there chatting on the phone. At five past two Kara heard the front door buzz and there she was, hair blown across her face, coat already half off, searching her briefcase for papers.

Kara stepped in front of her. 'Jackie, Ms Barker, could I have a word?'

Jackie pulled out some papers and tucked them under her armpit. 'Kara is it? I'm just rushing a bit, love, can it wait?'

'Could I see you after Mrs Simpson?'

'No, I'll have to cut her short as it is − I've got to be back at the Council for a meeting.'

'It's just that Helena said you did genealogy – you know – tracing people?'

'Did she?' Jackie flushed with pleasure. 'I didn't know she knew. Yes, I do a bit of detective work sometimes for people. Was it for you?'

Kara felt embarrassed talking in the public corridor like this about her private affairs but what could she do? 'I want to trace my biological dad. I've got some details.'

Instantly Jackie was all attention. Her face folded into a professional expression, eyes concerned, mouth smiling as she placed a hand on Kara's arm. 'Oh, darling, how significant for you,' she said, 'of course I'll try. Just a minute.' The papers under her arm fell to the floor as she retrieved a phone from her overstuffed shoulder bag. 'Give me his name, sweetie.'

Kara told her but added, 'There may be another name, a bit of a weird one, I don't know whether it's middle or first or what.'

'Ok. And have you got his date of birth?' Mrs Bandhal was making her way down the corridor towards them with the accountant and Jackie glanced at them and back to her phone. 'As quick as you like.'

'Yes.' Kara told her the date.

'Got it,' Jackie said, 'but I've got to scoot now. I'll get back to you as soon as, don't worry,' and she was gone. Kara's heart thudded as she walked away as calmly as she could.

At almost the same time Anna was tapping Robert's father's date of birth into a search box for marriages. Lindo Johnson and Mary Ryan. There they were so Robert had remembered the date correctly but to be thorough she double-checked the date he had given her of Lindo's death, too. Now she could order the marriage and death certificates, one of which, she hoped, would give Lindo's father's name and occupation and one would give Lindo's birthplace. His widow would have been able to tell the registrar that, surely? It would probably be Jamaica since so many of the Windrush generation of immigrants came from there but there were a scattering of men and women from other islands in the Caribbean, too. If it was Jamaica she was in luck because their archives were excellent.

That done, Anna could concentrate on the more urgent task of compiling a list of books to take to her first session at Church View which would be tomorrow afternoon. She would need to call by the library on her way home but there were some favourites that she had on her own shelves so she should be able to take a selection of short stories, different genres and some poetry. That was never a problem living with George.

How to organise this task best? She could, of course, approach people individually and see if they would like her to read to them but that would be very time-consuming as half an hour spent with each resident would mean she only could cover four or five. Maybe a small reading group could be formed? That did look a bit like a nursery class but would they mind? She thought of Diane. Would they be able to hear? Would it be better to go round and take requests for books she could borrow for them? That would mean a much longer commitment than two weeks, of course. And she mustn't forget that the real object of the exercise was to chat to Kara and win her confidence if possible. The burning question was whether she thought Graham was her real dad. Could Anna take in a book which dealt with that issue so that it would seem natural to bring it up? It felt clumsy and contrived. She groaned.

'Fancy getting some fresh air and a coffee?'

'Oh, Steve, that sounds great. I forgot my sandwich for lunch and I'm running on empty. Shall we go to the café on the quay?'

The large open office was almost deserted anyway when they left but Anna did wonder what people thought their relationship was. Suzy knew, of course, and Ted probably guessed and would be pleased because Steve, with his advanced knowledge of information technology could have been head-hunted at any moment and a commitment to Anna would tether him at Harts. What an awful thought, she mused, displeased by the image of Steve staked to a post with her name on it.

It was overcast but dry outside and they walked quickly for the physical release of it for ten minutes and then ducked into the café and grabbed a corner table. Steve had to take a call so Anna went up for the lattes and while she waited scanned the scant array of wraps and baguettes which were a bit threadbare at this time of the day. In any case she needed something hot. 'Have you got any soup?' she asked hopefully only to receive a shake of the head.

'Toastie?'

'Cheese and tomato.'

She turned to look at Steve who was still talking on the phone and, with his other hand, cleaning the top of the table with a napkin. Were those needles of grey in the close cropped dark hair above his ears? She could still hardly believe that they were together even after two years. The first six months had been so joyful, so full of excitement and then there were the blissful weekends away while Faye looked after Alice which had now stopped, of course. They had waited a long time to be together and it was as though the torrent of passion had rejuvenated them –as though they had turned back the clock to the giddy salad days of youth. An image flashed into her mind of Steve when they had been staying in North Wales one time and he had got up in the morning to make them some tea and had stood, naked and smiling, at the window gazing out at the splendour of Snowdon at sunrise and scratching his left buttock. It was nothing and yet it was everything.

Her smile drooped. Where could Alice fit into this scenario? She was too young to be put in her own room alone and the idea of a jealous child in a cot next to their bed was unthinkable. Now their relationship was not so hectic but as the excitement had ebbed a little, the pleasure of familiarity had grown.

Steve sensed her looking at him as she waited for the toastie and caught her eye questioningly. She blew him a kiss and he smiled his blue crystal smile and that look could still make her stomach lurch.

When the food and drinks were set down Steve leaned over the little table and kissed her on the mouth. 'Have I told you lately that I adore you?' he said.

'Once or twice,' Anna smiled. Actually, that had taken a bit of getting used to as Harry had been loving in all sorts of ways but didn't often just come out with it in words and neither did she but she had learned that it was very important to Steve that she vocalise her feelings. 'I might feel the same way about you, you never know.'

He took her hand just as she was about to pick up a section of her hot sandwich. 'You always make light of it, make a joke of it, but I'm serious, Annie, I want to spend my whole life by your side.'

'I know and it's wonderful, Steve, and I love you very much, too, but I just don't know how to say it without sounding silly.' She bent and kissed his hand. 'Sorry.'

'Go on then, wolf your food, I know you want to, and I'll tell you how you can make it up to me.' He leaned over towards her and winked. 'I have a cunning plan.' The cheese was perfectly melted inside the toast and just the right amount of salt had been sprinkled on the tomato and Anna bit into it appreciatively. She had only eaten a spoonful of granola for breakfast as Ellis had almost finished it and the morning had been busy with three new jobs from Ted so her appetite was keen and after this she might even indulge in a piece of rocky road tiffin which lurked seductively behind glass on the counter. 'Do you want to know what it is?' Steve said.

'Mm. This is really good, you don't know what you're missing.'

'I think we should get married now, not wait any longer.'

Anna choked and spluttered. 'What?'

'Don't you see, it's perfect! Alice is very into weddings at the moment so she would have a part to play as our bridesmaid and it would sort of set us up as a unit, the three of us.'

'You want us to get married to cheer Alice up?' The hot tomato was burning her fingers.

'Well that is the long term plan, isn't it? I mean for us to get married?' Steve had withdrawn a little and was not smiling any more.

'Yes, of course. It's a bit sudden, though.'

'But think about it.' He hunched forward again. 'It would do what marriages are supposed to do, or used to do – it would ceremonially mark a change of status which Alice might be able to understand better. So, she and I leave from our house, the wedding happens, we take our vows and then the three of us come back as a sort of new family.'

'To your house?'

'Of course.' He took her hand again. 'You saw how she was about Briony and Kimi getting married – it could be just the thing we need for her to understand that you wouldn't be taking me away, you'd be joining us – making her world bigger not smaller.'

So many thoughts were chasing round Anna's head that she didn't say anything. Steve genuinely seemed not to understand that a marriage between them was just that, a marriage of two people, two adults, not a vehicle for accommodating the feelings of a demanding little girl. They say that the way a marriage is planned is how that marriage will turn out and Anna had no intention of letting

Alice run their family life. Already, in the minutes it had taken Steve to voice his plan she had become resentful of the child – imagine how she would feel if this was a permanent arrangement where Alice's needs were always put before hers? And what was this assumption that she would move into their house? It had never been discussed and she didn't want to do it.

'What about dad and Ellis?'

'Diane might want to move in.'

By a huge effort of self-control Anna kept her mouth shut. Certain things said at this point could cause hurt and resentment for years. 'Let's give it some thought,' she managed to say, finally, 'and we'd better get back before Ted lets out the bloodhounds.' But all the way back to the office something inside her was shouting no, no, no.

The two young women sat perched on hard pink satin chairs and waited silently. They were beginning to droop despite the excitement of helping Shell choose the dress. This was the fifth bridal shop today and the tenth to date together with endless internet searches and one bridal fair at the NEC, itself a test of stamina and, as it happened, hope deferred. Both Lauren and Kara were beginning to suspect the source of the problem.

'She's got a picture in her mind,' Lauren said, 'of how she'll look, but she won't look like that, will she?'

'She's not fat,' Kara replied, 'it's more that she isn't the shape that suits the dresses she chooses.'

'I'm not going to be the one to tell her.'

'Me neither.' They lapsed back into silence.

But, fortunately, the manager of this emporium was made of sterner stuff than either of Shell's friends and after the bride-to-be had presented herself in yet another mermaid like sheath which barely concealed the nipples on her large breasts, the woman said, 'I think you might find that a more sophisticated look works better on you – brings out your elegant shape without being too obvious. How about this?' And in a twinkling she was holding up a white satin full length gored gown, the upper part crusted with sequins on lace with wrist length sleeves and a plunging but narrowly cut neckline. 'You see, a lot of people wouldn't have the class for this, but I feel you do.' All three gazed at the frock imagining themselves wearing it. The saleswoman let a moment of silence pass, knowing very well the effect the dress was having, and then added, 'It's the nearest you'll find to Kate Middleton's when she became Duchess of Cambridge.' Shell practically snatched it from her and ran to the changing room.

Sure enough, the slim deep V of the lacy top and the discreet covering of the upper arms and shoulders turned Shell from a wobbly stack of flesh into a statuesque beauty. When she reappeared she was smiling and they all knew the search was over but for one thing.

'How much is it?'

'As it happens, I'm running a reduction on that dress at the moment so it's come down twenty per cent. It was here just waiting for you, dear.' She named a price and they all sucked in their breath.

'Kara's doing your hair,' Lauren reminded her, 'so you won't have to pay for that.' Kara wished she didn't make it seem like a money-saving scheme. In any case, that money saved was nothing compared to the price of the dress.

'You do look amazing in it.'

'Go on then,' Shell said, 'twisting and turning to see herself in the big shop mirror. 'I'll have it. I'll just have to sweet-talk dad into coughing up the extra.' Kara tried to imagine sweet-talking Graham into anything and then remembered that he wasn't her dad after all. Robert Johnson would be a very different kind of father. Hadn't Elise said that he had loved her at first sight? She hugged herself and smiled.

She had changed her mind about confiding her secret because it was simply too big to keep to herself but the reactions of her friends to the news that she had broken up with Gerry and then discovered that Graham wasn't her father had been satisfyingly supportive. They were outraged that Vicki had never told her the truth and thought Graham had behaved very badly in blurting out such a bombshell in the way he did. Shell said she'd never liked Gerry anyway - Kara was far too good for him. Since then they had all played a game of pointing at random strange men and saying, 'Is it him, do you think?' choosing the oldest and least attractive and then shrieking with laughter. Kara enjoyed it as much as the others because she secretly knew what her dad would be like: nice-looking, of course, and with kind, soft eyes and a low voice. He would be dressed in fashionable casual clothes and would take her to visit interesting places while he explained how much he loved her and how desperate he had been to have lost her.

On Monday she arrived at Church View for the second shift in time to see Helena stepping out of a taxi, a bright scarf knotted about her neck. Helena waved at her as the driver took her bag into the lobby.

'Have you had a nice time?' Kara called out.

'It was fine,' Helena said. 'Please come and have tea with me when you're able to, will you?'

Kara smiled and nodded. She loved the way Helena made it seem like Kara was doing her a favour by visiting rather than the other way round. She's gracious, she thought to herself, that's what it is. So far nothing had come back from Jackie but Kara glanced into the office to see if she might be there anyway. Mrs Bandhal, having greeted Helena as warmly as she did all her residents, whispered to Kara, 'Would you mind helping out with clearing up lunch, dear? We're two kitchen staff down.' Dealing with congealed food and slippery, sticky cutlery was not Kara's favourite thing but she went to help cheerfully. There was usually a quiet time around three-thirty before afternoon tea when she might be able to slip into Helena's room and have a chat.

But by mid-afternoon she was hurrying. Geoff Baines wanted his glasses fetching for him when she'd finished her other jobs so she ran to his room and got them, catching him up as he settled in the lounge. 'Thanks, Chick,' he said, 'those are the ones. Can't see to do my crossword without them.' He put them on, glanced round the room over the top of them and whispered to Kara, 'Who's that?'

Sitting near the window with Edna Simpson was a woman Kara had never seen before. She was smiling around at everyone and leafing through a book. Kara wondered if she was one of Mrs B's many relatives with her shoulder length dark hair and brown eyes but then she caught Kara's look and stood up, keeping her place in the book with one finger, and came across. 'Hello,' she said, including Geoff and Kara in the same glance. 'Can I introduce myself? I'm Anna Ames and I'm volunteering for a couple of weeks to read to people who'd like it.' She looked down at Geoff who was impatient to get on with his crossword and then at Kara. 'Could we have a word?' She glanced at the name badge all the staff wore. 'Thanks, Kara.'

They stepped outside the lounge into the corridor and Kara tried not to look at her watch. Precious minutes she could be spending with Helena were ticking away. Mrs Ames seemed to pick up on Kara's restlessness. 'I'm sure you've got lots to do,' she said, 'so I won't hold you up but if you can think about which residents might like to be read to, could I check back with you? It would be better than me going round asking, I think. Mrs Bandhal says you've been here for some time so you'll know everyone and the residents like and trust you.'

Oh, so that was it. Every now and then Mrs B had someone come in under some kind of pretence who was really checking up on the place to report back. Kara didn't mind, in fact, she thought it was a good idea to have these informal checks. The nightmare scenario Mrs B dreaded would be if an undercover reporter from some television programme came in and caught a member of staff behaving badly. In fact, she had little to worry about because she was a good employer and paid higher than the minimum and promoted conscientious and popular workers so there was a much lower staff turnover than for most care homes - it was only good management to employ spies where there were vulnerable people, Kara thought. But right now she was in a hurry. 'I'd be glad to,' she said, 'but can I get back to you the next time you're here? When would that be?'

Anna smiled and thanked her. 'I'll be in every afternoon for a couple of weeks,' she said, 'I'd be so grateful if you could help me.' She had a nice voice, Kara thought, educated but not stuck-up.

'See you tomorrow, then,' Kara said, and fled down the corridor to Helena's room.

In fact, Helena seemed just as anxious to see her and snatched the door open the moment Kara knocked. 'Oh thank goodness,' she said, 'I thought you'd got waylaid and weren't coming.' She stepped back, flushed and seeming excited. 'Come in, sit down. Do you want tea?'

'No, I'm ok,' Kara said, 'I'll have to get off in about ten minutes.'

Helena pulled her own chair over to Kara's but before sitting down produced an envelope from her jacket pocket and waved it at the young woman. 'Guess what?'

Kara's heart sank. 'You've seen a house you like.'

'What? Oh no, no. This is for you – it's from Jackie. She popped in while you were doing the lunches and couldn't stop so she asked me to give it to you.' She sat down and leaned towards Kara. 'Oh, darling, she's found him – she's found your father!' Kara stared at the envelope, unable to move. 'Shall I open it? May I? It's so exciting!' Kara nodded. It was unbelievable and yet this is just what she had asked Jackie to do. Somehow she couldn't quite absorb the possibility that there was a living, breathing father in the same world as herself who even now might be chatting or driving or eating.

'Tell me,' she said in a tiny voice. 'Tell me what she says.'

Helena tore open the envelope, unfolded a single piece of paper and cleared her throat. '*Dear Kara, I followed the information you gave me and the weird name helped a lot as there were two Robert Johnsons, can you believe, with that birth date who could be him. One is a plumber living in Chesterfield but with no other name but the other may well be the man you're searching for! He is Robert Grenville Johnson – how about that? He lives in Redditch in a nice house (look on Google Earth and you'll see what I mean!) and has his own business (which I think is something to do with property) in Erdington. I can't find a photo but I've written down both addresses. Good luck! All the best, Jackie. p.s. Let me know how you get on!*'

Kara and Helena stared at each other with huge eyes and then squealed in unison. Helena leaped up and grabbed her laptop asking Kara, 'What shall I look up first?'

So they did a Google search which returned nothing and ditto a Facebook search. Then they turned their attention to the house and the business. The house was easily found and they moved the cursor back and forth to see what it was like from all angles. No doubt about it, it was a substantial red brick detached house with double garage and a wide cobbled drive. Helena looked at Kara, her eyes gleaming. 'When do you finish today?'

'Seven o'clock.'

'Shall I drive you out there?'

'I'm not ready,' Kara gasped.

'No, not to knock on the door, just to look at it. What do you think?'

'I can't tonight, I promised Shell I'd go round and it'll be dark. Can we go tomorrow morning before I start work? Say round 10.00?'

'Where shall I pick you up?'

'I'll wait outside on the pavement.' Without discussing it they both knew that going out with a resident was not something staff would be expected to do without it being for a good reason approved by the office.

They couldn't find anything for the business but that information could be out of date. Secretly, Kara thought she would go to that Erdington address and see what she could find out. She could go on Saturday and then there would be no danger of running into him until she had prepared herself. Robert Grenville Johnson. The name sounded so posh and alien.

When she left Helena folded her into her arms and gave her a long hug and Kara would have sobbed if she was not still so shocked. So, if her father was a businessman with a fancy house and premises in town maybe he wouldn't want to know her after all? But, maybe he had tried to trace her but wouldn't know her under the name of Brandon? She wished she had done better, could tell him she was at university or something. She had hoped for someone nice and ordinary who would be proud of her and now she felt overwhelmed by the new knowledge. She could hear the clatter in the kitchen and hurried to the dining room to start serving the tea and cake.

The visitor, Anna, was sitting with two residents and showing them a book but they didn't really seem interested in that, they just wanted to talk to her. She was having a bit of a struggle Kara could see because, unknown to her, the two elderly women were fierce rivals and were talking over each other to win her undivided attention. Kara smiled at her and made sure she got a cup of tea, too.

12

When Anna got home she could see the shed light was on so she went upstairs to get changed and tapped on Ellis' door. There was no reply so she opened it and saw him lying on the bed with his ear buds in and his eyes closed. She glanced around at the messy floor and saw that sticking out from under Bobble's elephantine posterior was the frilled edge of the dress shirt which Ellis must have flung in the corner. The dog, probably feeling that good manners were in order from someone in the room, raised himself to greet Anna and uttered a fog-horn bellow, bashing his tail against the wall.

Ellis opened his eyes. When he saw Anna he closed them again.

She perched on the end of his bed and tapped his arm. 'Do you fancy a snack?' she asked, 'George hasn't started cooking yet. Would you like some toast and Marmite?'

'Just trying to chill, Mum.'

'Did you know that Bobble is lying on your Poser shirt?'

'Don't care.'

'Sweetheart, talk to me. What's the matter?'

'Nothing. I've left the stupid band. I just need some space, ok?' He turned over on his side away from her so she got up and went over to the dog who was managing to look both pained and beseeching.

'Come on, you,' she said, 'let's leave him to it. I'll take you across the park and we can have a word with Joan, ok?' Bobble tried to put a grateful paw on her shoulder but she dodged him and got outside to the landing where he bounded ahead of her down the stairs and stood, quivering with excitement, by the front door. She grabbed his lead from the coat rack and pulled on her warm parka.

The days were lengthening and it was still light as she made her way across the pathways with the huge animal trotting beside her. Sometimes she felt guilty that he didn't have a long run very often but then, as George said after he had been taken out to Safe 'n' Sound, he didn't seem very interested in strenuous exercise. She was the one getting the work-out having to jog to keep up with his loping stride. Every now and then he would stop to examine a compelling splash of urine and she would get a chance to rest and breathe – he always attracted attention but she was used to it by now, the most common query being an astonished, 'What kind of dog is that?' to which she had no answer except, a bloody big one.

Joan was sitting on a stool in the grocery shop with a steaming mug in her hand. 'You'll never guess what,' she said in greeting, 'Piotr's cousin's brother-in-law has offered to do my roof for cost but they've made me promise to stay on even after it's paid for! Isn't it good?' Anna agreed it was good and refused a coffee as Bobble was too much of a handful in any kind of shop. 'But what about the roofer who said he'd let you pay in instalments?'

'Oh, he doesn't mind. I phoned him about it and he said he's got so much work on he'd be glad of one less job.' She studied Anna. 'Are you ok? I always know you're not when your eyes get that brooding look – like an action heroine on a film poster.'

'Just a bit worried about Ellis. He and Mike have fallen out and he's upset about something and just not being his normal sunbeam self, you know.'

'Hormones?'

'I suppose, but it's just so unlike him to be moody and closed down like this.' It would have been good to confide in Joan about the Steve and Alice dilemma, too, but she felt that would be disloyal and she really needed to figure that one out on her own. 'I'm making some progress with the daughter of the client who's in prison, though. I even had a brief conversation with her today.'

'Well, if anyone can sort it out, you can,' Joan said, supportive as ever, 'but can you get that hound's nose out of the potatoes?'

'Ok, I'm off. Glad it's working out for you.' She gave Joan a hug and kiss and body-shoved Bobble outside.

On the walk home she decided to call Mike's mum and see if there was any break-through from their end but Maggie said nothing had come out so far. 'There is one good thing, though, that's cheering him up despite missing Ellis.'

'Good. So what's that?'

'He brought a nice girl home yesterday evening – very pretty – called Kirsty. I think she's going to sing with the band. It was very sweet, actually, I went in to take them a cup of tea and they were sitting on the sofa plugged into their music holding hands! He's never had a girl-friend before, of course, so I'm in new territory and trying not to put my foot in it and embarrass him.'

Anna sighed. 'I'm sure you won't. Well, let's hope the thing with Ellis blows over soon.'

As she and Bobble strode back across the park she wondered whether to say anything to Ellis or not. The mystery of his resentment of Mike was now solved but she couldn't decide whether to let it ride or to speak to him. Had this ever happened with Faye? She vaguely remembered her being ditched by someone but Faye was not the kind to be upset about that sort of thing, she was the kind to get revenge by quickly moving on. Perhaps she should talk to George about it, he was better with delicate things like this than her and Ellis wouldn't feel as wounded by him knowing, perhaps.

Did Kara have a boyfriend, she wondered? She already had a good impression of the young woman whom she had observed chatting cheerfully with residents, never impatient despite being busy with all the teas, and who she would get to have a longer conversation with tomorrow. She liked the way Kara smoothed her hair up into a cute top-knot that burst into a foam of curls and, of course, she had those sloping dark translucent eyes so like her dad's that gave her face an attenuated, feline delicacy. She wished so much that she could tell her about Robert but it just wasn't possible, at least not yet, so she must work on trying to find out whether the girl even knew about his existence.

When she got in Faye was rifling through the kitchen drawers. Bobble staggered into the living room and collapsed on the sofa as though he had run a marathon so she joined her daughter in the kitchen and switched on the kettle. 'Tea?'

'Where's dinner? I'm starving,' Faye said without turning her head. She was making a pile of implements on the counter top.

'Not that paring knife, Faye, that's Pops' favourite – put it back.'

'Why isn't he in here cooking?'

Anna sat down at the table with her own mug. 'I hate to seem inhospitable,' she said, 'but you don't actually live here anymore, do you? Unless I'm missing something.'

'Jack's out with his mates. Can I have this, then?'

'That's a turkey baster. What can you possibly want that for?'

'We're going to drip paint over all the kitchen units and the chairs and table – this would be brilliant for it.' She scrabbled some more. 'Look, you've got egg-cups in here you never use.'

Anna sipped her tea and saw with quiet joy that Faye was happy. Yes, she was demanding, selfish and outrageous (presumably Jack liked that or at least was prepared to put up with it), but living with him had calmed her, there was no doubt about it. There was a new serenity about her. She stood up on impulse and went to put her arms round Faye's waist and her cheek against her slim back. 'It's all going well, is it?'

Faye turned and bent to give her a proper hug draping Anna in a tumble of fragrant red-gold hair. 'He is so lovely, Mum.'

The back door flew open and George rushed in bringing a blast of cold air with him. 'Sorry, sorry, sorry,' he was saying, 'oh, hello Faye - I'll go out right now and get us all some fish and chips. Is Ellis in?'

'I can go, Dad.'

'No, no, mea culpa, mea maxima culpa and all that,' and he rushed out into the hall.

'Brill,' said Faye, 'I timed that right. Curry sauce, Pops!'

Anna pulled open the dresser drawer and started laying the table with knives and forks. 'Put some plates to warm, will you? And can you be nice to Ellis, please, love? He's a bit low at the moment.'

'Why?' Faye added a spatula to her heap.

'Oh, you know, it's hard being his age.'

'Balls not dropped then?'

'Actually, Faye, that's just the sort of joke I'd rather you didn't make if you don't mind.'

'Ok. Poor little bugger, I'll be nice to him.' She pulled a plastic bag out of the tube they were stuffed in and tipped her booty into it. 'Didn't you make me a cup of tea?'

Kara couldn't sleep. It had been a useful distraction to mess with Shell's hair while she taught her how to use the pin comb properly, she had even let her keep it to practise, but now she was alone she couldn't stop worrying about her new-found father. Would he be ashamed of her? How could she approach him? Now she knew he was posh it was all much more difficult. By three o'clock she had given up and switched on her laptop.

Half-heartedly she did a Facebook trawl of various friends from school and from Church View but the images were mostly plates of food or photos of them screaming with laughter at the camera in their night-out clothes. Elise had accepted her as a friend but her page was all happy family shots that made Kara sad, like Elise and Connor and his dad doing things together. What would Robert Grenville do in his spare time? Kara didn't know anyone well off. Golf? Yachting? How could she engage with that? Finally she turned to Tassie's blog, half resentful of her as usual but also a little worried after that last entry.

The photos were all of scenery – mountains as brown as dried leaves and as crumpled looking and a long road that stretched out ahead as though the photos were being taken from the front seat of a car or bus. One was of a solitary figure in the far distance across a grey, rocky plain surrounded by what looked like dark coloured bushes but which were probably goats or something. Yes, Kara could see the reflection of a window faintly across the image so Tassie had to have been in a vehicle of some kind. The commentary was bleak, too, with not one exclamation mark, in fact, it was quite bad-tempered. 'Can't wait to get to the other side of this sick plateau,' she had written, 'roll on four-star hotel and wi-fi – sorry mum and dad but I need it and you said the card was for emergencies.'

Kara felt bad but she couldn't help being pleased that Tassie wasn't having a perfect day either. The trouble was that instead of feeling more connected now her dad had been traced, she felt more lonely. Vicki and Graham had more or less stopped bothering with her at all as though they could now drop the pretence of being a family but that wouldn't have mattered so much if she still had the fantasy of a caring, cuddly dad just waiting to be found. She berated herself that he could still be a really lovely person – she shouldn't be so judgmental about him being well-off. After all, he hadn't been left the money, had he? He'd grown up in the same neighbourhood as Elise and her mum so he must have made the money by working hard and being clever. He wouldn't be a snob. Thinking this made her feel better and she slipped back under her duvet to try to get a couple more hours.

It was cold but bright in the morning and Helena turned out of Church View drive exactly on ten so Kara didn't have to hang about long. 'I bet you couldn't sleep for excitement,' Helena said, smiling warmly at her so Kara just nodded and smiled back.

It wasn't far to Redditch from Bromsgrove but Kara didn't want to speculate all the time about Robert Grenville Johnson, her nerves were too raw for that, so she asked Helena about her weekend away. Helena gossiped easily about the hotel and the food she had had and how pretty even in winter the little harbour was. She had visited the town museum and even gone to church on Sunday so she could enjoy singing hymns but the thing she had liked best was a long chat with a stranger who was walking the same path as herself across the headland. 'You know how it is,' she said to Kara as though they were the same age, 'you can talk to strangers more easily than people you know sometimes about private things.' She paused and added, 'This woman was Australian but her mother, who had just died, had grown up in Devon so it was a sort of sentimental journey of a kind for her.'

'Is there something that's worrying you?' Kara said, wondering if she was over-stepping an unspoken limit.

'No, I'm fine,' Helena said, but the way she said it was a warning not to ask any more. 'We're nearly there, I think, so let me listen to the blessed Siri because it's a bit complicated.'

They drew to a halt two doors down from Robert Johnson's house. On either side were equally large detached properties with two-car garages and fancy gates but there was something different about his. Kara had wondered if he was married with a family but there was nothing about this property to indicate that, in fact, there were no signs of home-making at all. It looked neglected with weeds growing between the cobbles of the drive and some rubbish that must have been blown into a nook by the front door. 'Of course he may not live here anymore,' Helena said, sensing Kara's bewilderment, 'Jackie's information could be out of date.'

Kara opened the car door and said, 'I'm going up to the front to have a look in. I don't think anyone's living there and we can't come all this way for nothing.' She was surprised at her unusual boldness but she was jittery and off-balance.

'I'll come with you,' Helena said, 'We'll say we're Jehovah's Witnesses if anyone asks.'

But it didn't seem fun when they got up the drive and peered in the downstairs window because what greeted them was a room scattered with a few pieces of old furniture, a coffee table covered with take-away wrappings and beer bottles and a curtain half-hanging off its rail. On the sofa was an unzipped, filthy sleeping bag.

Helena stepped up to the front door and flipped open the letter-box to peer in. 'Just junk,' she said, 'and lots of cardboard boxes.'

'Come on,' Kara called, 'let's go. It's making me feel a bit funny.'

Not far down the road was a pub which advertised morning coffees and Helena turned into the car park. 'I know what's happened,' she said firmly to Kara, 'he's rented it out for some reason – that's exactly the sort of mess that students leave.' As they got out of the car and walked into the pub, she developed the idea. 'Redditch is on the train line to Birmingham, isn't it, and it stops at the university so maybe he's filled the house with tenants – or they could be young working people or anyone.'

Kara knew that Helena was trying to cheer her up, which was nice, but this was not the sort of neighbourhood where students lived – even she knew that. But what other explanation could there be? Maybe he was just a slob, or his wife was if he had one. In any case it had been depressing to see that squalor in what should have been such a nice home.

When their coffees arrived Helena asked brightly, 'So, what's the next step, eh?' but Kara didn't want to tell her so she said she was thinking about it.

Helena watched her quietly for a moment and then asked how Shell's wedding plans were going so Kara took a deep breath at last and told her about the triumph of the dress and how she was going to be the one to do her hair just as Helena had suggested.

'And what will you be wearing?' Helena's hands were cupped around her mug and her grey eyes were alight with what seemed to be real interest and Kara was grateful not to be quizzed about Robert Johnson.

'I got her to agree that we'll be in red and purple, me and Lauren,' she said, 'and that means I can wear that lovely top you gave me. I showed it her and she was so jealous! Thank you so much. Lauren's got a similar one from Debenhams but,' Kara whispered, 'it's nowhere near as nice!'

'You'll look a picture,' Helena said, 'can I make a suggestion?'

'Yeah!' Kara leaned forward eagerly, 'Anything.'

'Try to get the bride and bridesmaids not to wear too much makeup like so many do at weddings,' Helena said. 'Are you having someone do it?'

'Not for us, just for Shell.'

'Good,' said Helena, 'just use the minimum, what you normally wear, and one of those eighteen-hour lipsticks, I'll tell you how to apply it, so you won't need to fuss after you've eaten and you won't leave lipstick all over people's cheeks when you kiss them. You could suggest it to the others.' She smiled at Kara with such affection that Kara felt her spirits rise even further. 'You're a beautiful young woman and not just in looks, don't ever forget that. And I know what I'm talking about!' She glanced at her watch and lifted her coat off the chair. 'Come on then, love, we'd better be getting you back.'

On the way back to Church View Kara sat quietly savouring that 'love' and half-wishing that she had never started to hunt for her real father if it was going to be this confusing.

In the lounge Anna Ames was waiting, as promised, but Kara was too busy to speak to her until the residents were all fed and escorted to where they wanted to be. Eventually she was able to go over and sit next to the visitor, not quite sure how to tell her what she had discovered by asking around, but she was saved by Helena appearing in an elegant dove-grey leisure suit and making a bee-line for her. Smiling, she sat down on the other side of Anna and held out her hand. She introduced herself and said, 'Kara's told me about you, it's very good of you to give up your time.'

'Well,' Anna began, 'books and reading are very important to me - '

'Of course,' Helena interrupted smoothly, 'but the thing is it's better usually to take your cue from the residents and what they want.'

Was Anna blushing? Kara thought Helena had gone a bit too quickly to the point. 'They do like reading if they can,' she broke in, 'but, um, they're not always too keen on being read to, you see.'

'Oh,' said Anna, 'ok,' and closed the book on her lap. 'I didn't know.'

'Some can't hear very well and some feel it's a bit like being treated as a child,' Helena said, smiling, 'because most of them are quite able to read for themselves.'

'I would hate to come across as condescending,' Anna said, and yes, she was getting red in the face, 'I just wanted to help.'

Helena leaned towards her, the perfectly blended coral lipstick and carefully applied foundation glowing against the silver of her hair and eyes. 'Of course you do, I didn't mean to imply anything else, but I do have a suggestion if you're not averse to working with a group.'

'No – I used to run groups in the library.'

Helena beamed. 'What most people here really enjoy is to talk, not to listen. They like to have a good old chat especially about when they were young and their families and what they got up to. But they need a sort of facilitator because otherwise one person hogs the time or just keeps repeating themselves and the others potter off.'

'What about if I brought in a poem about some interesting experience and then asked them to talk about one of theirs?' Anna said.

Helena leaned back in her chair. 'That would be perfect.' She looked across at Kara. 'We could rustle up a group for tomorrow afternoon I should think?' Kara nodded, pleased both because she had not had to break the news that Anna's original idea had not sparked any interest and because she was being included in the group idea. 'Ok, I'm off – I'll go round now and have a word with anyone that's awake.'

Kara stood up, too, but Anna asked her if they could still have a little chat so she sat back down again. 'I have a friend whose daughter is thinking of working with elderly people,' she said, 'I wondered how you were finding it?'

Mindful of her earlier suspicions about Anna, Kara replied that in a retirement home as well run as Church View it was mostly an enjoyable job but she did know that carers in nursing homes where residents may be quite incapacitated were not always so happy. 'Here, people are elderly so they have a few things wrong with them, but they're still up for a chat and I like hearing about the lives they've led - and most of them are really grateful for the things we do.'

'Are your parents happy with your decision?' Anna asked, which seemed a bit odd to Kara.

'Oh, my mum never expected me to be a brainbox,' she said.

'And your dad?'

'I'd better get going now,' Kara said standing up, 'I'm a bit behind with my jobs.'

'Would you be able to help me with the group, I mean introduce people, make them feel comfortable to have a familiar face and so on?'

'I'll check with Mrs B. If she says I can, I'd like to,' Kara said. 'Bye for now.'

When she turned at the door to glance back, she saw that Anna Ames was packing the books that she had brought back into their bag so she left her to it feeling satisfied that she had said the right things and also that Helena would be part of the new project so she could see more of her.

13

After the dishes had been cleared away that evening, Anna put on her coat to walk down to Steve's. She hadn't seen Alice for days and was hoping that things might have improved, especially since she'd asked Faye to pop down and say hello when she'd been round pilfering kitchen utensils. She'd hardly even seen Steve at work as he'd got some kind of assignment from the NCA or something and had his door firmly locked and the blinds closed.

As she glanced into neighbours' front gardens she saw with a frisson of delight that strong green bulb fuses were poking up from the dun-coloured detritus of winter. It was still February but there was that pledge of new life to come that made her heart lift. And her plan to get to know Kara was coming along, too. She found that she had unconsciously drifted alongside Robert, her prior misgivings forgotten, and now wanted his daughter to know him, wanted to be able to assure him that she didn't think of Graham as her 'real' father. Perhaps the first reading for the group could be about fathers? Was that too manipulative? It was an odd position she was in, being able to speak to both father and daughter when they themselves were so separated, but she knew now, she thought, that they would get along very well indeed. Kara did not seem to be the sort of girl who would hold Robert's violent act, which, after all, was to protect his mother, against him, and Robert would be such a loving father to her when he was released. But everything must be done as he wanted and she must be on her guard not to let anything slip or, in fact, not to romanticise the whole situation as she was in danger of doing. Anyway, it was still very early days so she could take her time. Robert wasn't going anywhere, certainly.

Steve answered the door wearing an old T shirt over his jumper in lieu of an apron. He was smudged with flour and gestured Anna inside calling, 'Anna's here, sweetie,' but no patter of eager feet rose to greet her. 'We're making biscuits,' he said, 'for a party at school – I've forgotten what it's for.'

'It's for National Cookie Day,' Alice said as they walked into the kitchen, ignoring Anna. 'I told you.' Steve wrinkled his eyebrows in disbelief at Anna who laughed.

'They look good. I didn't know there was such a thing.' She sat down and admired the circles of dough covered with brown sugar ready to go in the oven.

'I'm not lying,' Alice said coldly.

'We've got Bobble into a new class,' Anna said, smiling at her and refusing to feel irritated, 'Ellis and George are there with him now. They had an awful time getting him into the car.'

Steve slid a spatula under the biscuits and slipped them on to a greased baking tray in neat rows. 'I'll just pop these in.'

'So how's school these days?' Anna tried again.

'I'm going to watch my video,' Alice said, and walked off into the front room to turn on the television.

'Just for half an hour,' Steve called, 'and then it's time for bed.'

'I'm not going to bed till she's gone,' Alice called back in her high, clear voice. 'Tell her to leave.'

Steve closed the oven door, set the timer and started to clear up the mess on the table. He smiled at Anna and kissed her on the top of her head. 'Don't take any notice,' he said cheerfully. But Anna felt that *he* should have taken notice of Alice's rudeness. Ok, she was upset by Faye leaving but that was weeks ago. She and Harry would never have let their children get away with speaking to an adult, or even another child, like that.

'Actually, Steve,' she said cautiously, 'to be honest, I don't think it's good for her to get away with talking to someone like that – if you don't mind my saying so.'

Steve swabbed down the table with a dishcloth and frowned. 'She's tired. I'll have a word with her tomorrow.'

After she had counted all the way to ten, Anna said brightly, 'How did it go when Faye came down last night?'

Steve rinsed the cloth, hung it neatly on a hook and peeled off his T shirt to stuff it into the washing machine. 'She breezed in all full of bonhomie, you know what a force of nature she is, but I'm afraid Alice wasn't in the mood for it so she stomped off up to her bedroom – I'm sure you're familiar with that tactic from Faye herself as a child. She and I had a nice chat, though, about the project she's on at work. She's a clever girl, full of ideas, I was impressed.'

Anna knew what he was doing. He was gently reminding her, while complimenting Faye, that she had been just as awkward as Alice but had turned out all right despite Anna and Harry not being able to tame her either. But, Anna thought, at least they had tried and Faye did know, in theory anyway, how to behave politely.

He came round and sat in the chair next to her, pulling her close to him. 'Can you come round later?' he whispered, 'I can text you when she's asleep.'

Anna kissed him on the lips and shook her head. 'I have to talk to dad about Ellis and then I need to prepare for a session at Church View tomorrow. I've been given my orders by a rather classy lady so I'd better come up to scratch!' By the time she'd explained about Helena's idea and Kara's part in that, Alice had returned and was standing in the doorway with her arms folded, glowering. All she needed was a rolling pin and curlers, Anna thought, getting up and picking up her coat so as not to provoke another hostile comment from the child which she may not be able to resist responding to.

It took a while for her to search through her dad's poetry books for something suitable for the group and there was nothing about fathers that wasn't bitter, like Sylvia Plath's *Daddy*, or weird in some other way. Why would that be? But she did find one by a small press poet about misunderstandings on a first date. It was light-hearted and would be fun to read. When she got back into the house Ellis was slouched at the kitchen table with a can of fizzy drink in front of him and his phone in his hand. He was pretending to read it. Sitting there rather than in his room was, Anna felt, tantamount to saying he wanted to talk. Maybe she would tackle the situation rather than slough it off on George, tempting though that was.

'How did you get on? Where's Pops?'

'There's something on at the Gudwara he's gone to. The dog instructor said she thinks Bobble's part deer-hound,' he said without looking at her. 'He's been barred.'

Anna sat down opposite him and tutted. 'Why this time?'

'It wasn't his fault – he just got over-excited with all the other dogs there so he barked and they barked and he barked and they barked and none of them would shut up. She told us to take him out so we did and walked round a bit and then went back in and it all started up again so she said we had to leave because he was a disruptive influence.'

'Bad Boy Bobble!' Anna laughed.

Even Ellis managed a little crooked smile and she decided to seize the moment. 'Ell, I don't want to intrude but I did wonder, is this thing with Mike about Kirsty? I mean Mike and Kirsty? Don't bite my head off.'

Ellis sunk down even lower in his chair, a faint flush coming up his neck. His skin still had the peachy bloom of childhood but there was a darkening around his upper lip and shadows like bruises on apples under his tiger eyes. She wanted to hug him to her but she knew she couldn't.

Finally he looked up at her, his face wide open with hurt. 'He knew I liked her, Mum. He knew and he took her anyway. That's what I can't forgive – the treachery of it. He's supposed to be my best friend.'

Anna let a space stretch open and then said, 'Is it possible, love, that it was Kirsty who fancied him and she made the move?'

Ellis shut his eyes and groaned. 'That's worse.'

'No, it isn't. She's not to blame for liking him and he's not to blame for liking her. He may not have betrayed you at all, he couldn't make her fancy you if she didn't – he never has gone behind your back before, has he?' She reached out and touched his long white hand quivering on the table like a damaged paw. 'We sometimes do fall for people who don't fall for us, Ell. It's hard but that's just how it is. But there will be – there may be at this minute – girls out there, just as nice as Kirsty, who are wondering how they can get you to notice them.'

His eyelids clicked open. 'Do you think so?'

'Yes, I do. So, will you make it up with Mike?'

Scraping his chair back, Ellis unfolded his long body and tucked his phone in his shirt pocket. 'I think he should make it up with me. Don't you think we ought to re-name Bobble to something more street if he's such a delinquent?'

'Like what?' She stood up, too, thinking that a glass of wine and a spot of telly might be just the thing.

'I don't know, Mr B? Big B?'

'While you're being creative can you have a think about your room? It needs a makeover badly.'

He stopped on his way to the hall. 'What's the budget?'

'Come up with the ideas and I'll see what we can do. We can run to a new bed, at least, but the rest's up to you – within limits, of course – don't knock any walls through.'

'Sweet.' His footsteps on the stairs definitely sounded more cheerful.

Anna pushed Bobble's bony rear end over to make a small space for herself on the sofa and switched on the tv while she took the first sip of her wine. As she flicked through the channels she realised that she had left her phone in the kitchen so she wouldn't hear it if Steve called to say good-night, but she was comfortable tucked up in her own living room in her own home and she decided to leave it there.

Wind was whipping rubbish up into skittering missiles that blew against her legs as Kara walked quickly along taking another turn past *R J Letting* and clutching her coat more tightly about her. It had taken two and half hours and three buses to get here and now she was here she had no idea what to do. She had glanced quickly to her right the first time she had passed and seen the 'Open' sign on a door which was fortified with steel mesh. In the window were photographs of properties but she hadn't stopped to examine them. She hadn't expected the business to be open on a Saturday but then, she hadn't expected it to be an estate agent.

The third time she passed by she looked through the window but could see no-one at the desks so she re-traced her steps, took a deep breath, pushed back her hood, smoothed her hair, and went in. She stood for a while looking around and thought that the place could do with freshening up so maybe business wasn't so good – that would account for the lodgers that Helena had suggested were staying at the Redditch house. Wasn't it true that it was a difficult time for estate agents? But *was* her father an estate agent, was that what Jackie had meant when she had said he was into property? She had assumed something much grander but still, he obviously owned the business so she couldn't relax as though he was on her level.

Suddenly a cry and shouting came from somewhere at the back of the shop and a door was snatched open. Then came sounds of some knocking and banging and a man's voice swearing. Kara sprang for the door but just as she pulled it open a boy rushed past her and out and before she could follow him, the door was firmly closed with her on the inside.

'Can I help you?' he panted, keeping pressure on the closed door.

Kara, as alarmed as she was, still absorbed in a flash his appearance. He had dark curly hair beginning to grey by the ears, very dark eyes and skin the colour of porridge. He was not tall but broad and heavy with the beginnings of a paunch. He was still slightly out of breath and on the intake she thought she could hear wheezing. He was staring at her as though she had accused him of something.

She had to speak. 'Mr Johnson? I'm thinking of moving to this area and I wondered if you had a flat to rent.' It was her prepared cover.

He dropped his hand from the door and stepped back. 'No,' he said, 'I haven't and I'm just about to lock up – I thought I had, it's past closing for Saturday. Look online.' He opened the door and raised his eyebrows at her to leave.

'No,' Kara said, quickly coming to a decision, 'I'm not really looking for a flat.'

The wary look had returned. 'What then?'

'Are you Robert Johnson?'

'Bob Johnson, yes. What of it? Who are you?'

Kara felt as though blood was draining down from her entire body and that at any moment she might disgracefully sink to the floor. She dropped her eyes. 'I think I'm your daughter.' A long silence followed and Kara remained immobile, eyes locked on to a patch of worn grey laminate.

Finally he said, 'How old are you?' and when she told him he nodded and then asked in the same business-like tone, 'Who's your mother?' so she told him that. After a few seconds he asked, 'Where did I know her?' and Kara named the school in Nechells, feeling as though she was being interviewed by police or somebody like that. At this he seemed to relax and stepped back into the shop space, pulling out a chair for her and then seating himself at another. He was looking intently at her now but with a different kind of look, a more interested and less suspicious one. 'Has she told you to come after me?'

'No. She doesn't even know I'm here. She married someone else and I only just found out he isn't my dad.'

'And, not that I'm denying it, what makes you think I am?'

'There's a woman at work who does genealogy as a hobby. She found you.' His voice was not what she had expected because there wasn't a trace of a Birmingham accent – he sounded almost posh, but she knew people often deliberately shed the accent if they wanted to get on.

'You haven't told me your name.' He nodded when she did and then said in the same matter-of-fact tone, 'You can call me Bob. What are you after then? What do you want?'

Kara straightened her back feeling misjudged. This was not at all how she had imagined their meeting. 'Nothing, I don't want anything. I don't need anything from you, I just wanted to get to know you.' She felt the blood rush back into her body and stood up. 'I'm sorry to have bothered you. I'll be off now.'

Bob laughed at this. 'Oh come on, I had to ask, don't get all offended. It's not every day a pretty girl walks into my agency and says she's my daughter – just give me a minute to take it in, will you?'

So she sat down again and looked round the room for something else to look at. It was just the usual stuff – filing cabinets, office furniture, a couple of rather grubby computer terminals, so eventually she had to look back at him to find that his body had relaxed and he was now slumped in his desk chair, revolving it slightly to left and right as he studied her, a smile on his face which made him look much more pleasant. She half-smiled back and breathed deeply.

'There's a café on the corner,' he said, 'can I buy you a coffee or something, darling?' She nodded and stood up. He shrugged on a dark coat and turned off the lights and in a moment they were out on the windy street and he was locking the door. The sudden chill made Kara tremble and she flipped up her hood and dug her hands into her pockets waiting for him. He had said she was pretty and called her 'darling'. He may not be exactly what she had imagined but he had a nice smile and, most important of all, he wanted to get to know her. Of course he had had a shock when she told him who she was, what did she expect?

The café was only yards away and packed with people steaming up the windows and making a racket. He took one look inside and turned away. 'Let's go to the pub,' he said, 'it'll be quieter,' and she was grateful for the way he took charge and knew what to do and it felt strange and new, but not in a bad way, to be walking swiftly by his side.

The pub had scrubbed wooden tables and plastic-covered tub chairs but there were only a few elderly couples eating and men staring at their phones with pint glasses beside them so he found a corner away from the others and went off to get the apple juice she had asked for and whatever he would be having. Kara finally let herself relax and feel a rising pulse of excitement. The bar was at right-angles to where she was so she could see him clearly in profile and, on an impulse, took out her phone and snapped him. She looked at the photo under the table and zoomed in on the face. Yes, it was clearly in focus and a good likeness. Elise had said he was mixed race but light-skinned enough to show a blush and it wasn't unusual for mixed-race people to have that oatmeal-coloured skin. He looked Italian, she thought, or Greek, and he wasn't bad-looking. As a young man with less weight he would be ok and Vicki might well fancy someone as ambitious as him. Perhaps she had got on his nerves and he'd dumped her and that was why she'd said he was no good. She certainly wasn't the easiest person to live with. Kara sometimes thought the only reason the marriage to Graham had lasted was that he was away most of the time, but that was mean. None of us know what other people have gone through and what heavy burdens they have, she reminded herself sternly.

'Now then,' he said, setting down her glass and then his own tumbler, 'I want to hear all about you, Kara. Tell me everything.' Kara flushed again with pleasure. 'But first, I was wondering, if you didn't know that Vicki's husband wasn't your dad, how did you find out? Did your mum decide to tell you?'

'Oh no,' Kara said quickly, 'Graham did. He got mad with me about something and just came out with it so I confronted her. She didn't want me to find you, she wouldn't tell me your name, it was you that gave it to me!' She grinned at him, risking the dimple showing in her left cheek, but he just stared at her so she went on, 'You signed my birth certificate only two days after I was born at the Women's Hospital. That was my starting point. Then,' she went on in a rush, 'I talked to my auntie, mum doesn't have anything to do with her but I tracked her down, and she told me that you and mum and she had been at the same school and she found your date of birth. Then Jackie, a work colleague, went from there.'

'Ok, I see.' He sipped at his drink and studied her. 'So she won't want to meet me? Your mum.'

Kara had never thought of this as a possibility and was a little shocked although, of course, it was a natural enough question. 'Oh, no! We don't even live in Birmingham, we moved out to Bromsgrove when I was just a toddler. No, she won't want to meet you.' Kara wondered if she should say anything else but decided to be honest with him. 'She doesn't like you any more, I'm sorry to tell you. She hasn't said anything, I mean told me anything, but she tried to put me off finding you. She said you were no good. Sorry.'

But far from this revelation distressing her father, he seemed even more cheerful. 'I probably was a bad lad,' he laughed, 'she's probably right, but, to be honest, darling, I don't want to meet her either. It could be awkward and – embarrassing - you know?'

'Fine,' said Kara, 'that's easier for me, too. We don't get along that well.'

'So,' said her father, leaning back in his chair, 'let's forget her and hear about you.'

All the way home, standing for ages at cold, windy bus-stops and crammed on noisy buses Kara hugged what had happened to herself like an invalid with a hot-water bottle. She had found him and he wanted to know her. Her phone never left her hand and it was always showing that photo – that face – the person she had not even known existed until a couple of weeks ago.

They had talked for over an hour before he had had to go but he'd arranged another meeting, dinner this time, at an Indian restaurant in Redditch in a few days. He'd written it down for her and, to add to the excitement, had told her to get a taxi from near her house and he would pay. No-one had ever done such a thoughtful thing for her. Gerry would pick her up if they were going out together when she was with him but had never offered to help her get somewhere otherwise. Graham had more or less ignored her for years. But now it would be different – now she had a proper father who listened to everything she said and didn't interrupt and when they parted he'd said the most wonderful thing. Even on the bus with all the kids shouting around her she couldn't help smiling because he'd said, 'It was a good day for me the day you walked into my life, Kara,' and he had kissed her on the cheek just like in television programmes about families meeting each other after years apart.

By the time she'd walked home from the bus stop in Bromsgrove she was cold and hungry because she'd missed lunch but she was still glowing with pleasure, so when Vicki shouted at her for not taking her outdoor shoes off quickly enough, she blurted out that she had been to meet her father and then stood, shoes in hand, feet cold on the tiled floor, wondering what on earth Vicki would say.

For a while Vicki didn't say anything but just stared at her with her mouth half open. 'Where?' she said, finally. 'Where did you meet him?'

'At his business in Erdington.'

'At his business in Erdington?' Vicki repeated as if stunned. 'What do you mean?'

'He's well-off,' Kara boasted, unable to contain herself, 'he's got a big house in Redditch and an estate agent's.' But Vicki was still staring at her. 'I like him, he wants to see me again.'

'He's well-off?' Then Vicki seemed to gather herself. 'Did he ask about me?'

'Of course he did! I had to tell him your name and how you met at school but that's all I know – you've never told me anything,' and then she explained about the birth certificate and Jackie and she didn't care if Vicki shouted at her and said mean things because now she was not alone.

'How did you know all that?' So Kara explained and Vicki's lips tightened. 'Elise,' she said, 'interfering bitch.'

Kara pulled out her phone. 'I've got a photo of him.' Her fingers trembled on the key-pad but there he was. She zoomed in to the face. 'See! That's him, isn't it?'

Vicki took the phone and looked at it for a long time, expressionless. 'He's well-off, you say?' Kara nodded, proud that he had made something of his life. 'It's been a long time,' her mother said, 'but it looks like you've found him.'

Kara snatched the phone back and ran up to her room. She couldn't wait to tell Helena and wished she had her mobile phone number so she could text her. There was no point in going to Church View to see her because she was away in North Wales for the weekend. She emailed the photo to herself and then brought it up large on her lap-top. There was an alert for another one of Tassie's blogs but she didn't care. Tassie taking her lonely trip round the world could wait. This was far more exciting. 'Dad,' Kara breathed almost inaudibly, touching the screen lightly with her forefinger, 'Hello, Dad.'

14

A small lounge had been made available and Helena was shepherding people in and seating them around a circular table just as Anna had requested. Some people would be hard of hearing and some would be shy and this arrangement was the one which in her experience at the library had always worked best for groups of older people as the deaf ones could lip read and the shy ones didn't have to speak but wouldn't feel left out. As people shuffled in and found places to prop their sticks and hang their bags and cardigans Anna glanced surreptitiously at Helena, intrigued by her. Kara herself had not yet put in an appearance but Anna was hoping she would. It was, after all, the whole point of the exercise.

After introductions and the distribution of stickers and pens for names, Anna decided to try to loosen things up a bit as most of the old people seemed to have more pressing things on their minds and were staring off in different directions. 'Ok,' she said, 'I know you all know each other but I don't know you, so can we just quickly play a game? Just to get started?' The level of distraction and boredom in the group increased visibly. 'The idea is that any one of you can tell us an outrageous thing about yourself and the rest of you have to guess whether it's true or not.'

'What do you mean?' Edna Simpson asked, frowning. 'What sort of thing?'

'Anything. It can be true or made up and we've got to guess which.'

A tiny woman with a crocheted beret said subversively, 'I'm the Queen of Sheba,' and there was a little ripple of approval. Her name sticker, printed in pink, read 'Barbie.'

'Something that might be true,' Anna explained trying not to sound defensive and thinking that if this went on much longer they'd be leaving. 'Anyone?'

Geoff Baines, polishing his glasses, said, 'I won the lottery once – six million pounds – or I would have done if my wife had bought the ticket with the money I gave her instead of buying her ciggies with it.' He didn't appear to be sabotaging the game, his tone had been regretful, if anything.

'Ok,' Anna said brightly, in her best facilitator mode, 'So what do we think? Is it true or is it a lie?'

'Well, it would certainly explain why you're divorced,' Edna said drily. 'Except that I don't believe a word of it.'

'Typical man, couldn't even be arsed to buy your own lottery ticket,' Barbie said. 'That sounds fucking believable.'

'Anyone else?' Anna asked, but she sensed the gambit had almost played itself out. 'Ok, let's vote. Who thinks Geoff's telling the truth?' One hand went up. 'Who thinks he's lying?' Five hands out of eight went up. 'Ok, Geoff, reveal all.'

He took off his glasses like an actor using his prop, held them up to the light, replaced them and then said calmly, 'It's true.' At this there was an outcry from some of the group until a blanched man without a name sticker, who had sat quietly throughout, leaned forward and tapped on the table.

'I've known Geoff here since we worked at the car plant together and what he says is true. Back then he showed us the numbers he always did and they were the ones that came up. If Shirley had bought that ticket he'd be on his own island in the Caribbean, wouldn't you, mate?'

There was a group intake of breath. Anna couldn't resist asking, 'What did you say to her when you knew you would have won?' Everyone was now listening intently.

'Well,' Geoff said, 'I didn't speak to her for three days and I've never bought a lottery ticket since.'

'Very restrained of you,' Helena said, smiling.

'And,' Geoff went on, 'the reason I'm divorced, not that it's anyone's business, is that she ran off with a chap she met at Bingo that turned out to be married so serve her right. I'd had it with her by then.'

Anna wondered if this really would be a good time to bring up first dates but decided to plunge ahead anyway and just as she announced the title of the poem, *May Date*, Kara slipped into the room. Anna indicated the seat she had kept free next to her but Kara sat down next to Helena. The poem, about a date which ended badly but comically, went down well and there were a couple of snorts of laughter. Kara was smiling round the group at the old people enjoying themselves Anna saw approvingly. Time for anecdotes. 'A funny thing happened the first time I dated my husband,' she began, hoping to set an example, 'he turned up in his - ' but she got no further.

'I remember a date Easter weekend 1952,' Barbie broke in loudly, 'with a fit chap from Old Hill Farm near Belbroughton.' Her mouse eyes sparkled.

'Near the Bell pub?' the pale man asked.

'Yeah. Not called that now though. He was a lovely fella, Andy, great big hands and arms, you know! And that wasn't all.' The women, except for Edna, laughed and the men looked down at the table. 'We didn't waste much time on sweet nothings I can tell you, he took me in the barn and you can imagine the rest.'

Although Anna was a little startled by this revelation having expected something more innocent and romantic, she was pleased they were opening up and looked round the table to see who might be next. She glanced at Kara but the girl was looking away and she hesitated to ask Helena since she was certainly confident enough not to need prompting, so she was just about to ask for more volunteers when Edna rose to her feet, scarlet in the face.

'You poisonous bitch!' she shouted at Barbie, 'telling filthy lies! I was the one he married, wasn't I? He didn't want used goods like you!' Silence fell round the table and now everyone except Barbie was looking into middle distance and trying not to giggle or show embarrassment.

'And you're so special, I suppose?' Barbie said spitefully, 'I remember you at school, Edna Billings, all mouth and no knickers!'

'Ok,' Anna interjected, standing up - which she could, at least, do more quickly than the two women – 'I think we'll end this session for today, shall we? It must be nearly tea-time.' At these words people began to heave themselves out of their chairs muttering and rolling their eyes. She looked for Kara and saw her helping the white-faced man get a grip on his walker so she went quickly over to her. 'Any chance of a chat?'

Kara glanced up at her in surprise. 'It's a busy time, now,' she said, and just then Helena appeared at Anna's elbow.

'Perhaps you'd like to see one of the rooms?' she suggested, 'Why don't you come to mine and I'll make us a cup of tea.'

As they walked down the corridor, Anna said how surprised she'd been that some of the residents had known each other before they came to Church View and Helena replied that it wasn't usual that they went as far back as Barbie and Edna who'd been at infant school together but many of them had lived in the area for a long time and often had a connection of some sort. 'People come from all over the place to live in Bromsgrove,' she said, 'but they seem to like to stay.'

'What about yourself, if you don't mind my asking?' Anna said as Helena halted outside one of the doors.

'Oh, I'm one of those people who aren't from anywhere,' Helena said, showing her in.

The room was flooded with light and Anna smiled as she looked around. Clearly, this room was furnished and decorated with Helena's own belongings and she was delighted by the fresh, pretty look of the place. There was a bed tucked away in a large alcove with a white quilted throw on it very like her own treasured item which Faye still lusted after. 'You've made this so attractive,' she said. 'I could move in here myself!'

'Assam, Earl Grey or Camomile? That's all I have at the moment.'

'Earl Grey would be lovely, thank you.' While she waited for the kettle to boil, Anna added, 'That little spat was a bit of a surprise, and what Geoff said about winning the lottery – I wonder what else will come out in our next session! I was expecting something much more mundane.'

Placing the tray on a small table and sitting down herself, Helena said, 'We've all had lives, haven't we? We haven't always been old,' which Anna took as a rebuke and felt herself bridle a little. Helena sipped her own tea watching her. 'Tell me about yourself. What brought you here, I mean, to Church View?'

'Oh, I'm between jobs and wanted to volunteer on a short-term basis.'

'Why here?'

'Picked it with a pin,' Anna said easily. 'My husband and I used to come out this way and bring the children to the spring fair so I had happy memories of the town. Were you living around here before you became a resident?' It was pleasant having this talk with Helena and Anna barely registered her own deception. She was much keener to find out what this intriguing woman was doing here and it would pass the time until Kara might be free to chat with her as she planned to ask directly about her family if she could. Anna noticed how fluidly Helena moved and how clear and intelligent were her eyes so it couldn't be that she needed assisted living, surely?

Helena put down her cup and saucer on the tray and folded her elegant hands together. 'And what is your interest in Kara?' she said, ignoring Anna's question.

'What?' Anna flushed with surprise. 'What do you mean? I have no particular interest in Kara.'

'I suspected you were lying when you gave your reason for being here,' Helena went on quietly, 'but now I know you are.'

Anna felt sweat prickle along her hairline and her thoughts raced. She couldn't tell anyone the real reason for being here and if she couldn't convince Helena of her cover story she may be reported to Mrs Bandhal and an investigation may happen and all sorts of trouble might come from that including Ted taking her off Robert Johnson's case, the last thing she wanted to happen. She stalled for time, 'Why do you say that?' she asked, noting with concern that the smile had faded completely from the older woman's face and the grey eyes were now cold.

'I used to run a model agency,' Helena said, 'so I am used to protecting beautiful young and often naïve girls from predators of all kinds – not limited to those of a male gender.'

'What?' Anna's thoughts whirled and she felt her cheeks glow hot. 'No, no, you're wrong.'

'I've been watching you since you came here,' Helena went on, this time with an unmistakeable edge in her voice. 'I noticed your interest in Kara but assumed that it would extend to all the staff. From time to time the management likes to have someone around under a pretext of some kind to see how staff behave when they don't know they are being observed. Kara herself thought that you were here for that reason.'

'No – I'm not - '

'But I soon saw that it was only Kara who was of interest to you. Your eyes follow her constantly when you are in the same room and you take every opportunity to spend time near her. I don't know whether you saw her before you set up this so-called volunteering or whether you were immediately struck by her when you first came here but your interest in her could be seen as a cause for concern, Mrs Ames.'

'No, really - I wish I could tell you what it is but I can't,' Anna said miserably, 'but believe me, it's not some kind of weird obsessional interest in Kara, it's – oh – it's who she is. I can't say any more.'

Helena stood up. 'No, I don't think you should. What you have said makes no sense, but I think it will be better, won't it, if you don't return? I'm sure you can find some excuse for cutting short your time here and if you attempt to contact Kara for any reason outside this place she will let me know because you have made her feel uneasy by targeting her and she has confided that to me. I would then have to speak to Mrs Bandhal about you.'

A small measure of self-control had returned so Anna could gather her shocked thoughts and feelings during this speech and she stood up and picked up her things. 'Helena, I'm glad you're looking out for Kara and I now understand how odd my being here and trying to get to know her must have seemed, but I can assure you that the situation is not as you imply. In due course I hope to be able to explain it to you but I will approach you and not Kara first if that time comes.'

In answer Helena walked to the door and opened it. 'I'll walk you to the main entrance,' she said, 'and if I have misjudged you I would be glad to know that, but so far all I know is that you're here until false pretences by your own admission.'

'Fair enough,' said Anna, and in less than a minute she was walking to the car park desperate to drive away and have time to process the bizarre twists and turns of the afternoon.

By the time she drew up in her own drive Anna had still not managed to find the funny side of Helena's implication but the embarrassment of the whole thing was beginning to lose its sting. Ironic, really, that she had thought she was observing Kara when all the time they had been assessing her. Just as well she didn't have to make her living as an undercover cop since she clearly had no talent for it.

Of course, she should have gone into Harts – there were a couple of hours left in the working day – but she couldn't face it. One thing did now seem more urgent; she should visit Robert and get him to agree to her telling Kara about him because otherwise she could not give him any more reports on the young woman's welfare. She was also hoping that the morning's work post would include at least one of the certificates she had ordered to help her trace Robert's family back into the heat and colour of the Caribbean. She rested her hands for a moment on the steering wheel and let her mind fill with images of foam-edged jade water beating on yellow sands, parrots and fishing boats, corals and palm trees. Then she noticed that the paint on the porch had peeled and lifted revealing bare wood in places and possibly the beginnings of rot. Her phone pinged and she saw that Ellis had sent her a text: 'have to clean up tennis club room after school pls take bb for walk??? soz.'

She let herself into the house and was immediately assaulted by Bobble himself. It was like having a large rag rug and a clutch of broom handles thrown at you, she thought, as she wrestled him down into a standing position. 'Sorry love,' she heard George call from the kitchen, 'he slipped out when he heard the car.' When he had calmed down a bit she took off her work coat and draped it on the newel post and went into the kitchen to greet her dad. 'You're home early,' he said, glancing at the kitchen clock. 'Are you all right?'

Explaining was too much of a hassle right now as there were one or two things she had avoided mentioning to him, but she might tell him later. 'Mm, finished early. Ellis wants me to take this one out as he's apparently at the tennis club?'

'Oh yes, he went there straight after school – they put a group email out last night asking for volunteers to sort the place out before the spring membership drive.' George peered at Bobble over his glasses. 'I could take him – it's not fair on you to have to do it.'

'Actually, Dad, a walk is just what I need. Come on, Big B, let's strut our stuff in the park.' Neither Ellis nor she had told George of their joint decision to take him off the dog-walking rota. He was seventy-four and healthy enough, but his lungs had not completely recovered from a nasty bout of pneumonia he had had a couple of years before and Bobble was just too much of a handful. 'Do you want me to get anything for dinner?'

'No, all under control,' George said, 'I'm just about to get started.'

Bobble was in many ways a daft dog but he had learned that if he stood still to have his lead put on the yearned-for walk would happen sooner, so he let Anna prepare him and waited, tail wagging furiously, while she put on her warm parka and walking boots. 'Has Ellis made it up with Mike yet?' she asked, panting a little as she bent over to tug the stiff laces.

'No, I'm afraid he hasn't. I had a word with him last night and he seems more chipper about it all but insists that Mike should make the first move. I suspect words have been said that we don't know about aside from the Kirsty stuff. Best not to interfere, I suppose.' His voice was muffled by the pantry door as he rooted in the potato bag.

Anna stood up and grabbed Bobble's lead. 'Maybe, but I don't like it. I'll speak to him later,' she said, 'and if he won't budge we might need to organise some kind of meeting – what do they call it now? An intervention – only less formal. He's such a nice kid usually that he hasn't had much practice at backing down gracefully from confrontations and probably neither has Mike.'

The stiff, chilling wind that had made the last few days feel miserable had dropped and there was even a weak gleam of sun as Anna strode out beside Bobble down the road to the park. She looked up at the sky and saw that the sun was visible as a blurred pewter disc through a shroud of stratus cloud as though it was hiding behind a thin scarf and she tried to remember the word for that. Bobble jerked her to a standstill as he found the first enticing trickle by the park gatepost and she waited, shoulders hunched, while he sniffed at it with deep interest. Perlucidus or was it translucidus?

Now that some time had passed she was beginning to think along new lines. Helena had accused her of inappropriate feelings towards Kara although the girl herself had maybe not tried to avoid Anna, she had just needed to get on with her work. That was understandable, especially if she suspected that Anna was a plant to observe her work practices. So, perhaps Helena had herself become over-involved with the young woman? After all, she was so different from the other residents she must often feel lonely and befriending a girl like Kara would brighten her day. It would be a short step from that to becoming over-protective. Even so, there was a nuance in the way she had talked that Anna found odd – she had certainly not had sufficient reason to imply, as she had, that Anna was sexually attracted to Kara, so what was behind that?

The park was filling up with brisk dog walkers and kids strolling home from school seemingly impervious to the cold, swigging fizzy drinks and cramming their mouths with chocolate and crisps. Bobble was greeted by several of them and politely wagged his tail in return but Anna could see it was the dogs in the park he was most interested in. It was a shame that the classes had not worked out. Maybe she should look up some enclosed outdoor spaces where he might be allowed to run free and socialise because he was not a destructive dog, he just wanted to be friendly. 'You just want a few mates, don't you?' she said to him and he turned his head, flattened his ears and grinned at her, saliva gloop trickling down his beard.

After a full circuit Anna had had enough and turned back towards home. As she did her thoughts turned, too, away from work issues and towards Steve. The truth was she was missing him. In the past when Alice went to bed earlier and was not so hostile to Anna, she would go round most evenings and after the little girl was asleep they would cuddle together on the sofa and as often as not make love there on the rug in front of the fire, a chair pushed up against the door handle just in case. There had been so many years before without sex that Anna found huge joy in the intimacy and release it gave her, and the fact that Steve was so uninhibited and passionate was not exactly a surprise but certainly an unexpected bonus. Of course she loved him for many things – he had, after all, once saved her life – but their physical compatibility had charged the romance to a more intense level. She missed him, she missed it. Nowadays it was more like a guilty fumble with one ear open for Alice's foot on the stair.

'I think we need a weekend away *without* Alice,' she told Bobble, who agreed happily, leaning sideways to go for a quick lick of her face. 'His parents would love to have her. I'll suggest it tonight, shall I?'

They were now walking up the road towards home and Anna saw that Mike and a girl, perhaps Kirsty, were coming towards them on the opposite side of the road. She waved and Mike waved back and at that moment a black and white cat streaked across the street and Bobble, obeying the instinct of all sight-hounds, tore after it. The lead was jerked from Anna's hand and she staggered sideways just as Mike leaped into the road to grab the dog. There was a horrible, sickening noise of tyres screeching and then silence.

'Mike!' Anna ran into the road while the girl stood with her hand over her mouth as though she was frozen to the spot. It wasn't a large, powerful motor-bike, it was more of a scramble bike but it had been enough to lay Mike out, his limbs twisted, and there was blood in the road. Anna tore off her coat and draped it over him. Her hand was shaking so much she could barely hold the phone but she made the emergency call, kneeling in the road by his side.

Was he breathing, they asked. Was he? Yes, she could see the slight rise and fall of his chest. Was he conscious? She spoke to him but there was no response. No, he was not. They're on their way, they said, they're on their way, and it was only when the call ended that Anna saw another immobile body further up the road.

She beckoned the girl over and asked her to stay with Mike while she ran up to the other one. It was a lad not much older than Mike, maybe seventeen, and she saw the L plate on the back of his bike, but unlike Mike his eyes were open. 'Are you ok? Don't move if you're hurting,' she said, 'the ambulance is on its way.'

The boy had large blue eyes that stared at her over the bleeding graze on his freckled cheek. 'He just ran out,' he said, 'have I killed him? Is he dead?'

'No, no,' Anna reassured him, 'but he is hurt. I saw what happened and it wasn't your fault – he was trying to catch my dog. Are you all right?' The boy was slowly stretching out his legs and feeling his arms and then he sat up.

'I think so, but this arm, my left one – I think it's broken.'

'Can I phone someone?' and he gave her the number.

'Tell them it wasn't my fault.'

By this time various people had gathered on the pavement and after the call Anna leaped up to organise them, a couple to direct the ambulance depending on which direction it came from, some more to stop the traffic entering the road from the junction and from the park side and when that was done she phoned George. It seemed only a minute before he was outside with a mug of hot tea for the biker and a rug to put over Mike who was lying so horribly still. The girl was now crying and shaking and Anna wrapped her in her arms and shushed her. With one arm round the girl she phoned Mike's mum.

Finally they heard the sound of sirens and the paramedics arrived and got to work. The boy was able to walk into one ambulance but Mike was carefully examined, connected up to things and eased on to a stretcher, his head held straight and steady by huge foam flanges. He was still, Anna noted with distress, unconscious.

Maggie had not even put a coat on before she left the house and arrived, running, in her slippers, as they were loading him in to the second ambulance, her eyes wide. She went in with him, the ambulance sped off, and Anna led Kirsty into her own house.

George made the girl a hot chocolate while Anna phoned the number the boy had given her again, telling them which hospital he was being taken to and that he had been able to walk and talk. The police were examining the bike, she said, but she would be a witness that it had not been his fault.

'And here's one for you, Annie,' George said, 'I think it's about time you sat down.'
Ten minutes later Kirsty's dad arrived to pick her up and after a short explanation he left.

'I want to go to the hospital,' Anna told her dad, 'can you tell Ellis? He should be back soon.'

'I think you should wait,' George said, putting his warm hand over hers as she sat at the table. 'You're still shaking and I don't think you should drive – it'll be rush hour traffic. Not only that, Ellis will want to see him, so you can take him with you, if he does. Let's just take a breather, shall we? His mum and dad are with him.' He paused and looked tenderly at Anna. 'I'll look for the dog later if he doesn't come home on his own. Don't worry about that.'

So Anna sat and sipped at her tea trying to push away the image of her son's lifelong friend, a boy she had watched grow up and whom they all loved, lying immobile in the road, a puddle of blood under his head. She had seen that before, a much larger puddle of blood, and before there had been a dog, too. The same dog. Blackness came in patches and then nausea and a second later her forehead hit the table.

15

Steve drove Anna and Ellis to the hospital while George made a boiled egg with soldiers for Alice. Every now and then Anna glanced behind her at her son who was slouched on the back seat staring bleakly out of the window like a criminal caught in the act and now being brought in for questioning. She couldn't think of anything to say to him to make him feel better that wouldn't be painfully fatuous so they drove in silence to the Children's Hospital and Steve drew up at the main entrance to let them get out before he went to park.

They were shown to A&E and a small bay with curtains drawn across on two sides, but the bed with its heaps of creased pillows was empty. John appeared, his phone in his hand. 'Oh, hi, he's being scanned. Maggie's with him.' He gestured vaguely with the phone. 'I've been letting people know.' John was the kind of man that a son would admire and try to emulate when he was a child, briefly despise as an adolescent and then love as a friend for life. Would he and Mike have a life together? A series of snapshots clicked through Anna's brain in the second it took for her to step towards him – John with the boys fossil-hunting on Dorset cliffs, John scrunched up in a thick jacket yelling on the touchline while the rain beat at him, John running after little Mike on his first two-wheeler pretending to hold the seat but letting Mike control the bike until he discovered he knew how. She reached up and put her arm around his back.

'I'm so sorry, John, I'm so sorry.' When the tremor she felt in his big frame subsided she asked, 'How is he?'

'All I know is he's conscious. That's got to be good, hasn't it? But they won't tell us anything else because they don't know yet.' He sank down on to the stacking chair by the bed. 'I can't lose him, Anna, I can't.'

A quick movement caught the corner of Anna's eye and she turned to see Ellis running away down the ward and out into the corridor. 'John - '

'Go after him. There's nothing to be done here and I'll phone you when we know anything. Tell him we'll phone him, too.' Anna started away but John raised his voice to her. 'Get rid of that dog, Anna.' His eyes were burning into hers. 'Do it now. Don't wait for the third.'

As she hurried down the corridor a lift door opened at the end and Steve came out with his arm round Ellis. She grabbed him and held him tightly to her. 'It's not your fault,' she said in his ear, 'it's not your fault, Ell.' He stood stiff and trembling in her arms until she released him. 'We should go home,' she said to Steve, 'they're going to let us know.'

The drive home was as silent and miserable as the journey out but as Anna opened the front door she heard the unmistakeable baying of Bobble. Ellis stared at her, his eyes dark and afraid and again, there was nothing she could say. He ran upstairs. In the kitchen Alice was sitting at the table on two cushions cutting shapes out of dough and George was rinsing some dishes while Bobble sat on his haunches in the corner by the back door tied, she now saw, with a rope to the handle. He perked up his ears, barked again, and then flattened them and tried to crawl towards her.

George said, avoiding her eyes, 'I found him on the front step.'

Anna turned towards Steve. 'Would you tie him up in the back yard, please? There's a longer rope by the bins.'

'It's cold outside,' Alice said, stopping her task and frowning at Anna. 'That's cruel.'

When Anna didn't reply but began to fill the kettle, George said, 'No, it's not cruel, dogs like to know what's happening outside. He'll just do what he needs to do and bark at the squirrels and then we'll get him back in.'

'You wouldn't like it,' Alice said, pointing her cookie-cutter at Anna as she stood dully, waiting for the kettle to boil.

She couldn't lift herself to reply and when Steve came back in she said quietly, 'Thanks for taking us Steve, but it's getting late.'

'Ok, but I just need to have a word in the front room. I'll get your coat, Alice, so wash your hands and thank George.'

'I haven't finished!' Alice protested, 'they've got to go in the oven! Not fair!'

Anna mutely followed Steve down the hall hearing her father telling Alice that he would bake the biscuits and bring them round for her tomorrow. She was becoming a martinet and a spoiled brat, Anna thought, aware that those labels had been swimming closer to the surface of her mind for weeks. Steve closed the living room door and pulled Anna into his arms, leaning his back against it. 'This must be terrible for you, it must remind you.' She held her emotions as steady as she could like steering a car through fog on a motorway. 'We'll just keep believing that Mike will pull through.'

His chest, warm and musky and familiar and his arms holding her felt so good that she wished she could just switch off all thoughts, all feelings, all memories and bask in him, stay for a long time in this moment but within seconds she was releasing herself. Ellis needed her and her freshly roused guilt and grief over Harry would have to be sedated and stashed in a dark place.

'I'll call later. Thank you.'

When they had left she climbed the stairs to the big back bedroom and tapped on the door. 'Go away,' Ellis muttered. She went in. He was sitting on the end of his bed in the corner of two walls, his long arms wrapped tightly round his knees and she could see, even though he quickly dropped his head, that he was crying. She sat next to him, pulling up her feet so that she could reach him and cradled his head in her arms. 'Shush,' she said, 'shush, now. Let's hope for the best, eh?'

'I was such a bastard to him, Mum!' He choked and swallowed. 'He tried to talk to me, he wanted to explain, but I was hooked on punishing him and what if he dies now and I never get to see him ever again?'

'Don't torment yourself,' Anna murmured, 'people have misunderstandings and naturally you were hurt – you didn't know what would happen.' She stroked his springing hair, something she had not done for many years, and almost wept herself at his distress.

Ellis sniffed, wiped his nose on his sleeve and sat up straighter letting his arms fall by his sides so she sat back, too, against the headboard. 'There's something you don't know,' he said. 'It *is* my fault.'

'No, love.'

'He's done it before. Bobble.'

Anna froze. Had she let slip to the children what part the dog had played in their father's death? Surely not – she searched frantically for who could have told him? Maybe Diane or even Joan or Rosa, maybe they hadn't known that he had not been told? Steve or George would never have said anything. 'What do you mean?'

'He's run off. Twice. I couldn't hold him. Once was last November when that tool Dave Watts let off a firecracker by him when we were in the park and it took me hours to find him and then just about a week ago I was walking down the High Street with Bean and Dan and we were into talking about the band and he went off after a squirrel into the back of the supermarket car park – I just couldn't hold him. It took all three of us to get him back on the lead. I didn't want to tell you because I thought you might say we couldn't keep him.'

Anna sat silently for a while, taking his hand and stroking it. She remembered John's face in the hospital wearing an expression of grim fury she had never seen before. 'Did Mike know what had happened with Bobble?'

'He knew about the firecracker one – not the last one, because - '

'Ok.' She stood up and smiled at him. 'Come on, love, let's get something to eat – your poor old Pops has been slaving away for us and starving isn't going to help anything. We'll figure something out, but for now we just need to think about what we can do to help Mike and his mum and dad. Ok?'

In the kitchen Faye was standing with her hands in her hair saying repeatedly, 'Oh my God, oh God!' while George was explaining to her but when Ellis came in she went to him and hugged him to her which surprised him sufficiently that he hugged her, briefly, back.

So they sat down and ate the hotpot that George had made and, despite it all, the crispy potatoes were delicious and the gravy was rich and herby and comforting and by the time they were finished Anna's phone had chirped and Maggie was telling her that Mike would be ok. He had a mild concussion and some bruising to his ribs and his elbow was a scraped mess but he would recover fully, he would be fine. 'He told me to say hi to Ellis,' Maggie said, 'he knows he came here to see him. Maybe he could visit tomorrow? Oh, just a minute, John wants a word.' There was a rustling sound and then some footsteps so he must have moved away from the bed. 'Don't forget what I said, Anna.' John's voice was low but urgent. 'You have to do something about it.'

'I know,' Anna said, 'I know. Give Mike our love, won't you? Faye sends hers, too, and Ellis will want to come tomorrow. Let us know if there's anything you want bringing.'

So, slightly hysterical with relief, they cracked out a frozen sticky toffee pudding to celebrate and Anna went outside to untie the huge dog which had come so cheerfully and disastrously into their lives and to bring him back into the kitchen where he rushed about swiping things off the edge of the table with his broom of a tail. But while Faye and Ellis scolded him and laughed at his antics, George and Anna looked silently at each other and sighed.

Later, George sat with the massive hairy head on his lap on the sofa as both he and Anna pretended to watch Newsnight. 'I've had seven hundred and thirty hits,' he said, 'I don't know why I never thought of this before.'

'Well, it is a great poem.'

'It's a bit schmaltzy, Annie – I know that.'

'But people like that.' She wriggled her toes in their thick woolly socks and grinned at him. 'Fame at last, eh?'

He grunted. She had told him what John had said and what Ellis had confessed. They both knew that there must be a change and it must happen very soon. As the men and women in suits got increasingly tense with each other on the screen Bobble yipped in his sleep, his paws scrabbling in the air. 'Shall I speak to Diane then?'

'Yes. Do it first thing, Dad, please. If she can't have him at Safe 'n' Sound we're going to have to think of something else very quickly – something that Ellis can cope with.'

George gently scratched behind Bobble's ear. 'Poor old chap. Can't help your nature, can you? It is as it is.' He looked at Anna over his glasses. 'So what's happening with that girl you're definitely not stalking?'

'I'm *not* stalking her!' Anna protested feebly. 'It's gone a bit pear-shaped actually. I'm going to talk to Robert – try to convince him it would be a good idea to tell her – why wait? Everyone needs a proper dad, even one that never lets anything go.' She got up and, as she passed the sofa, planted a kiss on his scantily clad dome.

Kara decided to wear the red silk top that Helena had given her to meet Bob for dinner. As she stroked the luscious fabric she whispered to herself, 'I'm meeting my dad for dinner.' That's what she would say casually if anyone asked if she had plans for the evening, although when Shell had called and asked her to go round to pick out some honeymoon clothes she had made an excuse and hadn't told her about Bob. Too soon to share the secret? She didn't want to wear jeggings, that seemed wrong, but she found a short black skirt and some new black tights which would be ok. She wished she had smart shoes but she hadn't. All she had were some spangly ten centimetre spikes she'd worn on a night out with the girls. Otherwise she wore boots, or sandals in the summer, so she pulled out the cheap black artificial suede ankle boots and gave them a swift once-over with her nailbrush.

After she'd showered and scraped back her hair to straighten it into a bun, she checked her nails, tidied them with an emery board and glanced at the clock. It was still too early to get dressed – she didn't want to sit around in her smart clothes. She didn't wear make-up or nail varnish to work but for a moment considered putting on her party face for the evening, except that didn't seem right either. Gerry had loved her wearing a lot of lippie and eye stuff but he would. She picked up a lipstick and smeared a little on her index finger and then rubbed it into what Shell called the apples of her cheeks. It did brighten her up so she applied it to her lips, smacked them together and took most of it off with tissue and then smoothed salve over the top. She didn't want to look like a silly girl. Helena always said that less was more with make-up and she couldn't be bothered to mess with mascara and eyeliner because it always went in the wrong places and made her look like a clown. Looking at herself in the mirror she remembered that Elise had said she had her father's eyes. But Bob must be almost forty so at that age you might look different and he was carrying a bit of weight which might change the shape of his face.

There were still twenty minutes to get through before she met the taxi at the end of the road. She brought up Tassie's blog to pass the time but was immediately alarmed. The photos were of Tassie in a bar with a lot of gesticulating people, all red-faced and sweaty and grinning and every one had a glass in their hands. Most of them were men. In the background Kara saw, as she zoomed in, there were other men with serious faces who looked as though they didn't think much of what was happening. Under the photo she had written 'Who says booze illegal here? Having a blast with fit Aussies! Eat your hearts out girls!!!' There was no indication of which country she was in but Kara sensed something worrying, maybe something desperate in her expression. But, surely Tassie's parents followed the blog? They would do something, wouldn't they, if they thought she was at risk? No sign of Ben so it seemed he'd gone off or come home. Tassie shouldn't be so far away all alone. Kara began to chew a newly tidied nail and stopped herself.

It only took a moment to get dressed and grab her coat and bag but when she passed through the kitchen, Vicki was at the worktop chopping celery and stopped her. 'Your dad says Gerry has been asking after you. Why don't you phone him?'

Because he's not my dad and Gerry is a creep, Kara thought, but didn't say. Vicki was a bit different these days ever since she had told her about Bob and Kara liked that she was taking more of an interest in her life. It must be a relief to her that the secret was out. 'We weren't right together,' she said, 'what are you making?'

Vicki gestured with her knife to the other ingredients. 'Superfood salad – it's got that quinoa and red pepper and all that stuff in it. I found it in a magazine. I've got no intention of ageing gracefully, I'm going to fight it all the way.'

This was the longest friendly speech Vicki had made to Kara for ages so Kara said generously, 'You'll never look old, Mum, Shell said you look like my sister and you do.' Both of them then seemed not to know what to do or say next so Kara added, 'I'd better be off, enjoy your salad,' and left. Just for one second she considered telling her mother where she was going but why spoil the moment? And, Vicki might try to stop her. If the evening went well she may tell her later. As she closed the back door behind her, her phone trilled so she ran down the drive and on to the road to the waiting taxi.

As the car threaded through the dark streets and the driver complained about the road works on the dual carriageway, Kara mulled over how she felt about Bob. She had assumed, as soon as she knew he existed, that she would instantly feel a bond but that wasn't quite right. In fact, he didn't feel familiar at all but she had been foolish to think he would. She liked his dark hair and she liked the way he took charge of things but she couldn't get out of her head the squalor of the posh house in Redditch that they had glimpsed through the window and the run-down business. He did seem to have money, though, so he must be successful at what he did. Who was she to criticise anyway? He could have just turned her away and shown no interest but here he was treating her to a taxi and a nice meal out when he didn't have to. The best thing, she thought, smiling now to herself, was that he seemed to like her and after all, that was the main thing.

He was waiting at the curb outside the Indian restaurant when the car drew up. He stepped forward and opened the door for her like men did in old films and it made her feel cosseted and even a little bit glamorous. Then he paid the driver and they went inside, but when he tried to take her coat off to hang it up there was a little struggle as she hadn't expected it and she flushed with embarrassment. It was her parka, the only coat she had, and it seemed silly to treat it as though it was a mink jacket. It made her feel ashamed.

He must have sensed her discomfort because he stepped back a pace and held up his hands in mock surrender. 'Whoops! I forgot that men aren't supposed to treat women like ladies anymore! My mistake.'

'It's not that,' Kara began miserably and then didn't know how to finish so she said, 'Thanks for the taxi, it was lovely not to have to get the bus.'

But Bob was staring at her as they waited to be seated. 'You look very nice - gorgeous, if I'm allowed to say.'

'Thanks.'

'Let me guess – standard size ten?' She laughed and flushed again. He must think she was behaving like a thirteen year old to be so unsophisticated.

The waiter led them to a booth set in a quiet corner and brought menus. 'I didn't even ask you if you like Indian food,' Bob said, 'is this all right for you?'

'Yes, yes, of course,' Kara said, feeling again that confusing mix of pleasure and embarrassment. 'It's very kind of you.'

'Not at all – my treat. I'm astonished to have been responsible for such a pretty young woman.' He raised his hand to the waiter and ordered wine.

Kara felt between her fingers the thick linen table-cloth and noticed how every item of cutlery and every glass glittered in the concealed spotlights. There was even a tiny sparkling vase on the table with a real dark red rose and baby's breath in it. She glanced around and saw men and women with expensive haircuts and elegant clothes. She had assumed this would be the kind of restaurant she and her friends might go to at the end of a big night in a club but this was completely different. She whispered, 'I don't think I'm posh enough for this place, Bob. I might show you up!' but she smiled to show she was only half-serious.

The waiter appeared with a bottle, opened it in front of Bob and then poured a little into his glass which he sipped and nodded.

Both glasses were then filled. He leaned forward towards her. 'Do you know, my mum had a dimple like yours on her left cheek – just the same.' He tilted his glass towards her. 'And you could never show me up, Kara, you light up the room. Here's to us. Here's to getting to know each other much better.'

She lifted her own glass and tapped his with it. 'Yes,' she said. 'Here's to us.' She would never forget this, she realised, this was a golden moment and it made her feel both humble and proud. She thought of Tassie whom she had spent so many years envying and felt only pity for her because she had everything and didn't value it whereas Kara would treasure every second of this new amazing thing in her life.

Bob was looking at her even more intently and actually reached over the table to take her hand which was a bit awkward in front of other people but there was no way she would pull it away. 'Your coat,' he said.

'Sorry?'

'You're such a stunner, Kara, let me buy you a nice coat to wear instead of that thing you had on. Your top's great, you need a coat to go with it.' She stared at him in shock. 'Shoes, too – a coat and shoes, anything! You're a classy girl, you deserve clothes to match.'

'No, you don't have to do that,' Kara said, colouring. 'I don't expect you to do that.'

'I know you don't - that's what's so nice about you, darling, but I want to make up for all the years I've never even bought you a birthday present. I want to spoil you.' He squeezed her hand. 'Will you let me? Please?' Kara didn't know what to say so she dropped her eyes and at that moment the waiter arrived to take their orders. It seemed wrong to take gifts, especially clothes, from a man you've only just met – in fact, no man had ever bought her clothes – but what if that man was her father and could afford it? The compliments excited but unbalanced her – the best Gerry had ever said was that she had nice tits.

Later, the food arrived and was delicious although she could barely remember what she'd ordered because she was unfamiliar with many of the dishes and had just picked one at random. As he ate he talked so she had time to gather herself and begin to feel pleasure in the idea of being taken shopping by this worldly man. His words slid by her because he was just talking about countries he'd been to and food he'd had and so on – the kind of thing that Shell's mum and dad talked about as they were always going off on cruises and package holidays. She couldn't eat all of the huge plate of food so when she'd finished she put her fork down and studied him instead. He looked better than he had before. Because he was dark he must need to shave twice a day and last time she'd seen him he looked scruffy but this time his chin had an almost metallic sheen it was so recently done. His shirt was smart, too, a deep blue with a striped tie and a nicely fitting suit. She had to give him a chance to explain.

When he stopped talking about somewhere she'd never heard of she took the opportunity and said, feeling a little shame about the subterfuge, 'So, where do you live?'

'Got a house in Redditch.' He wiped his mouth with the napkin and took a gulp of wine. 'I don't live there, though. I spend so much of my time in Birmingham now I've got a flat there, an apartment.'

'So your house is empty?'

He glanced at her sharply. 'You're not undercover tax police, are you? Just joking. No, I'm renting it out at the moment. It's just an investment property really.' So Helena had been right and the mess was from the tenants. Kara almost told him he should check on them but stopped herself in time. How could she have thought he might live in such a state? Sitting in front of her now he looked completely different from that first time but, of course, she had taken him by surprise and caught him on a bad day. She had seen countless photos of celebrities looking awful while they went about their routine tasks – no-one looked perfect all the time. She felt bad that she had been a bit put off by him on their first meeting.

'Can I ask another question?' There had been something about his response to the last one that put her on guard but she wanted to know and even though she hated him thinking she was a nosy person, she had to ask. He put down his knife and fork and nodded. 'Are you married? Do you have any other kids?'

He laughed and went on eating. 'Was married, twice, but no, I'm not going in for that malarkey again. I've had enough of gold diggers and as for kids, well, I would have said I didn't have any before you made my day and turned up out of the blue. Who knows – I might have some others!' This seemed to amuse him so much that he needed a long drink of water to wash down his last mouthful.

'Can I ask one more?'

'Ask as many questions as you want, darling.'

'Do you want me to call you Dad?' As soon as the words were out of her mouth she regretted them.

He became serious and stared for a while at the tablecloth. She began to feel hot and awkward and wished she hadn't said anything. 'Do you want to?' he asked, eventually.

'I don't know – it seems a bit weird. I've been calling Graham 'Dad' all my life but I can't now. Just forget I said anything, it doesn't matter.' She was sure she was now bright red and sounding like a stupid kid.

'Let's not rush it,' Bob said. 'It's all new for me, too, you know. Just call me Bob and we'll see how it goes.' He pushed back his plate. 'Enough about me, I want to hear more about you, starting with any boyfriend I might have to make sure treats you right!'

So she told him a little about Gerry and much more about Shell's upcoming wedding and working at the care home. Every now and then she checked that he wanted her to go on, asking, 'Is this stuff boring?' but he always laughed and shook his head and told her to go on and tell him more. When she stopped he asked for the pudding menu and she chose a simple honeycomb ice-cream. He just got coffee.

'So, what about your mum? Vicki. You don't talk about her or Graham much. Don't you get on?'

'Oh, you know. She's very busy with work and the gym and friends and he's away a lot driving.'

He started to push the gold watch on his wrist round and round and she wondered if he, like her, was nervous. It may be stirring up old feelings to talk about her mum – she may have been his first love. Sure enough, he asked quietly, 'Have you told her about meeting me?'

Did he want her to? Was he wondering if there was any chance of a re-union? He said he didn't want another relationship but you heard plenty of stories where in later life people met their childhood sweethearts and married them. 'Not about tonight,' she said gently, 'but I did tell her I met you in person.'

'Really? What did she say about that?' He had stopped messing with his watch and was sitting forward, his eyes fixed on her face. How could she tell him how cool Vicki had been? She had already said to him that Vicki had warned her that he was no good, but, of course that was before Kara had actually met him.

'I showed her a photo of you.'

His face seemed to tighten. 'Where did you get a photo of me, Kara?'

'It was when we were in the pub and you were ordering at the bar. I took one then. I'm sorry – are you mad with me?'

'And you showed this photo to your mother?'

'Yes.'

'What did she say?'

'She said it had been a long time but it looked like I'd found my dad,' Kara said shyly and saw the tight muscles in his jaw relax and when she added, 'I told her how well you'd done for yourself,' his lips curved and broke into a smile. 'You were very young. Was she your first love?'

'Oh, I thought the world of her,' he said easily, settling back, 'but, you know, people change, especially at that age. After you were born she lost interest in me, and this doesn't reflect well on me, but I met someone else and then moved away. I was very immature, not ready for responsibility.'

Kara was so touched at his contrite look that she put her hand over his as it rested on his napkin. 'Oh, please don't feel bad. They looked after me ok and, to be fair, though I love her, of course, Mum isn't the easiest person to get along with.'

He looked rueful. 'She did give me a few tongue-lashings, I must admit.'

Kara glanced at her watch and saw that it was getting on for eleven o'clock. 'I'm sorry, Bob, but I'd better go – I'm on early shift tomorrow. I've had a really lovely evening, though, I can't thank you enough.'

The bill was already on the table and he paid with cash, peeling off a few notes from a wad he kept in his inside breast pocket. Kara had never seen anyone in real life do this. As he took her coat and helped her into it, he said, 'Give me a date when I can take you for those clothes.' She didn't need to check her phone – her only thing was to meet Shell and Lauren at the pub on Saturday night. What used to be the highlight of her week seemed boring now. 'I'm going to take you home so I know where you live and I'll pick you up at, what, 11.00 on Saturday?'

'I could meet you in the Bullring to save you the trouble.'

He laughed and pulled open the heavy restaurant door. 'We're not going to the Bullring, darling, I'm taking you somewhere a bit more exclusive than that. You're going to get the VIP treatment – only the best for my daughter.'

His car was an Audi and it was warm and quiet and the upholstery was leather and when he stopped round the corner out of sight of her house he leaned towards her and kissed her cheek. She floated home.

16

On the drive down the motorway to visit Kara's dad, Anna was counting her blessings. The last few days had been much better than the previous ones and things were looking up all round. Mike was doing fine but being kept in for a couple more days of observation and when she and Joan had turned up with chocolate biscuits and a bag of satsumas they found Ellis by the bed playing Mike a video on his phone which the band had put together. It was a pastiche of the jazz number, 'Won't you come home, Bill Bailey,' but with rather different words. Mike was grinning and replaying it over and over so the adults got to hear it whether they wanted to or not.

George had driven Ellis over and had appeared with a paper cup of tea as they all listened for the sixth time. 'I want a word with you,' he said to Joan mysteriously and the two of them stepped outside the ward. She must ask him what that was about. Anyway, it seemed that Mike and Ellis had somehow (no doubt using the teen boy code of modulated grunts which served to convey profound emotion) made up and the friendship was back on.

Not only that but Faye, who had only happened to be passing on the evening of Mike's accident, probably in search of kitchen goodies, but who was just the comfort Ellis had needed, had stayed to play with Alice who was then won over by an avalanche of hugs and kisses and compliments. The upshot of this was that the little girl had been promised a weekend play date at Faye and Jack's flat and had consequently been almost friendly to Anna in the mysterious way these things work. In the warm glow that followed Anna had suggested to Steve a weekend away for just the two of them and he had seen her point and was, he said, organising something to happen very soon. Paris had been mentioned.

The other thing which Anna was pleased about was that the certificates that she'd ordered had arrived at work and contained just the information she was hoping for. She couldn't wait to tell Robert what she'd discovered and it might even be that she could persuade him to let her put Kara in the picture. After all, she couldn't go back to Church View after telling them that she had to give it up because there was a family crisis (which there had been, to be fair) and, in any case, she'd promised the suspicious Helena that she would not contact Kara, a promise which she now regretted.

Diane had, bless her heart, agreed to take the dog – a decision that Ellis could just about bear since he could visit often and knew that Bobble would love the company of the other dogs. What he didn't know was that Diane had said it could only be temporary and they would be advertising Bobble for re-homing to a suitable place. Those were the rules of Safe 'n' Sound. Unless an animal had been so traumatised in its previous place that it could not be re-homed, in which case they would keep it, the charity had to move animals on so that others in dire need could be looked after. Bobble was not in the slightest traumatised, in fact, he had been indulged a bit too much, but he was a large, powerful dog and wouldn't be the first choice of any family living in a suburban situation. He shouldn't have been theirs.

Anna turned off the motorway and took the A road off the roundabout. She would arrive in about a quarter of an hour so she treated herself to a burst of *Sigh No More* by Mumford and Sons, singing along at full blast and ignoring raised eyebrows in juxtaposed vehicles at traffic lights.

When he was ushered into the same little room with the cameras and the table and chairs, Robert was already smiling. He quickly offered her his hand to shake and then sat down as if he couldn't wait a moment longer to hear what she would say. She had thought about what reason she could give him for leaving the voluntary work early and decided to say that after a few days she was concerned that Kara was wondering why she kept trying to chat with her. She told him Kara might be worried that she was being monitored covertly by the management, that she had had a complaint against her or something.

'Oh, I wouldn't want that,' Robert said quickly. 'I wouldn't want her to get into trouble or even think that she might be.'

Feeling as though she had got her feet tangled in a loose ball of wool with all these different narratives, Anna was grateful that he didn't pick holes in her excuse. It must be hard work to be a habitual liar, she thought, having to remember all the different versions you told people. 'I did get some photos, though. Just a couple and from a distance but you can see what she looks like. Did you find the Facebook page?'

He threaded his fingers together and steepled them almost as though he was praying. 'I think so, but the photograph had two other girls in it and they were all making faces – it was hard to see what she really looks like.' Anna found the photos and passed him the phone. He gazed and gazed at the first one sucking up every pixel and imprinting it on his brain. It showed Kara in three-quarter profile bending over Edna Simpson with a cup of tea.

'You can make it large if you like – zoom in on her face.'

Not touching the phone he peered at the controls and around the edge and she realised that, of course, he might not ever have used a smart phone, not unless he'd been in cahoots with more newly-arrived prisoners who might show him. The fact that he didn't know how to do this simple thing, zoom into the image, touched her deeply. More than anything else it brought home to her not only how long he had been incarcerated but how few must have been his contacts with other prisoners, how lonely he must have been. 'Like this,' she said, reaching across the small table and bringing Kara face up to fill the screen.

'Oh,' he gasped, 'Oh.' She waited a moment and then swiped the screen to the next image, enlarging that one, too. 'She's so beautiful. I can't believe I'm looking at her, how she is, how she was just a few days ago. My own girl.' He made no apology for the tears that now ran freely down his face and dripped on to the table but after another moment or so he wiped his face with both hands. 'Thank you. I don't know how to thank you.'

They sat silently then for a few moments as Anna realised that his joy had changed into a more complicated emotion and one hard to bear. Was he thinking of all the years he had missed out on or on whether he would ever really know her? 'Are you sure you don't want me to approach her, Robert? You have the right to let her know about you, surely?'

'I lost all my rights when I killed that man,' he said, and it was so weighty a statement she thought he was voicing something he had told himself, or been told, for decades and the sentence, both verbal and penal, had thickened a neural link in his brain by endless repetition until it had formed a noose around his self-respect. 'I know I was defending my mum, but I could have done it without killing him.'

'You were eighteen.'

'Yes - a man, not a child.'

'You've surely been punished enough. Let me tell her – let me arrange a meeting.'

'No Anna. I have a plan, you see.' Finally some lightness came back into his face. 'I'm applying to a college to take a degree and they're helping me to find a job when I get out and when I've done all that, when I'm, you know, worth something, then I'll think about it.'

'Ok. If that's what you want. There's no hurry, I suppose.' She bent down and picked a folder out of her big bag. 'On a different matter, I've been finding out a little about your father, Lindo. Shall I tell you?' He smiled properly then and turned that into a mock-fear grimace and she admired him that he still had a sense of humour. 'Don't worry, nothing horrible. I sent for his death certificate and on that is his country of origin. Your mum must have known it, of course, and told them.'

'Jamaica?'

'No, it's not. It's the Cayman Islands.'

'Where all those offshore banks are? Hey, man, don't tell me I'm a millionaire, eh?'

'Don't count on it! No, that didn't really get going until the '70's, I don't think, although the people on the island were forgiven their taxes some time in the eighteenth century because they rescued a member of the British royal family from a shipwreck, or something. That's why it's a tax haven now.'

'So it was a British colony?

'Still is – but they call it an Overseas Territory now. Maybe that's good for business so the local government are in no hurry to become independent. I read a little about it but you can find out loads on the internet. There's a group of three islands and they're all quite small and distinctive and really beautiful. Before they were settled with families, mostly from Jamaica, they were a hide-out for the remnants of Cromwell's dirty army who became pirates, well, buccaneers, anyway. There was one horrible man called Morgan, I think. The settlers bravely drove the pirates out – there's still canon there from the defences.'

'So that's where he grew up, my dad?' Robert's eyes never left her face.

'Yes, but that's not all. I got his marriage certificate, too, and on that is his dad's name, your grandfather, and his occupation. It seems he lived somewhere in West Bay on Grand Cayman but no more detail than that.'

'My grandfather?' It was as though Robert had never before contemplated the obvious truth that somewhere in the world he must have had a wider family, including a grandfather.

'Yes – he was called Stanley, and guess what his occupation was?'

'Oh man, I can't. Tell me.'

'You're learning about the stars, aren't you? Well, your grandfather was a seaman. He must have known how to navigate by the stars in those days, probably using a sextant or something – no computers or GPS then.'

Robert leaped up from his chair and actually began to jig around the room, laughing and cracking his fingers. 'Woah! This is fantastic! A seaman from the Cayman Islands! I have a place – I have a family to search out!'

'Yes, you're not alone,' Anna said, smiling at his exuberance which she had never seen a hint of before. 'You must have cousins and so on.'

He sat down and stared at her. 'Tell me how to look, please, Anna. Tell me how to find them.'

'Ok. You can go on *familysearch.org* to look for Stanley's date of birth and where he was born and then take it from there, but your Stanley Johnson may be one of several in the Cayman Islands so what may also help is that I found another son, your uncle, who stayed on the island and who has a very unusual name. In fact, I think it's a made-up name because I can't find any other record of it.' Robert hadn't blinked for seconds. 'It's Astrophile.'

'*Astrophile?*'

'Yes.' Anna wanted to grab his hands that were clasped in their steeple again on the table near her own but she resisted. 'It means "Star Lover."'

'Shut up.'

'No – it does.'

Now, in contrast to his dancing and whooping, Robert seemed to have been turned to stone so Anna sat still, too. She had seen this before and was always struck by how powerful was knowledge of a connection with family, an insight into identity and roots. When people discover families they think are lost it's as though time collapses and the empty space fills with chattering voices. No wonder companies are doing well out of DNA sampling and database management and why not? So many of us feel disconnected, she thought, so many of us *are* disconnected. Her own mother, Lena, had been a mystery to her until near her death and even now she had no idea of her mitochondrial origins. Perhaps that had been what attracted her to genealogy in the first place, the awareness of huge gaps in her own family history, gaps she had still not filled and in her resentment towards her mother she had been unwilling to attempt to do so.

Finally, Robert spoke. 'You didn't have to do this,' he said, so softly she had to strain to hear him. 'You did it to make me feel less alone and to help me with Kara. Give me something good to tell her, something in our blood and our history that is beautiful.'

'Well, um,' Anna began, uncomfortably aware that she had not been motivated by any nobler impulse than curiosity.

Robert stood. 'Thank you,' he said, and this time when he took her hand he held it for several seconds and it would have been crass of her to deny his assessment of the situation which would make him seem naive. He was not, she thought, at all naïve, he simply assumed the best of people which was a quality she sadly lacked. 'I'm going to find out every tiny thing, Anna, I'm going to *stalk* the Cayman Islands so all of them better watch out!'

She left the prison with the sound of his laughter in her ears.

Walking into the kitchen that evening Anna was pleasantly surprised to see Steve there with George and Diane all seated at the scarred old dining table and poring over OS maps. Anna paused by the door for a moment to absorb the sheer vitality of him. His hair, always stiff and unruly, had risen up and flopped over like the short end of a horse's mane – it must be due for a trim – and then his forearms, revealed by the pushed up sweater sleeves, were a pleasing tangle of muscle ropes thickened by climbing and covered with what she knew to be extraordinarily soft hairy skin. 'You're like an animal,' she had said to him once, 'with your hot pelt.' 'We're all animals,' he had replied laughing, flipping her around.

Now he was saying to George, 'Then you can cut across to the head of the glen here and finish the day at Oldpits Farm campsite. Let me look at your Caravan Club book again.' When he noticed her there he smiled and in his ruddy face, flushed by the heat of the kitchen and his interest in the task, his eyes were summer blue.

Ellis came in as she was putting the kettle on and flung his schoolbag down by the door. 'What is it with oldies?' he asked as he made his way to the fridge. 'What's this paper fetish you've all got? Look it up on your phones, whatever it is.' He opened the door and stared at the interior.

'You're letting all the cold out, Ellis, don't be so wasteful,' Diane scolded. 'And as for your precious phones, I always feel as though I'm looking at stuff through a keyhole. This way you get the whole picture.'

'This part looks steep,' George said, pointing, and Anna, loving maps as much as he did, leaned over him while Steve put his arm round her waist, and saw the section where the contour lines almost touched each other. 'It's not even a B road – I wouldn't fancy getting stuck on that – the van's not in its first flush.'

'Maybe you could swing south round that coll and miss that bit. Look, if you took the A road from back here - '

'Is there any cake or anything, I'm starving,' Ellis said, 'any ort will do.'

Anna stood up and smiled. 'Go on then, Ell, what's an ort? I've never heard of it.' George looked up from his map and beamed. It was so good to have their boy back minus the misery.

'What's the prize?'

'I know where the cake tin is.'

'It's a fragment of food, an ort, which is what this fridge needs. Wicked, isn't it? 1400's. I think we should trend it.'

'Yes, great name for a new cooking show – Orts and Tortes. The tin's on top of the piano – bring it in and we'll all have a piece.'

'Ort for Thought,' George suggested and then they all came up with silly stuff.

Dinner wasn't for an hour and it was already in the oven, a slow-cooked lamb and prune tagine that was George's speciality, so Anna fetched the tiddly-winks from the heap of grubby board-game boxes stacked against a now silent piano and asked Alice to have a game with her at the other end of the big table. She could sense Steve paying attention to the little transaction, although he was still helping George and Diane plan their spring trip since he knew the area north of the Great Glen better than they did.

Anna realised that for the first time in ages she felt relaxed. If Alice gave her a rude reply or walked off to watch something on tv then so be it. She was still elated by the visit to Robert and by how pleased he had been with what she had discovered. She could have gone on and found out much more but she hoped he would want to do that himself and it seemed he did. She had told him to email her if he got stuck on anything. She kept imagining how wonderful the meeting between that nice girl, Kara, and her lovely father would be. Was she getting a bit too involved? Helena's unpleasant insinuation rose up and indignation burned her; all her previous admiring thoughts about the woman had dissipated in a puff.

Alice climbed up on the chair that had her cushions on it and claimed the red tiddlywinks for herself. She was wearing a grey hoodie with a cartoon cat on the front and denim leggings and her bright thistledown hair had finally become long enough to go up into a tuft on top of her head. But her skin had not changed since she had been that desperately sick baby – it was still pale, almost translucent. After a few minutes of play she said to Anna, 'When can we go and see Briony?'

'Did you like her?'

'She's the most beautiful lady in the world. She's like a queen.' Alice flipped and missed the board. She glanced up at Anna. 'Why is she marrying another lady? Only men and ladies get married.'

Anna heard the grunt of amusement in the other group and knew they were all listening. 'People get married when they love each other,' she said, 'they don't have to be men and women. It means they want to be together always.' She glanced across to the others and saw Steve give her a thumbs-up.

'I'm marrying Steve,' Alice said decisively, returning to the game. 'I'll wear a big pink dress with fairy wings.' Anna flipped her own counter all the way down the table to the other end. 'You meant to do that!' Alice accused her, 'Play properly!'

'I've had a brilliant idea,' Ellis said, sitting down by Anna, 'about Big B.'

'Ok.'

'Rosa could have him. She's big and strong, she could handle him. I'm not being rude, I think she's great, but she *is* big and strong, and he could be her guard dog.' He leaned over and flipped a counter into the cup, fluttering his long black lashes comically at her. 'Will you ask her, Mum?'

The game was over and Anna stood up to clear it away ready for laying the table for dinner. 'I can ask, Ell, but don't get your hopes up, the boat's a small space for a huge dog.'

Then Steve took Alice home for tea and Ellis went off to his room so Anna got out some beers for herself and George and Diane. They both looked sweaty but excited now that the trip had taken shape and Diane was working on a list in her big, round hand. They had only been together for a few years but already they were beginning to look alike. When they first became an item Diane had tidied George up, but that had long been abandoned since they both were far more interested in being comfortable than smart. Anna knew there would be no clothes on Diane's list, they would both grab a handful of clean garments at the last moment and stuff them into a bin bag, probably. The list was for important things they mustn't forget like the spirit stove and hot water bottles. Anna looked at her father's straggly grey wisps of hair and Diane's thick thatch of shaggy white and thought a comb probably wouldn't make it on to the list (or into the bin bag) either.

'So what did you need to talk to Joan about at the hospital the other day?' she asked, sipping her beer.

'Not that it's any of your business.'

'Not that it's any of my business,' she repeated, grinning.

'It's this wretched Youtube thing you two put me on,' he said huffily to Diane. 'I wish you hadn't.'

'Don't be so soft – it's been a triumph,' Diane said, not pausing to look up, 'You should be thanking us. Dubbin.' She wrote it down.

So George told them that the poem's modest success seemed to have attracted the attention of other people, people he insisted could not be poetry lovers but who had picked up a name, an image of an old man, a sweet poem, and that was enough to hate him.

'You're being trolled?' Anna couldn't believe it. 'Dad?'

Diane stopped writing and looked up. 'What are they saying?'

George got up to take out the tagine to check the tenderness of the meat. 'Silly things, mostly, but the worst was quite vicious. I'm not telling you what it was.' He stuck a skewer into the meat and inhaled the fragrance of the spices. 'I know they're just trying to seem more important than they feel they are but it's depressing that people can be so hostile to a perfect stranger just because they think they can get away with it - that given anonymity some people actually *choose* to be cruel.'

'What are you going to do?'

George put the tagine back in the oven and turned with the meat skewer still in his hand. 'Ready in ten, I'll call Ellis. Do about it? I'm a Quaker, Annie, I will turn the other cheek which in this instance means giving it all a rest for a few months – the whole thing of Youtube, Twitter, all of it. I shall bow out. I shall, as the politicians say now, recuse myself.' He waggled the skewer in Diane's direction. 'Just promise me you won't do anything like that ever again.'

Diane frowned and nodded which was as near as she ever got to an apology. 'It was Joan's idea,' she sniffed, 'I think she's gone unstable since she's been working in that shop. She told me the other day that avocado is a superfood.'

'It is a superfood,' Anna said.

'Nasty, slimy things,' Diane shuddered, 'and no taste. We managed all right before all that foreign stuff came in.' Anna and her father dropped their eyes and went on with laying the table and putting plates to warm. Diane's legendary opposition to all foods 'foreign' was not up for discussion. It had caused several altercations between her and George in the early days so now George tended to negotiate himself round it and remind himself of Diane's many sterling qualities. It didn't put her off the Moroccan tagine, Anna noticed, it was one of her favourite things.

Later, Anna phoned Joan to talk about the trolling. She sighed but didn't seem as upset as Anna had thought she might be. After a few more minutes of chatting she whispered, 'You'll never guess, Anna, Piotr's father, Jakub, has asked me to go out with him for dinner! What should I do?'

Anna rolled her eyes. 'Do you want me to go and have a word? Find out his intentions towards you? Ask about his prospects?'

'You think I should go, then?'

'Free meal.'

'You are such a romantic, Anna Ames. I'll go and see what I've got in the outer reaches of my wardrobe! Isn't it exciting?' And Anna agreed that yes, it was, and that if Paris worked out as she hoped she'd be a little bit giddy, too.

17

Saturday was dry and clear but chilly and Kara's breath made little clouds in front of her face. She felt like a child waiting to be taken to a party as she hopped from one foot to the other and waited for Bob's car to arrive. Shell had not been best pleased to have their shopping plans disrupted but Kara had told her that Vicki needed her to fetch something for her from Birmingham. Shell knew that Vicki couldn't be argued with and accepted it but Kara felt bad lying to her, she'd never done it before. But, on the bright side, she may be able to wear her new clothes at Shell's hen do. She imagined a sparkly tunic, silver if possible, that would go with her party shoes and, if Bob was as generous as he'd promised, a new coat to go on top. She had seen a gorgeous black fake fur on a girl in Bromsgrove High Street. She could wear her silver and diamante stud earrings.

She was standing with her back to the wide green verge as she waited because of the sea-gulls. There were at least half a dozen quarrelling over some chips in paper which must have been flung aside last night and she hated them. Even their cries sounded to her like hopeless, starving babies. Vicki had told her that it was because she had had an ice-cream cone snatched from her hand when they had been on holiday in Newquay. Kara didn't remember the holiday or the incident which sounded, the way Vicki told it, almost funny. What she remembered wasn't amusing – it was like a nightmare - a terrifying flurry of bony wings bashing her face and yellow eyes and screeching sharp beaks. Sometimes she dreamed about them.

Bob didn't keep her waiting too long and it was delicious to slip into the already warm car on to heated seats. She had wondered if she should kiss him when they met like some families did but he immediately steered away from the curb so she just settled back. He asked her how work was going which made it easy to chat away for a while about the old people and her work-mates. She hadn't told Jackie or Helena about Bob and she didn't want to. They would be full of advice and questions and just too much intrusion. She wanted to keep him secret, at least for now.

'You sound as though you like it there,' he said, when she came to a halt.

'Oh, yes, I do. I know people don't think it's much of a career but I like it – at least for now.'

He glanced sideways at her, smiling, and she caught the look and tucked it away because he was handsome when he smiled. 'So what would be your ideal job?' he asked, 'I mean if you could do anything?'

She lifted her chin and thought about it. Tassie was taking foolish risks in her opinion and should never have gone on with the trip without Ben, useless as he was, but the places that she had visited so far, the scenery, had seduced Kara completely. She thought about the tall mountains covered with what looked like heads of broccoli dropping down to a white sand beach and blue-green shallows where people were running and splashing like kids. And even the deserts were fascinating because they were so different, so exotic, with their wide open spaces under huge skies. 'Something where I could travel,' she said vaguely, 'see new places, see the world!'

'There's a lot of world to see,' he agreed, glancing sideways at her. 'You wouldn't be scared?'

Kara thought of the stupid decisions Tassie had apparently taken so light-heartedly. 'I'm not thick,' she said, 'I know how to look after myself even if I haven't been abroad yet.' He laughed and seemed pleased by her answer and she felt proud and grown-up. It was true, though, that she was sensible and practical. Mrs Bandhal had complimented her only the other day on an idea she'd had to make it easier for the residents on sticks to get out into the little ornamental garden if they wanted. And she knew how to manage money, too. For all that she was on little more than basic wage she had still managed to pay rent to her mum and save a few hundred pounds – two hundred and fifty five pounds, in fact.

'What's your favourite place in the world?' she asked, feeling guilty that the conversation had been so one-sided and wanting to know about what he liked.

'Oh, that's easy. Right here, next to my daughter.'

Kara flushed deeply and kept very still to stop herself saying something silly and spoiling the moment. After a few seconds she whispered, 'Thanks.' What he had said would be another bright star to pin up on her memory wall, to savour last thing at night before she went to sleep. She imagined all the nice things he had said to her as being like the string of lights she had wound round her bedhead, glowing softly in the darkness and comforting her.

Instead of taking the Bristol Road straight into the centre of Birmingham he kept going through the tunnels and out the other side over the Aston Expressway and into Spaghetti Junction. She knew this way because Graham and Vicki liked to play crazy golf and there was a course at Star City which they had taken her to a couple of times when she was a kid. Eventually she asked where they were going and Bob said, 'To see my secret treasures!' Had he forgotten about the clothes? Kara felt a stab of disappointment but perhaps his promise had slipped his mind.

What she had not expected was for him to pull up outside his shop-front in Erdington. It was locked up and the light was off so maybe he just wanted to pick up some papers or something, she thought, until he came round to her side of the car and opened the door. 'Come on,' he said, 'I've got a treat for you.' She got out obediently and shivered while he unlocked the padlock on a chain and then twisted the key in the Yale lock and kicked the door a little to open it. A sour, musty smell oozed past her. 'Come on,' he said again, 'Hurry up. It's freezing.'

He snapped on the main fluorescent light, closed the street door behind him and locked it, and then walked quickly towards the back of the office. Kara stood waiting by the door thinking he must have to do something but he beckoned her to him, staring at her with a little smile. At the back of the shop was a short corridor with a storage room on the left containing boxes and bags and a toilet which she could see through its half open door. It was not very clean. On the right, opposite that room, was another door but this one was made of metal.

'Are you ready for your treat?' he asked.

Kara drew back a little. 'What is it?'

'I can't tell you, darling – that would spoil it. You're not frightened are you? You told me you didn't scare easily – you didn't lie to me did you?'

Was he teasing her? Gerry had teased her sometimes and she hadn't liked it. But this was her father so she must be able to trust him. What would he think of her if she didn't? He would be hurt and upset with her when he had been nothing but kind and generous so far. 'What's in there?' she asked instead of answering his question, and was furious with herself that her voice was wobbly.

'I told you, my treasures,' he laughed as he unlocked and unbolted the door. A dim light was already on. 'Don't you want to see?' He took her arm and half pulled her into the room.

Her first impression was that this was where that strange musty smell was coming from – the little room was heated and the air was fetid. On three sides were banked glass tanks from floor to ceiling and inside them she could make out in the low light that there were things moving. Bob had stepped close to a tank at eye-level and was peering into it. He began to murmur, croon almost, to the thing inside as Kara watched, fearful but curious. He turned to her and whispered, 'Come and see, this is one of my beauties.'

Kara took two steps to his side and looked where he was looking. A huge insect with long furry legs looked back, its eyes on stilts. Kara gasped. He looked at her sharply. 'You're not afraid of arachnids, are you? I thought you were far too sensible for that.'

In fact, Kara was not afraid of spiders. Seagulls, yes, but not spiders. 'No, of course not,' she said with relief. 'I just couldn't see what it was.'

'Good girl,' he said, seeming amused, 'good girl.' He turned back to the cage. 'This one is Queen Nefertiti – I give them all names – because of her long neck. She's Mexican, aren't you, darling?'

Kara looked round. There must be thirty tanks. 'You collect them?'

'I admire them,' he said. 'They're beautiful and powerful. Look at this one here,' and he sprang sideways and crouched down to a lower level. 'Can you see her?' Kara noticed a label on each tank with a pet name and what she assumed was the species written underneath in Latin. 'This one's a Red Widow Spider. Naughty girl, aren't you? Bought her in honour of one of my exes – she was a ginger nut, too.' He tapped the tank and made kissing noises. The spider was at least twelve centimetres long and had a red and white shield on her back like a ruby surrounded by seed pearls. Kara stared at the creature, part fascinated, part horrified. She straightened up, shivering slightly and thought, not for the first time, how cruel nature was. But then, some people weren't very nice either.

Bob stood up and sighed. 'I know, I know, I promised to get you some gear. I haven't forgotten, darling, I just wanted to introduce you to the rest of the family. Come on, let's be off.' He ushered her out and bolted and locked the door behind them before striding through the office to the street door where he paused after unlocking it. He frowned and faced Kara. 'Do you remember that day you came here looking for me?' She nodded. 'Did you see a boy run out? You might have heard a fuss, too.' After a pause she nodded again, less firmly. 'Silly kid. I wanted to hire him to feed them at weekends but he was scared and started yelling and carrying on. I didn't want him frightening them so I told him to shut up and he ran off.'

'Oh, ok.'

'Just so you understand,' he added, and opened the door to the frigid street.

It was near the end of the week when Anna walked the short distance from Harts' car park along the canal tow-path and up the steps to the plate glass doors. She didn't have to see anyone outside the office that day so she'd pulled on a warm fleece and her favourite navy cords. Ted said he believed in a cool working environment because it was healthier, which was just the sort of Ted-speak that made people look at the ceiling. There was that change of light that happens in February when it seems possible that spring really will come again and Anna had noticed with a lift of her heart the clumps of snowdrops gleaming bravely in her own garden borders. A quarter of a mile away in the city centre the skyline was a monochrome of grey blocks silhouetted against a pearl sky with a scatter of yellow-lit office windows like miniature post-it notes.

Josie raised a hand at her in that Nazi-salute way she had when she wanted to convey information. Anna swerved over to the reception desk. 'Hey, Josie,' she said, expecting to be given mail.

'He wants to see you later on,' Josie said, running a perfectly shellacked orange nail down her list of things that needed seeing to. 'Wait a minute – he said ten o'clock?'

'Ok. How are you?'

'I don't know. He told me yesterday I'm getting an assistant.'

Things must be going well, Anna thought, maybe she should ask Ted for a pay rise. For some reason unfathomable, every unexpected bill from whatever source seemed to turn up, spitefully, in January and February just when funds were at their lowest after

Christmas. The rotting wood on the porch couldn't be ignored much longer, either. 'But that's good, isn't it?'

'I don't know,' Josie wailed. 'What if I don't like her and I've got to put up with her all day? What if he's going to replace me?'

'What if he's going to promote you?' Anna asked, smiling. 'And it may not be a her, anyway.' Josie's eyes widened at this new set of possibilities and Anna left her and went on her way up the green glass stairs to the office.

Suzy wasn't in yet so she went straight to her own place after hanging up her coat. She always left her desk in order from the day before with the 'to do' jobs on the right, with a list if necessary, and the never-diminishing stack of professional articles about changes to the law, new sources of research and so on, on the left. In theory, she should read at least two of these updates a day but in practice she cherry-picked what she was interested in and the rest stayed where they were. There was a compost of financial and corporate directives at the bottom of the pile which was probably years old and which she hoped might become so out-of-date that she could at some point re-cycle the paper they were written on without guilt.

But today, right bang centre, neatly aligned with the edge of her desk was something quite different and she knew immediately what it was. It was a wallet with an airline logo on it and inside were two boarding passes for Paris for next weekend. She leaped up and ran out of the office and down the corridor to Steve's, bursting in with a whoop of excitement. He picked up a coffee, not from the office machine, and a chocolate chip croissant in a see-through bag and offered them to her. 'Better get in some practice.'

She snatched them both like a teenager. 'Have you booked the hotel, too?'

'In the Marais. And something else. A treat for us.'

'Not a frog-eating restaurant? If so, you can cancel it – I can't bear how you actually see their tiny joints -'

'Of course not, Annie. The Moulin Rouge.'

'Isn't that horrendously expensive?'

'Yes. I can afford it.'

'You're paying for all this? Really?'

He drew her to him, for once unconcerned about decorum in the office. 'Of course. I plan to make you so grateful I can have my wicked way with you.' He laughed into her face and she felt his arm tighten round her waist.

This was Steve, lovely Steve, but she registered a tiny shock. She and Harry had been partners and equals in everything, earning and worrying about bills together, planning together and spending together. They had only one account, a joint one. There had never been any question of their money not being available for both of them to use at will. Anna had heard friends or colleagues talking about how they had 'asked' their partners or husbands for a new outfit or defiantly gone ahead and bought something expensive for the house expecting a row to ensue. But Anna couldn't live that way. It struck her, possibly because of the porch niggle, that Steve earned much more than she did. Deep down she had always known it but not wanted to admit it. Not only did he have his Harts' salary but also he was paid on contract by the Government for his cyber-security work. He had not been with Cathy long and so had spent most of his adult life being in charge of his own finances. Would he expect her to feel, even a tiny bit, dependent on him when they lived together – would he expect her to be grateful because of the imbalance of their incomes?

He must have sensed her motionless withdrawal because he added, sounding a little confused, 'Joke, Anna.'

'I know. I know that.' Nevertheless, she moved away from him but managed a smile. 'Thanks so much for the goodies and for organising everything. I'll bring the spending money.'

He was taken aback. 'There's no need.'

'I'd like to,' she said, trying to make her smile more enthusiastic as she reached his office door. 'It's only fair.' Then she silently cursed her costly high horse wondering where on earth the money she had offered would come from.

Suzy was standing by her desk. 'What's this, what's this?' she asked, holding the airline wallet. 'Tell me immediately!' She was wearing her blonde hair longer these days, styled to corkscrew discreetly forward into her cleavage, and her lipstick today was a glossy pillar-box red. But set against the Mad Men image and retro glamour was always the ironic twinkle in her eye. Men who confused her appearance with a matching 1950's girlish self-effacing personality usually left her presence whimpering.

Anna put her coffee and croissant on the desk hoping that Suzy wouldn't hang around too long. One piece of toast for breakfast now seemed like a whole morning away. 'Steve and I are going to Paris this weekend,' she said. She had almost said, 'Steve's taking me to Paris,' as though she was a child.

'Ooh, brill, lucky you two.' Suzy stared her down and pulled up someone's chair. 'So what's the matter?'

'He wants to pay for everything.'

'Even better.' She noticed Anna's expression. 'Or not?'

Anna groaned. 'Am I being unreasonable to feel put down by it? I'm just not used to it, Suzy, and it feels horrible, like I'm some little bimbo that should squeal and be grateful or, I don't know, put up with things.'

'Like me, you mean,' Suzy said, amused.

'When have you ever been grateful?' Suzy laughed and Anna sighed again. 'It's hard to explain but I'm a bit worried about how things will be, you know, if – when - we do finally live together. He's already taking it for granted that I'll move to his and I don't want to, Suze, and now this – this head of the household, breadwinner stuff.'

'Explain to him.'

'How can I? I can't even explain to you without feeling ridiculous.'

'Do you mind if I make two suggestions as your only bimbo-feminist friend?'

'Go on.'

'First,' she held up an index finger doing a good impression of Alice in hectoring mode, 'this feeling of being put down by Steve paying for you once in a while – it's new for you but there will be different special gifts you give him, it's just another way of showing love - don't complicate it.' She raised her middle finger, 'Second, and this is *not* a gift, do you want to borrow my purple felted wool coat and beret you're always on about? You can't go to Paris in that undertaker's uniform thing you wear.'

'Suze,' Anna said soberly, 'you have gone above and beyond the call of duty and I may even bring you back a fridge magnet of the Eiffel Tower. On me it will be trench-coat length but that's fine. Can I have the gorgeous scarf you wear with it as well?'

As Suzy glided off Anna opened the bag with the croissant knowing that the awkwardness she felt over Steve's money had not been dissipated by a bit of banter but that her friend was right. It had to be understood and dealt with. The coffee had gone cold.

At ten o'clock she was tapping on Ted's door with the usual mental scanning of her recent work performance that a summons from him brought on. Actually, it had been a good month and she'd solved a couple of lucrative probate mysteries but she didn't imagine for a moment that Ted had asked her to see him to congratulate her. It was, after all, her job, and which assignments a researcher got was usually a matter of chance so someone else would have probably done just as well. He barked something and she went in.

The change in his appearance was subtle but unmistakeable. His cocky stance was now a slouch, his facial hair was back in the form of an unshaved chin and he was wearing a pilled woolly turtleneck. He glanced up from the papers in front of him and regarded her dully. 'What?'

'You asked to see me, Josie said.'

'Oh. Yes. Tell me about that girl you were tailing – that murderer's daughter.'

Anna bit back a facetious reply since Ted looked in no mood for correction. 'Kara. I have met her and talked to her a little but I had to give up the volunteering as it wasn't working out.'

He regarded her from under his eyebrows. 'What do you mean, wasn't working out?'

'Um. A resident felt I was taking too much interest in one particular member of staff.'

Ted sat back in his huge desk chair and assumed a sour expression folding his arms across his chest. 'It was a bad idea, Anna, bad professional judgement on your part. Harts could have ended up looking disreputable if not fraudulent.'

Ted had never been this harsh to her before and she instinctively straightened her back and sharpened her attentiveness. He had been keen enough on the plan to flesh it out for her before. 'No damage has been done.'

'You say. What about the father, the one in prison. Is he ready to meet her?'

'No, he wants to wait until he's out and has something good to show for himself – you know, a job, somewhere to live, that sort of thing. He doesn't want her to be ashamed.'

'So, there's no progress on that and none likely in the short-term.' It wasn't a question. He unfolded his arms, picked up a piece of paper which he glanced at and asked, 'Have you been using Harts' resources to pay for certificates for him, Anna?'

The question was so unexpected that Anna almost gasped. Of course, strictly she shouldn't have sent for Lindo Johnson's death and marriage certificates through the company since they were not necessary to her remit but it was so automatic to put in requests for legal documents for searches that she hadn't thought twice about it. Ted would not ask such a question if he didn't already know the answer.

'Yes Ted,' she said miserably. 'Two – so he would know where his family came from.'

Ted stood up and put his hands on his hips – a familiar sign of censure. 'So, what you're telling me is that you've blurred boundaries all over the place, haven't you? You are a probate researcher, Anna, not a private detective or a social worker or whatever other fantasy role it is you're playing at, at our expense. You will reimburse Harts for the two certificates and you will watch your bloody step in future if you want to remain as an employee here.'

'I'm sorry, Ted,' Anna muttered and turned to go.

'Oh, and finish that case and send me your hours and expenses – not to Accounts – to me by tomorrow morning, and make sure they're all legitimate work for this job. Tell Robert Johnson I'll be sending him my bill and I would appreciate a rapid settlement.'

Anna closed the door behind her and stood for a moment in the corridor churning with anger, shame and disappointment but by the time she'd reached her desk she had to admit that Ted had a point. She also surmised that the Governor was no longer a 'friend'. A minute later she almost went back to his office to tell him in no uncertain terms that she hadn't wanted the blasted job in the first place and that it was he who had talked her into it.

But then she thought of Kara – the sweet-natured girl with her father's eyes – and she sighed and started assembling the data Ted had asked for.

18

When they got back in his car Kara couldn't stop herself asking, 'Are we going to the Bullring?' She was hoping for Zara although H&M would be great, too, but he had given her no hint.

She had rubbed moisturizer into her skin after her shower and used some jasmine-scented hair lotion to make her hair shine and smell nice when she moved her head because he had asked her to wear it loose which she almost never did. Now it tickled her cheek and got stuck down her collar and she felt untidy but it was a small enough thing to do to please him. He was wearing a navy overcoat which she wanted to stroke it looked so soft – probably cashmere – but under it a grey open-necked shirt and dark trousers. The outfit was fine, of course, for Saturday, but she would buy him a scarf, a striped city scarf, to complete the urban look, with some of the fifty pounds she had taken out of savings. She didn't want him to think she was just going to sit back and let him spoil her – she wanted to give, too. He wore his good clothes carelessly and the coat could do with a clean. She would look after him. The corners of her mouth tucked and rose with pleasure at the thought.

'No, darling, none of that tat. You're going somewhere exclusive.'

He was now nosing the car down a tangle of old back streets which looked like shut-up factories and offices, it being the weekend, and stopped outside a narrow, tall house squeezed between two shabby concrete warehouses. There was no sign outside and no number on the door and, as she got out of her side, Kara could see that the windows from bottom to top of three stories were blinded. She glanced around. Down the road a man was trundling bales of something on a dolly and in the distance the city high rise buildings loomed up a long way away. The place was deserted. She kept one hand on the door handle. 'Where are we?'

He glanced over at her as he locked the car. 'Doesn't look like much, does it?' Then, seeing that she didn't move to join him, he walked round to her side and lifted her hand free. 'Don't you trust me?' His eyes in their nest of fine creases looked tired in the dull light and she noticed for the first time that there was a small silver scar on his cheekbone. She wished she had told Shell about him, told her about this so-called shopping trip, and then felt cowardly and disloyal. She shivered and nodded.

There was no bell or knocker on the door but someone must have been watching because it opened as soon as they crossed the tarmac pavement and then she was inside. What she saw was so unexpected that she couldn't help staring around her. There was no hallway, they were immediately in a room the width of the house and it was brilliantly lit – there were floodlights, she saw, three of them. All the walls were white and so was the floor and set against the far wall was a sort of ski-slope of white cloth. Tucked against the side wall were tripods and cables and high stools and to her right a large upholstered chair.

The woman who stood in front of them now with her arms folded, looking Kara up and down as though she was an exhibit in a museum, was very tall and dressed from head to toe in black. Skin and bone, Kara thought, remembering something Edna Simpson had once said scornfully about a slim young care-assistant but this wasn't what you'd call slim, this was skin that looked shrink-wrapped to ancient neck tendons and skull. Skin and bone and eyes so deep-set you could never know the colour.

'Hi Gret,' Bob said, sitting down in the chair, 'How's yourself?' and then, without waiting for an answer, 'This is my girl.'

Kara felt something was expected of her although the woman had not spoken. 'Hi,' she said.

'Take your coat off.' Kara had heard that voice before, not the accent, but the coarseness and knew that it told of a lifetime of heavy smoking although there was not a hint of stale tobacco about the place. If it smelled of anything, it was plastic. She slipped off her parka and then didn't know what to do with it. The woman nodded behind her and she found a row of hooks and hung it up. In the white room it looked drab and tawdry and the fur trim looked cheap. 'Come,' the woman said and opened a white door in the white wall, beckoning Kara brusquely.

Kara swallowed and looked at Bob. She was not a child. 'What's this about, Bob?' she said. 'I don't want to be rude but I don't know what's going on.' The front door, after all, was only metres away and had not been locked or bolted and she could be out of it in a moment. She recognised this feeling and she didn't like it – this was how she'd felt when Gerry used to tell her, without even checking her mood, to get undressed.

Bob rose from the chair and opened his arms. 'Sweetheart, darling,' he beamed at her, 'I'm so stupid. Come here.' She stayed where she was and he moved towards her and took her by the shoulders. 'I didn't explain, did I? I wanted to surprise you, but you knew I was treating you, didn't you?' Now he was gripping her shoulders a little and she tried not to squirm. 'Let me make the introductions.' He turned her towards the tall woman who was still standing by the door looking bored. 'This is Grete and she, my dear, was once a doyen of the Paris fashion houses, weren't you, Gret?' No response. 'Come on, Gret, crack a smile for Kara if it won't break your face.'

The woman left the doorway and moved to Kara, taking her hand. 'I have some clothes for you to try on,' she said seriously, 'that's all. Come with me, please,' and then, sensing Kara's reluctance, 'they are nice clothes, better than any you have ever worn.'

Bob had returned to the chair and now took out his phone. 'I'll be here when you're ready to show me,' he said skimming messages, so Kara felt she had no option but to follow Grete deeper into the house. Now that this scary-looking woman had spoken to her, if not kindly, at least normally, and Bob had explained who she was she found that there was a pulse of excitement in her alarm. This was another world, Bob's world, and she, it seemed, was about to try on the poshest of posh clothes. Nothing like this had ever happened to Shell and Lauren she was certain so she would remember everything to tell them some time. It comforted her to think of them while she was in this weird place with this skeleton woman.

In the next room Grete told her to take off all her outer clothes but there was no changing cubicle. 'Where?' she said, but all the woman did was bring two hangers and wait so she stripped down. This room was a little smaller than the front one but had a large triple mirror set into its own stand and again, the lighting was fierce. Scattered untidily around the walls were racks of clothes of all kinds so when Grete took Kara's clothes away and returned with an ugly unbleached cotton dress for her to put on, she pulled back from it.

For the first time a hint of a smile touched the stretched face. 'It's not clothes,' Grete said, 'it's a toile because there is no time to measure and tailor. Bob says you are standard UK ten but this will quickly show where you are bigger, smaller. Put it on, please.' So Kara did and stood, feeling foolish like a little kid. Grete smoothed and pinched fabric with her fingers here, there and then said. 'Ok, you are ten but four centimetres smaller waist. I will tell Bob to get you better lingerie. This bra does not support as it should so the line of the clothing will be compromised.'

'I'm not a model or anything,' Kara said shyly, thinking that Bob could do with explaining a great deal better to people than he did. There was clearly a misunderstanding. 'I'm his daughter.'

Grete stopped removing the toile and stared at her. 'His daughter? Bob's daughter?'

'Yes.' Perhaps she shouldn't have said anything – she remembered his hint about keeping it between the two of them, but why should she? 'I found him not long ago. I thought the dad I grew up with was my real dad but he isn't. It's Bob.' There was a silence so shocked that she added, 'He was very pleased once he knew the truth.'

'Take off, please,' Grete had got past her moment of astonishment and spoke as though nothing had been said, 'I will bring proper clothes now and take photographs.' She indicated an SLR camera sitting on a chair.

But as the clothes accumulated on a rack Kara became more and more confused. They were beautiful clothes, some lined with silk, all expensive fabrics, and with each outfit she was asked to put on three-inch heels until Grete had looked and photographed and then ordered her to try on the next. Sometimes a dress would come with a little jacket, sometimes it would have three-quarter sleeves. Adult clothes. The coats were of different styles, fitted or swinging loose and draping elegantly from her shoulders so when she moved the fabric swung obediently around her. So this was why some women looked so good, why Helena looked so good. Money. The colours were mostly subdued – dark greys and navy or a green so deep it was almost black. Some clothes Grete hung on a rack and some she returned to where they'd been.

In the mirror she saw a business woman. A beautifully dressed and striking-looking (it had to be admitted) business woman. Why? At no point had Bob ever asked her what she wanted but she had assumed that she would choose. Who didn't choose their own clothes? Where would she wear these things – what kind of life did Bob imagine she lived?

Grete had gone off to one side and now came back with a hand mirror and a lipstick. 'This is the shade you must always wear,' she instructed.

Kara twisted the cylinder and up rose a deep crimson bullet. 'Are you sure?'

'Yes. Apply now, please – I will show you how to apply and blot. No other make-up except translucent powder which I will give you and mascara. Your fragrance should be La Perla. I will tell Bob to buy it.' She indicated the rack. 'These are the best clothes for you.'

'I usually choose my own,' Kara said shyly.

'Yes, so do all women who do not know how to dress,' Grete replied shortly. 'I know what suits you. Fortunately there are no bad parts to cover up and you are a beautiful young woman so it's easy. Now, casual.'

And so it went on through rack after rack of what Grete called casual and what Kara thought of as unbelievably dressy. Now there was colour and she found that she could wear yellow and white which she had never done before. For each successful outfit, as judged by Grete, a pair of shoes or boots was selected from the heap of boxes by the door and put neatly underneath the outfit on the rack of chosen items.

Then came the evening wear. Kara didn't talk any more, she just put on, posed, took off one outfit after another, shocked by how glamorous she looked. One, in gold lace on black net, made her gasp but Grete was not pleased. 'For this,' she said, prodding Kara's cleavage, 'the right bra you must have.'

'I don't really go anywhere to wear this kind of thing but I love it,' Kara breathed, turning and gazing in the mirror.

Grete looked into the mirror too and met her eyes with her own expressionless black ones set deep in their sockets. 'Now you know Bob, you will go to places to wear these things,' she said.

But Kara had a new worry. Her wardrobe at home was tiny, just a single one because that was all there was room for, but on the rack there were already twenty outfits. And what would she tell Vicki? One new coat, yes, she could tell her that Bob had bought her that, but all this? Vicki would know they were quality – they didn't even have labels in them! She would say horrible things in all likelihood or want to get involved and spoil it all.

But Grete had now finished and said matter-of-factly, 'I will accessorize these for you with jewellery, hose etc. but you must make sure of the lingerie and the fragrance. I do not carry those things.'

When Kara walked back into the front room in her own clothes Bob seemed disappointed. 'I thought you were going to show me?' he said to Grete.

'No time. You were late and I have another client. These are the photos.' She passed him her camera and he began to swipe through them, smiling more and more broadly. 'Yes, she is a very beautiful young woman,' Grete said, as though she was sad about it. 'You will need to take her to buy lingerie from this house,' she passed him a note, 'and also this fragrance which can be bought in John Lewis.'

'Look, she needs a proper coat now,' Bob said, glancing at Kara but speaking to Grete, 'I'll take the black one with us, ok? We're going to the club for a while.' Grete went back through the door and Kara whispered, 'I haven't got room for all this,' but Bob just laughed.

She returned carrying the black swing coat and a pair of black suede boots with three-inch stacked heels. The red lipstick was in Kara's pocket and still on her lips. 'Yes, pop those on now, darling, will you? Otherwise you're ok. You can leave your bag in the car. See to those, too, will you, Gret?'

'Everything will be fully accessorized,' the woman said as if offended and it struck Kara that Grete didn't like Bob very much but that she wasn't afraid of him, either, which was reassuring.

Bob threw the parka into the back of the car as though it was a rag, which she supposed, to him, it was, and she climbed gingerly into the front in her new warm, collarless coat so that her hair, instead of getting knotted and stuck, sprang out in a retro afro. She looked and felt like someone else altogether.

Bob smiled across at her and patted her knee. 'Well done, kid,' he said, 'it's a whole new world, isn't it? Relax and enjoy.'

'I'm really grateful,' Kara said, moving her shoulders slightly to enjoy the satin lining, 'but I don't know where I'll put these things when Grete sends them. They'd fill my whole room!'

Bob swung the wheel so that they were back on the dual carriageway into the city centre. 'Oh, she's not getting them delivered to you,' he said, 'they're coming to me. I told you I had an apartment in the city, didn't I? I didn't want you put in an awkward position with – um – your mum.'

'So when will I wear them?'

'When you're out with me, of course, darling. Wait and see, eh? Wait and see. I knew you'd scrub up nicely and you've done me proud.'

Anna had felt out of sorts all day about the nasty scene with Ted and her thoughts rolled round the possibility of reasoning with him to keep Robert's file open and how she would break it to Robert himself. It was very unlikely that Ted would change his mind and, really, should she be so involved with it? Kara was safe and seemingly happy enough with her family and job and wasn't going anywhere and Robert's plan to set himself up before meeting her, if he did, made sense but there was some nagging anxiety ticking away in her subconscious. Sometimes, these worrying intuitions which she had had before turned out to be misplaced and foolish but sometimes they were spot on. The trouble was that she had no way of knowing in advance which kind they were.

Most of the office had gone home but if it was not her turn to make dinner Anna liked to use this time to sort out her desk and prepare for the next day and, hopefully, avoid the worst of the rush hour traffic. Steve always left early to pick up Alice from the after-school club. She glanced out of the window and saw that a thick wool of dreary clouds had lain itself down over the city. She sighed and checked her phone.

There was a missed call from Rosa and she remembered Ellis begging her to ask about whether Bobble could go there. It was always a pleasure to talk to her and, as the dialling tone went on, Anna realised that Rosa now felt much more like a family member than an ex-employee. What would that be? Not a sister, she was too young for that, but maybe a neice?

'Hiya.'

'Hi Rosa, you ok?'

'Not really,' Rosa said calmly, 'I've had a break-in.'

Anna stood up and started throwing things into her bag. 'Are you all right? I'm coming over. I'm so sorry I didn't see your call earlier. Is there damage?'

'They bashed the door to break the lock so that's knackered but they must have been disturbed because there's nothing much gone. Just food from what I can see.' She must have been looking around because her voice got fainter. 'I didn't phone you about that, though. It's Len.'

'What's happened?' Anna's step-brother was usually a source of bizarre anecdotes rather than serious problems but she was more aware than most that anything can happen to anyone at any moment and she was instantly alarmed.

'Oh no, he's ok. It's not that. You know he's away on this gig, tour, whatever, with the group?' Anna grunted, having completely forgotten. 'Well, he's sent me this card. I'm sorry to ask if you're busy, Anna, but is there any chance you could come by? The van's battery's flat or I'd come over to you.'

By-passing the clot of traffic on the A38 in Selly Oak, Anna found the back lane to the canal where Rosa's boat was moored and tucked her car into the usual spot. She pulled her hood up against the fine mist in the air and opened the boot to change into wellingtons for the muddy bank. It was slippery on the moorings' access path and she stayed safely away from the water's edge as she squelched along but it was good to see a spiral of blue smoke coming from the stack on Rosa's boat and she knew the kettle would be on and fresh tea in the offing. The painted doors were lying in the stern in pieces and would need completely replacing but she saw that Rosa, probably with the help of the other permanent boat-owners, had contrived some temporary security with a makeshift board and padlock. She called out.

'Just a minute,' she heard Rosa say, and then the panel opened to reveal her substantial upper body. 'I had to undo the padlock on this side first.' She looked at Anna hunched on the bank. 'Can you get on or shall I come up?' Anna's short legs managed the long step without slipping flat on her face on the edge of the boat and she clomped down the three steps.

It was warm in the cabin and, sure enough, a pot of tea sat on the tiny counter-top next to a plate of chocolate digestives. Rosa was comfort personified. Anna sat on the padded bench and looked round, munching. 'I can't see anything amiss,' she said, 'but did you lose much food?'

Rosa, dressed gorgeously as ever in layers of purple and red woollies, topped off today with a rainbow beanie, settled back on her own side and picked up her mug which she waved towards the galley area. 'I don't begrudge it,' she said. 'They only damaged what they had to, it wasn't malicious. There are a lot of hungry people about and they can't all get referrals to foodbanks.' She sipped her tea in her usual delicate way and not for the first time Anna felt soothed simply by being with her. There was something about that firm bulk of flesh, the fresh colouring of her face and her clear hazel eyes together with the comforting Black Country voice, that settled Anna and, of course, it was no wonder that Len had been drawn to Rosa so immediately and strongly. She was, it had to be said, the antithesis of their brittle and selfish mother.

'So you've heard from Len? Is the tour going well?'

Rosa flashed a mischievous look at Anna. 'He said "Ok here," so, you know.' Len had never been garrulous and generally went straight to the point which meant that he and Faye lived in a state of poorly-managed hostility at most family get-togethers. Rosa put down her mug and picked up her sewing. Even now, Anna marvelled that having had her home invaded she would embroider. She leaned over to look more closely at the piece and Rosa lifted it to show her a printed roundel of swallows chasing each other around a Tudor rose which Rosa was bringing to life with tiny stitches of silk. 'Got the commission last week,' she said, 'it's pretty, isn't it?'

They settled back, Rosa to work and Anna to watch. 'So?'

Rosa seemed reluctant to begin but Anna waited and eventually she said. 'You've spoken to me about Len before. You know, how he fancies me?'

'You said you weren't interested in him like that.'

'But people can't just leave things be, can they?'

'What's he said?'

'He's said he wants to ask me something when he comes back and I think he means he's going to propose. He was working up to it before he left.'

To everyone who knew them, a romantic relationship between Len and Rosa was as obviously right as fish and chips. The only exception to this view was Rosa herself who clearly liked him and enjoyed his company but had always cut off any talk of anything more intimate.

Anna said gently, 'And is that not welcome?'

Rosa continued to sew but when Anna glanced at her face she saw, in the soft yellow cabin light that Rosa had tears in her eyes. She got up and went to her and, unable to hug her large body, took her arm and wrapped her own round it. 'Oh sweetheart,' she said, 'What is it?'

Rosa wiped her face with a man-sized tissue. 'I can't tell you the reason, Anna, not even you, I've never told anyone, but I can't marry him.' She stopped sewing and looked down at her hands. 'I mean, I can't have sex with him – or children.'

Anna thought of her own no-nonsense campaign to initiate Len into modern standards of personal hygiene which had involved baldly stated home-truths and a joint trip to explore the exotic wonderland of the men's toiletries department in a local supermarket where he had shaken his huge head in disbelief at what was expected of him. But that was years ago and now, apart from an eclectic clothing style to which Rosa certainly would not object, Len was comparatively fragrant so it couldn't be that.

'You don't care for him that way, you mean?' Anna asked trying to be tactful.

'No, I could. I mean, I do – sort of. It's not that.' Rosa wiped her face again and took up her sewing. 'I'll just have to say no.'

'I'm sorry, I don't understand.'

Rosa suspended her needle over a fine curve on a bird's tail and stared at it. 'Something happened to me when I was little,' she said. 'I don't want to talk about it. I can't marry anyone.' Anna waited and waited but she knew Rosa would say no more now. The cabin had become a place of shadows and silences, of ancient darkness shifting and stirring. Finally Rosa asked, 'Is George all right?'

Anna took the change of topic. 'Mm. He and Diane are planning a camper-van trip to Scotland. There was something Ellis asked me to ask you if you don't mind.'

'Is it the dog?' Rosa sewed on.

'How did you know?'

'He sent me a text saying had I ever considered I might need security on the boat.' Rosa snorted with amusement, 'So I put two and two together.' She turned the embroidery frame to a fresh spot. 'Funny, isn't it, that I got broken into after that? But then, we often do have uninvited guests.'

'So, what do you think?'

'No, Anna. I'd like to help Ellis out, I know how much that dog means to him but it needs space, not confinement. He'd go potty here and I can't commit to walking miles with him twice a day. As for security, if someone was determined to break in they'd just poison the poor animal and I couldn't stand that.'

Anna gathered her coat and bag and edged round from the table to get up. 'That makes sense – I'll tell him. But Rosa,' she hesitated, 'do you want me to say anything to Len when he gets back?'

Rosa looked up at her. 'Yes, thank you, I was hoping you'd offer. That would be best. But let him know I am fond of him.'

'Have you got jump-cables? We could get your car battery going.'

'Oh thanks, but no, Freda from the next boat is going to do it 'cos I've got a long drive tomorrow morning so it'll charge it up if there's any life left in the battery.'

It was dark now on the bank and Anna took small, careful steps along the beaten mud and grass until she reached her car. She was thinking of how bitter it was that someone as kind, as giving and sensitive as Rosa would have had a terrible experience as a child, something so bad that it couldn't even be spoken of to a close friend. She had a sudden image of that man in Bromsgrove, that strange, disordered, violent man, and again she had the feeling of skating care-free along a smooth surface when underneath, barely glimpsed except in nightmares and heart-stopping disclosures, were seething demons.

19

Kara decided to keep the coat to take home. It was so soft and warm to touch and satin-slippery inside that just easing herself in and out of the car was a treat. A new world, Bob had said, and this was just the start. As he drove on she thought of those clothes now waiting to be packed and transported for her use to some smart apartment in the city. She would have, she realised with a start of surprise, a secret life, something she had never particularly thought of or wanted but that now it presented itself had a thrill to it. Of course, she could tell Vicki about what was happening, which was simply that Bob wanted to have her in his life, natural enough and exciting in itself, but Vicki was Vicki and had the knack of evaporating joy with a word.

'Bob,' she asked, coming out of her reverie as they drove back into the city, 'where are we going now?'

'Sorry, darling,' he said, 'I'm not used to telling people what I'm doing. Just keep asking if I forget.' He wore driving glasses, she had noticed, and looked somehow both more approachable and more distant in them which was odd. 'We're going to a club in town which I've got an interest in. It's just the usual thing, you know, a bit of music, a bit of dancing, drinks, food and so on – of course, it's closed to the public now but there's someone I want you to meet.' He stared ahead at the road and then stopped at traffic lights and turned to look at Kara. It was a serious, questioning look and she tensed. 'After you've met this person I might trust you and tell you something that's very important to me and ask you to make a decision, but we'll see.'

'Ok.' When Kara had learned to swim at the local baths with the school, there had been a moment when the teacher, kneeling at the side of the shallow end, had instructed, 'Take your feet off the bottom now, feel the water lift you up,' and she had done so and it had been both scary and exciting. This felt like that – she felt that today might be when she lifted her feet off the solid ground and felt a new force hold her.

They pulled in to a parking bay at the side of a drab brick building and it struck Kara that for all Bob's obvious financial success, the places where he worked fell far short of glamour. He came round and opened the car door for her and she slid out, tossing her bag on the back seat as ordered. The little black boots and the lovely coat bolstered her courage as she waited for Bob to unlock a steel side door and she felt grateful to him that she had the correct armour for whatever encounter would follow – the tatty parka and synthetic textile boots she had put on this morning would have made her feel like a skivvy.

Inside were narrow corridors with rooms off and then they were in a large windowless space with tables scattered around and chairs tipped up on top and an old man vacuuming a dark red, stained carpet. At one end was a small stage with a central pole. Kara glanced away. At the far end was a long bar with stools and a tired young man checking things off a list. It all looked, in full overhead strip-light, shabby and dreary. Bob made a gesture to the cleaner and he switched off the machine and disappeared through a side curtain. The bar-man continued with his list. Bob pulled down three chairs from a table near the stage and indicated to Kara that she should sit down.

'Drink?'

'Oh, no, I'm ok, thanks.'

Bob turned to the bar-man and called, 'Two coffees.' He nudged Kara's arm. 'Doesn't look much, does it? But you should see it when it's open. It's a miracle what lighting and music and so on can do for a place.' The table they sat at was plastic-topped and Bob tapped it. 'Tonight this will be spread with white linen and a vase of imported roses and candles in tall glasses and there'll be jazz, be-bop of course, and beautiful girls dancing and you'd think you were in Soho, Paris, New York.' He sniffed with satisfaction. 'The entertainment business is all about illusion, darling, smoke and mirrors - '

Kara felt rather than heard someone behind her and whipped round. The man who was examining her didn't just look tired like the barman, he looked so hard-used it was as if he was carved out of old leather. There wasn't an ounce of fat on him, she thought, it was all muscle, sinew and unpadded skin which was exposed at his neck and arms by the tight black t-shirt he wore. His chest looked so hard you could knock it like a door. But for all that, she did not feel frightened, she was proud to note, because as well as her dad being there, there wasn't a trace of hostility in his face. It was calm, set as though it never changed, so when he sat down at the third chair and said, with some kind of accent, 'Good afternoon, Miss,' to her, it was intriguing rather than worrying. Also, she had never been called 'Miss' before and it sounded old-fashioned and chivalrous.

'Good afternoon,' she said back, as though she was in school assembly replying to the headmaster. Two black coffees arrived and were placed in front of the two men and Kara wished she had asked for a hot chocolate. She had thought that Bob meant an alcoholic drink when he'd asked her before.

'This is my daughter, Kara,' Bob said, and smiled at the other man who nodded. It was the first time he had introduced her as his daughter and the blood rose in her face. 'Kara, this is Jan.'

'You are how old?' Jan asked, and when Kara told him nodded again and then asked, 'You have passport?'

Bob seemed as annoyed by this question as Kara was surprised. 'This is a social call,' he said to Jan, 'we're just getting to know each other. Christ, man, don't you have any small talk?'

The look which Jan gave Bob startled Kara. She had assumed, maybe because of the T shirt and the tough looks of the younger man, that Bob in his cashmere coat with his worldly air was the more important of the two but now she was not sure.

Jan swivelled his eyes back to her. 'Tell me about yourself,' he said, sitting back with his hands crouched like two of Bob's giant spiders on the bare table. 'Tell me who is Kara.'

Was this some sort of interview? It was exciting being with Bob but she was really getting fed up of being the victim of minimal information and a throb of irritation rose up in her. She liked people to say clearly what they meant and she didn't like surprises. She glanced at her father for direction but he was looking sulkily at his phone. 'Perhaps you could tell me why you'd like to know?' she said as politely as she could, but she felt Bob stiffen beside her.

Jan's face eased a little in what may be his version of a smile, she thought. 'Good. Girl have spirit.' He picked up the coffee cup between two huge fingers. 'Your Bob, your dad, and me have an enterprise – a thing we do with some others. It might be of interest to you, too, since you are family.' She heard Bob chuckle at something on his phone. 'He don't explain things good.'

'No,' Kara said, a little too quickly for politeness, 'he doesn't!'

'But before you decide if you want in, we decide if we want you. Understand?'

The clothes were beginning to make sense, maybe, although it seemed odd to buy them first – they must have cost Bob a fortune. 'What do you want to know?'

So, she told him about her family, her work, her friends, and then, when he continued in attentive silence she told him about her dreams for a bigger life, a larger meaning to her existence. Bob had stopped messing with his phone and was listening, too. 'I've always felt as though I'm just sitting by the side of the road while other people rush by in their exciting lives,' she said, finally, thinking of Tassie and Shell. Both men were now looking at her thoughtfully. The irises of Jan's eyes were an unusual milky brown punctuated by the black dot of his pupil but there was no white visible. Beyond the clay disc was only a hint of reddish darkness before folds of flesh spiked with pale lashes lipped the ball. They reminded her of something but she couldn't think what it was. 'I have been going on, haven't I?' she said, to break the silence.

'No, not at all, darling,' Bob said, 'very interesting.'

Jan got up and nodded at Bob. 'Set it up,' he said, and then, turning to Kara and offering his hand, 'We will meet again.' Bob half rose in his chair and then sank back and again Kara had the sense that he was deferring to a more powerful man.

'So what did you think?' he asked eagerly when Jan had gone.

'Of Jan?' She reflected. 'He looks scary but somehow he isn't.'

'Good girl. Good instincts. Look, I'm going to have to put you in a taxi, darling, because I've got to be somewhere but I'll be in touch.' He was pulling on his coat and seemed anxious to be gone.

'But what about this thing, this enterprise that Jan said you were in? Aren't you going to tell me? You were going to ask me to make a decision.'

'Yeah, yeah, but not today. I'll phone you. You can come to the flat next time.'

A taxi was waiting outside and it was only a minute before she was in it and driving away from the club. She hadn't thought to kiss him goodbye after all his generosity so she texted him to say she had had a fun time and the clothes were fantastic. She thanked him for introducing her as his daughter to his friend.

It was only as they drove through Rubery that she realised what Jan reminded her of. When she was in the Juniors the class had been taken to Dudley Zoo and they had all run up to the enclosure of a brown bear. She couldn't remember whether there were bars or chain-link or a pit to keep the bear away from them, or them away from the bear. All she remembered was that the huge bear stood quite still looking intently at them, its massive paws hanging by its side and its head high and silently focussed on their giggling, bobbing group. The expression in the eyes of the brown bear had been the same as in Jan's.

In the end she didn't tell Shell and Lauren anything. When she got home Vicki and Graham were out so she hung the new coat in her wardrobe and put the boots beneath it. After she'd got herself a snack of microwave chips, salad and a cup of tea, she lay on her bed for a while thinking about the day and how odd and unreal it had seemed. She must have dozed because when her phone woke her up it was Shell saying they were outside waiting for her so she grabbed the parka and ran out with that.

In the pub the talk was all of Shell's hen night but Gerry was there at the bar with Maz and the others and Kara wondered what she had ever seen in him. He was just a boy, really, he would be totally intimidated by Bob and Jan. He kept glancing back at her and, although she was wearing clothes she'd bought herself, it was as though the memory of how she'd looked and felt in those smart expensive clothes still stayed with her body so she held herself straighter, made more conscious movements, ignored him.

Just before they left Lauren asked if Kara minded if she started going out with Gerry and Kara almost laughed at the thought. She stroked Lauren's arm. 'Of course not, Lol. You go for it – I don't want him,' and she raised her eyes and looked straight at him, red-faced and sweaty, bawling and whooping with the other boys as he was, and he caught the look and cringed a little.

New worlds were opening up to her: enterprises, travel, gorgeous clothes and a proper father who looked after her and was taking her on his arm into his life. She was wanted, praised, admired. She didn't need to tell the girls about all this – how could they understand?

To avoid the Friday evening rush to Paris Anna and Steve went early on Saturday morning from Birmingham airport to Orly and Steve insisted on a taxi into the centre even though they could have easily caught the Metro. Early as it was, the day was already bringing surprises when Steve spoke to the driver. When he settled back she gently punched his arm. 'I didn't know you could speak French.'

'See. *Mais oui, bien sur.* Who knows what other impressive talents will be revealed?'

'When did you learn? And don't say at school, because I so-called learned at school and I can't remember anything.' They were driving through a mixed industrial and agricultural area but every now and then a pretty house with shutters or street signs in French would appear through the morning greyness and remind her of where she was.

'You'd be surprised. Believe me it would all come back to you if you lived here for a while.'

'I'm being kidnapped, am I?'

'Don't think I haven't considered it but I decided you're too gobby to make a good hostage. My nerves couldn't stand it.'

'Hey!' She took his arm and snuggled down. 'Tell me, then.'

'I had two months in France before I went to university. Grand-dad had a mate from his sea-going days who had set up a *gite* in the Auvergne and wanted a general dogsbody. That sort of ex-pat hostelry thing was newish then and I loved being there soaking up the sun and cycling round the lanes. All you learn at school comes to life.'

'Your grandfather was at sea?' She thought of Robert and Stanley and wondered how the internet search was going.

'Yes. That's why my dad moved to Derbyshire – to get as far away as possible – from the sea, I mean.' Anna looked up at him to say more. 'Grand-dad died not long after I went to uni to do physics but even so I'd only met him three times in my whole life before that. My dad always said he and his brother felt as though they were raised by a single mum. Some women could have coped fine with that but my gran found it very hard, not just because of having to do everything herself and take care of all the emergencies but because she worried about the house being broken into, the children attacked, things like that – stuff that sells newspapers. Dad said she checked every door and window before she went to bed and kept a poker by her pillow. Then, when dad and his brother left home, she had a sort of breakdown as though she'd been holding things together so long she'd snapped, and she hardly left the house after that. She was the sort of person that needed a husband to be a support and a soul-mate to her, a constant companion, and she never got that. Even when he was home between jobs he wanted to socialise with other men, not with her. Dad vowed that when he married he'd never leave the woman he loved to manage everything on her own and he hasn't as you know.'

'Your parents are very close,' Anna murmured, trying to imagine how it would have been for her bringing up the children if Harry and then her dad had not been around. She couldn't get a picture of what Stanley's life would have been like as a 'seaman' either. He could have been on inter-island cargo tramps, maybe, or the trans-Atlantic route to Europe. He could have been a fisherman or a ferry-master. It would have been fun to do the research herself but much more so for Robert, probably. She must go and see him soon albeit on her own time.

The traffic was getting thicker now and horns were blaring as they twisted and turned through the inner city roundabouts and boulevards. Anna craned her head, 'Look, look, there's the Eiffel Tower! Let's dump the bags at the hotel and find a café for coffee and pastries, shall we? Let's do every touristy cliché we can pack in.'

'Including the siesta?'

'Isn't that Spain? Isn't this February?' Anna cried, feeling suddenly skittish, 'What can you be suggesting, *monsieur*?' She fluttered her eyelashes. For answer Steve grabbed her, tickling and nuzzling into her neck until she lost her breath with giggling and fighting him off.

'*Anniversaire de marriage en argent*?' the taxi driver asked as they stopped outside the hotel.

'*Mais non*,' Steve said, 'We just met at the airport.'

After coffee, exquisitely served in small cups and saucers instead of pint mugs, they wandered down the Boulevard Saint Germain to look at the Louvre (but not go in) and then down the Seine to the Quai D'Orsay and on through the tangle of squares and little streets up to Montmartre. But all too soon, when they stopped at yet another café or strode together, arm in arm, down blustery boulevards, it was not about Paris that they talked. She wondered if all tourists did this, reverting quickly to familiar preoccupations as they gazed at the great monuments and land-marks and sampled the food and drink of another country. It was on the Rue des Trois Freres in Montmartre where they had stopped to buy a bottle of wine that Steve mentioned Alice for the third time and Anna registered a small puncture to her frivolous mood. The balloon wasn't burst but there was a slow leak. She wondered how many text messages he had sent since arriving.

'It's amazing how strong she is considering what she had to go through, poor kid,' Steve was saying. 'Don't let me forget to call her at four home time, I promised I would.'

'Ok,' Anna said, turning up Suzy's coat collar and pushing past incoming customers to get out of the door on to the now damp street, trying to dissolve the flick of resentment which had just pinged her solar plexus. 'Look, we've done loads and it's great but we had such an early start, love, how would you feel if we crash back at the hotel for a while until then?'

'We'll get a taxi.'

They showered together first, luxuriating in the intimacy and sensuality of it and Steve whispered into her steaming ear, 'Why haven't we done this before?' as if he didn't know. It was fascinating to watch the water bounce on his shoulders and find its way like a flash flood over boulders down between the mounds of muscle, straightening the black hair on his chest and groin and she held him to her so that the same water could flow over her. He soaped her from head to foot with gel, turning her, kissing her, gently massaging every inch of her body until they could take no more and fell on the bed still wet and urgently in need of each other. When the release came it had been so long overdue that Anna found she was crying and laughing at the same time.

They lay side by side until they could breathe normally and then Steve said, 'I'll get the wine,' and found he needed a corkscrew and called Room Service and knotted a towel round his waist. She needed more, much more of him, so while he answered the door Anna rolled over to his side of the bed and switched off his phone.

After the wine they made love again, slowly this time. Between the curtains the sky deepened into dusk and the amber glow of the street light outside their window was the only invader into their space. Finally, they rolled apart and spread out, lolling their limbs over each other. Steve eventually spoke into the darkness. 'I love you so much, Anna. There were times in the past when I thought that I would never have this bliss.' Then he kissed her lightly on the forehead, switched on the bedside lamp and stretched to check his watch on the side table.

'Shit!' Anna had never heard him swear before. He picked up his phone, stared at it, and then turned to her. 'My phone's off. I promised Alice I would phone – I put an alert on it!'

Anna pushed her hair back from her face. 'I just wanted you to myself for another hour, Steve. It's not late.'

'What?' He leaped out of bed. 'Are you crazy? Anything could have happened, anything! She could have had an accident, she could need me! What were you thinking?' He tapped frantically at the keys and muttered, 'Two missed calls – shit, shit -' and Anna rolled over away from him on to her side and stared at a knock-off Impressionist print on the wall. In a few seconds he was talking to Alice who was watching something about crazy weddings on television and giving only half her attention to responding.

Steve was not the kind of person to simulate an emotion he didn't feel and dinner limped along between his puzzled questions and her defensive answers. Yes, they were in Paris and the waiters wore long white aprons and black bow ties and flourished the food and drink and it was all exactly as she had hoped except that it wasn't. What could she say? That she thought he over-indulged Alice and let her behave badly? That she was jealous of Alice? Was that the truth? Of course she couldn't say that, so instead she kept repeating how much she had missed him physically, how deeply she had needed this time alone together, which was also true - but only the silver lining, not the cloud. She apologised for switching off his phone and then despised herself for doing it.

The glitzy show at the Moulin Rouge helped to lift the mood a little but they walked soberly back through the frigid late night streets to the hotel until Anna suggested hailing a taxi. When they got back to their room the tension had returned and Steve sat on the side of the bed running his hands through his hair, his gesture of bafflement. Finally, he said quietly, 'It's the deceit I can't understand, Anna. It's you doing it behind my back. That's what I can't get my head round.' He shook his now crested head. 'And what if something had happened and my mum and dad couldn't get hold of me?'

Anna perched on the club chair by the window staring out into the night. She was not going to apologise again but she didn't want to risk saying something that might throw a lance between them that could never be pulled out. What was it her father had said once? Some words are never forgotten. Better for him to think she was sulking or ashamed than to say anything bitter about his relationship with Alice.

'We're tired,' she said, getting up. 'Come on, let's get some sleep.'

They fell asleep lying on different sides of the bed and at some time in the dark Anna woke and lay reflecting sadly on what had happened. She had been wrong to do it. With the family history of sudden loss through a random tragedy, Steve must always have a part of his consciousness anxiously scanning for disaster and the phone was his only guarantee that this minute, now this minute, nothing bad is happening or someone would contact him. Phone silence, she realised too late, was his peace of mind. It had been childish and selfish of her. She sighed and eased out of bed needing to move, to not be trapped by her own thoughts, to be distracted. She went to the window, cosily double-glazed against the chilly night, and stared out down to the street where even at this hour a few people were hurrying by.

Quietly, she lifted the club chair and placed it nearer to the glass and then went to the bathroom for a robe to wrap herself in. This was the time of night, they say, when murderers confess their crimes, when the world can drift from its moorings.

She thought about Harry and how easy and natural their marriage had been, looking back at it. They had rows, of course, mostly about ridiculous things - like what? Oh yes, the episode of the staff Christmas do at the school where he was head of department. It was true that she had possibly had too many festive drinks but only because she was so bored by them all talking about the kids all the time – on their holidays, at a party! What was it with teachers? She didn't even fancy the chap she'd grabbed and kissed under the mistletoe, she'd just wanted to do something outrageous to shut them all up for a minute. But it turned out that he was gay and it hadn't gone down well at all as everyone had assumed she was making some sort of political point. At first the row was real but as the years went by it became comedy and then farce, a joke enjoyed by them both. She couldn't ever remember feeling side-lined when she was with Harry.

But was it jealousy that she felt over Alice? Steve really did indulge the child beyond what was reasonable and it really was an issue whether she or Alice would be in charge of any joint living arrangement. Anna knew her own nature and would not be able to meekly step back on all occasions when Alice wanted her own way. She sighed and leaned her head on her hand.

'Come back to bed,' Steve said quietly into the darkness, 'please, love.'

So she went back and crawled into his arms and he stroked her and kissed her and she pressed her cheek against the hot rubber of his flesh and hoped he didn't feel a few tears ooze on to it. 'It's hard for you,' he said softly, 'I know it is. You probably think I don't notice but I see how difficult things are for you with Alice. But, sweetheart, I don't know what to do either. Can we just keep trying?'

She pulled herself up his body and took his face in both her hands. 'Thank you for saying that – I was feeling very alone.' She kissed his mouth and smoothed his hair back. 'Yes, let's keep trying. After all, it's only twelve years till she goes away to college.' Steve grunted in amusement and they were friends again and lovers again and hours later they ate breakfast together in a subdued mood only because they were exhausted. Another day of sight-seeing was looming so they put the sign on the door and went back to bed to sleep.

20

Anna got into work on Monday morning to find a long email from Robert waiting for her. She carefully hung Suzy's delectable purple coat on a hanger and hooked it and its scarf and hat on to a coat-stand in the corner of the office and then hurried back to her desk to read it.

The name Astrophile had been as productive as she had hoped. Because of his exemplary record and imminent release the Governor had given permission for Robert to make contact through Facebook and he'd found a cousin of that name still living on Grand Cayman (though not in West Bay), who was Stanley's brother's grandson and who was only a couple of years younger than Robert and delighted to hear from him. Az, as he called himself, put him in touch with the family that had stayed behind when Lindo had left. There were photographs of all of them, cousins, uncles and aunts popping up with every log-on and greeting him with affection and curiosity. What did Anna think, Robert asked, stopping himself in mid-flow, should he tell them where he was? He didn't want to deceive them but he didn't want to risk losing them.

But the most exciting and amazing thing was what he had learned about his grandfather, Stanley. Although Stanley's older brother had been given that made-up 'star-lover' name, it was Stanley who learned the stars and even as a small child had been able to name the constellations, spending hours each night lying on his back on the little jetty that poked out into the North Sound, suffused with delight at the sight of the seven sisters, the beautiful Pleiades, shining out from a crowded sky with the other astral bodies. From being only a boy he had gone to sea with his father fishing for turtles travelling further and further as his skills grew until sometimes they would be away for a week or more. In his late teens Stanley had been recruited by a shipping company to run cargo to Cuba (before Castro) and to and from Miami and on that ship he had learned more about navigation and had become a second mate before he was twenty-two.

'How was it?' Anna whipped her eyes away from the screen, from the sun and spray and the smell of hot wood and metal and saw Suzy smiling at her.

'Good. Yes.'

'Don't sound so enthusiastic!'

'No, I was just caught up by this email. No, it was lovely, Suzy, just what we needed.' Anna remembered the coat. 'Do you want me to get it dry-cleaned? I felt very svelte in it, thanks so much.'

'Not unless you were using it for a picnic blanket which I doubt given that it was literally freezing on Saturday night in Paris.'

'Was it?'

Suzy laughed. 'You did have a good time, didn't you? Good for you. Fancy lunch out later?' Anna nodded and let Suzy get half way across the office to her own desk, torn between remembering Paris and finding out about Stanley before she eagerly went back to Robert's email.

Then, he wrote, the Second World War started and merchant shipping was under attack from U boats in the North Atlantic.

The email stopped. Anna scrolled down and down and then, smiling, saw this. *'If you want to know more, come here and see me! It's amazing, Anna, but I want to say it not write it!'*

She sat and thought about it, realising that a visit couldn't be during the week now that Ted had axed the case, but it could be on Saturday. She typed a quick reply saying yes, she was hooked, and would see him at the weekend for the next episode. She added that she was very happy for him (and for Kara) that he was now connected with his family. Perhaps they could talk when she saw him about the dilemma of revealing, or not, his situation. She sat back in her swivel seat thinking of Kara and groaned with frustration that she couldn't jump in the car and go out to Church View and tell the young woman everything. Well, she would get on with the jobs in hand because that was all she could do, so she went back to the list of emails and started going through them, all fifty-four of them after the weekend, consigning to the bin nine out of ten.

At eleven fifteen her phone pinged and she saw that she had a text from Kimi saying that Bri was driving her mad with wedding nonsense and that as far as she was concerned they could go to the Register Office in their jeans and cagoules and be done with it in fifteen minutes. Briony wanted a 1930's theme with a cool jazz duo and matching dresses in heavy silk – no suit for Kimi, no way, they would both wear female Hollywood glamour outfits. Anna texted back that she thought Kimi could do a Veronica Lake very well if she marine-varnished her hair flat, and received some very rude emojis in response.

The afternoon seemed endless and, although Steve was friendly when she popped into his office hoping for a chat, he was clearly snowed under with work so she left and dragged herself back to her desk.

Romance seemed to be in the air – Briony and Kimi, Len possibly declaring himself to poor Rosa, and even Joan out for a date with Jakub Nowak. Anna picked up her phone and texted Joan to ask if she could pop round for a catch-up that evening but Joan texted back that she was off to the cinema and didn't know when she'd be free next. So Anna texted, 'Going well then?' and got a row of exclamation marks in response. So she went back to her computer screen and decided that, all else having failed, she would have to do what she was paid for, no further distractions were on offer.

A promising smell greeted Anna when she opened the front door that evening so she hung her coat in the hall and went straight into the kitchen. George was beating time to Abba with a wooden spoon while he consulted a piece of paper weighted down by the salt and pepper pots. The surfaces were littered with used bowls; it seemed like every one they possessed had been put to work.

'I'm doing a L'Escoffier recipe for you,' he said, 'in honour of Paris and all that.'

'Wow.'

He beamed at her. 'I've got a supermarket steak and kidney pie in the freezer if it turns out you really do need to know what you're doing.'

'Tea?'

When the two mugs were placed on the table George stopped and sat down, uttering that little 'ah' sound which seems to be part of the old person survival kit. 'So, Paris was good?'

'Mm. Good in parts.'

'Too much walking? Too many people?'

'No.' Anna believed that talking about her relationship with Steve to her father was something she shouldn't do because it would put him in a difficult position and, in any case, it seemed disloyal to Steve, but he had been her confidante all her life. The earliest problem she remembered telling him was that her friend Lizzie at nursery had a green T shirt with a scary picture of a witch on it which was giving her nightmares. 'We had a bit of a falling-out because I turned his phone off secretly.'

George drew his brows together and set down his mug. 'Why did you do that?'

'I wanted him to myself for an hour.'

George sat back and sighed. 'Alice.'

'I don't know how to handle it, Dad. It's not just the day to day hostility from her, it goes deeper than that.'

'Mm. Yes, it does. Steve is her protector as well as loving her and it says good things about him that he takes his responsibility so seriously – but it's hard-wiring as well. Every cell in his body is alert to her vulnerability especially after what that family's gone through, and the little girl herself.' He traced circles on the table with a puddle of spilled custardy goo. 'You'd be the same if you were Alice's mum, but of course you're not. It leaves you in a difficult position because you and Steve should have emotional space to sort yourselves out, you know, who's in charge of what, where the boundaries are, that sort of thing, but the existence of Alice constrains that.'

It was so good to talk over her feelings to her dad that Anna blurted out, 'He expects us to live at his house and I don't want to!'

George thought for a while and then stood up. 'Go and look out of the window, Annie.'

'What?'

'Look out of the window.'

She got up and went to the wide window over the sink that looked past George's shed and down the garden to the tall ash trees at the side and at the end. The year was lightening and the late-afternoon sky was a sheet of galvanised steel. 'What?'

He came and stood beside her. 'Every year you say, "Look at the trees, spring is coming."'

'Do I?'

'Yes. Look carefully, Anna, and you can see that very first stipple of dark red that you always check for, before the brightness, before the lime green. It's like a mist, a life-blood mist over the branches. You almost can't see it but then one day you can. Renewal, re-birth - hope. The promise of regeneration.'

The grass on the patchy lawn was dun and there was no colour in the beds yet apart from the light brushstrokes of lilac crocus but as Anna strained against the dullness she saw that her father was right and her heart lifted at the sight of the millions of tiny leaf buds once again, miraculously, piercing tough old bark.

The smell of burning jolted them. George rushed to the pan on the hob, grabbed a tea-towel to snatch it off and plunged it into the washing up bowl full of water. Anna opened the freezer and got out the family-sized steak and kidney pie. 'Thanks, Dad,' she said.

The building wasn't a swish glass tower block as Kara was expecting, it was a beautiful old house, sparkling white, with big windows and four steps up to a covered entrance with pillars either side. She had walked at least half a mile from the bus stop on the Hagley Road and was awestruck by the size of the mansions she had passed. This one had a tall wrought iron gate with spikes on each rail but Bob had given her the code to get in so she could walk up the broad drive to the house. By the side of the door were six brass plates with numbers on them and next to each one was a lighted bell push. She pressed the bell for three and looked round to see if there was a speaker, noticing that half a dozen security cameras were fixed at different angles, but instead of Bob's voice she heard a click and found that the door had been opened.

Inside it was quiet. The kind of quiet you get in a museum. On the walls were large splashy paintings and on the cream-tiled floor a massive colourful rug which she knew was called kilim because Shell's mum had a much smaller one of the same kind. Which one was number three? Bob, yet again, had given almost no directions. She tiptoed round the wide foyer and could only see numbers 1 and 2 so she crept up the thickly carpeted stairs which curved to left and right at the top. It was almost as grand as the Art Museum in town but much more luxurious. At any moment she expected someone in uniform to pop out and shout at her.

Number three was to the left and she raised her hand to press the bell but the door was flung open and Bob was standing there, grinning. 'Watched you having a look round,' he said.

'I wasn't... How did you know?' Bob stepped back and waved her in. To the right of his door was a small bank of screens revealing the front gate, the front door, what must be the garden and terrace at the back, and the shared areas inside the house. 'I was just trying to find your door,' she said, a little flustered, 'I wasn't being nosy. You didn't tell me which floor you were on.'

'More fun that way,' Bob said. 'Coffee?'

'Yes, please.' She followed him into a spacious kitchen area feeling humbled and out of place but determined not to show it. There was nothing on any of the gleaming surfaces, no clutter at all, and she thought how much her mum would love this. 'Have you been living here long?'

He looked around as though surprised to find himself where he was. 'Um. Few months.' He pressed buttons on a complicated looking machine and placed a mug under the spout.

'It's amazing.'

'It's all right. Your gear's come. I'll show you where it is in a minute. Milk? Sugar?'

Metres from the kitchen area was a cluster of sofas on three sides of a low, glass coffee table on which Bob placed the mugs, waving for her to sit down, too, but she couldn't resist a detour to look out on the back garden with its long lawns and huge trees. 'You can't believe this is in the middle of Birmingham,' she said.

'Oh yes,' Bob said, 'Birmingham's full of surprises. Did you want a biscuit or something? I haven't got any.'

'That's ok.' Kara sat down carefully, pleased that she was wearing the classy boots and Helena's silk top. Bob had flung her expensive new coat carelessly over a chair and she wanted to grab it and hang it up but she suspected that rich people did treat their clothes disdainfully because they didn't have to worry. She had washed and de-frizzed her hair (as far as it would cooperate) and now it was fluffed out in the afro he had said he liked. She was also wearing the lipstick Grete had given her, applied and blotted twice as instructed.

'Look, darling,' Bob said, wheezing a little as he leaned towards her, although he was not really fat. 'I was hoping to have the whole day with you but something's come up.'

Kara felt disappointment like something physical dropping inside her. 'Ok.'

'So I'll have to cut to the chase.'

But having said that he went silent, sitting with his head bowed and his hands clasped between his knees. Kara told herself not to make demands on him and to distract herself glanced around the flat again thinking this must be what a luxury hotel suite would look like although she imagined there would be massive vases of flowers as she'd seen on tv. There were no photos on the wall which, she supposed, would be too down-market, but there were two huge abstract paintings. At school the art teacher had given them a whole term on doing abstracts and she had loved it – it was making paintings look like things she was hopeless at. She glanced back at Bob who was wearing another dark outfit that hadn't been hung up overnight, she thought.

Finally, he looked up at her. 'You met Jan, right?' Kara nodded. 'What did you think of him?'

Kara thought it would be rude to remind him that she had already told him what she thought of Jan so she said, 'He seemed polite - he listened to me chattering on without interrupting.' The image of the bear standing still and gazing intently came back to her.

'Mm. He's a bit of a hard man but he's had it hard. Have you heard of Moldova?' Kara shook her head thinking it might be another club in Birmingham. 'Not many people here have. It's next to Romania, Eastern Europe, you know, a small place and very poor. I want to tell you about Jan so you can, you know, get the picture.'

'Ok.' Kara wondered if this had to do with the decision she would be asked to make.

'Jan had a bad start in life because he was an orphan and the orphanage was so hateful he ran away and lived on the streets when he was only a kid. He had to stand up to all sorts, you can imagine, I don't have to spell it out. Well, by the time he was sixteen he was the king of his block, his manor, because he wasn't just hard he was smart, too. He knew how to manage the low-life and the police in Chisinau – that's the capital city. Well, when he was twenty something went wrong and he got in a knife fight and put in prison.' Kara sat very still, hardly breathing while she listened to her father talk. A different world, he had said, and this was another different world. 'When he got out he was in danger from enemies he'd made but he got himself to England all on his own.'

'So he asked for asylum?' Kara said, remembering a documentary she'd seen.

Bob gave her a worried look. 'No. No. You have to understand, darling, that he didn't know anyone here, he didn't know who he could trust, he'd never been able to trust the police.'

'So he's illegal?' Kara was trying hard to understand and not appear naïve.

'Look, that's not the point. That's not what I'm trying to tell you. Just hear me out, but all this is totally, I mean *totally* confidential, ok?' Bob narrowed his eyes in a way Kara hadn't seen before. 'Jan and I think we can trust you but you have to keep everything I tell you now between us, ok? Promise me?'

'Ok.' It was a bit like being in a Hollywood movie thriller right here in Birmingham.

'Good girl. When Jan came here he worked hard and he made himself valuable to people who didn't care too much that he didn't have papers because he was so useful to them. But he never forgot where he came from, his life on the streets and how badly he'd been treated.' Bob smiled at Kara. 'He's all legit now, of course, and got a nice little nest egg for himself but he wants to help those others, those kids back in Moldova who don't have anyone to look out for them, so he got together with some friends who came over like him and some benefactors from here and they set up a sort of charity.'

'A charity?'

'Yes. It's called New Life. It brings kids off the streets of poor places in Eastern Europe over here and gets them homes, new lives, fresh starts, you know.'

'That's wonderful,' Kara said immediately, sitting forward on the sofa. 'And are you involved, too? Is this what you were going to ask me about because I would love to help with that.'

'You're a sweetheart – I knew you would.' Bob stood up and pushed his hands down in his pockets and started walking round. 'It's just that there's a problem. Jan said this would happen and it has. The Moldovan authorities don't want the world to know about how badly they treat their own children so they won't let us go and talk to these poor street kids to tell them about the opportunities here. Naturally, the kids are suspicious at first. But the government have banned anyone connected with New Life from entering the country.'

A surge of excitement propelled Kara to her feet. 'They don't know about me!' she cried, 'I could go!'

'Oh, no, I couldn't let you do that, it might be risky, I was thinking you might do some paperwork here or something,' Bob said, shaking his head.

'But I want to go! You'd have to tell me what to do, I've never been abroad before but I'm sure I could do it. The old people at Church View say I'm a really good listener and they tell me all sorts of things so I think I could get the kids' confidence as long as I had a translator to help. But,' a thought struck her, 'how do you get them out of the country if the government doesn't want you to help them?'

Bob stood up, put his hands in his pockets and rocked on his heels. 'You've heard of the Kinder Transport?'

'Oh yes, one of my friends at school's granny was in that – it was so good. They got all those children out of Germany in the war who would have been gassed just because they were Jews.'

'Well, we have something similar but I can't even tell you what it is because it's so top secret.'

For the next fifteen minutes Kara asked questions and Bob answered them but the reality of this plan was all the time sinking in and she realised that she had some problems, too. The main one was how she would explain to work and to her mum why she was away from home. She did have two weeks holiday owing to her which she'd planned to take in the summer so she could use the time for this. But what about Vicki? 'What do I tell my mum?' she asked.

Bob had a solution. 'She knows you meet me?' Kara nodded. 'So tell her I'm taking you on holiday to make up for all the holidays I've missed having with you.' He looked at his watch. 'I'm sorry, darling, I'm going to have to go but I need to know. Are you on board?' he was already shrugging his coat on and handing her hers.

'Bob, do you think I can do it?'

'Course you can. You're my daughter, aren't you? Now then, there's going to be a get-together of those friends of Jan I told you about and they'd like to meet you themselves, so you can wear one of your outfits, can't you? Why don't you pick something out and take it with you today?'

'I'm on the bus,' Kara said helplessly.

He stared at her open-mouthed. 'On the bus? Oh, bloody hell, I didn't think. Ok, I'll get you a taxi. Go and look now will you? Get the accessories, too, smart day wear, ok?'

Kara found that all the clothes that had been selected were hanging in plastic covers in a double wardrobe in the spare bedroom. The shoes were placed underneath in transparent bags which also contained jewellery. There was nothing else except the new stuff in there. She quickly chose a dark olive day dress which she had liked best during the trying-on session and saw that Grete had picked gold earrings and a fine chain necklace to go with it. The latte coloured suede shoes had three-inch heels and toned with her skin. They even had a small gold motif on the heels. And there was a matching bag. She saw immediately how sophisticated she would look and anticipation bubbled up so she grinned at herself in the mirror. 'Bob?' she called, 'I've found something but I think I should have my hair up with this outfit?'

'Whatever,' he called back. 'Hurry up, darling.'

It wasn't until he was opening the taxi door for her that she remembered something. 'I never told you, Bob - I didn't think until now. I haven't got a passport.'

'You don't need to worry about that. They'll sort it out. I'll be in touch.' Then he was gone, striding up the drive to where she supposed the residents' cars were kept, already talking on his phone. Clearly, she would have to be the one with her head screwed on because he hadn't even asked her for a passport photo which they would certainly need, so she would get some taken and pop them in a card to send him with her details. She was beginning to suspect that he wasn't very well-organised as well as being terrible at explaining things. Everyone has their faults and since she was so practical she would be able to help him. This idea made her smile and, as the taxi turned into busy traffic and slowed down, the smile deepened as she remembered the important work she had volunteered for. Her dad was a good man, a man who had committed himself to helping the poor street kids and she felt ashamed of her previous doubts about him.

Finally, she was going to have her very own adventure and she felt sorry for Tassie who was only trekking selfishly round the world on her parents' money and not doing anything for anyone else.

21

They weren't in the small, sterile room this time. They were allowed to use the library where the computers were so he could show her, not just tell her, what he had found out. It was good to be here and to think about things which had nothing to do with her own life. Steve had been surprised that she wanted to go on visiting Robert and she didn't like the feeling that she had to justify her decisions to him but then, as always, came the self-doubt about whether she was being over-sensitive to potential power in-balances as Suzy had implied. Perhaps he was just concerned for her? Perhaps she had made more of his reaction than it warranted. Oh, let it go for heaven's sake.

Anyway, she was professionally interested in the place and strolled quickly round the shelves checking how recent were the books and how well-shelved and so on. It was a sunny February day but the blue sky was smudged by dusty windows and the intrusive low-angled light made everything look tired. The periodical section was, as always, dog-eared but otherwise it seemed orderly if limited. When they went in she had smiled at the man on the desk who was glaring at a screen but he didn't glance up so she postponed the pleasantries she had hoped to exchange. It would be interesting to know which were the most popular books and so on but there was something about him that suggested she keep her distance. He had a dull, crunched look with his foggy glasses and sparse hair, like a screwed up ball of waste paper. Anna noted this sour observation and rallied herself to focus on Robert.

He led her quickly to a table and when the officer on duty gave a nod, logged on. His eyes and fingers darted about the keyboard and then stilled as he turned the screen to her. She was looking at a black and white photograph of a handsome young man leaning against the counter of what appeared, from the collection of bottles, to be a bar but it was too dark to see properly. He was smiling at the person taking the picture and Anna wondered if he was in love with whoever it was because his face was lit up, the eyes and teeth points of brightness in the dark features. But what might be a glow from a raised shutter or an open door also showed up the modelling of the straight nose and high cheek bones and the soft crumpling of the parted lips. One bare arm lay resting on the bar and one hand was curled round a shot glass next to a pack of Camel cigarettes and a Ronson lighter. If it was someone he was romantically involved with holding the camera, she had done well to have such a steady hand, Anna thought.

'Is it him?' she asked.

'Yeah. Stanley, Lindo's dad.'

'Your grandfather. He's good-looking, isn't he?' She wasn't then able to add that he looked very much like Robert with his sloping eyes – that seemed to be crossing some kind of line. She peered closer and noticed epaulettes on the grey shirt (or was it blue?) and asked, 'When was this taken?'

'It was around 1938 they think. He had just been made second officer on a US merchant ship, the Nortonburg.'

'But he's so young!'

Robert couldn't conceal the pride in his voice. 'He learned navigation so fast once he was on the ship that he got promoted in only three months. It was a record.'

'So what else do you know about him?'

Robert gave her a mock-stern look and wagged one finger at her. 'Not yet, lady, you have to wait for the whole show before I tell you that!' Anna's throat constricted at his teasing tone remembering the dropped head and shrinking presence of the almost monosyllabic person she had first met. Finding his family and, of course, knowing that his daughter was well and contactable, had given him life so visibly it was as though a long dried out cactus had plumped and flushed green after a deluge of rain.

He took her through the messages and photographs and face after smiling face came up as he eagerly described each one. 'This one, Claudette, is a teacher and this one,' he tapped again, 'is Michael her brother, he's a programmer for the government. Then look, these are his twins, see? So beautiful.' Anna watched his face as much as she watched the screen. Could anyone, even someone finding a treasure trove of Saxon gold in a muddy field, look more ecstatic? These are my people, this is my tribe. This is where I belong. The very cells in his body seemed to have opened and refreshed their DNA.

She saw their houses, too, which were mostly single-storey bungalows stretching themselves out among palms and oleander and tall trees which Robert said were mango and poinsettia. The sun bounced off the cars in their drives so brightly that she could almost feel the heat of the metal. One house was two storeys, painted pale blue, with a deep balcony on the shade side and Robert stopped at that one and grinned at her. 'You know what they call this kind of house?' Anna shook her head. 'An upstairs house. Cool, man. This one is the family house of Stanley and Dorothy which they built just before the war, not long after that photo was taken, maybe. That's where they had Lindo and then Bernice. Another grandson, Barry, Bernice's boy lives in it now.' Robert kept the image up and zoomed around so Anna could see the conch shells in a decorative line bordering the creamy marl path to the door and the scarlet hibiscus bushes in the raked sand front garden. 'Behind the house is their little beach and the sea. The water is unbelievable, Anna, it's blood heat, Michael says, can you imagine? Man, it's like paradise.'

The last comment sounded wistful and Anna wondered if he was contrasting his own 'better life' which his father had come to find in England with the life he might have had if Lindo had stayed but what would be the point of asking him? The world had changed and changed again many times since the 1950's when she knew from her own research that the Cayman Islands would have been a very different place. Grand Cayman was infested with mosquitoes and roads outside Georgetown were bad or non-existent in heavy weather. Work would have been hard to get and poorly paid.

'Are you ready for the big finale?' Robert asked, tapping once more and turning the screen back to conceal it from her. Again, the playfulness was a revelation of the man he could be, must have been at one time.

'I am.'

'Ok. You see this here?' On the screen now was a photograph of a medal and she recognised it at once. The university library where she had worked had had a significant collection of war medals because of a donation from an emeritus professor of history whose life-long avocation had been to collect them.

'That's the North Atlantic Star!'

'Very good! Not many people our age would know that.' Anna didn't mind at all being bracketed with thirty-eight year old Robert into 'our age.' He tapped again and turned the screen towards her. 'And look at this. You get to be a big-head if you know what this means?'

The photograph showed another medal but, unusually, on the ribbon was a silver oak leaf emblem which Anna had never seen before. 'Just a minute, just a minute, let me get my head round this.' Robert turned and settled in his seat, his hands patiently folded. 'You said that Stanley was second mate on the Nortonburg which was a US cargo ship. How on earth was he involved in the battle of the North Atlantic?'

'I've been reading about it, getting some background to what Az has been telling me. There was a problem with U boats sinking merchant ships in the First World War but they really came out in force for the second. They were fast, invisible and deadly in the early years of the war and they was sinking merchant shipping carrying supplies to Britain in bad numbers. It wasn't just ships that had to be replaced, it was crew, too. Seamen like Stanley, men from the British Caribbean islands, volunteered immediately war broke out but it wasn't until a few months had passed and things were really bad in '40 and '41 that the Admiralty put its prejudices away and took them on. They were British subjects, after all. Stanley was posted to *Aldgate*, a British carrier running from Canada to Portsmouth.'

'Was that one of the Liberty ships?'

'No, they were American and came later when the US had to build ships fast, too fast, some say. Az says there's one of those wrecked on the reef off the east of Grand Cayman.'

'So, you're saying that your grandfather was an officer in the British Merchant Navy in World War 2?'

'Can you believe it?' They sat in silence for a while thinking about the tragic losses of men and cargos, the desperately slow race across stormy seas in gale force winds of the heavily laden ships with their all too few Royal Navy escorts. Anna imagined them as though she was looking down on the rough seas, willing the brave little ships on while all the time steel sharks darted and circled under the green fathoms looking for them to destroy them. Steve had said that his grandfather was also a seafarer but hadn't mentioned the War although he must have been of a similar age to Stanley. She would ask him about it.

Anna dragged herself back to the quiet room, the smell of books, the shuffling of other computer users on other tables and to the image on the screen. 'I've just thought of something. Was the North Atlantic Star only given to men who died in service? I'm so sorry.' So did the handsome man stay handsome? Did he never get old?

Robert shook his head. 'No, it was given to people who survived, too – those who had given over six months' service. But you're right, he didn't survive. Az is sending me some photocopies of Stanley's war record because that has more details so I'll know more then, but he did send this photo.'

'What's this medal, then?' It seemed more ordinary than the Atlantic Star.

'It's the War Medal that everyone got who served at least twenty-eight days in a combat zone but this one is very special because of the emblem.'

'A silver oak leaf?'

'Yes.' Robert seemed fixated by the image and Anna was just about to ask again when he said, 'It means that Stanley got the King's Commendation for Brave Conduct.'

'Oh, Robert.' She took a deep breath while she stared at the screen but when she turned to smile at him she saw that his face was expressionless, the same blank wall that she had seen the first time they met. Was this the shield he used to hide his joy and pride as well as his suffering?

Then a prison officer was behind them, tapping his watch at Anna, and she rose obediently to leave. Robert turned to her a face stripped of all defences. 'And here am I,' he said softly, 'a convicted murderer, a disgrace to the family. How can I tell them that?'

Anna drove home soberly thinking about Robert's painful dilemma and was still in a sombre mood when she let herself in despite noticing Faye's Micra on the road, but then she heard a shout and pulled the door open again letting in the rawness of the February afternoon. The weak sun had long ago disappeared behind a lowering wad of nimbostratus and some icy drops were already falling on the front step. Ellis dashed up the drive round her car with, she was surprised to see, a girl.

'Quick! Come inside.'

She led the way into the kitchen and the teenagers tucked themselves in at the table on high alert in each other's presence as well as at least one of them feeling the nervousness induced by a mother who might at any second say something.

'Milk, sugar?' Anna offered, slinging tea bags into mugs.

'What kind of tea is it?' the girl, introduced as Shona, asked.

'Ordinary.'

'Do you have any Chai?'

Anna did not point out that chai is the Hindi word for any kind of tea and shook her head. 'I've got some camomile or – um – green tea, I think.'

'I'll just have water,' Shona said with an air of resignation.

'Me, too,' said Ellis and Anna, with her back turned to them, rolled her eyes deciding not to make bacon sandwiches as she had been just about to, unless asked. It was two o'clock and it seemed reasonable to close the kitchen. Besides, she was very aware of Faye clomping about upstairs and wanted to talk to her.

'Ok, well, you can get that, can't you, Ellis? Faye's here and I just want to see how she is.'

Faye was in Anna's bedroom listlessly rooting through her jewellery box. Her entire body oozed dejection and Anna marvelled at how she had always been able to fully inhabit an emotion in this way. Faye put up no screens between herself and the world, unlike Robert, possibly because she had not yet needed to. She pulled out a lump of air-hardened modelling clay which had a hole bodged in it for a leather string and had been splashed with glittery green paint. 'You've still got the pendant I made for you when I was in Infants,' she said.

'Yup.' Anna sat down on the bed. 'The trouble is I never go anywhere smart enough to wear it.' Faye managed a half-smile. 'What's the matter, love?'

'We're just so hard up, Mum. We never go out any more like we used to, like our mates do. We can't even think about a holiday. There's so many bills!' She stretched her eyes wide to show Anna how shocking this situation was. 'You have to pay for everything, even water! It's not right, and that's on top of them taking tax and National Insurance off your pay!'

'Are your friends, the ones with more money, are they still living at home?'

Faye nodded, missing the implication, and picked up a string of amber beads, prettily separated by tiny gold florets. 'This is nice. Do you wear it?'

'Can you stay a bit longer? Shall we sit down and work out a budget? It's so much easier when you know what has to go out and what's coming in. Unless you want to do that with Jack.'

'Oh Mum, he's hopeless with money. He bought a new game the other day but I made him take it back. He was really grumpy about it. He's such a kid in some ways.'

'And after that,' Anna said, getting up, 'shall we pop down and see Steve and Alice? I know they're in this afternoon and they would love to see you.'

Understanding that this suggestion was part of a bargain and not a request, Faye calmly agreed and they went down together to the kitchen to look for pen and paper. Ellis and Shona had disappeared but the sound of Jerry Lee Lewis was blasting from his room and Anna made a mental note to check again with their elderly neighbours that they were still conveniently deaf.

Vicki and Graham were out somewhere so Kara crept into the main bedroom with its floor-length mirror to look at herself in her outfit. She had showered using a creamy lotion that left her skin feeling wonderfully smooth and a shampoo she had had for Christmas that was peach scented. It was Sunday and in the distance she heard the bells of St John's church ringing in the morning service. The rain had stopped and the day was clear and still which was a relief because she had nothing posh to cover her carefully pinned up hair if it rained. She would buy a black umbrella from the pound shop to have handy in future.

She turned this way and that marvelling how the tailored olive wool dress with its narrow belt flattered her figure and made her look neater and slimmer and with the shoes on and her hair pinned up high she really did look amazing. She looked amazing. She saw that the lipstick shade that Grete had insisted on made her look fresher, dewier, more adult and sexy. She tripped back to her own room for the earrings and other gold jewellery and then ran to the mirror again to see the effect. She wished there was someone there to enjoy it with her, to exclaim over how lovely the outfit was and how well it suited her. She wished Shell was there.

Tonight the girls were meeting at a new bar that had opened, not for a late night because it was work the next day, but just to chat without any boys present. Maybe she would tell her about Bob – not everything, of course, she had been sworn to secrecy – but just something, maybe? Bob had said not to wear a watch so she checked the time on her phone and then slipped it into the mocha suede clutch Grete had chosen for this outfit, pulling on black gloves. The taxi would be here in five minutes so she twirled one more time and then picked up her coat and stepped carefully down the stairs in her high heels. The meeting place was on the other side of the city, somewhere in Staffordshire, he said, so they would go in his car from his apartment. She saw with satisfaction that the expression on the Uber driver's face changed from boredom to interest when she emerged from her front door and she straightened her back and tried not to let her ankles wobble as she strode forward.

Bob was, in fact, waiting for her outside the elegant Edgbaston house and flashed his lights at her to get in. She tried a little skipping run like women did on adverts when they were hailing a taxi in New York or somewhere sophisticated and it crushed her toes a little but it made her feel silly and grown-up at the same time which was another new feeling in this new Bob world.

He was wearing his driving glasses and tended to hunch over the steering wheel in a way that couldn't be good for his back but she decided not to mention it yet. There was something about the intensity of his driving that made her think he had things on his mind and she didn't want to seem like a foolish chattering girl. He had given her one swift glance and nodded and hardly said anything else.

After twenty minutes she cleared her throat and asked if he could tell her a little more about the people she would be meeting and at the sound of her voice he jumped as if he had forgotten she was in the car. 'Businessmen mostly – they want to do their bit – put something back, you know the sort of thing.' Kara felt this wasn't helpful.

'No women, then?'

'Um. Oh. Business people I suppose – there may be some women.'

'Will Jan be there?'

At this Bob seemed to finally realise that she needed a proper response. He glanced sideways at her and grinned. 'You taken a fancy to him?' Nothing could have been further from Kara's mind – Jan was ancient. He must be at least in his thirties. She shook her head, perhaps too vehemently. 'Oh, well, no, he won't. He's the contact person as he speaks the language, of course, but these are the ones that put up the money. Philanthropists, you could call them.' Kara slipped her phone out of her bag and looked it up, the dictionary kindly altering 'fil' to 'phil'. A philanthropist was someone rich who did good things for less fortunate people. She sighed with satisfaction.

'Texting someone?'

She didn't want to admit she hadn't known the meaning of the word so she said, 'No, I just wanted to check the time I'm getting together with my girlfriends tonight. We will be finished, won't we?'

'Oh, yes. I'll have you back for five or six at the latest. These meetings don't last too long and then there's a snack, you know.'

They were driving through grey, sodden countryside but every now and then a red-brick cottage or a cluster of shops and garages would appear or some horses standing disconsolately in fields in their waterproofs. She wanted to find out more while Bob's attention was with her. 'So, are you going to introduce me to people or should I mingle?' Bob smiled. 'What do I say if they ask who I am?'

'The people who matter know you're my daughter – I don't give a damn about the others so you don't need to tell anyone anything. If people ask just say, I'm here with Bob, or something like that, ok? You won't come into the meeting until you're invited and then it's just so they know who you are. Some of them might ask some questions which you'll answer. Just tell the truth, darling, they'll love you, but no need to bang on. After you leave the meeting I'll explain to them that you may be willing to go over and help contact the kids who want to come here for New Life.'

'Oh no, I definitely want to,' Kara broke in, 'there's no maybe about it.'

'Never a good thing to seem too available,' Bob murmured. 'Just leave it with me.'

Clearly, she was being interviewed for the task, which she was now thinking of as a mission, even though Bob didn't say so or hadn't thought to tell her. He probably didn't want her to be nervous. They drove for five minutes in silence and then Kara had to ask one more question. 'Will they know that I'm only a care worker?' she said quietly, 'I only got four GCSE's.'

For answer Bob burst out laughing and continued snorting for several minutes before he patted her knee and said, 'Believe me, darling, you're overqualified.'

Kara flushed, feeling that she was being made fun of. 'What do you mean?'

'Look - you're pretty, you're nice with people, you're willing and you're smart. Who cares about whether you can do trigonometry or reel off the Kings of England?'

The compliments slipped down inside her like the creamiest hot chocolate. She turned her head to pretend to look out of the window so that she could let herself smile without Bob seeing. He believed in her and it felt so good that it was as though she could take deeper breaths than she had ever taken before. 'I won't let you down,' she said solemnly.

Eventually, Bob turned the car into a driveway with huge gates set in a high brick wall which opened as they approached so some device must be reading the number-plate, she imagined, like they do in supermarket car parks. A drive went between trees and then curved to the left in front of a pretty house. It was half-timbered, the plaster painted cream with the wood left a weathered silvery brown as if it was covered by snail trails. The entire height of the end wall was hidden by creeper which must turn orange in the autumn, Kara thought, and rose branches were clipped back and trained round the porch so she could easily imagine the riot of blossom in the summer. Some dogs ran out barking and she half-expected to see children run out, too, in little rubber boots with maybe a smiling woman holding a baby in her arms. 'Oh,' she breathed, 'oh, Bob, it's gorgeous!'

Bob pulled the car round and parked it under some trees next to half a dozen others. 'Not bad. Bit chocolate-boxy, but it's only the dower house, of course. The main house is up there.' He waved vaguely at the drive which went on up a hill and out of sight. No-one came out to greet them but Bob walked in through the unlocked door without hesitation so she followed him, patting her hair at the sides and wishing she had asked him about a ladies' room where she could check her appearance. She hoped very much that Bob hadn't got it wrong and they would find everyone in tweeds and jumpers. A small woman with tightly permed grey hair met them wordlessly and took Bob's coat and then hers, disappearing into a narrow corridor off the square hall.

Kara plucked his sleeve. 'Is there a loo?' she whispered.

'Down there, hurry up, we're late,' he said, so she ran off and was back, feeling more settled, in under five minutes. The mirror had revealed that her hair was still in place and that she looked just as good here as at home and her confidence soared. She had taken three slow, deep breaths. 'Stay by me and smile,' he instructed as he pushed open a heavy door. Inside were about a dozen men and a few women. The men were animated, chatting with each other in groups, laughing loudly, showing off to each other, Kara thought. The women seemed bored, glancing around at the pictures on the wall or checking their phones, although one or two were hanging on the arms of men and cuddling into them as though they were afraid to let go.

'Here's our Bob!' called a man with a red face and slicked-down silver hair. 'Hey, Bob, who's this lovely young lady?'

'My daughter,' Bob said firmly as Kara stood proudly by his side not allowing herself to slouch or look nervous.

'Tell that to the Marines,' someone muttered, but then men were stepping forward and shaking her hand and one man even kissed it which made her feel as though she was in Downton Abbey. The women looked hard at her and then away.

'Now Bob's here, what say we get started?' the red-faced man said. 'In the dining room those who are coming, you know who you are.' But not all the men shuffled out, laughing and slapping each other on the back, some stayed behind looking a little downcast. Kara saw a window seat and went to it, perching on the cushion and looking out on a side garden with a stone fountain pedestal and cobbled pathways.

'Like a film set, isn't it?'

Kara turned and saw that one of the bored women had come over to talk to her which was kind. 'It's beautiful. I'd love to see it in the summer.'

'Well, you might. Who knows?' The woman leant against the thick wall and folded her arms following Kara's gaze. Kara glanced at her and smiled to show she appreciated the conversation, noting the heavy gold chain round the woman's neck and the careful fall of thick blonde hair. 'You've not been before, have you?'

'No.' She was going to go on to tell the woman how and why she had found Bob but she had got the impression that Bob didn't want her confiding in these people, much as she would have liked to. 'Are you here with someone in the meeting?'

The woman stared out at the dull garden. 'For my sins.'

'Do you know my dad?'

'Not well. He was at school with my husband, that's all.'

Kara was shocked. This woman with her upper-class accent and expensive clothes and jewellery didn't seem the kind to marry a man from inner-city Nechells. 'Really?'

'Mm. In the Borders somewhere.' The woman was still staring out of the window but not as though she was seeing anything out there.

Kara hesitated. It was rude to contradict people but she couldn't let this go. 'I'm sorry but I think you may be mistaken. My father went to a school in Birmingham.' Although Bob had done well for himself, of course, and there was nothing to say that this woman's husband couldn't have done the same.

Two grey eyes, perfectly outlined in taupe kohl, stared into hers. 'Oh, of course,' the woman said, 'I have a terrible memory – take no notice.' She looked Kara up and down. 'You're very pretty,' she said, and her voice sounded sad like Grete's had done but it must be hard for women who had been beautiful and were now getting older, 'and you have perfect taste in clothes. Well done.' Pleased, Kara was about to respond with a reciprocal compliment when the door out of the sitting room opened and Bob was there beckoning to her.

There were no women seated round the polished oval table but the red-faced man was clearly in charge, staring at her with frank interest and asking almost immediately for her to, 'Speak up for yourself, darling.' She liked Bob calling her this but not a stranger and her discomfort must have registered in her face. 'Come on, come on, I won't bite. Come and sit yourself down.' Someone pulled out a chair on her side of the table opposite the bossy man and she obediently sat. 'So tell us a bit about yourself, Bob's daughter. Tell us what you like doing.' At this there were some subdued sniggers but Red-face frowned at them and they stopped.

This was Kara's chance. 'I like helping people,' she said earnestly. 'I work in a retirement home and some people might find that boring but I like it because people can't help being old and finding things more difficult and it's a privilege to help them and hear their stories.' She hoped this didn't sound as rehearsed as it was because the little speech was followed by silence.

Red-face shuffled some papers and coughed. 'Very commendable.'

'How do you feel about travel?' the man to the left of Red-face asked. 'Have you been abroad much?'

'No, not yet,' Kara said, adding quickly, 'but I'd love to go. It's not that I don't want to, I just haven't had the opportunity.' She thought of Tassie who had been taken off on foreign holidays since she was a baby and who had only complained about the long waits in the airports and had never told her about the exciting places she'd been. Kara knew she would never take the opportunity to travel for granted but Bob had said she mustn't say too much so she left it at that. Better not to mention New Life or Moldova because maybe she shouldn't know about the enterprise.

'Is there a boyfriend?' asked another man whose face she couldn't see because he was on her side of the table. The one masking him leaned back helpfully and revealed a thin, dark-skinned face with penetrating black eyes staring at her.

'No,' she said feeling free and powerful, 'no one.'

'A girl-friend?' the black eyes persisted, and at first she thought he was joking but then saw he wasn't.

'No, not like that.'

'Still living at home, Bob says,' Red-face stated.

'Yes. With my mother and her husband.'

'No doubt they dote on you, right?'

Kara wasn't entirely sure what this meant, so she said, 'I'm an adult, they don't tell me what to do. We have separate lives.' The truth of this chilled her for a moment.

'Thank you, Kara.' Red-face seemed to have finished with her and turned to Bob. 'Ok, she can leave now.'

It was only then that Kara noticed that Bob was not sitting at the table with the other men but was off to one side in an alcove. Next to his chair was a small desk and on it a silver laptop. He rose and smiled at her and she turned to go out of the door. As he opened it for her he whispered, 'Well done, darling,' and she flashed him a grateful smile.

On the way home he seemed to be in a good mood, whistling and grinning to himself – what Edna Simpson would call 'chuffed', but the only thing he said to her was, 'Book your two-week holiday off work, darling, soon as you can, and let me know the dates, ok?'

'But what about my passport? I've sent you some photos and the details they'll need, have you got them yet?'

'Oh – very efficient. All in hand, don't worry.' So that was another compliment to add to the list.

22

Kara decided to leave her hair pinned up for the time out with the girls because she couldn't bear not to, it looked so elegant. She had a reputation for doing hair which was why Shell was trusting her with her styling for the wedding and it did help that Shell had lent her the proper equipment to practise with. The curling tongs were much better than the cheapo ones from the chemist and the pin comb was great for teasing out strands to soften the structured effect. Shell had ordered the extensions and the silk flowers to pin into the curls and they would have a proper run through to trim them to size next weekend since the ceremony was going to be at the end of March and there would be too many things to organise nearer the time to worry about perfecting a style.

She hung up the olive wool dress and pulled out her jeans and a loose top. Kara liked Shell and she and Maz were well-suited but she felt no envy about the wedding. It was a relief not to have to pander to Gerry all the time and she was too young to settle down. Wouldn't marriage just be more of the same? Work, housework and sex - with evenings out at the pub for a social life. Still, if you loved the person, she supposed it would be ok and Shell wanted to be just like her parents who were still devoted to each other. It all seemed so dreary and limited now that she had linked up with Bob and he had taken her into his world.

She hadn't liked to ask him why he wasn't seated at the table but she thought she might know. All the men had been friendly to him but you could tell that he was tighter with Red-face than the others. She'd noticed on the way out that Bob had been drawn to one side and the two had been deep in conversation away from the others. She reckoned that he was like a secretary to the group or something like that; there were important people called Company Secretaries, weren't there? He was probably keeping the minutes on his laptop. That meant that he was at the centre of things, one of the most trusted people. Some things that had puzzled her were beginning to make sense. No wonder his estate agency was dusty and neglected looking – this, the New Life enterprise, was what he really wanted to give his time and energy to. And it made sense. He'd come from nothing – a mixed-race boy with only a widowed mother living in a council flat in a poor part of Birmingham and he'd really made something of himself. No wonder he had such a passion for street children who had no-one to help them climb out of poverty and worse. It was all meant to be – a purpose to her life – all of it had been just waiting to happen.

Lauren and Shell were already at the pub as they'd walked down together from their side of Bromsgrove but they'd only just ordered so Kara got her lager in and joined them at a high table. The pub was nicely re-done and they commented on that for a while and then Lauren told them both (but Kara thought Shell already knew) that she and Gerry were now an item. Kara thought of his pasty grey buttocks and dirty fingernails and told Lauren she was very happy for her because, really, he was just like many of the other lads, no worse, and she was pleased he had moved on so she didn't have to feel guilty and Graham would let it drop.

Then Shell came in with her big news. She and Maz had planned to live in his family's house, since it was bigger than Shell's, while they saved for their own place but, unknown to the couple, her parents had got together with Maz' mum and dad, who only had him, and had raised enough to put down a deposit on a house on the estate just being completed near the big roundabout. This was huge and the girls talked over the ramifications and marvels of it for the next hour.

They were just beginning to sigh and look at their watches when Kara took a deep breath and said, 'I've got something to tell you, as well.' She could see from their puzzled expressions that they had no idea what she, with her predictable, ordinary life might have to say. 'I've found my real dad,' she said.

'No! Already?' Then the questions rained down on her and she answered most of them but couldn't stop herself adding, 'He's bought me a whole wardrobe of designer clothes – they're beautiful, you should see. He's really generous and he lives in this, like, mansion in Edgbaston – not all of it – but a really big apartment. He drives me to places in a massive Audi.'

At this there was silence. 'So what's your mum said?' Shell asked eventually.

'I don't tell her much. She knows he's well-off but she doesn't ask anything and he doesn't want to see her which suits me.'

'Can we come over and see the clothes?' Lauren asked. 'You're about my size.'

'I've only got one outfit and a coat at home, my wardrobe's so small. You can come and see those. He's keeping the others for me at his flat in the spare bedroom wardrobe.' At this Kara saw Lauren and Shell exchange a look.

'Where did you buy them?'

'It wasn't a shop, it was the house of a woman who used to be a couturier in Paris. She had loads of clothes there and she picked some out for me. She knew just what suits me and they feel lovely to put on.' Shell and Lauren stared at Kara.

'Have you got a photo?' Lauren asked, so Kara showed them the one she had taken of him on their first meeting at the bar, and they peered and zoomed and then sat back thoughtfully.

'Well, at least he isn't ugly. Your life will change,' Shell said.

'Actually,' Kara smiled, 'it already has. I'll tell you some time, but I can't tell you now.'

'Lucky you,' said Lauren, grabbing her coat and sliding off the high stool, 'you won't want to know us soon.' Kara knew she was being sarcastic and it stung.

'That will never happen,' Kara said firmly. 'We're mates, that will never change.'

Shell hugged her. 'Yes, don't be jetting off to the Caribbean or somewhere when you should be doing my bride hair, Kar!'

'No chance of that,' Kara said, 'I wouldn't miss your wedding for the world.'

The temperature had dropped to freezing when they left the bar and the girls hurried off in their different directions, Kara pulling the string tight on her parka hood and thrusting her hands deep into the pockets as she walked quickly up the steep hill to her estate keeping a sharp eye out for Wally Wanker who may be harmless but it was best to avoid trouble.

Although Shell seemed pleased, Kara was disappointed in her friends' reactions. Perhaps they didn't believe her, what had happened was hard to believe, but she'd never lied to them so they should have taken her word. Lauren had been a bit nasty but she was like that and may have hoped Kara would be jealous of her hooking up with Gerry. Anyway, it had taken the shine off the day when all Kara had wanted was to share her good news with her two closest friends. She certainly had no intention of telling Vicki.

The house was in darkness when she turned her key in the lock and she realised that she was hungry. The snack Bob had mentioned had not materialised and she had had nothing since a piece of toast that morning so she put her shoes into their bag and padded about the cold kitchen tiles making a cheese sandwich and a cup of tea to take up. By the time she'd cleared up the preparation area and polished the granite top and climbed the stairs with her shoes in one hand and plate and mug in the other, fatigue hit her.

Alice had been more at ease with Faye on this visit and Faye had behaved impeccably and played tiddly-winks and threading beads and so on for a good hour until she glanced at her watch, then at Anna and received a nod in recognition of job done. She skipped out promising Alice that she would see her again soon and Alice merely made a song out of saying 'bye-e-e' so that was a step in the right direction, too.

Steve and Anna made a chicken and mushroom pie since Steve liked making pastry and Alice formed little people and dogs out of the cut-off bits and insisted on putting them in the oven. While the pie was cooking Alice wanted to watch her Frozen DVD so Steve poured a couple of glasses of wine and sat down with Anna in the kitchen

'My idea of heaven,' he said, smiling at her, 'the last couple of hours. It's just what I've wanted for years.'

It felt slightly wrong to Anna to agree since some of those years Harry would have been alive and her feelings for Steve during that time had torn her up with guilt but she didn't want to spoil the pleasant time they were having so she responded lightly, 'What? Not hanging off some overhang in freezing rain? You amaze me.'

'She's coming round, isn't she? Alice? I knew she would.'

'Maybe seeing Faye made her realise that people come back from time to time.' Except for Harry, of course, no coming back there. She felt lonely, suddenly, cooking in this kitchen which was not hers with this man who was not him.

'Weddings seem to be in the air this year,' he said, pouring her another glass. 'Maybe we should abandon ourselves to the zeitgeist? Give Alice a hat-trick.'

I should marry you so that Alice gets to play some more dress up Anna immediately thought defiantly and then felt ashamed of herself. This foolish and hostile attitude of hers to Alice had to be dismantled not indulged and she forced herself to say, 'Maybe we should go for a themed do – possibly Comicon? Then she can really go to town with the costume. So could we – I could be Superwoman.'

'Mm.' Steve stretched out a hand to stroke the back of hers. 'I can just see you in blue and gold sparkly tights.' He smiled at her. 'So you will? Is that a yes?'

For answer Anna got up and opened the oven door. 'I've fallen down on my sous-chef duties – the pie's done, and the roasties, but no greens – I shall bestir myself forthwith.' Steve must have taken the hint because he said nothing but when she looked back Anna saw that the smile had left his face.

As she washed and chopped the green beans and broccoli spears she thought about Robert, probably by now in his cell or room or whatever it was in an open prison and she pictured him writing in the journal he had told her he had kept from the day he had first held Kara over twenty years ago. Of course for most of that time he could only record his thoughts, his wishes and fears for her, but on her birthdays and at Christmases he had allowed himself to speculate on what she might be doing, what presents she might like, what games she might be fond of. Sometimes Anna wondered if the new reality of Kara, her grown-up look, her work, her address, the ordinary and yet, to Robert, hugely significant facts of her life had exploded that parallel fictional life he had given her so that there may be times when he even regretted the loss of it. The fantasy would have been tailor-made to comfort him but reality brought demands, responsibilities, even conflict if he asked to see her and Vicki refused.

Anna paused at the chopping board struck by the disturbing thought that it was not only Robert who had pursued a pleasing fantasy future that had turned into a less dreamy reality. She loved Steve, she really did, and yet she knew, if she was forced to be honest with herself, that it wasn't just Alice who was complicating the situation. She tossed the pile of greens into the pan of boiling water and pulled open the unit drawer to finish laying the table. Steve had disappeared.

At 11.52 Kara was woken by a cheep from her phone. She rolled over and switched on the bedside lamp. It was Shell. She got up on one elbow and read the message: 'Bit worried about you, babe. Who is this man says he's your dad? Can we talk just you and me? I can come to yours tomorrow after work if you like. Don't be mad with me cos I love you - you know that. Shell.' There was a worried emoji and two kisses. Kara put down the phone and turned on to her back to stare at the ceiling. A tear ran from the corner of her eye down her cheek and into the pillow and it was only then, only with Shell's caring message swelling her heart, that she let herself admit that she was just a tiny bit scared herself.

Mrs Bandhal's secretary, Sheila, was a bit huffy about the short notice but since Kara didn't normally cause any bother she sighed and filled out the requisite forms – late winter wasn't popular among the staff for holidays so no inconvenience was involved. 'Going anywhere nice?' she asked to show there were no hard feelings and Kara said, 'Just away for a break with my dad,' which passed without comment. In fact, Kara realised as she said it that she wasn't sure whether Bob would be going to Moldova with her or not. As with so many things, he just hadn't said, hadn't explained. She made a mental note to ask him about it when she told him the holiday dates. Just eight days and she would be at Birmingham airport boarding a plane!

'Hey, I was hoping I'd catch you!' Kara turned and saw that Jackie was throwing her coat over the hook and dumping a bulging folder of papers on the photocopier.

'Not there,' Sheila said frostily, 'I'm about to use that.'

Jackie grabbed the papers again and hustled Kara outside on to the corridor. 'How's it going, sweetheart? Did you find him from what I told you?' Her round cheeks were shining with rain and Kara felt slightly exasperated that a professional woman like Jackie could have forgotten to bring an umbrella despite the forecast. How did someone get to be a social worker who was so scatter-brained? But she must have been clever at school and university which seemed so far above Kara's horizons as to be completely inaccessible.

'Oh, yes. I've been trying to catch you, too, to thank you,' Kara said, blushing. 'He's not what I expected at all but he's very nice.'

'Looks as though he's got a bob or two at any rate,' Jackie said.

'Sorry?'

'Done ok for himself.' Jackie winked.

'Mm. I felt a bit intimidated at first – he's got a really posh apartment in Edgbaston aside from the Redditch house and a nice car but he's not stuck up at all.'

Jackie glanced at her watch. 'Sorry, love, I'm going to have to dash, glad it worked out for you – happy to help,' and she was off again at a fast lope down the corridor towards the residents' lounge.

It was only five minutes till her break and Kara was desperate to see Helena whom she had decided to confide in about Bob – not everything, just what was allowed. Shell's text had both comforted and alarmed her. If Shell also knew about New Life would she be reassured or even more worried? More than she had realised she relied on her friend's common sense to be a sort of sounding board since she couldn't talk to Vicki about anything important. When she had been going out with Gerry, Shell had never made a negative comment, in fact, hadn't commented at all, but when she told her he'd been dumped Shell had immediately said, 'I think you did the right thing, babe, he isn't good enough for you,' when her parents were telling her she was mad to let him go. The other person whose opinion she had come to rely on was Helena. She admired her, of course, everyone at Church View did, but the most important thing was that this classy woman seemed to genuinely care for her. It was nice to feel special and before Bob Helena was probably the only proper adult who made her feel that way. She pretended to check the residents' toilets for something to pass three more minutes until her break. If she went into the lounge she could be at everyone's beck and call for her whole fifteen minutes.

Helena opened her door and pulled Kara inside. She was flushed and seemed excited. 'Oh good, I was hoping you'd come by. I've got news!' The laptop was open on the desk and revealed a photograph of a long curving beach and a house on a rock that jutted out at the far end. 'Let me show you and then I'll make tea – I know it's your break.'

Kara was disappointed that her whole break would probably be taken up by whatever it was that Helena wanted to show her but it would be rude and unkind not to be a good listener. 'Ok. What is it?'

'You know I told you I was looking for somewhere and I would know when I found it?' Kara nodded, her heart sinking. 'Well, last weekend and I saw this little place in the window of a travel agent. Isn't it the sweetest thing? It looks out to sea and there is a land bridge but it's almost completely isolated. Do you see? Self-catering, of course, but they'll lay in supplies – whatever you want.'

'It's lovely,' Kara said, confused by the travel agent reference. Did Helena mean estate agent? 'Are you going to buy it?'

Helena looked away from the screen reluctantly. 'No, no, not buy it. But I am going to go there.'

Kara took a relieved breath. 'Oh, for a holiday. I thought you meant for good.'

Helena smiled and closed the laptop down. 'Now, what about you? I can see from your face that you're bursting with news. Forget my place – tell me what's happening while I make tea.'

'I've met him, my dad, Bob. He's really nice and rich and, oh Helena, there's so much to tell you.' She seized on the thing that might interest Helena the most. 'He's bought me a whole wardrobe of couture clothes! Everything! A beautiful coat I've got at home and a dress and shoes but lots more. I would love you see them.' At least Helena wouldn't be jealous and snide like Lauren had been.

Helena turned, stirring the pot. 'Couture clothes? Where from?'

'Oh, it was so weird – not the shopping malls at all. There was this sort of street of factories in Birmingham and a strange house with the windows covered and inside was all white and I think it was a photography studio and this woman called Grete and she...'

'Tall, very thin, very serious?'

'Yes. Do you know her?'

Helena took both mugs to the little table and set them down. 'I may have done – a long time ago.' She added quietly, as if to herself, 'I didn't think she'd ever come back here.' She sat down and stared at Kara. 'Who took you there?'

'Bob. He said to call him Bob, not dad, just yet. He took me there. He said he wanted me to have the best to make up for all the years he didn't provide for me.'

'That's nice,' Helena said neutrally. 'And he paid for it all?'

'I didn't see him pay,' Kara admitted truthfully, 'but who else would have done?'

'So, go on?' Helena was now fixed on her in that focussed way she sometimes had and Kara felt a little uncomfortable. She had promised not to tell anyone about New Life and she needed Bob to know she was the sort of person who could be trusted. She thought of other things she could say that would put Bob in a good light.

'He took me out to a lovely Indian restaurant, a really nice one with proper flowers on the table, and to a club he kind of part-owns, I think, to meet one of his friends.'

'What about your mum, does she know all this?' Helena's expression was now almost scary it was so intense.

'I showed her a photograph I took and she said it was him but really, she's not that interested.' Kara added, 'I don't want her involved either, she'd only make trouble. That sounds nasty but I just want to have this amazing thing for myself. Not have it ruined.'

Helena looked away, finally, and sipped her tea. She must have overslept, Kara thought, as she was wearing a navy blue fleece dressing gown over what looked like grey satin pyjamas. It was the first time Kara had ever seen her dressed like this, she was always in day clothes, but perhaps she had been about to take a late shower. She had been looking forward to confiding all this about Bob but, like Shell and Lauren last night, the telling of it seemed to fall flat and she didn't know why. Finally Helena said, 'Have you got the photo on your phone?' so Kara passed it to her and she studied it, enlarging it with her elegant fingers. 'I thought I might know him if he moves in the fashion world but, no, I don't think I've ever seen him before.'

The pretty clock on Helena's desk told Kara she needed to leave – her break was over. She wanted to say more, tell her about the extraordinary event which was about to take place where Kara would be (a bit like Princess Diana who Vicki was mad about) on a rescue mission which would transform the lives of all those poor kids who had nothing and no-one. She would ask Bob if she could tell people, only Shell and Helena, after it was over. Or maybe, she would just swear them to secrecy except that she knew how that went and she daren't risk it. He needed to know he could trust her.

When she opened the door Helena said, 'Forgive me asking, Kara, but has he – um, is he affectionate with you?'

Kara laughed. 'He calls me darling and kisses me on the cheek sometimes but he's not used to having a daughter, of course. Half the time he's so busy with his phone I think he forgets I'm there. He doesn't seem to be a touchy feely sort of person at all, but that's ok. I don't mind.' She glanced into the corridor. 'Sorry,

Helena, I have to go. Thanks for the tea and I'm glad you found your special place.' She hurried down the corridor to find that Edna Simpson, who was just going into her room, had trodden a dropped bourbon biscuit into the carpet.

23

'I'm coming round after work tomorrow and you can't stop me,' Anna had said to Joan yesterday afternoon, 'you can't be out every night. I want to talk to you about something so you'll just have to take a break from Love's-Young-Dream.'

'You're very silly,' Joan had replied, rustling something which was probably one of the paper bags the grocery store used. 'I've got customers, I'll see you after 7.00, ok?'

Actually, there were a couple of things Anna wanted to chew over with Joan who filled the vacant position of mother in her life. The quiet order of Joan's house with its high-backed unfashionable sofa so deliciously comfortable, and the box of shortbread always at the ready helped Anna relax. Joan herself seemed unflappable, possibly because the shocks and losses of her life had made her stoical and empathetic.

It was another work day but Anna skipped up the steps to Harts smiling because it was the first bright blue day of the year. March, and the sky was bustling with white and blue and grey, clouds forming and reforming in the turbulence of the upper air announcing, almost shouting, that new life was erupting everywhere from cosseted garden to broken paving slab, from secret pale blue eggs cosied by warm breasts against the still-bitter winds, to staggering lambs trailing their dark cords across grass sedgy from winter. The bloom of blood red on the trees was changed now to lime, a froth of it as if splattered from a flicked brush.

To add to her good mood, Josie handed her a thick envelope with an HMP crest on it which must be the photocopies of documents about Stanley that Robert had promised her. She ran up the stairs, wiggled her fingers at Steve in his office and pulled off her coat as she crossed to her own desk. Ted wasn't in yet, there was no light on in his office, so she tore open the envelope and pulled out a stack of folded sheets of A4.

Some of the papers were copies of newspaper articles from the Cayman Islands and Jamaica and one from The Times of London dated 1941 but others were crew lists and other shipping information about cargoes, itineraries and so on. Among them was a short list of instructions to Merchant Masters from the Admiralty telling them what to do in the event of U boat attack. Anna pulled that one out and read it marvelling at its brevity and surety of tone and contrasting that with the chaotic horrors that are the eternal nature of war. It reminded her of the US instructions to school-children that in the event of a nuclear attack they should Duck and Cover as if that would do any good.

Robert had helpfully included a narrative for which the documents provided evidence and she was interested to see that he wrote fluently and vividly in a pleasingly open hand with no egotistical flourishes or excitable punctuation. He probably could have used the computer, she imagined, but had chosen to tell the tale in more personal hand-writing.

Anna finished Robert's account, sat back and sighed. She thought of Ellis, currently in double-maths, his head full of excitement like the morning sky had been. No doubt Shona figured in there but also, jostling for attention, would be the archaeology club he was starting with Mrs Whittington, the tennis club about to begin its season, worries about Big B, The Posers' first gig at a class mate's fifteenth birthday party, and things she could never know - but all infused with passion, optimism – life. Some of those seamen who had died on Stanley's ship either in the shattered engine room or swept from the plunging deck might only have been Ellis' age. They would have had heads full of hope, too. Again came the vertiginous slip in her heart because of the fragility of peace and the menace of the seething, ever-present, poorly bridled beast that feeds off the worst in us all – fear, hatred, greed, the lust for power and dominance. The thought of Ellis or Faye being caught up in the maw of that beast made her clench her fists.

As she was tidying the papers back into their envelope she saw that Robert had added a message on the back. 'I've decided not to go to university when I'm released,' he wrote, 'I've been looking into training for the Merchant Navy. There's a place called Clyde Marine Training in Scotland where you can qualify to start as a trainee officer and then I may be able to work my way up if I was good enough to be Master one day. They sponsor you so I wouldn't have to find the fees up-front either. It feels right. It will be my way of honouring my grandfather – honouring all of them.' He finished by wishing her well and saying he had been given a date when he would be discharged and there would be some day releases as well so he could acclimatise a little.

And another thing. He had decided that he would tell Az and the family in Cayman what he had done and where he now was, and about the only good thing he had, a daughter. He would tell them the whole truth because even rejection wasn't as bad as deception. He would then have to wait and see how they reacted.

By the time Anna turned into Mill Lane that evening to where Joan lived, it was dark but the lamps were visible in her front room because she had hospitably left the curtains open for Anna to feel welcome. At the open front door she hugged Anna. 'Come in, dear, come in and get warm. That wind's not died down.'

When they were settled and Joan had drawn the curtains, Anna asked her how it was going with Jakub. 'Are you still on?'

Joan rolled her eyes. 'You younger people are so romantic,' she said, '"still on"?'

'Ok, then – how is your courtship with the amorous Polish gentleman-caller progressing?'

Joan clasped her mug with both hands and looked gleeful - there was just no other word for it. 'He's a very nice man,' she said. 'He makes me laugh.'

'So, dinner, cinema, what next?'

'I know what you want to know,' Joan said crossly, 'and it's none of your business.'

'Nonsense,' Anna grinned, 'of course it is.' Joan laughed.

'The family came over here fifteen years ago because he had a brother in the city,' Joan said, 'there's Jakub, his two sons and their children but only Piotr is in the business, it wouldn't support more than two of them, and me, of course.'

'More input,' Anna said, crunching a petticoat tail, 'and less about the business.'

Joan's face took on a glow. 'He's a widower, that's why they came, really, because his wife had died and he felt there was nothing for him in Krakow and his children were wanting to have new opportunities, of course.' She sipped her tea looking into the fire. 'I like his company, Anna, I hadn't realised how lonely I was.'

Neither had Anna. Joan was always busy with something, always cheerful, always available to help and it had never crossed Anna's mind to wonder how her friend coped with spending so much time on her own. Self-sufficient as she was, there must be times when it would be wonderful to have a close companion. 'Good for you. Maybe if it goes well you could set up house together at some point in the future.' As soon as she said it, she realised that she must be unconsciously wanting to talk about her own issue.

'Oh no,' Joan replied briskly, 'for now we've decided to be friends with benefits.' Anna almost choked on her tea. 'We both like our own houses and we're used to doing things a certain way and, quite honestly, having some private space, too.'

'Ok.'

'It didn't work for George and Diane, did it?' Joan said. There had been a period of about three months when George had gone to live with Diane at Safe 'n' Sound and she was right, it had not gone well.

Anna decided that now was the time. 'Actually, Joan, I wanted to talk about something much along these lines to you anyway – about me and Steve. He's great and we're fine really but he's expecting me to move in with him and to be blunt, I don't want to, I want to live in my own house, not his.' She thought best not to mention the Alice factor at this point or at all since it did seem critical of Steve and she didn't want to moan or seem petty or both.

'And it's not just how *you* feel, is it?' Joan said.

'What do you mean?'

'How could George pay the mortgage on his own? We know Diane wouldn't move in, not that she's got much income anyway, because she would never leave the animals.'

'I suppose Steve would say I could go on paying the mortgage out of my salary even if I moved into his.'

'Could they move in with you? I have a friend who wanted to live with her partner and sold her own place and bought out half his house. A win-win situation, really, if people want to live together.' Anna considered this and knew immediately why it was impossible, but didn't know whether she could bring it up, but if she couldn't run it past Joan, who could she? It wasn't something she could talk to her dad about.

'I don't know if I could deal with – um - '

'Making love to Steve in the bedroom you and Harry shared.'

Anna grimaced at Joan. 'Yes, even apart from Steve and Alice's feelings about leaving their own house. Especially with Ell down the landing.'

'Understandable.'

'You don't think I'm being a bit over-sensitive?'

'You feel what you feel and to be fair, Anna, I'd probably feel the same. In some ways it's been a long time since you were properly with Harry but in other ways it hasn't been, if you know what I mean.'

'You're saying, give it time.'

'Well, there's no rush, is there?' Not for me, Anna thought, but what about Steve? Would he take her stalling on the marriage and the living arrangements as a rejection? She sighed.

'Thanks Joan, it is a relief not to feel pressured into it all, by you, at least.'

Half an hour later Anna was leaving, her coat hunched up against the chill, and feeling more resolute but with nothing properly sorted out. Joan was right, she wasn't ready for a major move. Meanwhile, a weekend away here and there, an English country hotel, a city break, would possibly buy time for both of them until a solution could be found, although of course the other problem, the Alice factor as she was unkindly calling it, was no nearer to being settled.

Kara would have preferred to meet Bob at his beautiful apartment or even at a restaurant for the indulgent novelty of it, but Bob has asked her to come to his scruffy shop in Erdington and must have his reasons. She was by now a seasoned Uber user and since she was never involved with paying it was a luxury that was still thrilling. By bus it would have taken her at least two hours and two freezing waits at stops but this way she was just wafted in warmth and comfort to the door of wherever they were meeting. Another world.

This time he had promised to answer any questions she had about the upcoming trip to Chisinau and give her proper instructions so she had bought a little notebook to write it all down. She had passed on her holiday dates as soon as they were booked with Church View and she couldn't believe it was now only just under a week away. There were all sorts of practical things to worry about – she didn't possess a suitcase for a start. Would she take the clothes she would need home from Bob's apartment or would he expect her to leave for Birmingham airport from there and how would that work? Had the passport arrived? There must be some kind of emergency procedure, she supposed, if you paid extra. And that was another thing – she had amazing clothes and the airfare was paid but how much money would she need to take and in what currency?

Google had said euros or dollars would be acceptable – should she have bought these? She had noticed that Bob didn't seem to realise how little money she had, how little of anything she had, and he may be assuming without thinking about it that she would provide her own money for day-to-day needs. New Life was a charity after all.

The Uber driver wouldn't let her get out until Bob arrived, following instructions he said, so they chatted for a while about nothing while Kara peered up and down the street. She was getting to know her father, she thought. Not only was he always in a rush, really bad at communicating and sticking to plans, but also he was often late. He needed someone to organise him – someone to keep his diary in order, remind him of things, to generally look after him. If his daughter couldn't do that after all he had done for her in the short time she'd known him, who could? Last night, lying awake in her narrow bed and staring at the ceiling, she had imagined a future where she might (having gained his approval from the success of this trip) be always by his side as he met important people, raised funds, organised everything for New Life. Her own new life.

A sharp tap on the window meant he had arrived. He pulled open the door for her to get out and, forgetting to greet her, hurried to unlock the shop door. In seconds the taxi had left and Kara was shivering on the pavement in her old parka. As he ushered her in he said irritably, 'What are you still wearing that for? Wear the coat you were bought when you're with me – I can't stand seeing you in that chav tat.'

'Sorry,' Kara muttered miserably. She was keeping the good coat for best but maybe people like him didn't do that. It was cold in the office and she didn't know whether she should take it off if it offended him or not. He was still wearing his own with the collar turned up. There was no sign of the striped scarf she had given him last time they met and which had cost her thirty-five pounds.

He pulled together two grubby office chairs and cleared a stack of papers off to one side of a desk to make space. Kara had been going to make a teasing comment about the place needing a bit of a makeover but she hadn't seen him in this mood before and she kept quiet. From his inside coat pocket he took a brown envelope.

'Are you paying attention?' She nodded, feeling as though she should be apologising for something, as though she was in detention at school, a disgrace that had only happened to her once when Tassie had persuaded her to cut the last lesson of the day and they had been caught. He lifted the flap of the envelope and took out a maroon passport with gold lettering. 'Here,' he said brusquely, 'don't lose it.'

Kara opened it and turned the stiff pages. At the back was a photograph of her and some printed information and a little hard pellet under laminate. She didn't like to show her lack of sophistication by asking what it was because something more puzzling had struck her. The photograph was not the one she'd sent Bob. It was her, though, so when had that been taken? In this one her hair was loose but in the one she'd sent it had been pulled back in her usual style. Grete? But that was before she knew anything about New Life. She pushed that to the back of her mind to think about later because Bob was now on to the next thing. His mouth was set in a sour downturn and he seemed to have his teeth clamped together. He hadn't smiled once since he'd arrived.

He unfolded two pieces of A4 paper stapled together. 'E-Ticket,' he snapped, 'your itinerary is on there – make sure you're at the airport at least two hours early, take one on-board bag, enough for a few days, nothing sharp like scissors or they'll take them from you at security, nothing liquid, you can put make-up and toothpaste in a see-through bag to show them.' He stopped talking and looked at her, frowning, 'I can't believe you've never been on a flight – I thought all you young women were forever jetting off to Turkey or Ibiza or somewhere.'

'Not me,' Kara said quietly and then had to cough because the words had stuck in her dry throat. 'Can I ask you something?'

'What?'

'I thought I was taking some of my new clothes but if I'm only taking a carry-on bag I couldn't fit them in.'

'Oh. Ok.' He sighed. 'I never check luggage into the hold, a couple of spare shirts does me, but I suppose you do need more being a girl. Well, you'll have to do that but don't take one of those bloody huge things.'

'Right.' There was a market stall on her High Street that sold luggage very inexpensively so she would buy a bag for herself, she didn't want to ask him for anything the mood he was in. 'When should I pick up the clothes I'll need from your apartment?'

Bob now looked exasperated and sat back in his chair. 'All right, let me think.' He frowned. 'Change of plan. The flight's not till early afternoon so I'll send a taxi to yours at 9.00 a.m. Got that?

You bring your case and your other stuff and pack what you need from the gear at my flat and I'll make sure you get to the airport in time. Wear nice clothes to travel in, you're in business class.'

'Will you come with me?'

'No.' He frowned again. 'Don't tell anyone you know me, ok? Don't mention my name. Have you got that?' His face was so stern that the eyes seemed even darker than usual and she noticed for the first time a yellowish tinge around his mouth that made him look mean.

Kara was beginning to tremble slightly and she took a deep breath to steady herself. 'Will someone meet me in Chisinau, or should I just take a taxi to the hotel?'

'Hotel.' He unfolded another piece of paper from the envelope. 'This is where you're staying – it's all paid for – but don't chat to anyone. There's always English tourists in these places and they're bored with their holiday and want to talk. Just tell them you're on business and cut them short, ok? One of Jan's contacts who speaks English will meet you off the plane and take you about. He'll be with you all the time you're working – just do whatever he tells you.' He reached into his back pocket and took out a wad of money. 'Here – euros. You shouldn't need much, it's just for emergencies, he'll pay for everything.'

Now the trembling was visible so Kara hid her hands in her lap hoping Bob wouldn't notice. 'I'm a bit scared,' she said, 'I don't want to let you down.'

There was silence so she glanced up at him from under her lowered eyelids and saw that his face was registering astonishment and something else, something she couldn't identify. It didn't matter because it wasn't irritation any more. He leaned across the desk and patted her upper arm. When he spoke his voice was different, it was like it had been when she'd met him before. 'I'm sorry, darling,' he said, 'I'm so used to dealing with men, you know. I've spooked you, haven't I? Look,' he scooted his chair closer to her, 'I've just got a lot on my mind, sweetheart, but you've got to believe we have every confidence in you. You'll do a first-class job, I know you will, and they'll all love you.'

'I hope so,' Kara said.

'Of course they will. Who wouldn't? You're a sweet, pretty girl and they'll believe every word you say. You just tell those poor kids the truth, you know, that they'll have an amazing new life here in Britain if they'll just trust you and they'll follow you like the Pied Piper of Hamelin.'

'So I'll bring them back with me?'

'Oh dear, oh dear. Let me explain, ok? Jan's contact, I don't know his name cos we like to keep things on a need-to-know basis, he'll take you to where they hide out, where they sleep at night, you know, and you'll chat with them and then he'll tell them where to go and what the deadline is. It's a kind of church hall they're told to go to, part of our organisation, and there's nice people there who feed them and give them a shower and fresh clothes – we give them all school uniforms.'

'Why?'

'Because that's how we get them out, you see. There'll be two coaches and the pretend teachers have all the papers ready except for the photos, they do those last minute, and we bring them in like it's a posh school trip to the UK. Then we sort them out to where they're going once they're here. That's top secret, by the way – but you know how to keep your mouth shut, don't you? Your job is to tell them that kind families are waiting to give them comfortable homes and they can go to school here, too. They'll never be hungry or scared again.' He laughed. 'You can't believe, can you, that starving street kids actually want to go to school when our own obese little monsters can't be bothered?'

'Mm.' Kara tried to remember her questions. 'So it's boys and girls under twelve?'

'Oh, not this trip, darling. It's just boys. We find it easier to get them through if we take one lot at a time. Oh, one more thing. I know it's tragic but some of these poor kids are disabled, you know, or sick. I feel so sorry for them but we can't take them, they'd jeopardise the whole rescue.' Kara nodded, relieved at his kinder tone. This was the father she knew.

'You'll be the heroine of Chisinau,' Bob told her, smiling now, 'and I'll be a very proud dad!'

'I've learned a few words off the internet,' Kara admitted.

'Great – good girl. I knew you were right for the job.' Bob had stood up and was pushing the chair back to its place.

'Would you like to get a coffee?' Kara asked, remembering the cafe nearby.

'Oh, sorry, darling,' Bob said, 'I can't today, there's a bit of a rush on. There is a favour I'd like to ask you though – it's why I met you here – I'll just phone for your taxi.' As he gave instructions on the phone, he was walking to the back of the office and out into the short passageway. When he realised Kara was not following him, he stuck his head round the door frame and beckoned. When she caught up with him the phone was back in his pocket and he was unlocking the heavy steel door to the spider tanks.

The same fetid smell rolled out at her as the door opened and she couldn't help choking a little and coughing. Bob was laughing at her. 'They like it like this,' he said, 'wouldn't do for us, would it?' He bent down and opened a cupboard door which she hadn't noticed before. The tanks with their long-legged occupants looked exactly the same and she wondered at their appeal for him. They didn't seem to do much and they smelled appalling. Bob was getting a tub of something out of the cupboard and then rooted round for a scoop which she noticed was crusted with dirt. He looked up at her, 'Just one scoop for each tank, ok? You can sprinkle it in the top, you'll see where, and check the water drip's running – top it up if you need to but they don't need much.'

'You want me to feed them? Now?'

Bob stood up and dusted off his hands, smiling at her. 'No, no, not now. I'm going away tomorrow for a few days, darling, could you pop over and see to them? Day after tomorrow will be enough, I'll be back by the time they need feeding again. It'll be a chance for you to get to know each other, too.' He put his hands on her shoulders and added, 'all my darlings together, eh?' Kara blushed with pleasure.

'Of course I will,' she said. 'I'd be happy to.'

Bob was checking a second ring of keys. 'These are for the front door and this one's for this door, ok?' He pulled out his phone again, 'Oh, and I'll give you the Uber account number so you can come and go easily, give me your phone and I'll put it in. I know you won't take advantage.'

'No, no, of course not,' Kara said quickly, an idea already forming.

As Bob locked up the taxi arrived but he didn't rush off. Before he opened the door for her he took her parka hood in his hands and pulled it playfully forward so the fake fur framed her face. 'You're a beautiful, smart woman, Kara, I'm proud to have you as my daughter, but when you get home promise me you'll burn this, ok?' Then he leaned forward and kissed her forehead and his compliments and the warmth of his lips carried her home.

24

Alice was wearing her best clothes and had pinned a scarlet paper flower in her silver hair. She was sitting almost rigid with excitement in the back seat of Steve's Yeti with her legs stuck out in front and her hands clasped round the box of chocolates she had made Steve buy for her to give to Briony, explaining that 'ladies expect to get chocolates.' The plan was that while Alice was consulting with Briony about dresses, hair and protocols, Anna and Steve could go off for a walk round the farm so as not to get in the way. Kimi had not been mentioned. It was an arrangement that suited everyone and spirits were high as they drove into the countryside along lanes edged with greening woods and newly-slashed hedges.

Kimi was, as expected, in the stable yard, her wellingtons plastered with fresh horse manure and wearing a filthy padded coat. As she came over to greet them, Alice averted her eyes. 'Why don't you have a ride instead of a walk?' she asked, 'I could saddle up a couple of horses in no time. You'd love it, Steve.' Anna turned to grin at him. She knew why he would not accept this offer but was going to try to make him say it.

'If she wasn't here,' he said, jerking his head in Anna's direction, 'I would tell you that I can't ride because of a climbing injury or something, but since she is, I'm going to have to tell the truth and admit that I'm terrified of horses.'

'What? Why?' Kimi folded her arms and lowered her brows. 'They're magnificent creatures – nothing to be scared of.'

Steve looked at the ground and Anna couldn't resist. 'He fell off a donkey that bolted with him at Skegness when he was a tot,' she said, 'and bawled about it for hours afterwards, to say nothing of nightmares!'

'I'm not letting you talk to my mum ever again,' Steve laughed, 'far too much ammunition.'

'All the more reason you should overcome your fears,' Kimi said sternly. 'If I'm going to come climbing with your wretched club, then the least you can do is learn to ride. Anna loves it.'

'Shall we go in?' Anna suggested hastily.

Briony was in the spacious sitting room curled up on one of the Chesterfields wearing a boxy smoke-blue sweater and jeans with a bridal magazine on her knee. A stack of them were littered nearby on the floor. When she saw Alice she opened her arms and called, 'Darling! Come and kiss me, we have so much to do!' and Alice almost swooned on the spot with joy. Anna felt a little dizzy herself – this was a side of Briony she had never before witnessed.

While they were getting their boots out of the car and pulling them on, Anna teased Steve about the arrangement that seemed to have been clinched without his agreement. 'She'll have you bruising your tail with the sitting trot, you know,' she said, 'and she'll probably give you that big, bad-tempered stallion she keeps just to torment people like you!'

'Just shut up about it,' Steve said, nudging her so she staggered and had to hop about with one boot on and only a sock on the other foot. 'I'm thinking of developing an allergy.'

'She'd probably rub your nose in some beast's mane to cure you!'

'Oh, hell, she probably would. Stop laughing.'

Although the fields were damp and spongy and the paths criss-crossed with trenches of thick mud, it was glorious to be out striding along together in the fresh, sweet air. Anna linked her arm through Steve's as they splashed along talking over George and Diane's trip to Scotland and how soon Alice's grandparents might have her again so they could have a weekend to themselves. This reminded Anna of what she wanted to ask.

'You know your grandfather was in the Merchant Navy?'

'Mm.'

'He must have been the right age for the Second World War and I was wondering if he was in any of the terrible sea battles there were, like the battle for the North Atlantic. Was he?'

Steve tucked his chin down into the collar of his fleece. Their breaths were turning into clouds as they spoke. 'I don't know. It's never been mentioned but dad rarely talks about him – I'll ask when I call him about a date to have Alice. Why?'

So Anna told him about Stanley's war record and how profoundly it had affected his incarcerated grandson. 'I think Robert's making a mistake not letting me tell Kara who he is,' she added, 'especially now that he's told his family in Cayman. Kara is on Facebook, too, and they might contact her if he doesn't make it clear he hasn't and in any case, she should know, she's a lovely girl and I think she would be open-minded about where he is and what he did and she'd let him explain to her.'

'Mm. His decision, though.'

'I know.'

At a rise in the path where they could see the canal gleaming beneath them, Steve stopped and took Anna in his arms. 'Are we all right?' he murmured, and she noticed how his skin looked steel blue in the chilled hollows of his face.

'Yes. Yes, we are.' She was pressed into the warmth of his jacket and could feel the thumping of his heart. 'I do love you, Steve, we'll work it out.'

He bent to kiss her on the lips. 'That's all I need to know.'

By the time they got back to the stable-yard they were warm and pleasantly tired from the walk and Kimi was, thankfully, nowhere to be seen so no dates for Steve's induction could be settled. They washed their boots off under the tap in the yard and threw them into the back of the car hoping that a coffee might be on offer in the kitchen. The back door was unlocked so they let themselves in but the house seemed deserted. 'Hello?' Anna called, 'Anyone there?' There was a clatter of feet on the stairs and Alice appeared glowing like a Christmas fairy.

'Go away,' she ordered, 'we're not ready yet!'

'Ask if Briony minds if we make coffee.'

Alice shot off and then reappeared. 'She says you can and she wants a pressed one, but don't come upstairs!'

'Espresso?' Steve mouthed to Anna who shrugged and nodded. They found the necessary things and brewed up deciding to also try out the electric milk frother that was on the counter top. Anna had coveted one for some time and had almost decided to give one to George as a birthday present.

When Briony and Alice joined them for coffee and hot chocolate, it seemed that all important decisions had been made. 'I'm going to wear a rose-pink satin dress with a gold circlet – that's a crown that goes round your head,' she explained to Anna, 'and silver slippers, not shoes, Briony says, and carry a posy of lily of the valley, that's flowers.' It seemed that for these feminine matters Anna was the go-to adult rather than Steve although Alice would probably have far preferred Faye.

'Wow,' Anna said politely.

'We decided in the end that shocking pink with purple polka dots might be too unsophisticated,' Briony put in, winking at Anna.

'I've seen Briony's clothes,' Alice breathed reverentially as one who has been to the summit of the mountain, her mouth rimmed with chocolate foam, 'and I want some just like that when I grow up.'

'We need to get her measured for the dressmaker,' Briony said, 'could I borrow her next weekend and take her over there?' Alice gazed at her in awe.

'Of course,' Steve said, 'just let me know what time and I'll make sure she's ready.'

When they were back in the car and Alice was belted securely into the back, she said, 'I think that Briony is the most beautiful person in the whole world. I'm her best friend.'

'Well, as one door closes another opens,' Anna said before she could stop herself.

'You say silly things,' Alice remonstrated, 'Briony never does because she's a princess and a queen.'

The kitchen table was heaped with stuff and George and Diane were in a state. The campervan was to be packed this weekend so they would only need to buy food before they left in a few days. For reasons Anna was not going to question, Diane had brought her stuff to the house rather than leave it at the farm where the campervan was. Technically, it was George's turn to cook but that was probably going to be a task too far since it was already late afternoon. 'Dad, do you mind if we have a Chinese for tea?' Anna asked when there was a lull, 'I just fancy it.'

Ellis came in and flung his coat on the old chair. 'He's been an ergate all afternoon,' he said, nodding towards his grandfather but misjudging the mood.

'I'm not an idiot,' George huffed, 'I'm trying to cope with things that I knew where they were being moved!'

'Not an idiot,' Ellis said, laughing, 'an ergate. It's a worker ant characterised by the complete absence of wings and a very small thorax.'

'Give me strength,' Diane muttered. 'George, did you find that tarpaulin in your shed?'

'It's got holes in,' George said helplessly, 'I'll have to buy another one.'

'How about we leave you to it? I want you to help me with something, Ell. Just shout if we can do anything, Dad.'

'The footie's starting in half an hour,' Ellis protested.

'Ok, so let's make a start.'

Ellis' room was worse than when Bobble was in residence and something had to be done. She pulled open the old wardrobe door and they both stared at the contents. 'I haven't seen the back of this cupboard since I was a kid,' Ellis said, 'why can't it just stay this way?'

'There's a jumble sale next weekend at the church to raise funds for the women's refuge in town so let's just make some piles, ok? Keepers, jumble, tip?'

'How do you know? Do you ever go to that church, Mum?'

'I go and sit there sometimes like your dad used to. I've even been to a couple of services. I like it, I like Andrew, you know, the vicar – he's the real thing.' She picked up a deflated plastic football. 'What about this?'

'That's the one I scored the winning goal with two years ago, I want to keep that. Why did dad go?'

Anna stopped pulling things out and let herself remember Harry, especially the time near Christmas, it must have been about three years ago, when he had knelt at the side altar, his face softly lit by candles and tried to sing a carol. He hadn't known her but it had been comforting to kneel by his side. 'I think he found it peaceful,' she said. 'But I knew about the jumble sale because there's a poster on the supermarket notice-board.' She reached forward and picked up a sweater that was crisp with mud. 'I'm throwing this out.'

'I can't even remember whose that is,' Ellis agreed, tossing it on the tip pile. 'What happened to that woman you were stalking?'

'Oh, she's ok. That situation is in a bit of a hiatus at the moment but I'm thinking of giving it a shove forward - using my considerable powers of persuasion, of course.' She picked up a large rock with an ammonite in it and raised her eyebrows at Ellis.

'Definitely a keeper – I might make a rock garden up here.'

'No, you won't. How's – um – Shona?'

'Dumped.'

'Really? That was quick.'

'She's a bit of a snob, Mum, to be honest and she was rude about Bean.'

'Not having a go at you Ell, but posers are ok and snobs aren't? I always thought posers were snobs who didn't want to admit it.'

'For goodness sake, Mum,' Ellis groaned, dropping a hamster cage on the jumble pile, 'The Posers are not only ironic, they're making an important social statement, I don't know why you don't get it.'

'Maybe I'm just being eristic,' Anna said, nudging him with her elbow, 'do you get it?'

'Greek for a pain in the bum?'

Anna laughed. 'Not far off! Look it up.'

Kara was relieved it was only going to be her and Shell tonight. She'd known Lauren since they were in infants together but she could be quite catty sometimes and she didn't want to have to deal with that. As she walked quickly down the hill towards Shell's house, keeping a sharp look-out for Wally Wanker, she realised that she needed to explain at least something to her friend because to go away in between now and her wedding would seem just weird or even hurtful. From the flight schedules Bob had given her she saw that she would only be gone for five days, not a fortnight, and she wondered why Bob had asked her to take so long off? She hoped very much that it meant she would be involved in settling the boys in good homes. She could be a link between Chisinau and England – a friendly face they could trust.

'Keep out my fucking road!' It was him. He was swaying from side to side just ahead of her so he must have been waiting to jump out and even though the temperatures were below freezing he was wearing only a loose T shirt and saggy jeans. Kara rapidly crossed the road away from him and almost ran the rest of the distance down to the brightly lit pedestrianised High Street. Everyone said that Wally Wanker was harmless but that didn't stop him being scary. The gossip was that his mum and dad were brother and sister but that was just the sort of thing people said. It was true he'd never actually hurt anyone, as far as she knew, but it wasn't nice to have someone shouting and swearing at you.

Shell's house was up towards the park and Kara liked going there because her mum and dad made her welcome and sometimes she got to eat with them but it was too late for that tonight so Kara bought a cone of chips and was eating as she went along. She was trying to decide how much, or how little, she could tell Shell without breaking Bob's rules.

When she arrived they settled in Shell's room without delay as her parents were out and Kara saw that the extensions were laid out neatly on the dressing table with a block of little post-it notes, Shell's proper scissors and a comb. 'What are the post-its for?' she asked.

'Once we've cut them we need to know where they'll be pinned on the day. Do you see? I'll cut each one to curl a certain way but they have to be placed exactly the same as we do it today and I thought this would be a good way to remember – give each one a code, like F1 for Front One.

Kara immediately grasped the situation. 'How about I do a drawing of your head and we label each one to match the place on the drawing? I could do two side views and one back view – oh, and one top view.'

'That's brilliant, Kar!'

'So shall we pin them in now and then you can trim them?'

But Shell sat down on the bed and pulled out her dressing table stool for her friend to sit on. 'In a minute. I just want to see how you are – you've not said much and, to be honest, I am a bit worried about him buying you all those clothes when you hardly know him.'

Kara sat and thought about how much had happened with Bob and how she could possibly explain how huge it had all been – and would be. Her life had grown so big, almost as though she had won the lottery. Three weeks ago she worked as a carer, had a boyfriend she didn't like and parents who seemed not to like her. It had seemed ok, but now she saw it was a narrow, empty life. She realised that she hadn't checked Tassie's blog for over two weeks. Why should she? Her own life was much more exciting with taxis and meals out and gorgeous clothes but mostly, far better than all that, a proper father who cared for her and the chance to do good for those poor children. She thought about them each night, imagining how cold and hungry they must be, and whispered to them that she was coming, that she was on her way to rescue them.

'I know it must seem strange, Shell, but it's all right, honestly. I can't tell you much but my dad's involved with a charity and the clothes are so I can help him with that because people dress up for – fundraisers and things and he knew I couldn't afford them on my wages.'

'What charity?' Shell asked immediately.

'I can't tell you.'

'Why not?'

'I'll explain one day but I can't now. In fact, I'm going away to help them for a few days soon but it won't make any difference to your wedding plans, I'll be back in good time for that.'

'You're going away? You never go anywhere.'

'It's just a different world, Shell, that he's in. Please, be a friend, be happy for me.'

'Ok. Just promise to tell me if you're ever made to feel uncomfortable, ok? Promise?'

Kara hugged her. It would be good to know, when she was alone in a foreign country, that Shell was here thinking of her and was just a phone call or a text away. Bob hadn't told her she couldn't make a phone call, had he?

Then the business of the evening began and everything else was forgotten.

Shell's parents got back around eleven and her dad insisted on driving Kara home which was very nice of him because both girls were triumphant but exhausted. Helena had been right, the extensions gave Shell a full, bouncy head of hair that worked perfectly with the light veil she would wear.

As she passed the sitting room at home Kara called out a 'good-night' since she could hear that the television was still on, but there was no reply. She cleaned her teeth, brushed her hair and cleansed her face, patting moisturiser into the skin. She needed to make a list of things she should pack for the trip. Fortunately, she was on a late shift on Monday so she could pop down to the street market and get a case or bag of some kind. She had not told Shell she was going abroad, that just seemed too big a thing to reveal, but at least she had told her something and Shell had not freaked out about her being away between now and the wedding.

She climbed into bed and pulled the duvet up around her thinking about her other plan, the one Bob didn't know about. When he had given her the shop keys so she could feed his spiders she had immediately thought of what else she could do. For ages she had been aching to do something to help him, something a thoughtful daughter would do, and she'd been stuck for ideas but now she knew. The estate agency was in a dirty, neglected state and she knew why – he was too busy with New Life. It was no wonder no-one called about the properties in the window, it looked so messy and uninviting, but one thing she did know how to do was clean. There was running water at the shop and a kettle to heat it so she could just take a bucket and some cloths, a cleaner, some spray polish, a pack of screen wipes for the computers and she would generally tidy up. If she had time she'd mop the floor, too, but she'd have to go out and get a mop to do that if there wasn't one in the back room. She could imagine the look of surprise and delight on his face when he came back.

She turned over in bed and smiled to herself. He really did need looking after – his coat was a good one but he seemed never to brush it and from the way his shirts looked she was sure he just got them from the dry-cleaners and then threw them in a pile somewhere. And what did he eat? Apart from the Indian meal they'd had she'd never seen him eat anything and suspected that he made do with ready meals and bar snacks. That was probably why he was a bit moody sometimes and why his skin had had that yellowish pallor. If she was sharing his apartment with him there would always be fresh fruit in a clean bowl on the work top and a fridge full of salad and vegetables and posh sea-food. She imagined standing at the gleaming hob and cooking the only dish Vicki had ever taught her, chilli con carne, and he would be choosing just the right wine to go with it. She must remember to call in sick so she could have the whole day.

By the time the streetlights went off at midnight, she was asleep.

25

As Anna passed Steve's office at work on Tuesday morning he saw her and leaped up to open the door. 'Hi, are you ok?' he asked, sparkling down at her.

'More than – a little tired, but definitely worth it.' She regarded him lasciviously. 'I'm thinking of keeping you, if you're not careful.'

He laughed. 'Thank the Lord for inventing sleepovers, eh? I do have something to report, I didn't stop you just to get a rave review.' Anna snorted. 'I had a word with dad last night and asked him about grandad and the war.'

'Oh yes?'

'It's no wonder I didn't get told about it at my dad's knee when I was a kid. Grandad had the ghoulish job of fishing the dead bodies of airmen and so on out of the English Channel.'

Anna shuddered. 'What dreadful times they were.'

'So - are you busy today?'

'Mostly just routine stuff but I am thinking of leaning on Robert Johnson again to let me contact Kara. I don't know why it's bugging me but it is. It's like the feeling you get when you've forgotten something – I haven't forgotten her at all, quite the contrary, but I feel I'm missing something or there's something loose somewhere. I just feel anxious about it.'

'From what you've told me it doesn't make sense any more for him to hold off. Ok, he doesn't know if she knows Graham Brandon isn't her father but you would know how to tell her so she wouldn't be too traumatised and she's got to be told some time.'

Anna nodded and laid her hand on the arm holding open the door for a second and then moved off to her own desk. The room was buzzing with chatter and laughter, unusually so, and Anna looked quizzically at Suzy across the room. Suzy mutely pointed at Jonathon and then made a head-swelling gesture so he must have scooped a fat bonus for some case. But Anna knew it wouldn't just be the money, it would be the excitement of tracking down a lost beneficiary or a whole slew of them who had no idea they were just about to become a little or a lot richer and in some cases hadn't even met the person who had died. That made her think of the poor young men in the cold waters of the English Channel and then Stanley who had met his own untimely end. She opened her emails and scanned the list. There was one from Robert which she immediately opened.

'Hi Anna,
You'll never believe this but I got a message back from Az the next day after I told him. He says they all believe I acted right to defend my mum and have nothing to feel shamed about and, to tell the truth, I wouldn't be the first one in the family to be detained at her Majesty's pleasure! He says they're all getting ready for me (and maybe Kara?) to come out there. He says they are already filling the freezer with red snapper and conch stew for me!
So, I was wondering if maybe you're right? Maybe you should tell her? Would you do that? I know you'll know what to say.
What do you think?
Best, Robert
p.s. I'm so excited about everything I can't sleep!

Anna forced herself to think calmly for a minute. She couldn't rush off now as she was not officially employed to support Robert Johnson any more but she couldn't bear to put it off too long. Maybe she could just phone Church View and see what time Kara finished her shift? If she was on second shift it would be no problem to see her after work. In the light of Robert's email she didn't feel obliged to keep her promise to Helena to whom Kara could explain the next day anyway, if she wanted to. But what excuse could she give to the receptionist? Maybe instead she should phone Helena, tell her a relative of Kara's had asked to get in touch and get her to set up a meeting with Kara? She was, after all, on the spot, but Helena's peculiar accusation towards Anna made her cautious. Certainly Anna couldn't go to Kara's house.

Her mobile rang but she didn't recognise the number. 'Hello?'

'It's Helena. I think I need to talk to you.' Anna stared at the phone. She had just been thinking of the woman and whether to contact her and here she was. It was uncanny.

'From Church View?'

'Yes. How are you?' And how did she have Anna's private number? 'I hope you don't mind, I asked Mrs Bandhal for your number – I made some excuse about a book. A lie, obviously. She also told me you had worked for Harts Heir Hunters and I looked them up.'

Anna was tempted to say that Helena wasn't alone in bending the truth but was more intrigued by the conciliatory tone of voice. The last time Helena had spoken to her was very different. 'How can I help?' She wouldn't reveal that she still worked for Harts until she knew what was on Helena's mind.

'I don't know if you can, and I do realise that you might not want to after what I said, or implied, but would you at least meet me for a coffee, maybe, so we can talk?'

Helena was happy to take the train from Bromsgrove into Birmingham so she didn't have to negotiate the city traffic and they arranged to meet in Grand Central (a second-hand name that jarred on Anna) in Caffe Concerto on the mezzanine. If Anna walked fast she could be there in ten minutes and if she was late back she would just have to think of some excuse for Ted. Anything to do with Kara had to take precedence over the other jobs on her desk and what else could Helena want to talk to her about? So much for her avowed professional ethics, she thought wryly, as she left the building for personal reasons half way through a working day.

The atmosphere was still breezy and fresh as Anna made her way along the tow-path into Brindley Place to stride through the ICC and Centenary Square past the magnificent new library and down to New Street Station. It was good to be out of the office on a day that was neither wet nor cold but there was a nagging worry. On reflection, Helena had sounded a little desperate, as she must have been to swallow her pride and phone even after she had discovered the nature of Anna's work. And that was another thing – maybe this had nothing to do with Kara and Helena, thinking Anna was not currently in work, as she had told Mrs Bandhal, wanted to ask her to do some genealogical sleuthing into her own family which Anna would refuse.

The Bromsgrove train wasn't in when Anna arrived so she waited under the high translucent dome to see if she could spot Helena rather than going up the escalator to the café, but soon realised the folly of this. A passenger could come from any one of four directions or bypass the central area and go directly up the shopping and eating floor above and it would be easy for them to miss each other, so she took the escalator up and found a table for two overlooking the vast concourse.

In fact, she did spot Helena beneath her walking quickly past the Pret a Manger wearing a very long leaf-green trench-coat and grey slouch boots which suited her slim, tall figure and silver hair very well. People turned as she passed and it wasn't so much beauty, Anna mused, as confidence, what people used to call 'presence.' Hadn't someone mentioned something about her being a model, or having a model agency? Anna could well believe it and straightened her own back and ran her fingers through her windswept hair since gaining nine inches in height all of a sudden was unlikely to happen.

But it was Helena who seemed the more flustered as she threw off her coat and sat down. For a few minutes there was the distraction of ordering and then the two women faced each other. 'Thank you for seeing me,' Helena said.

'I must admit I was surprised to hear from you,' Anna ventured.

'Well, I did think long and hard before I asked Mrs Bandhal for your number but then, when she told me you were a probate researcher, I suppose she knew that from your references, I wondered if I had misjudged you.'

Anna said reluctantly, 'You were only looking out for Kara – I do understand how odd my interest may have seemed.' She was still fencing, still giving nothing away because, glamorous and interesting as Helena appeared, she was very much an unknown person and Anna had her own defences raised. What was Helena doing living in Church View anyway? The coffees and pastries arrived which Helena had insisted on paying for so there was a pause while both women sipped and nibbled. Anna wanted Helena to make the next move.

'But, I did wonder, because of your job, whether you wanted to see Kara about her father?' Anna stopped eating and waited because she didn't know what to say. Admitting to Helena that she knew Kara's biological father would be as much a betrayal of Robert's orders as telling Kara since Helena would be under no obligation to keep the news secret. The fact that Robert seemed now to want her to make contact didn't mean she could tell someone else before Kara herself.

'Her father?'

'Her real father – Robert Johnson.'

She stalled for time. 'Kara knows that Graham Brandon isn't her real father?'

Helena was now impatient, realising that Anna was revealing nothing. 'Yes, yes, she knows. She was told by Graham himself in a fit of anger only a short time ago.' She stared at Anna and added urgently, 'You know, don't you? You know about Robert Johnson?'

'Did her mother tell her?' Anna asked, still wary.

'Kara found her birth certificate and then got someone to help find him after her aunt had given her his date of birth.'

So all this had been going on when she had thought the situation was completely stable – Robert locked up and Kara continuing her normal daily life. The alarm bells, the intuitive anxiety had been right. But, this way could make everything easier for her, no need to explain after all. 'So she knows his circumstances?'

'Yes. She was quite surprised but seems pleased now.' Helena did not seem pleased, she looked worried.

'Pleased? How do you mean?' Much as Kara might like Robert, may come to love him when she knew him, pleased was an odd thing to feel after finding that your father is on a life sentence for murder. Also, it was a mystery how Kara could have found out about him. Records of term-serving prisoners are not easy to come by. Perhaps the same aunt told her what had happened in the week that Kara was born and that's how she knew. 'How did she find out?'

'The social worker at Church View, Jackie, was able to give her some details and then when she met him - '

Anna almost leaped out of her chair. 'Met him?' she shouted, so that some nearby customers turned and stared. 'What do you mean, met him?'

Helena was as startled by Anna's reaction as Anna had been by her statement. 'Well, I drove her to his house in Redditch but we didn't see him and then she took it upon herself to go to his business in Erdington and actually introduced herself. They seem to be getting on very well, and she's excited, of course, but I'm a little concerned.'

'No,' Anna said firmly, holding up her hand. 'No, Helena. This man, whoever he is, is not Kara's father. He is not her father!'

'But Kara's own mother confirmed it was him from a photo Kara took!'

'What?' Anna's brain was whirling.

'And Jackie researched the name and the date of birth – she found him.'

'Do you have her number?'

'Kara's?'

'No, Helena, this Jackie's. Do you have the number?'

Helena was beginning to stutter in the face of Anna's intensity. 'I don't, no, but I can get it. Sheila in the office could give it to me. But what makes you think - ?'

'Do it,' Anna said, 'call now.' Her thoughts were running fast and clear now. 'Don't tell her anything, ok? I don't want her contacting Kara. Just – um – just tell her you may want to trace someone and how did she find this Robert Johnson, something like that – don't alert her that anything's wrong but get the full name and date of birth that she used.'

'I don't know if I can - '

'Of course you can – you care about Kara, don't you?' She leaned forward. 'Helena, Kara may be in danger – bloody well do it.'

When Helena phoned Church View her voice was a little shaky Anna was worried to hear, but she wrote a number down on her napkin, entered it and took some deep breaths. When she spoke again, this time to Jackie, she sounded calm. Anna heard her make a plausible excuse and then some pleasantries and then she adopted just the right casual tone to get the other information, seeming as though she half knew it but was impressed with Jackie's skills over getting precise details. When she hung up she looked at Anna.

'Name?' Anna demanded.

'Robert Grenville Johnson. Kara said that her aunt had told her he had an unusual Christian name as well as Robert but she couldn't remember what it was – Grenville's unusual, isn't it?'

Anna heard the slight pleading tone in Helena's voice, an admission of concern, guilt perhaps, and wondered how long she had known that Kara believed she had found her real father. But that was for later.

Date of birth?' Anna asked, trying not to snap. She was using the small notepad she always carried.

'Kara told her it was the thirtieth of October, 1977. It must be a huge coincidence to have two people of the same name born in the same area on the same day, surely.'

'It would be,' Anna said tersely, 'but it's the wrong name and the wrong date.'

Helena reared back in her seat, the blood draining visibly from her face. 'I don't understand – was Kara given the wrong date by her aunt?'

Helena may not have understood but Anna did. She knew exactly what had happened; it was a mistake that all proper genealogists, professional or amateur made sure didn't happen, but her thoughts were racing ahead. This man must have known he was not Kara's father so why did he let her go on believing he was? And Vicki, Kara's mother, how could she identify him from a photo when she must have known it wasn't him? What on earth was going on?

'Anna?'

She was already finding the number for Church View as she answered Helena. 'Kara said thirteenth - Jackie heard thirtieth. That's why we write everything down.'

'Oh God,' Helena said, her hands to her mouth, 'oh God.'

After a minute's phone conversation Anna rang off and stared across the concourse while plans rapidly formed and re-formed in her brain. She leaped up and grabbed her coat. 'I have to go. Kara is not in work and I have to find her.'

'I'll come with you!' Helena cried out. 'Wait, I can call her now.' She found the number and then shook her head at Anna, 'Switched off.'

'Give me the number.' Anna quickly entered it in her phone. 'I don't want you to come with me – I need to move fast. I'll run back to the office and get a colleague to do some checks and while he's doing that I need to go after Kara. What you must do is find that address in Redditch when you get back and text it to me and the name of his business in Erdington if you have it.'

'Oh, please, let me help!'

'That's how you can help,' Anna said, 'I need that information from you as soon as you can get it. Don't tell anyone about this and don't try to contact anyone. Do you promise?' Helena nodded, ashen faced. 'When I know anything I'll tell you.'

Helena glanced at her watch. 'There isn't another train to Bromsgrove for an hour. I'll get a taxi,' but Anna was already out of the café and running across the mezzanine.

26

The Uber driver had given Kara a puzzled look when she got into his cab with a large plastic bucket full of bottles, sprays and cloths. She was wearing her oldest jeggings and hoodie and the parka which, of course, she had not burned.

It was freezing in the shop and for a few minutes she hunted for a heater of some kind but couldn't find one so she decided activity would solve the problem. She looked round the littered grimy office space and smiled. She would work a transformation. In the back room she found, against expectations, a new mop and put the kettle on to boil the first of several quarts of hot water. She would, of course, work from the top down so she would tidy first and then clean the computers, the desk tops and cupboard and shelf surfaces and then finally sweep and mop the floor. It would take a few hours but it would be worth it.

She started by stacking and tidying the papers in the in-trays on each desk and then put them to one side so that the desk surface could be wiped. There were three desks and she couldn't help noticing, despite working fast, that the documents, letters and so on were at least six months out of date. Had he actually gone out of business but didn't want to say? Certainly the photos in the window were faded and curling at the edges, but even if he had problems it would be a morale boost to see the place looking much fresher and it was all she could do for him at this point. She would feed the spiders last so that she didn't let out that horrible smell to breathe while she was busy. She had plugged in her ear-phones and jigged a little as she worked when her favourite songs came on.

By two o'clock she had done everything except the floor and was starving. She popped the steaming bucket of frothy water into the kitchen thinking that it would be quicker to top it up with more boiling water later and use that rather than start with fresh as she would have done at home. She locked the front door carefully and hurried down the street to the café. While she waited for her sausage sandwich she thought that she had accomplished far more than she had expected in a couple of hours and that it would only take her twenty minutes to finish up. Maybe she could do even more than she'd planned.

Back in *R J Letting* Kara looked round with pleasure. The computers and desks had cleaned very well and weren't old at all as she had thought. Brushing the upholstery of the chairs had brightened them and the whole place seemed cheerier. She was less sanguine about the potential of the floor which was badly scuffed and stained but she would do her best. Should she buy flowers to put on each desk? It would be expensive and Bob might think it silly so she decided against it. He didn't seem a flowers sort of person.

Lunch had given her new energy and sweeping and mopping the floor, although not as rewarding as doing the furniture, didn't take that long. It was, as she had suspected, more age than dirt that marred the laminate boards. If it had been her business she would have replaced the floor or put down a nice hard-wearing carpet. She looked around. To one side was a large filing cabinet and on the top a stack of papers in an old shoebox labelled 'Filing'.

She opened the top drawer and shut it again as the slings were not orderly and helpfully labelled, but were skewed and adrift and it wasn't at all clear what the system, if there was a system, was supposed to be. The second drawer down was just as bad but the bottom drawer didn't have any slings at all. She knelt on the floor and pulled out a brown paper packet which turned out to be a thick business-style envelope which was folded over and held closed with a rubber band. When she started to slip the perished band off, it snapped, so these packages must be years old.

Kara hesitated. She knew it wasn't right to pry into other people's things even in an office and she wouldn't need to use this bottom drawer if she was going to try to file things, impossible though that seemed. She was just being nosy. In any case, these old packages were probably just ancient property details or advertising and kept in the bottom drawer to weight the whole thing down so it didn't fall over when more than one drawer was pulled out. She opened the envelope carefully and peered inside. Yes, they were photographs but not of houses. She slid the first one out and saw it was of a boy of around ten or eleven. His face was dirty and his eyes were squinting at the camera. He wore a jumper with holes in it and had no shoes on his feet although it seemed like a cold place.

Could this be one of the street boys that New Life had brought to England? Had she stumbled on the pre-digital photographic records of the kids they'd brought over who might now be in their late teens or twenties – the same age as her? Of course there would need to be documentation for the charity to go about its business and it would make sense to photograph the children before they were processed. Nowadays, there would be no need for paper records. She turned the photograph of the boy over and saw a name scribbled on the back – just a first name which she couldn't read – and a date which could be a date of birth. One by one she drew more photos from the package trying to imagine what these children would now be doing. They could be studying at university, or even married with children of their own and would have become British citizens, wouldn't they? She hadn't realised New Life was such an established charity but then, Bob told her so little.

She put the package back and picked up another one. There was no rubber band on this one so she unfolded it and took out the first photograph. At first she couldn't understand what she was looking at and turned the photograph round to try to understand. Then, horrifically, she saw exactly what it was and threw it from her with a cry. She wanted to jump up and run out but a dreadful fascination, almost a disbelief, overcame her and she took another photograph and another from the envelope until she turned and vomited her sandwich on the still-damp floor.

'You stupid little bitch,' Bob said. How long had he been standing by the door? She hadn't heard or seen him come in.

She wiped her mouth with the back of her shaky hand. 'Someone's been using your office to store this disgusting, wicked pornography,' she said, feeling the bile rise again in her throat, and her heart hammer in her chest, 'you've got to call the police!'

But Bob turned and locked the door with the keys she'd left on the nearest desk and bolted it and then he took three strides towards her and yanked her to her feet by her hair so that she screamed. 'Shut up,' he spat at her, 'shut the fuck up.'

Then he half-dragged, half-carried her down the passageway and, holding her against the wall by the force of his forearm across her throat, he unlocked the steel door and shoved her inside so that she fell badly and hit her head. The next thing was her bag being thrown at her and the door slammed shut. For a few minutes there was silence except for the ringing in her ears and then the door opened again and Bob came in, shutting it behind him.

When Anna burst in to Steve's office he didn't have to be told that something serious was happening and he let her talk without interruption. 'It may not be dangerous,' he said, 'just some lonely man who wants to believe he has a daughter and doesn't correct her or he may even believe she is his if he put it about a bit when he was young.'

'Maybe, but Steve, I have to try to find her and I have to talk to Vicki. Will you phone me if you discover anything about him? You don't have to say his name, you can say it in code, I'll understand.'

'Ok. I'll be in touch. But be careful!' She heard him lock the door after her and drop the blinds and she knew he would be bringing up the NCA site on his dedicated computer.

Ted was strolling down the corridor towards her, peering in through the big windows to check his researchers were all working. 'Ah, Anna,' he said, 'So good of you to pop in on a working day.'

'I can't explain now, Ted, but I've got to go. Just dock my pay or something but I have to.' Without waiting for an answer she rushed past him, catching his elbow with her shoulder bag and shouting an apology back at him as she ran. Steve was right, of course, it could be perfectly innocent but her gut told her it wasn't.

The traffic out of town wasn't too bad yet and she drove as fast as she dared down the A38 towards Bromsgrove. Where could Kara be? She had already tried her three times but the phone was still off. Again, there could be a reasonable explanation – she could have forgotten to charge the battery or be on a course or at the dentist, anything. She tried to calm herself down by thinking of any possible scenarios which would involve a man believing or pretending to believe that the pretty young woman turning up out of the blue was his daughter. And, it seemed as though this had been going on for a few weeks. And what about Vicki? The only possible innocent explanation was that Robert Grenville happened in some extraordinary coincidence to look like Robert Lindo.

Just as she was turning into Kara's estate her phone went and she pulled over to the side. It was Helena. 'Yes?'

'I'll tell you the address of the Redditch house and then text you to be sure,' Helena said breathlessly. 'Have you found her?'

'No. I'm on my way to talk to Vicki.'

'I couldn't find the business in Erdington but it's something to do with property, Jackie said. I phoned her again but I was very careful.'

'Ok.' Anna was scribbling in her notebook. 'There's something I wanted to ask you anyway. You seem to have known about this Robert Grenville Johnson for a while. What made you concerned? Why did you call me?'

Helena couldn't keep a tremor out of her voice. 'She told me about the wonderful couture clothes he had bought her and I asked where from and she said not a shop, but a place like a studio in the city centre and when she said the woman's name, the woman in charge, I knew it – the name.'

'Tell me.'

'She said her name was Grete so I checked that it was the same one by her appearance, extremely odd and distinctive.'

Anna was staring out of the car window trying to make sense of this. 'How did you know her?'

'I used to have a model agency in Birmingham and in the nineties there was a scandal around this woman who also had an agency. There had been gossip for some time that her models were far too young - most of them were from Eastern Europe - but she always insisted they were at least sixteen and she had written consent from their parents. We thought they were more like twelve but she kept them closely guarded and no-one ever got a chance to talk to them. It was when some unscrupulous fashion houses were promoting heroin chic, of all things, and very thin, pale girls and boys were in demand. Well, the next thing we knew the police had charged her, the girls had disappeared and her agency was shut down. To cut a long story short, she served time. I never thought she would ever come back to Birmingham but perhaps she had nowhere else to go.'

'She was involved with trafficking?'

'We didn't call it that then. At that time we probably thought that the girls' families were exploiting them for money and that what she was doing was a bit dodgy in taking advantage of that.'

Anna chewed on her index finger and tore a nail painfully. 'What else do you know about the whole situation? Tell my anything, everything.'

'I don't think he's behaved inappropriately to her sexually, Bob, I mean. I asked her if he did anything to make her feel uncomfortable and she laughed and said no. She seemed to be almost protective of him. Of course he may believe she is his daughter. He may have had several girlfriends when he was a young man.'

'Yes.'

'She has a very close friend, Shell, short for Michelle, I imagine. She might have said more to her?'

'Ok. I'd better go. Thanks.'

Anna texted Steve the Redditch address and sat for a few minutes trying to sort all this out in her head but only coming up with more questions. She glanced at her watch. It was three-thirty and Vicki may well still be at work but she had to do something. She drove on slowly until she reached Kara's house, noticing that the four-wheel drive was parked at the front. She locked her car and walked up to the door to ring the bell. After the second ring the door was snatched open.

'For crying out loud...' a man began and then stopped. 'What? What do you want?'

'I'm here about Kara,' Anna said, 'are you Mr Brandon?'

'What's she done?' He narrowed his eyes. 'Who are you?'

'I'm representing her biological father,' Anna said, mentally crossing her fingers and reviewing how professional she would look to him. Fortunately, he could only see her severe black coat and not the fleece underneath.

He passed his hand over his close-cropped hair. 'I don't know anything about all that,' he said, 'I'm just the sap who's put food on her plate and a roof over her head for twenty years. Look, I've just driven down from Scotland and I'm cream-crackered so - '

'I need to talk to Mrs Brandon. Is she in?'

'No.'

'Can you tell me where I can find her?' He gave her the name of an optician on the High Street and she walked away knowing that he would phone Vicki the minute the door was closed. He had looked exhausted but she didn't get the sense of any guilt. Rather the opposite.

Not knowing where else to park she went back to the supermarket and then crossed the street and went up to the pedestrianised shopping area. A man with a walker told her where the optician was and in less than ten minutes from leaving Graham she was stepping inside to confront Vicki. Anna knew immediately which one she was because of the hostile look in the woman's eye. Vicki was carefully groomed and had the kind of toned body that only comes from a gym, shown off by a smart suit that was just a touch too tight. When Anna introduced herself, using the same phrase as she had to Graham, Vicki opened the door of a small examination room and nodded her in.

'What do you want?' she said, the minute Anna was seated on a stool.

'It's about Robert Johnson,' Anna replied, 'I think you might be able to help.'

'I haven't clapped eyes on that bastard for twenty years,' Vicki said.

'But you recognised him in the photo on Kara's phone?'

'How did you –   Look, I don't know what she's told you but I know nothing about him. Ask her.'

'You did know he was serving a life sentence? Didn't it surprise you to know that Kara had met him?'

Vicki rolled her eyes. 'They let them out after five minutes these days.'

'So you're certain the man on the phone photo is Kara's father?' At this Vicki's eyes flickered. Anna decided to press hard. 'Isn't it true that the man in the photo was not the Robert Johnson you knew, not Kara's father?' She held her breath.

Vicki barely paused. 'He could have been. He had dark hair. How do I know what he looks like now?' but she did not seem surprised at Anna's question. 'I have to get back to work.'

'You haven't asked if Kara is ok,' Anna pointed out.

'Why shouldn't she be, she's at work, isn't she?'

This was getting nowhere, so Anna asked for Shell's number and place of work and got up to leave.

'He's not done anything wrong, has he?' Vicki said. 'He bought her a lovely coat.'

Outside in the street Anna tried again to get an answer from Kara's phone with no luck so she checked one more time with Church View only to get the same, more irritated answer. She was stamping her feet against the cold and wondering what to do next when Steve called.

'I can't tell you on the phone,' he said, but she caught the intensity in his voice. 'Come back in – we need to talk and we need to gather as much information as we can.' Talking to Shell would have to wait until later. Anna strode back to her car and drove into Birmingham trying not to let her imagination whirl out of control.

27

Kara had not got up from the floor as she didn't trust her legs to hold her she was so nauseous with pain from the blow on her head. She was pressed into a corner of cupboards so that one of the metal knobs dug painfully into her back but she sat very still clutching her bag Bob that had thrown at her because it seemed the safest thing to do. The instinct to stay small, stay still, (predators are excited by movement) came from some ancient, animal part of her brain. But the sick feeling in her stomach came only partly from fear of what might happen; the images she had seen had imprinted indelibly on her mind and she knew that she would never in her whole life be rid of them. She had no idea such things happened in the world.

If Bob hadn't said anything she would have assumed, as she told him, that these old packets of photographs had nothing to do with him, but he had said something so now there was no doubt. He knew they were there and he knew that because he was implicated in the evil exploitation they documented. It took her only seconds to understand the bitter irony of the New Life enterprise and what her role would have been in it. Bob's laughter and words in the car came back to her – that she was overqualified. Of course she was – what they wanted was exactly what she was offering: naivety to the point of stupidity, friendliness, enthusiasm, to be an example in her lovely clothes of how well people lived in the UK, so that the starving, desperate street boys would listen to her, be a little seduced by her, believe what she promised and follow her to hell.

Bob was still looking at the spiders in their tanks, tapping the glass to check each one was alive and mobile. He started talking in his usual way as though nothing had happened. 'You know why I keep these creatures,' he asked, 'I keep them to remind me of how the world is. People don't like thinking like this but the natural world, so-called God's Creation, or even more ironic, Mother Nature, has one principle that rules the whole thing – might is right. The strong live and the weak die. These spiders are no different from daddy polar bears that hunt down their own cubs and eat them. Life is about survival not sentiment.' He looked round to make sure Kara was listening.

'Or hyena packs that follow a zebra separating herself from the herd to calve. They follow her because they know she will be helpless when she's giving birth so they can move in and kill her.

With the bonus of the tender new-born foal, too, clever little doggies. Every creature uses the toolkit life has given it to exploit all other creatures for its own needs. The mistake people make is thinking humans are any different.'

Kara made no response. She wanted to ask him what was going to happen to her now but she daren't. His calm narration was like a documentary sound-track. He was not frightened or rattled or threatening and there could be only one reason for this, couldn't there? She was never going to be able to tell anyone what she had seen, what she knew, who she knew. He had already made that decision. Her mother had told her he was no good and she had ignored her. Something like a high-pitched humming was making it hard for her to hear him and she was glad of it. She wished he would shut up.

But Bob wanted to continue the lecture. 'That's where do-gooders go wrong because they think that human animals are different from these creatures here who wait patiently for little innocents to make a mistake – including their own species, their own lovers in some cases. We're not different - we eat, shit, and fuck just like all the other animals. We just like to pretend we're better – most people are hypocrites or fools. Why do we have so many laws, so many prisons, so many ways that we're taught to feel guilt and shame? Why? Because we are just as ruthless as any other animal, that's why, and the big beasts that are at the top of the heap get there by exploiting the suckers any way they can. The tough ones like me, the winners, want what we want and we'll destroy anything that gets in our way because we're animals and the world is a jungle and we know it.' His tone changed from calm reason to irritation, 'What's the matter with you, lost your voice?'

Kara made a huge effort. If she could keep him talking something might happen, someone might come. 'There are good people,' she said, almost choking on the words her throat was so tight and dry.

'Typical bottom-feeder wishful thinking,' he laughed. 'The big con that all the little boys and girls get told, that everyone should behave nicely and obey the rules. That's great for those at the top – great for life's winners who take just what they want because those obedient, good little proles make life so much easier for them, for us. So what do we do? We pat the good, docile ones on the head and tell them how wonderful they are so that no-one notices how efficiently we take everything from them. Look at wars – the profiteers and stay-at-home politicians are the real winners, aren't they, not the saps that get killed and maimed and get given medals for it. That's what ceremonies are all about – blinding people to how they've been used.' He snorted derisively. 'It's always been the same. It's the nature of the beast.'

'But those children - ' Kara began.

Bob dropped the lecturing voice and started shouting. 'You think they're so innocent? They'd cut your throat for a penny if they could! They're worthless scum – they're nothing. Don't give me your comp school witless sentimental crap – children are as selfish as anyone else!' He thrust his hands into his trouser pockets and glared at her.

He seemed to have talked himself out and sank down to the floor. What was he waiting for? Surely he didn't care what she thought of him now so why was he going on like this? But it was a relief not to have to listen to his voice and she realised that among the pain and fear that throbbed through her body was a sort of weeping deep inside that the man she had thought was a kind, loving father who cared for her was lost. He was no good – she had been warned and hadn't listened. But he hadn't finished.

'If you'd been to a proper school,' he said contemptuously to her as she watched him silently, 'you'd know there's only two kinds of people, masters and slaves, winners and losers. You learn it behind the cricket pavilion, you learn it at night in the dorms, you learn it fast when you're small and weak and you never forget it. The ones you'd call the nice ones get the worst of it.'

Cricket? Dorms? It sounded like Harry Potter or Downton Abbey or something, but definitely not Nechells comprehensive. What was he talking about? The woman at the cottage had said he was at a different school with her husband somewhere – Kara couldn't remember where – but had then corrected herself. A huge hope leaped up in her. Maybe he was not her father at all? But if she said anything, if he knew she had figured that out, did that make her more or less vulnerable? After all, despite her fears he hadn't hurt her, except when he threw her into this room and he hadn't threatened her. Maybe he would treat her better if he believed he was her father. She took a deep breath through her nose trying not to inhale the filth in the air.

Anna had to tap on Steve's locked and blinded door to be let in. He opened it and she slipped in wordlessly seeing he was on the phone. 'Yes,' he was saying, 'yes, I'll see what I can find.' He made a small gesture with his head and she sat on one of the two swivel chairs as he paced. All the Harts' screens were crowded with icons but there was one screen which appeared blank. She knew that he wouldn't let even her see classified material and she respected him for it. After a couple more minutes of grunting he ended the call, sat on the other chair which he scooted across to his desk, and turned towards her.

'Have you found her?' he asked. Anna shook her head and he sighed. 'It's bad. I'm sorry.'

'What?' Anna was aware of that familiar draining away of emotion that she now could identify as shock, a useful survival mechanism allowing the brain to function. Those intuitive alarms about Kara's vulnerability, those little nagging anxieties, why had she not taken them seriously?

Steve ran his hands through his hair so that it stuck straight up which would have been comical if his expression had not been so worried. 'Robert Grenville Johnson is well known to NCA – they've been trying to pin him down for years but each time he's slipped the net.'

'Drugs?'

'Worse. He's a procurer and probably a perpetrator, Anna. He transports vulnerable kids from Eastern Europe for people over here.'

'Trafficking? Why don't they just arrest him?'

'There's no evidence that would stand up in court. He keeps changing the border scam for getting the kids in and then they disappear. Not one of them has ever been tracked down and interviewed.'

'So how do they know it's happening? I don't understand.'

Steve stared at Anna miserably. 'The only ones they find are the dead ones. Canals, gravel pits, two thrown down a mine shaft. Over the last three years there have been twenty-two of them, boys and girls, all under fourteen. You know how good modern DNA identification is and forensics generally, well, they've traced them back to places in Eastern Europe. Of course some police authorities have better data gathering than others but street kids and runaways may sometimes have a DNA presence on official records because of petty crime and so on. The investigators were pretty rigorous following stuff up even though no-one cared about them in some jurisdictions. But there's nothing solid to link them to the traffickers and users. Not just Robert Johnson's bunch, of course, there are dozens of cells here.'

'So from the numbers of dead children found, they know there must be live ones?'

Steve nodded. 'And the investigators have been talking to the kids who are still over there on the streets and once they'd got their trust the older kids told them about those they knew who had gone, who had been taken away to have what they were told was a new life here – the specially selected attractive, healthy children. "The lucky ones" the older kids called them in the reports I've been reading.' Steve stood up as though sitting was too passive, too impossible. 'From what they were told the investigators think that there are hundreds over here just from his operation who've disappeared into various kinds of exploitation.'

Anna stood up too, rubbing her upper arms and trying to make sense of this. 'But Kara is a grown woman, Steve, so she wouldn't be of interest, would she? And why would he risk letting a stranger like her into his world? He must have known she wasn't his daughter?'

'I don't know why – it is strange for such a secretive man. He may have believed she was his.'

'But wait, did he grow up in Birmingham?'

Steve glanced at some densely written notes on the pad he always kept by his computer. 'Just a minute.' He turned a page. 'No, he was born in Warwickshire and grew up in Knowle – must have had a well-off family because he was educated privately in Shropshire, it seems.'

'So, if Kara told him that he met her mother at a high school in the centre of Birmingham, he would know that he was not her father, wouldn't he?'

'Mm. But we don't know what Kara's told him, do we?'

'We need to find her but I don't know how,' Anna said. 'She's not answering her phone, she's not at work, her mother doesn't know where she is. What can we do, Steve?'

'Ok. Give me her number and I'll pass it on. They can track a phone even if it's switched off and if they have his as well, which I was just going to follow up on, they might be able to locate the phones at least, Anna. They've had the Redditch address for some time and now a flat in Edgbaston but they can't find any evidence of his activities at either place. He's too smart to leave a trail.'

'Isn't there a business of some kind in Erdington – a property business?'

'Yes, *R J Letting*, but it's been pretty much abandoned. The team would like to get in and poke around but they've got no reason for a warrant and it seems he's never there anyway. The local traders say they've never seen him – don't recognise photos of him, although they may just want to stay out of a police investigation.'

'Or they're scared.'

Steve took her hands in his. 'Look Anna, it's horrible, but there is no reason to believe that Kara is anywhere near him right now. She might just be skiving off work for the day – he may be out of the country or anywhere. There's nothing to put them together so try not to worry. Keep calling her and get Helena to call, too, since Kara trusts her but aside from that I don't see what you can do.'

'Ok. I'll let you get on. I need to talk to Ted anyway if I'm going to keep my job and then I'll phone her friend, Shell.'

As soon as Steve locked the door behind her she was off down the stairs, struggling into her coat and calling out to Josie on Reception, 'Tell Ted I'll phone,' and then through the glass doors, down the blue-brick steps and along the canal to Harts' car park. In the car she googled the address, set her sat-nav and accelerated fast out of the security gates.

Bob now had his back to Kara and was crooning endearments to Brucie, his favourite. Kara realised that for almost the first time they had been together, he was not in a hurry to leave. Why? He had not taken off his coat despite the close, rank air in the spider room and seemed almost relaxed now. A horrible, terrible thought struck her. Was he waiting for someone? Was he waiting for someone like Jan or Jan himself? Now, in this new reality, Kara remembered neither the compliment Jan had given her or the politeness with which he had addressed her – she remembered only the brown bear with its unflickering eyes, its steady, predatory gaze.

She softly drew open her bag, grateful there was no zip or clasp to make a noise, and put her hand inside to grope for her phone. She felt the familiar objects, the tissues, the little purse with an owl motif, the scarf she had taken off and stuffed in when she arrived so it would not absorb the nauseating smell of the spider room. Her fingers probed, searched.

'Looking for your phone, darling?' Bob said kindly, not turning round. 'Not there, is it, sweetheart?'

'I need to phone mum,' Kara croaked. 'She'll be worried.'

'I doubt it,' Bob said thoughtfully and turned round to face her. 'I've never met her, of course, but I somehow don't think she's the type to bother. Just a feeling, I could be wrong.'

'No, she will. She'll be worried. Where is it?' And it took that long, those five seconds for Kara to take in what he had said. Should she ignore it? How could she, he had said it deliberately. She had to respond. 'What do you mean, you've never met her?'

Bob opened the cupboard door and slowly measured out one scoop of food. 'Here you are, precious,' he murmured to the end cage, the one nearest the door. 'Look what Daddy's got for you.' He tapped gently at the scoop until it was empty and then turned to look at Kara. 'Attribute this quotation,' he ordered, '"Man is the cruellest animal" – no? Oh, I forgot, you're only a state-educated semi-literate aren't you? What about this one? "People don't want to hear the truth because they don't want their illusions destroyed." No? Well, I'll tell you then. Friedrich Wilhelm Nietzsche. Heard of him? Why do I bother asking?' He shook his head from side to side as if in despair. 'Ok, I'll try an easier question. Why on earth would I – even at the priapic age of nineteen - disgust myself by having sex with trash like your mother?'

'My mother isn't...' He was on her in a flash, his hand choking her throat.

'Don't contradict me, bitch,' he said. The fingers loosened and she was free and gasping for air. He stood up, the livid yellow around his mouth like a curry stain. 'Look what you made me do – bad move.' He stepped away breathing heavily and bent again to the spider food cupboard.

So he was not her father. Was that better or worse for her? She couldn't think straight. 'Where have you put my phone?' she asked in a thin voice. It was her only connection, her only possible way out of this. 'I've got all my numbers in it. Just let me phone my friend. I won't tell her anything but she'll be worried – we're supposed to be meeting up.' Of course Shell wouldn't be worried, she wouldn't have even finished work yet but what else could she say?

Bob spun round from the second tank. 'Meeting *up*? Meeting *up*? You can't even speak English can you? God, no wonder this country's in a mess.' He turned back to the tank. 'Here you are Dolores, *mi amor, te ves guapa, no*? Come to Papa.' His voice changed. 'You can stop whining for your phone, you must remember it accidentally fell out of your pocket into that bucket of hot water you were slopping about like a skivvy.'

'No, it didn't…' Kara's voice tailed off.

Bob again turned to look at her. He sounded genuinely puzzled. 'What the fuck were you doing anyway?' Kara bowed her head. He kicked the foot nearest to him. 'What?'

'I was cleaning to make the shop look nice for you.' She did not look at him.

Bob yelped with delight. 'You really *want* to be a slave, don't you? The poor really do rejoice in their chains! Ha! Why don't you come here and lick my boots, darling, really humiliate yourself. Would you get off on that?'

Stung, Kara raised a defiant face to him. 'You wouldn't understand. I was trying to do something nice but I'm glad now that you're not my father. You're sick and you're evil.' He didn't punch her or throttle her as she half-expected, he just tapped the tank of the first spider he had shown her – the Sydney Funnel-web spider.

'Did you hear that, Brucie?' he asked. 'Did you hear what this low-life said to your Daddy? That's not nice, is it?'

Her blood up, Kara demanded recklessly, 'What are you going to do with me? Tell me!'

Bob turned away from the tank. 'Me? I'm not going to do anything. I'm not even here, you see, so I can't. I never was here today – I'm actually in Eastbourne at a meeting. I popped back for my laptop, my special one, and here you were, stupid cow. But this one, Brucie, he might do something because you might carelessly put your hand in his tank when you feed him, mightn't you? He doesn't really like you any more now you've been nasty to me, do you, my pet, and he can be a bit irritable if he's upset, so, you know, accidents happen, don't they, and I have this funny feeling that one is about to happen round about now.'

He was silent and Kara's heart beat so high in her throat she thought she would choke, but then he spoke again. 'I'm going to be so broken-hearted when I hear the news – it will be like losing you twice. Hey, that's good. I'll use that when I'm interviewed by the police, make a great headline for one of their tabloid chums. It's not my fault that you deceived me, is it?'

He left the tank and kneeled beside Kara, lifting her chin with one finger until she was forced to look at him. 'Think it through, Kara,' he whispered, so close to her face that she was forced to breathe his breath. 'Even a silly girl like you can work out how this story is going to end.'

Kara closed her eyes.

28

Anna parked in an adjacent road and walked back to *R J Letting*, her hands thrust deep into her pockets. It was very cold and raw, one of those bitter March days that make it hard to believe that spring will ever come. She walked quickly past the estate agency only glancing at the window but it seemed deserted. Mesh grilles covered the windows and there seemed to be no light on inside despite this being a working day. She turned and walked back more slowly and then stopped and pretended to look at the properties mounted on grubby panels. They were all over two years old.

So would the shop be a cover? For what, though? What purpose could a defunct agency serve? She cupped her hands around her eyes and peered into the space beyond the listings to see if she could discern anything. Near to the window it wasn't hard to see a desk and chair with a computer and filing trays on it looking surprisingly clean. It seemed from the grey shapes behind it that the entire space was taken up with other desks as might be expected. But as her eyes became more accustomed to the dim interior she thought she could make out a faint source of light coming from the back right of the office space and then, with a shock of recognition, she saw draped over the back of a desk chair, a dark green parka. 'Shit,' she breathed. 'Shit.'

Outside the convenience store in the next street she phoned Steve. 'What? You're where? Anna!'

'I know it could be anyone's, I know that. One in two women are wearing them this year but Steve, I had a really good look at hers when I followed her to Church View that first time and I think it is the same – the fake fur trim is a little bit ratty like they get after being worn for a while and it's the same shade of green.'

'I can't get them to produce a search warrant on the basis of you seeing some ratty fake fur,' Steve said with a touch of irritation and then, more kindly, 'Even if she is there for some reason it doesn't mean he's around.'

Anna had an idea. 'I'll call you back.'

She fumbled in her bag for the little note pad and pen and then walked up and down the roads within fifty yards of the agency. Most of the parked cars were work vehicles of some kind or had registrations before 2016 – this was not an up-market area. Only two vehicles stood out – a BMW with the current year's plate and an

Audi with last year's code. The BMW had a briefcase on the back seat but there was nothing in the Audi. Anna called Steve again to give him the makes, models and plates and then found her own car and got in turning on the engine and the heater up to maximum.

Shell answered almost immediately sounding wary. 'Yes? Who is this?'

Anna suddenly realised that introducing herself was going to be tricky because she didn't want to reveal anything about Robert Lindo or, come to that, about where she worked since she was officially off the whole case. On the other hand, she needed to get Shell to trust her. 'It's about Kara,' she said, 'I'm a probate researcher working on behalf of her biological father. I need to talk to you.'

There was silence on the other end. 'I don't understand,' Shell said at last, 'he isn't dead, is he? She would have told me.' Smart girl, understandably confused.

'No.' Anna took a deep breath. 'Look, Shell, I'm going to tell you the truth which even Kara doesn't know. This man she thinks is her real father isn't. There's been a mistake so he is either pretending to be or believes he may be her dad.'

'Is she in trouble?'

Now it was Anna's turn to pause for thought. Eventually she said, 'Probably not, but please don't say anything to anyone. The police and other people are working on finding him and her right now so please don't say anything in case it gets out to the wrong people.'

'How can I trust you?'

Good question. Anna stalled for time. 'I've seen Vicki and Graham but they don't seem to know where she is.' She thought about telling Shell about volunteering at Church View in case Kara had mentioned her but that wouldn't help. Helena might have warned Kara off her so Kara might have told Shell that she was a weirdo of some kind. 'Please, Shell, I can't prove at this minute that you can trust me but I really am working with her genuine father. We had no idea until today that she thought this other man was him but this other Robert Johnson could be dangerous and we're worried. Did she say anything about where she was going today?'

'She isn't at work?'

'No.' Anna couldn't keep the disappointment out of her voice. Clearly, Shell couldn't help.

'She told me she's going away next week with him or for him, I couldn't be sure. She said she had to keep it secret but he wanted her to help him with his charity. She wouldn't tell me what it was. I thought it was strange but she just seemed so happy to have found him and he's been buying her clothes, really nice ones, and - ' Her voice trailed away.

'Have you got my number? It's Anna Ames.'

'Yes, I've saved you.'

'Please don't tell anyone about this yet, Shell. We don't know what's going on – nothing may be. But if she contacts you - '

'Yes, yes. I thought it was weird, but - ' Shell's voice was shaking. 'I should have stopped her – I should have said something.'

'You couldn't have known – neither could she. She's probably fine. Look, I have to hang up now but I'll call you when I know anything, ok?'

When she got out of the car the day had darkened and the street lights were coming on. People were hurrying along pushing toddlers in buggies wrapped up against the cold and dropping their faces into their scarves. Everyone was hunched and anxious to get home as if they had just heard that a tornado was approaching. Anna wished she had a hat with her and a warmer coat but she couldn't leave. She took another turn past the shop but this time, now it was darker, she saw that there was a light showing at the back of the room, a very faint one, but definitely a light. The parka was now appearing in silhouette, the outline of the fur hood looking like a terrified cat crouching on the back of the chair. When her phone rang she jumped.

'It's the Audi,' Steve said, 'it's registered to him.'

Anna knew what that calm tone implied because Steve and she had been through crises before. 'She's in there with him, isn't she?'

'Both phones checked out. Are you ok?'

Anna almost yelled at him. 'So what? What now?'

'Ok, listen. There's a special police unit on its way but there'll be no noise, no sirens, no marked cars, nothing to make him alarmed if he's watching. They'll just creep up until the place is surrounded and then the commanding officer will make a decision. They have full authorisation to make an entry.'

Anna had crossed the road to be out of sight and now stared at the shabby shop front. 'Steve, he'll kill her if they do that. I've spoken to her friend, Shell, and they had her lined up for a trip. I'm sure she doesn't know anything about what he's involved with but she knows too much for him to let them interview her.'

'I'll pass that on.' She could hear him breathing and for a moment felt giddy with the need to have him here, beside her, but what he was doing was far more useful for Kara's safety.

She took a deep breath herself and said quietly, 'I'll be staying here.'

'I know. I've told them.'

Anna moved off again so as not to look suspicious and decided to stand in a bus stop to get out of the wind and give herself cover. She could still see the shopfront and nothing had changed except that it was now almost completely dark. Some parking spaces had opened up outside the line of shops as workers went home and as she watched one car slipped in here and another one there and she straightened up and began to count. They must not break down the door. The cliché of the police ramming open someone's front door (that seemed to happen on every news bulletin these days) was a horrible possibility. Did they think that Robert Grenville and Kara were having a cup of tea and a chat in those squalid premises?

Men and women began to get out of cars and cluster together by the adjacent shopfronts and it would be crystal clear to anyone watching as attentively as Anna was who they were in their black quasi-military outfits and bulky belts. 'Oh God,' she breathed, 'take care, take care.'

'Mrs Ames?' The voice was so close to her ear that she gasped as she span round to see a stranger regarding her intently. The woman flipped an identity card at her.

'You can't batter your way in!' Anna hissed, 'She's innocent – she doesn't know what he's into but he won't let you take her alive, I'm sure of it.' The woman's immobile face remained unaltered.

'We don't know what she knows.'

'Oh for goodness sake,' Anna muttered, turning back to look at the shopfront. 'What are you planning?'

'We need you to remove yourself from the scene.'

Was that a Geordie accent? 'No. I won't interfere but I'm not leaving.' An inspiration struck. 'She knows me and that may be useful.'

The woman turned away. 'Just make sure you stay on this side of the road,' she said, 'or we will remove you.'

Anna watched closely, her eyes flicking from one knot of officers to another, none visible from inside the premises, unless there were cameras covering the street, had they checked? She began to tear at her index finger nail with her teeth and then stuffed her hands in her pockets.

Suddenly the quiet was shattered by a large van careering down the street with tyres screaming as it braked opposite *R J Letting*. Two men and two women tumbled out clutching cameras, cables and lighting.

Anna swore as she had never sworn before.

The police moved swiftly to contain the pulsing, frantic activity of technicians and reporters as it grew by the minute. They were like a swarm of wasps zoning in on nectar. More vans and cars screamed up and it took long, expensive minutes to herd them behind tape barriers and impose some sort of control while Anna hardly dared to breathe. Kara was in there, Kara was in danger and this was a desperate waste of time: silence and the hope of a covert operation were gone. Tactics were being reviewed moment by moment as the noise of excited chatter mounted and the media were joined by curious passers-by and local residents. Spotlights flared revealing shivering presenters checking their hair and notes and speaking rapidly to camera.

Anna leaned her forehead on the cold Perspex of the bus shelter and tried not to yell or weep. The early TV news would have its story, the tabloids would have their headlines and by tomorrow the broadsheets would have picked them up, too – social media would go crazy. Even now phones made small spots of light among the swelling crowd, looking incongruously festive like Christmas lights, as footage of the *R J Letting* shop front and the tense knots of officers promised the possibility of lucrative sales to media outlets hundreds, thousands of miles away. It was a feeding frenzy held at bay only by five-centimetre plastic tape.

And yet there was no change in the still centre of everyone's attention. The shop front was dark with only that same faint gleam of yellow from the back. There was no movement, nothing to see. Gradually, as the minutes passed, the chatter of the crowd became muted and the chill wind tossed the day's litter around the street and some onlookers shook their heads and slipped away to home and warmth. One or two of the luckier presenters had blankets round their shoulders but the lack of action and the raw March night subdued the restless crews like puffs of smoke into a hive.

Anna, her hands and feet aching with cold, texted George to say she would be late home and not to wait dinner and wondered if it was possible that Kara and Bob were not in there at all, even though their phones might be. But that would be worse, wouldn't it? Wouldn't that mean that Kara had been taken somewhere else, to an untraceable location, or she might even – Anna gasped at the thought – she might already be dead either in the building in front of them or in a ditch, a back street, a wood. The lack of movement in front of scores of watching eyes may be because all life had ceased.

'Anna.' Helena was beside her suddenly and was holding out a thick paper cup. 'Coffee – warm you up.' In reply to Anna's puzzled look she added, 'It's on Twitter already – hashtag "brumstakeout."'

'But how did you know to come here?'

'I saw the name on the shopfront on 24 hour news and Googled it.' Helena pointed to the crowd. 'Like most of them, I suppose.' Anna sipped the hot drink thinking that in some ways, good and bad, social media has made villagers of us all. 'How long have you been here?'

Anna glanced at her watch and was astonished to see that it had been less than three hours since she had arrived because it seemed so much later with the empty, cordoned-off street and the numbing darkness. 'She may not be in there,' she said quietly, voicing her best hope and worst fear, and she heard Helena's breath draw in sharply with the same understanding of the implications of that thought.

The police unit seemed to have come to a decision. After some of them had slipped away, possibly to surround the shop as far as possible, the rest of them in close formation moved towards the shop door and in the lead was a black figure with a battering ram. Anna put her hands over her mouth. The noise level among the encampment behind the tape abruptly rose in response but just as the team got to the door they fell back as one body as if some electro-magnetic field had been switched on and repelled them against their will. The officers in the rear stumbled at the unexpected change of direction and one fell on his back. Anna stared so hard into the shifting darkness to try to see what was happening that her eyes ached.

Then the reinforced door opened slowly and Kara walked out.

She had no coat or bag and she stood for a moment in the bitter cold like a person turned to stone noticing neither the tense posse of armed police a metre from her or the buzzing crowd down the street. She started to walk across the road towards the bus stop, stumbling a little as though she was drunk.

Anna rushed forward tearing off her own coat, ignoring the commands of the police, and caught Kara in its warmth as the girl sank to her knees on the filthy tarmac. Kara was now shaking so hard that her teeth were chattering audibly and her eyes were rolling back in her head. Anna cradled her as tightly as she could and Helena took the other side, wrapping her arms around her.

'Stand back!' someone ordered angrily but both women ignored the command. It seemed an age before the close embrace and the warmth penetrating through to Kara's trembling body began to have its effect and her eyes focussed a little before they closed. Minutes passed as they huddled together and all Anna could think of was that whatever had happened to Kara in there she was, at least, still alive.

A gentle Birmingham voice spoke now, close to Anna's ear. 'It's ok, ladies, we're not going to do anything, take as long as you need.' Some kind of covering was draped over Anna's exposed back and she could see that Helena, too, was being wrapped up as she crooned to Kara over and over again that she was safe, she was ok.

Finally, Kara opened her eyes and there was consciousness in them. She looked from Helena's face to Anna's and back again but said nothing. Someone must have been watching carefully because now two new women in green and yellow jumpsuits nudged forward, crouching to be close to the three huddled on the ground.

'We're medics,' one said calmly, 'we need to get you to hospital, love. Kara, is it? We're taking you to hospital so we can look after you. Nothing bad is going to happen, we just want to check you over, sweetheart, ok?' Then, without asking permission, the two put their arms forward and gently and efficiently took Kara from Anna and Helena and lifted her upright. They scrambled to their feet reluctant to let her go.

'Can we go with her?' Anna asked, but the medics had moved off and now a policeman was with them.

'No, we need to interview you so you need to come with us to the Station.'

'No,' said Anna quickly, 'if you want to interview us you can do it at the hospital.' She turned to Helena. 'My car's nearby, let's go.' They ran towards the ambulance driver to get his destination and then ducked under the police tape and pushed away microphones and cameras until they were clear of the mob. While Helena checked there was no-one following, Anna drove off through a zig-zag of side streets until it was safe to turn on to the main road.

At the hospital they were firmly told that they would not be allowed to see Kara but they could wait in a small family room. Anna checked her phone, running through the list of worried texts from Steve but stopping at the latest sent only minutes ago. It was a long message and she re-read it several times. She knew Helena was waiting anxiously for any news she could give but she wasn't ready to do it yet. Instead she opened a text from George telling her that a portion of hot-pot had been put aside for her and that the neck of lamb had turned out especially tender. He had signed it, 'love ever, Dad,' and added a smiley face which was the extent of his interest in emojis. She paused on the screen to let the comfort and sanity of home unfreeze her shock.

'Kara's going to need every friend she's got,' she said finally to Helena.

'Did he hurt her?'

'No.' Anna wondered if it would be better for Kara if he had – bruises, abrasions, nothing too serious, of course, but visible evidence.

Helena's voice was low when she spoke again. 'Did he molest her?'

'I don't know.' Anna straightened her back and looked Helena in the eye. 'I'm going to tell you what happened because I know you care about Kara but it can't get out – it can't be leaked. If it does, I will know you are the source. Do you understand?'

Helena nodded, her fine brows already drawn tightly together. 'Did she find a way to lock him in there?'

'No.' Anna paused, not wanting to utter the words. 'She killed him.'

Helena's hand flew to her mouth. 'How?'

'There's a special kind of comb – I've seen it at my hairdresser's – it's got a metal spike tail.'

'A pin comb,' Helena said immediately.

'Yes. She must have had one in her bag for some reason.' Anna took a deep breath. 'She stabbed him through his ear into his brain.'

'Oh, God.'

'She must have used all her strength to do it – it penetrated five centimetres through his skull.'

The two women sat silently staring at nothing but the appalling image in their minds. Kara had a light build and a sweet, accommodating personality. What on earth had happened in that shop to drive her to such a brutal act? Anna didn't know her very well but she suspected that she would have suffered even rape rather than do such a violent thing. So what had Robert Grenville done or what did she believe he might do that would force her to kill him?

An alarming thought struck her. She brought up the news on her phone and saw that Kara Brandon's name was out – her Facebook profile photo splashed all over the stories. Interviews were being scrambled together with her friends, her co-workers at Church View, any source the media could trawl. Detectives were filmed removing her computer from her home although there was no sign of Vicki or Graham. 'Kara, the Carer who Kills,' was just one headline. The thought that had come to Anna was that Robert Lindo would see all this in prison. What terrible effect would this have? He might try to escape – he would do anything to reach her if he believed she was in danger or distress. He only had days to his release, if he did go AWOL he could face years longer inside, probably in a closed prison.

Since he had no phone she rapidly emailed him to say, 'We are with Kara, don't believe news reports, I will keep you informed but STAY THERE!' Then she phoned the prison administration and asked for the officer in charge. When she was connected with him, he was calm. 'We know,' he said. 'Robert saw the early evening news and as soon as he heard the name he was off.'

'But this could set his release back weeks, months - I don't know!' Anna wailed.

'However,' the calm voice went on, 'it seems that before he reached the perimeter fence he was – um – detained by another inmate on urgent business and he is currently sedated and confined.'

'Oh, thank goodness. Thank you. Please let him know that we are doing everything we can for his daughter and that she is safe and unharmed.' There was, she suspected, a great deal more to the incident than had been revealed but she didn't need to know. 'Tell him not to believe the news reports.'

'Does anyone?'

The door to the family waiting room opened. 'I'd better go, thank you again,' Anna said and prepared herself to talk to the two police officers. It was tricky – neither she nor Helena should know what had been discovered at the back of the shop, but would it be worse to pretend not to know if they knew she did know? If she admitted what she knew would Steve be charged with breach of confidentiality, or official secrets or something, she had no idea what trouble he could be in.

'We need you to come to the Station, Mrs Ames. Ms Stansfield, you can go, but stay where we can contact you. Miss Brandon is sleeping and there's no need for either of you to be here.' It was not a request.

Anna stood up with her mind clear. 'I'll come with you but I'd like my lawyer to be present,' she stated calmly. She would phone Briony.

29

Impressively, considering it was now evening, Briony appeared within the hour at the police station looking fresh and alert in a sharply tailored black suit, ivory shirt and spiky heels. Anna felt grubby, hungry and uncomfortable but most of all, worried sick.

While she was waiting she had found no solution to the problem of being honest with the police without dropping Steve in it. He had broken confidentiality because he loved her and made her concerns his own instinctively and that had resulted in the first and probably only breach of security he had ever committed. She couldn't bear the idea of exposing him and she wished she had not told Helena. She had fidgeted on the moulded plastic seat while they all waited for Briony to arrive and tried to separate information she could reveal and intelligence which could have only come from the NCA or some similar agency via Steve.

Obviously, the result of the phone triangulation must be covert as would be Robert Grenville's known criminal associations. Most important of all she must remember that there would be no way she could know that Kara had killed Robert so that knowledge must be hermetically sealed off from anything she told the police. Steve probably had deleted his outgoing text to her but it was still on her phone she realized with a prickle of sweat down her back. What if they confiscated it? Could they do that?

On the other hand, she could tell them it had been Helena's casually imparted information about Bob over coffee which had triggered Anna's alarm about Kara and she had immediately checked for the cause - Jackie's shoddy tracking of the supposed father. Ok. But why had she been outside *R J Letting* – that had been information from Steve. Anna chewed her fingers. No, wait, hadn't Jackie told Helena that he had some kind of property business? Couldn't a rigorous internet search by her have brought up the name? Possibly. So, her concern for Kara and her discovery of a potential business in his name could have taken her to the location in Erdington, but the timing – that was hard to explain. Why would she hang around an apparently deserted premise for no reason? Well, she thought she had recognised Kara's coat which was visible through the window in daylight and having got no answer to her calls she had decided to wait until Kara came out to speak to her. She could tell them she had become tired and cold waiting and if they hadn't turned up when they did she would have gone home. She tried not to look worried.

Briony asked for a private room, listened intently while Anna explained the whole situation and then told her what to say and what not to say. She must always tell the truth, Briony instructed, but it didn't have to be the whole truth. The important parts of her story checked out – the mistaken identification and the living proof of Robert Lindo and his known history together with his own testament that Kara was his daughter but didn't know it. Vicki would corroborate his name even if she had reacted ambiguously to the photo of Bob on Kara's phone. Anna might be censured by Ted for going beyond her remit but that was not a police matter.

If the police did touch on intelligence that she should not have had then she could, in the last resort, say 'no comment' Briony said, but only as a last resort. Her best approach was to appear open, co-operative and, within limits, informative. If they asked why she wanted a lawyer present when she had not been arrested she would say that it was normal professional protocol with police interviews since probate researchers often knew things about clients that were confidential and she needed advice so as not to cross that line. Robert Lindo Johnson was her client.

'Eternal gratitude, number one superhero,' Anna whispered when Briony had finished, 'don't leave my side.'

Briony allowed herself a knowing glance at Anna. 'Well,' she murmured, 'it could be said that I owe you.'

In fact, the police interview was over in twenty minutes. Once they had facts they could verify and a plausible story they let Anna go. On the way out, when Anna had politely expressed her gratitude to the interviewing officers, Briony muttered drily, 'Better thank the universe for making you white, educated and middle-class. Goodnight.'

In her car Anna called Helena, sent another brief email to Robert Lindo and then phoned George. He picked up the weariness in her voice immediately. 'You don't have to explain anything, Annie, just drive carefully and I'll have your dinner on the table, piping hot, when you walk in. There may also be a glass of wine.'

While she had been waiting in the police station Steve had sent a brief text: 'Will phone when I can,' which she took as an instruction not to phone him so it was 11.30 before he called and George had gone to bed. 'Just wanted to check you're ok,' he said, and again she sensed that warning in his voice. Anna told him what she'd told the police and that Kara was now in hospital being checked which he almost certainly already knew. 'Any chance you could pop down to mine for a nightcap?' he asked lightly.

'How could any girl resist?' she answered, matching his tone. She turned the guinea fowl to the wall, shrugged on her coat and ran down the road.

Steve opened the front door as she turned up his short drive and pulled her to him urgently, 'I'm ok, love, I'm ok!' she cried, her voice muffled by his woolly chest. 'I was never in any danger.'

He led her to the big sofa in the living room and pulled her down into his arms. 'He was a wicked person,' he said, 'and he wasn't working alone by any means. You must be vigilant, Anna. The minute news of his violent death gets out there will be panic among some powerful people both here and in Moldova – it's such a poor country, you know, one of the old USSR satellite states, and the main place in Europe for trafficking women and children for prostitution and slavery. Not just here, of course, but in the Gulf States, Turkey and other places. They take desperate people from the rural areas and the city streets and promise them jobs and hope just like Bob was doing. We only hear about foreigners doing the trafficking on the news but, of course, they wouldn't do it if the demand wasn't here. Bob and his ilk.

'I know. I'm worried about Kara.'

It seemed that piercing Bob's eardrum and brain might not in itself have been enough to kill him but in her panic Kara had worked the steel shaft back and forwards so there had been a massive bleed which had eventually finished him. 'He must have lived for minutes – we can't even imagine what happened, what Kara witnessed.'

'Self-defence,' Anna said. 'Thank goodness she had that comb.'

Steve hesitated and stroked her hair but then said, 'There's no mark on her, Anna, no evidence of sexual assault either.'

Anna reared her head. 'But he's a known villain!'

'He's still got civil rights – no-one is allowed to kill him or assault him in any way even though he's spent years inflicting appalling misery on children.'

'Well,' Anna reassured herself, 'once she wakes up, Kara will be able to explain what happened. I know her, Steve, she's incapable of violence.'

Steve bent his head and kissed her as she lay in the crook of his shoulder and then he said quietly, 'And yet she killed a man, so it would seem she is as capable of violence as any of us might be, given cause.'

Kara opened her eyes. In front of her was a bedside cabinet she had never seen before – where was her dressing table? The light was all wrong, too, because there were vertical blinds at the window which made stripes of beige and grey which sliced the sky into iron strips. She lay very still. She was not at home – she was not in the room she had woken to almost every morning of her twenty years. She moved her eyes cautiously round. She realised what sort of room this was because she had seen it on countless television dramas and one time for real when she had visited Gerry after he'd fallen off the back of Maz' motor bike and fractured his shoulder and leg. She was in hospital. Why? She was feeling no pain.

Without moving her head she stretched out her fingers and then her toes but there was nothing unusual so she rolled her shoulders to lie flat on her back along the bed facing the door not the window. Her body felt as it always did. She pulled her hands from under the sheet and examined the palms. The right one was sore so she brought it up to her face to see better. Across the palm was a row of tiny bruises, some of them bearing pin-pricks of dried blood. It was an odd kind of injury but surely not one to put her in hospital?

She needed to pee. Carefully, she rolled on to her other side, checking first that she was not connected to any intravenous lines, and swung her legs over the side. She was wearing a hospital gown. Where were her clothes? A young nurse appeared and stared at her with wide eyes as though she was wearing a Hallowe'en mask or something. Was there something the matter with her face? Was that the injury?

'I need the toilet,' Kara said, 'could you show me where it is, please?' The nurse jerked a hand to indicate an internal door Kara had not noticed so the room must have its own facilities. Kara frowned at her in bewilderment. 'Why am I here?' She sounded like one of the Church View dementia patients, she thought. 'What's happening?'

'Someone will come,' the nurse said in a rush, and left the room almost running.

Kara went into the roomy bathroom and used the toilet noticing that there were no curtains in the shower and no towels so, much as she would have liked to, she couldn't wash herself. She soaped her hands and ran them under the tap studying her face in the mirror above. It looked the same as usual. What had alarmed the nurse? True, her hair was sticking out all over as it always did in the morning but it wasn't that scary, was it? She splashed her face and dried it off with paper towels from the dispenser. She needed to get her phone to call Shell and find out what was going on. Instantly, something stalled in her brain. It was as though a pause button had been pressed in her thoughts. She shook her head to clear it and went back to the main room.

A man and a woman were sitting by the bed and the man was writing in a little book. The woman was staring at Kara just like the nurse had done. Both wore lanyards with ID badges – police – Kara swallowed. What on earth had happened? She thought back to when she had just used the toilet. Was she sore or bleeding? Had she been raped? No. It had been normal.

The woman spoke fast and introduced herself and the other officer but the information swam past Kara as she climbed back into bed, there being no other chairs. She propped the pillow up so she could at least sit up straight. 'You are Kara Brandon of 46 Elgar Crescent in Bromsgrove?'

Kara nodded. 'Is everyone ok? My mum?'

Instead of answering the woman said, 'We need you to talk to us about Robert Grenville Johnson, Bob, can you do that?'

'Has something happened to him?'

'How do you know him?'

'He's my father, my biological father. Is he ok?'

The two police officers glanced at each other as though they wanted to check that each was thinking the same thing but didn't reply. 'Can you tell us about your relationship?'

Kara didn't like to show annoyance under any circumstances but especially not with people in authority who should be respected but it was frustrating and a little worrying that they wouldn't answer any of her questions. Perhaps if she told them whatever they wanted to know they would eventually explain why she was here. So she told them, hesitantly at first, and then with more enthusiasm how she had not known Graham was not her father until quite recently but once the truth was out she had found him and he had been kind and generous to her. (Remembering Bob's repeated cautions to her she did not go as far as telling them about the meeting at the cottage or his work with New Life.)

When she had finished telling them about the expensive clothes they looked at each other again. 'What did you do for him in return?' the woman asked and there was something nasty in the question.

Kara flushed deeply. 'Nothing. He said he was making up for all the lost years he didn't know me. He's,' she hesitated, not wanting to show off, 'he's not short of money – he's got a house and a lovely flat.' So they asked her more questions but still she kept her promise to him and said nothing about New Life or her upcoming trip to Moldova to help those poor kids.

'How did he make his money?' the man asked.

'I don't know.' Bob seemed like the kind of person who just had money and she had never thought about how he had acquired it.

'But you were happy to take his gifts even though you knew they had a luxury price tag?'

Kara said nothing. It seemed that something very unpleasant was being implied, as though she had taken advantage of Bob instead of him being fond of her and wanting to give her things. The woman leaned forward. 'When was the last time you saw him?'

Kara usually had a good memory for facts like times and dates but a kind of grey blizzard was silently whirling in her head and it took her a while to work it out. It must have been when she was at his shop – the time he gave her the plane tickets and hotel reservation and so on. She told the detectives about that time but left out the part about the travel arrangements. 'It was last Saturday,' she added, 'I'm sure it was.' It seemed to Kara that she had now done all they asked of her so she repeated her earlier question. 'Is Bob ok?'

The woman lowered her eyelids as though she scorned the query and her phone beeped. 'You'll be discharged from hospital later on today,' she told Kara coldly as she stood up, 'and you will then be transferred to the police cells at Birmingham Central Station.'

'Why? What have I done?' Kara cried, her heart pounding painfully, but they had already left.

The next day brought new revelations – rather too many for Anna. She saw Ellis off to school and left for work as normal. Luckily Ted was away at a conference so the fancy foot-work round the truth that would be vital in an interview with him could be postponed. She was hoping to visit Kara in hospital if the police allowed it.

At ten-thirty Steve approached her desk smiling with the seemingly casual suggestion that if she was not too busy they might get a breath of air and a coffee at the canal-side café. She yawned, stretched, glanced around and winked at Suzy who was watching her from the other side of the office with eyes full of mischief and got up slowly to go with him.

'Let's just walk a while,' he said, once they were outside in the chill breeze and there was tension in his voice. The lumpen gobs of stratus cloud that had been idling over the city for days were breaking up to reveal a clear, dazzling blue. Anna lifted her face to the sky letting the colour flood her eyes but the serenity didn't last long after she asked Steve whom she should approach to get permission to see Kara.

He stopped, looked down at her, his stiff peak of earth-coloured hair bending and bristling in the wind, and said, 'You can't, Anna.'

'Helena, then?'

'No.' He took Anna's hands and held them tightly as if she might suddenly dart away. 'I have news which you can't share with anyone.' The morning had brought the sensational story of Robert Grenville Johnson's macabre death so that was now public knowledge and she felt guiltily relieved that her passing it on to Helena may no longer be an issue. The wind was whipping along the canal ruffling the surface of the black water and causing moored boats to creak and knock each other. A thin humming sound came from the taut steel wires supporting pennants and flags as they frantically flapped.

'Ok.'

'They've been to see her,' Steve said, 'and it appears she has no memory of what happened yesterday.'

'The shock of it has put her into denial?'

'Or she's lying.' They stared at each other. Steve didn't need to say, she thought, that he was giving the police hypothesis not his own.

'But what do they imagine her motive would have been? She was so happy to be reunited with him as she saw it and it seems they got on well – she liked him. Helena said she seemed almost protective of him.'

Steve coughed and sunk his head lower. 'When the police went to her house and searched her bedroom they found things, Anna: euros, a plane ticket to Chisinau International, a hotel reservation and, worst of all, a forged passport.'

'What?' Anna was stunned. Kara? All she had seen was a sweet girl living an ordinary life. It was unbelievable.

'Bob was the organiser for the syndicate bringing children from Eastern Europe,' Steve went on unhappily, 'and it seems on the facts that Kara had been recruited to help him.' Anna tried to make sense of this and failed. 'You see, that stuff was at her home, it was not with her at the shop. If it had been, then you could maybe make the case that he had asked her to do something she revolted against and in the ensuing struggle she'd tried to scare him off but accidentally killed him in panicked self-defence.' He lifted his head and looked at the dark water nearby. 'She certainly knew about the sexual exploitation.'

'No, Steve, I can't believe that.'

'There were old photos in the file cabinet at *R J Letting,* very disturbing and graphic ones, and forensics have found her fingerprints on them.'

Anna buried her head in her hands. 'It's like you're telling me George is a serial killer.'

'You know your dad,' Steve said quietly, 'you don't really know Kara.'

When Vicki put her head round the cell door it was the first good thing that had happened to Kara all day. Past resentful feelings were forgotten as, twisting and turning in the confusing events that had unaccountably hijacked normal life, she finally saw a familiar face. She leaped from the bed to hug her mother. Vicki allowed that for a moment but then pulled away.

'What's going on?' she asked sharply, 'What have you done?'

Kara slumped on the narrow bed. 'I don't know! I don't know what's happening – they won't tell me. I just remember being on a dark street and it was very cold and then the paramedics came and I was in hospital and then the police brought me here. They keep asking me but I can't remember anything.'

'Shit,' Vicki said, sinking down beside her, 'I might have known you'd end up in trouble with the police. It's in your blood.'

Kara grabbed her arm. 'Don't say that! I've never been in trouble in my life! Why are you saying that?'

Vicki answered her gloomily. 'Him – your real dad, Robert Lindo Johnson – he's a murderer.'

Kara's blood froze in her veins. 'No.'

Vicki glanced at her and then away. 'You look like him – the same eyes, the same shape of head and colouring. Every time I see you it's like he's haunting me, never letting me be free of all that nastiness and shame.' She turned abruptly to face Kara. 'How hard have I had to work to live down having the child of a murderer? I married Graham, I moved house, I cut away from my friends and family. I try to make something of myself – but every time I see your face I see him – that jailbird that brought me nothing but misery and disgrace. So, this is how you thank me. It's history repeating itself.' She burst into tears and sat beside Kara sobbing, the water running unchecked down her cheeks and splashing on to her hands knotted together on her lap.

Eventually Kara said in a small voice, 'I haven't done anything.'

Vicki rounded on her. 'Liar! You must have done something, girl, something very bad if you can't or won't remember it yourself!'

Kara sat very still like a cornered mouse. 'Who did he kill? My dad, who did he kill?'

'Oh, some crack-head his mother was shagging. That's the kind of people he had.' Vicki blew her nose furiously and scrubbed at her face. 'I've tried not to think of it for twenty years and now this!' She stood up and threw a plastic grocery bag on Kara's bed. 'They told me to bring some things you'll need so I have but that's the end of it. I want nothing more to do with you.'

After she had gone Kara lay for a long time on the bed staring, dry-eyed, at the ceiling, her mind a blank. This must be an old part of the building, she thought at last (because it was a small, safe thought), as the ceiling plaster was fissured in several places. Towards the door the cracks made a kind of pattern and Kara tried to identify what it reminded her of. Perhaps someone in the room above had dropped a heavy object or maybe a tall and powerful person had been in this cell and had punched the ceiling above his head. The lines radiated out and in between them the plaster was flaking. Suddenly, she recognised it. The pattern was like a spider's web.

Kara gasped and sat up. She ran to the cell door and pounded on it, screaming as loudly as she could, 'Help, somebody! I've remembered! I've remembered!'

30

By late afternoon Kara had been interviewed repeatedly and Shell had been brought in to explain the presence of the comb in Kara's bag but she also had to admit the other thing Kara had told her – that she was going away to help Bob with his secret charity. The staff and some residents at Church View had been questioned. Kara's laptop had been thoroughly investigated and the drowned phone had yielded what data they could retrieve. Grete had disappeared as had Jan. Kara had only the sketchiest memory of the location of the Staffordshire cottage but an analysis of Bob's satnav was in progress. The spider room had been examined and sealed to await the removal of the arachnids to a safe place.

Nevertheless, either scenario concerning Kara's innocence or guilt could be argued. Kara had been an innocent dupe of her supposed father and known nothing of the real business of New Life or she had known everything and agreed to be part of it, possibly for financial reasons among others. The police would soon have to make a decision to release or charge her.

Up to this point Steve had been kept informed by a friend and colleague at NCA who was also a climber but this source was abruptly terminated by a text at 5.06. He had been expecting it, he told Anna, because it wouldn't take long for them to make the connection between himself and Robert Lindo's researcher at Harts: same workplace, same street and in a relationship. He had become too much of a security risk even though she was, they would think, only tangentially involved in the case.

Just as Anna was sitting down at her kitchen table with a mug of tea and her tablet's news feed, Helena rang. She'd been given permission to visit Kara in her cell the next day and wanted to ask Anna's advice on what to say to the young woman who found herself in such appalling circumstances.

'I don't know, really,' Anna said, 'she may want to talk rather than be talked to. She must be very scared and confused so seeing a friendly face would be the most important – someone who's on her side. Please tell her I'm thinking of her.'

The door from the utility room opened letting in a blast of cold air and George hurried in with his cardigan flapping from one button. 'Dad! It's freezing out there!' Anna protested. 'Where's your coat?'

He re-filled the kettle and switched it on. 'It's warm in the shed – it must still be in there. I'm ok, don't fuss, I just realised the time.'

'Don't worry about it,' Anna said wearily, 'I can knock something up.'

George glanced at her, made his tea and sat down opposite her. 'God invented frozen pizzas for times like these,' he said sternly, 'and we should not take his bounty for granted. I happen to know there are two in the freezer.'

Anna smiled at him. It had been a while since Diane had taken her kitchen scissors to his hair and it stood out in shaggy tufts and clumps around the pink dome of his crown, the unkempt effect being compounded by his wiry eyebrows leaping crazily in all directions. She didn't even examine his beard which was, at the best of times, chaotic. 'You need a trim,' she said, 'You can't go away looking like that. I've got Faye's dress-making scissors in my drawer upstairs – shall I have a go?'

George said tenderly, 'If you want to, Annie-get-your-gun, I'd appreciate it. You couldn't do worse to it than it's had.'

When the children were small and money was tight Anna had cut everyone's hair, letting her own go for months between appointments at the no-frills hairdresser's on the High Street. She had forgotten the pleasure of it. George sat still, a tea towel draped round his shoulders to keep the clippings off his cardigan, as she combed and lifted the strands between her fingers and snipped her way round. Soon, the kitchen tiles looked as though a goose had been plucked. She wondered if she would ever acquire her father's talent for tact. He had not asked her one thing about the current crisis, understanding that to keep going over it would only increase her anxiety. He knew she would approach him if she needed to and he knew that when she was ready she would tell him about it.

The razor-sharp, open scissors were poised over George's twitching eyebrows when the front door slammed shut and as she straightened up, George took a deep breath and Ellis burst into the room looking for food.

George was rinsing the pizza plates ready to go into the dishwasher and Anna was taking her coffee through to the front room to catch the evening news when Helena phoned again. She made no attempt to conceal the agitation and excitement in her voice. 'They're letting her go!' she said, 'They want me to pick her up and I can, of course, but Vicki won't have her at home and there's nowhere at Church View. Can she come to you? I don't know who else to ask. I can't bear the thought of her being alone in a hostel.'

Anna snapped into action. Kara must have the best bed, there was no way she could put her on the couch after her night in a police cell. She could unfold the camp bed in Ell's old room usually kept for the children's friends to stay over but it would do for herself. She pulled the denim striped duvet set out of the closet on the landing, noting in passing that the stack of linens seemed considerably reduced, and in fifteen minutes the double bed was freshly made and white towels were stacked on the ottoman with a blue facecloth on top. She turned off the main light so that the yellow walls glowed in the soft illumination from the table lamps. She wanted Kara to feel safe, to be cosy if that was remotely possible. She popped the hot water bottle with the plush spaniel cover into the bed.

She wondered if Helena would say anything to Kara about Robert Lindo and hoped she would not. The poor young woman was already dealing with a huge shock followed by the trauma of remembering the ghastly events and being interrogated about them, to say nothing of the terrible rejection by her mother when she needed her most. One criminal father at a time seemed more than enough to deal with.

There were already two cars in the drive so Helena parked on the road but Anna had been watching for them and flung the front door open as they hurried up to the house. Kara looked very pale, her freckles standing out like coffee splatters across her nose arch. Anna drew the girl to her in a brief hug and then guided her into the living room. 'Make yourselves comfortable,' she smiled, 'I'll get you both a hot drink. What would you like?'

Kara regarded her seriously as though this might be an important question. 'Hot chocolate, please,' she whispered politely. Anna had not thought to turn the television off in her hurry to prepare the bedroom and *Coronation Street* was now on. 'I watch this,' Kara said in the same small voice, turning her gaze to the screen, 'I like Craig.' The older women's eyes met over the girl's head. What better comfort at this moment, family and friends being unavailable, than to sip hot chocolate and watch your favourite soap?

If anyone needed escapism then surely Kara was that person. It was at least a start on what may be a long road back.

Kara awoke in a different bed for the third night in a row. She lay for a while looking round the room. It was still dark outside but Anna had told her she could leave on as many lamps as she wanted. Her body was comfortable but her thoughts were not. There had been dreams which had been forgotten with consciousness but they had left her tense and scared.

She couldn't think about Bob yet. When she had been forced to during her account to the police her attention had kept sliding away and they had had to prompt her to continue. She turned on her side. Vicki's tear-swollen face confronted her with the terrible revelation about her real father. Where was he? She imagined a street person scuffling from one dark corner to another or maybe he was in prison? Jackie had told them all how horrible prison was these days with the over-crowding and drugs and violence and to think of her own flesh and blood, no matter what he had done, to be in such a place for years and years made her heart swell in her chest.

She turned over to her other side. A new thought came - that Church View might give her the sack now that she had been involved in a crime. No, she must face it, she had not just been involved in a crime because unbelievably, horribly, she had killed someone. Could you inherit a murderer gene? It was too much. The terrifying thought was that another person, who was not the child of a killer, could have dealt with it all differently. She had been naïve, yes, but she had also been viciously violent. No, she couldn't deal with it. She rubbed her face and sat up.

There was no sound in the house so she got up and tiptoed out on to the landing. It was cold so she returned for the fleece robe that had been placed across the foot of her bed. Downstairs she trod silently along the hall and into a big, square kitchen. She could see fairly well without turning on a light as the moon was full. It was better to be up and moving about but not much. She went back down the hall to the living room and closed the door quietly behind her and then curled up on the sofa. Anna had said she should make herself at home but the truth was she had no phone to contact Shell and no laptop to divert herself with social media sites and she felt utterly disconnected and alone. Her finger on the volume control of the remote so as not to wake the house, she turned on the television and the flickering images of a couple checking out sunny homes was just enough to distract her from the clamour in her brain and the knot of pain in her heart.

At seven o'clock Anna found her there, curled into the foetal position in front of a breakfast show, her thumb in her mouth, fast asleep.

By Sunday afternoon Steve's security purdah had been lifted as proof of Kara's version of events had been found and he was back in the information loop. A DNA analysis had been done on the dried vomit on the floor of the shop near the file cabinet but, more wretchedly, records had been reviewed on the deaths of the trafficked boys. Three of them, it turned out, had been killed by the atraxotoxin venom of a Sydney Funnel-web spider. One had been found in woods in Surrey two years earlier, one in a quarry in Wales and one, the most recent, had been the gruesome prize of a dog off its lead in a cave in Yorkshire. The connection between the three had not been made before. Of course, international investigations were being rigorously conducted as well as a flurry of arrests of the men and women who had met at the picture-postcard cottage in the country.

Kara seemed permanently glued to the tv unless the news came on when she switched channels. She did eat a little but shrank from contact with Steve or even Ellis. George and Diane had gone to Scotland and sent anxious texts almost hourly. The young woman spent all her time curled up under the plaid fleece throw on the couch. She spoke to Anna a little but it was only when Shell came for a couple of hours that Anna heard the murmur of conversation from behind the closed living-room door.

Anna had a problem. She had to go back to work on Monday but couldn't leave Kara in the house without female company. Helena would probably come but she didn't seem quite the right person to be with Kara all the time – she was maybe just a bit too brittle? There was something about her that made Anna wary, an air of locked cupboards and secret compartments.

When the door opened and Shell came down the hall into the kitchen Anna looked up from her laptop hoping that a solution would be announced. But it seemed that Shell herself needed comfort. 'She's asleep,' she said, and burst into tears.

Anna hugged her, made tea and listened. Shell blamed herself for not being more alert to Kara's situation because her own head had been so full of wedding plans. 'I had a feeling it was all a bit weird,' she said, 'but I just pushed it away. She could have been killed by that horrible monster.'

'But she wasn't,' Anna said gently, 'she was brave and resourceful and, looked at another way, you were the one to give her the means to defend herself, although you didn't know it, obviously.'

Shell shuddered, 'I don't think I can ever use that kind of comb again. And there's something else. I wish I hadn't told her now, she's got enough to deal with but it just came out.'

'What?'

'There's a weird man in Bromsgrove that goes round shouting and swearing at people but he's harmless. My mum knows his mum and he's got some sort of brain damage. Everyone calls him Willy Wanker which isn't very nice but I don't think he knows.'

'I may have run into him once,' Anna said.

'Well, he's dead. Some teenagers kicked him to death round the back of Asda.'

That horribly familiar slippage – the mask knocked sideways, the beast revealed in the shape, not of Willy Wanker as it turned out, but of those cruel young people. 'I'm so sorry.'

'What is the matter with them?' Shell cried, 'He didn't hurt anyone. He couldn't help being how he was. Anyway, I wish I hadn't told Kara.' She started sobbing again.

When she was calmer Anna was just opening her mouth to ask if Shell could take Kara home with her to stay at her house when she said, 'I wish she could come back to mine but my aunty's come to help with the wedding and there isn't a bed.'

After she left and Anna had checked on Kara who was deeply asleep, she went back to the kitchen and phoned George. 'Bit of a problem, Dad.'

'Kara?'

'Yes. It seems Shell can't have her and - '

'She needs to be kept an eye on.'

'Mm.'

'I did have a thought.' Anna could almost see him scratching his shorn but stubbly chin. By the time she'd finished trimming him he had looked like a bespectacled fledgling ostrich. 'Who has seen us through a couple of difficult patches, Annie, and is a very safe pair of hands as well as Earth Mother personified?'

'I'll phone now.' Of course, Rosa with her calm strength and caring ways would be perfect for Kara but was she available? She would be needed all day for five days this week but maybe not for longer if Kara recovered well - but could she ask Rosa to ditch existing long-term jobs just for one week? She had made her living for years by giving respite care to families of dementia sufferers and had no other income. All Anna could do was try. If she could do it, they would worry about how to pay her later.

Anna quickly explained Kara's situation and her present shocked condition. 'I've been meaning to come round for a chat,' Rosa said, and her comforting Black Country voice let Anna relax a little.

'Len?'

'Yeah. But that can wait. This poor woman is the most important now – I saw it on the telly.' There was a rustling noise. 'I'm just looking on my calendar.' Anna visualised the paper calendar decorated by Rosa herself with birds and butterflies hanging on a hook in the tiny galley of the boat. No smart phones for Rosa. 'Right, this is what I can do this week coming, ok?'

'I'm listening.' Anna grabbed a pen and paper as Rosa went through her commitments and it turned out that she could either be at Anna's house or pop in every couple of hours for the whole of the next week. Anna leaned back in her chair and let her spine rest.

'I'll come over tonight and say hello to her, will I?'

'Come for dinner, please, Rosa, I'd love to see you and Ellis won't be back till late so it would be a good way for the two of you to meet.'

Kara was still in the same position as before, now snoring slightly which probably meant she'd had little sleep the night before, but Anna didn't want to disturb her. It was a huge relief that Rosa could help them out as long as Kara took to her when they met. But, who wouldn't? She put the concern aside and phoned Steve who was with Ellis and the climbing club on the Roaches escarpment, and then sent a short text to George.

Next, she opened her emails to write to Robert Lindo who must be desperately awaiting news. They had been contacting each other several times a day, always by email, and he was grateful that Kara was safe with Anna but he, more than most, knew that taking another person's life is a scarring experience and he was worried about Kara's state of mind. She opened the one from him sent at 8.06 that morning. He blamed himself for not letting Anna tell her before because if he had, the false father and ensuing horror would have been avoided. What could Anna reply except that he had had good reasons for delay and no-one in their wildest imaginings could have known what would happen?

Anna stared at the screen thoughtfully. Certainly, Kara knew Graham was not her father but was she ready for another father to pop up so soon? Understandably, she was knocked sideways by what had happened and Anna feared that another bombshell would be too much. In her current withdrawal it was impossible to gauge her state of mind. She emailed back saying she would play it by ear.

She stood up and rolled her shoulders. It was late morning and she needed fresh air. She stepped through the utility room and out of the back door pulling one of her dad's old coats off its hook as she passed and then was outside admiring the duck-egg blue sky. She made her way slowly round the garden enjoying the fresh breeze and noticing clumps of purple and gold crocuses around the bole of the sycamore tree and the masses of narcissi, the tete a tetes that she and Harry had brought back from a holiday in the Scillies a dozen years ago, now about to burst out of their papery sheaths into sunshine yellow. There were tiny new red leaf buds on the viburnum bush and if she looked closely even the roses had crimson warts on their stems. Spring. Sparrows and blue-tits dashed about mad to mate and nest. She crossed her arms and stared up at a few puffs of fair-weather clouds dreamily floating along high above and thought of Robert and Stanley and navigating by the sun and the stars.

An idea was forming in her mind. She pulled out her phone from her back jeans pocket and called Joan expecting to have to leave a voicemail but Joan answered. She sounded a bit moody. 'What's the matter?' Anna asked, 'Surely the orgy of silver sex hasn't got you down?'

Joan grunted. 'Not exactly but, well, I've been making my own decisions for a long time.'

'What does that mean?'

'He's started taking over a bit.'

'Like what?'

'We were in a restaurant on Friday night and he said the tiramisu was excellent there and I said I didn't really like it and would have the cheesecake but he went and ordered them for us both and then smiled and said, "You'll see I'm right.'''

Anna sucked in her breath. 'Oh dear. What did you do?'

'I left it, wouldn't eat it, and then there was an atmosphere, you know, so the evening was spoiled. But that's not the only thing. He wants me to go and live with him in his house and I don't want to.' Anna bit her lip and said nothing. 'I said nicely that I thought it was too soon and we were fine as we are and I liked my own house but then he went all wheedly and asking why I didn't want to spend all my time with him like he did with me.'

'Whoops – bit of a red alert, I agree.'

'We're already in the shop together most of the day and the thought of never having any time to myself makes me feel like dashing for the exit.'

'Do you think it's winding down?'

Joan made an exasperated sound. 'Why can't it stay like it was? It was good when we saw each other a couple of times a week but he wants more all the time.'

Anna absent-mindedly poked at the damp ground with the toe of her slipper and then wished she hadn't as she saw a clump of mud had stuck to it. 'Would you like an excuse to have more time to yourself and not to move?'

'Yes, but I can't think of one,' Joan wailed. 'He's a nice man, I don't want to hurt him.'

'I've got an idea,' Anna said, 'pin back your ears.'

Rosa took the tea Anna had made into the front room where Kara was owlishly gazing at a game show and looking drained. 'Do you mind if I join you?' she said easily and Kara turned her head and stared at her. Rosa was wearing her rainbow striped cardigan and a pink beret perched on her now emerald green hair. Her impressive build was in itself enough to make people look twice but she did love colour and couldn't care less about what anyone thought. She seated herself in the armchair, put her own mug to one side and pulled out of her bag a square of embroidery trapped in a circular cane frame. 'Who's winning?' she asked, nodding at the television.

'I'm not really watching,' Kara said without taking her eyes off Rosa.

'I'm Rosa, a friend of the family,' Rosa went on, 'but Anna's busy in the kitchen so I've left her to it. What do you think of this?

I'm not sure which of these pinks to use on the outside petals.' She showed Kara the cluster of cabbage roses she was working on and fished a bundle of silks from her bag.

Kara sat up a little. 'Have you done all that?' Rosa nodded. Kara examined the selection of colours. 'I like that one best – it's a bit darker so the other petals would show up against it.'

Rosa considered this seriously. 'I think you're right.' She cut a length of silk with her swan-necked scissors and then carefully pulled the skein apart so that she was working with three threads. She took out a scrap of aluminium with a fine wire loop at the end and threaded the silk through it and then through the eye of the needle.

Kara moved to the end of the sofa closer to Rosa. 'That's a good idea,' she said, thinking how hard some of the residents at Church View found threading a needle. 'Where can you get those?'

When Anna went to the front room to call them in for dinner she found Kara with a scrap of linen in her hand doing a practice row of chain stitch while Rosa sat beside her in comfortable silence. The television whooped but neither of the women looked up.

Nothing, Anna thought, was more comforting (unless you were a vegetarian which she hoped Kara was not) when the weather was cold than a steak and onion pie with a short-crust pastry cap. She had needed to fill her time in the kitchen so as not to crowd Rosa so she had been especially artistic with the leaves and buds decorating the lid so the golden varnished result did look mouth-watering. With it she'd done a mixture of broccoli, carrots and frozen peas so if Kara didn't like one there'd be other choices. Also, she had indulged herself by making roast potatoes instead of mashed even though she hardly needed the extra calories. She had even par-boiled the potatoes before roasting to occupy a few more minutes. The meal was almost up to George's standards.

A subdued email had come back from Robert and she thought how ironic it was that when she was pushing him to tell Kara, he'd held back, and now he was pushing her and she was holding back. But he did have a photograph which he forwarded. Stanley's body had been pulled out of the freezing North Atlantic waters and taken home to Grand Cayman and the photograph showed his grave in a cemetery which sloped down to a beach edged with oleander and revealing the turquoise sea beyond. There was an image of Stanley in naval uniform, framed and protected by glass, set in the pale headstone. After his name and dates, the inscription read: '*A Quiet Hero Loved and Missed by All Who Knew Him. He Laid Down his Life for his Friends. We Will Meet Again by the Grace of God.*' Anna stared at it for a long time thinking of the great-grand-daughter so close by.

Over dinner Anna and Rosa talked about small things. Anna told them about the bulbs appearing in the garden and Rosa said that she was planning to give the decking on the boat a fresh coat of varnish when the weather warmed up. Kara stopped eating.

'You live on a boat?'

Rosa explained and added, 'You could come and see it if you like but wrap up warm. It's cosy once the heat's got going but it strikes cold at first.' Glancing at Kara's engaged expression, she added, 'I could take you over tomorrow morning if you like – I've got to come this way to be with a client. Pick you up around eleven?' There was silence.

Anna was just about to ask if anyone wanted more pudding when Kara asked shyly, 'Who'll be there?'

'No-one. I live on my own. There are other boats nearby, of course.' Another long moment of silence.

'Can I come back here afterwards?' Kara asked Anna.

'Of course you can. I'll be out at work but I'll give you a key. Rosa has one as well from when she was looking after my dad when he had pneumonia.'

Kara stared at her spoon which was half full of sticky toffee pudding and custard. 'Thank you,' she said, 'I'd like to do that.' It seemed as though the whole house took a deep breath of relief.

By the time that Ellis came in, tired and muddy, Kara had gone to bed so Anna was able to have a word with him in the kitchen about what had been arranged. Before she'd gone up Kara had asked Anna if she would go with her on Monday evening to pick up some clothes from her house. 'I know it's a cheek to ask and I could go on the bus but I don't know how mum and Graham will be with me.' Anna was glad to do it, and more pleased that Kara was up to making practical plans at least for the next few days.

Ellis listened while Anna told him Kara would be around for a while and Rosa would be popping in as he ate the meal she'd saved for him and then said, 'Kirsty's bailed on the band. We need to find another vocalist.'

Anna translated this as, 'Message about visitor understood, don't go on about it, over and out.' Faye would have been less polite and simply said, giving her mother a black look, 'So?' She suggested the vacancy be posted at school or on social media or whatever was appropriate and they could hold auditions.

'Yeah, Dan's done that but no interest.'

'Other schools? Churches?'

Ellis pushed his chair back from the table. 'You'll be suggesting the supermarket notice-board next. I'm whacked, Mum, can I do the dishwasher tomorrow?'

Anna stood up, too, and gave him a brief hug. 'I'll do it this once, love, you get off to bed but have a shower first.'

At the kitchen door Ellis turned and looked at her. 'Did Diane say anything before they went away about Bobble?'

Anna had not thought of the dog in days. 'No. Why?'

'What will happen if no-one wants him, Mum? Will they put him down?'

'Oh, I'm sure they won't do that. Try not to worry. Night-night.' But she wasn't sure at all. What Ellis didn't know was that George was paying Bobble's food bill at Safe 'n' Sound as they were always strapped for cash despite the best efforts of their volunteers, but they did have their rules, she supposed, and the eventuality of Bobble, who was a young dog, not being re-homed hadn't really been discussed. As it was he was settled enough at the refuge but naturally Ellis worried and missed the companion he had had from a puppy and his twice-weekly visits only seemed to make him feel the separation more keenly.

Still, Anna reflected as she began to stack the dishwasher, it hadn't been a bad day all round. Kara had moved towards Rosa like a small boat slipping into a safe harbour out of a storm. Her affection and admiration for the girl was deepening by the day. Kara had been put through a nightmare situation when the person she loved and trusted had not only betrayed her but promised to kill her but she was sensible and resilient and was beginning to heal. Anna hoped she would come to see herself not as perpetrator or victim but rather as a survivor.

Steve called and she leaned back against the counter top to chat. Alice had been asleep all the way home in the car after he'd picked her up from his parents in Ambleside and he hadn't woken her to undress her to go to bed. She would be furious in the morning that she'd slept in her day clothes being a stickler for the correct routine being followed but he just hadn't the energy to sort her out and didn't want to risk waking her and then having to spend an hour getting her back to sleep.

'Get them to put her in her pj's and clean her teeth next time before she gets in the car,' Anna advised.

'We tried that but she threw a fit and said it wasn't bedtime.'

'Mm,' Anna murmured, wanting to say, well, that's how you're letting her be – difficult and demanding – but stopping herself. Instead she told Steve about Rosa and Kara.

'Are you seeing Ted tomorrow?' Steve asked. Anna put back her head and groaned.

31

Ted didn't even let her take her coat off. He was standing at the end of the corridor with his door open when she got to the top of the stairs and barked at her, 'In here. Now.' She was not asked to sit down and he remained standing himself, his arms folded and his expression grim.

'Talk,' he ordered.

'Look, I know the case was closed, I do know that, Ted, but I got some information that really worried me.'

'How?' Anna knew he wasn't interested in why she was worried, he was asking how she got the information.

'I didn't go looking for it. A friend of Kara approached me because she was concerned.'

'And did you see this so-called friend on Company time?'

'Yes.'

'And did you recklessly, as an employee of this Company, allow yourself to be filmed by the world's media sitting on the road with that girl in the middle of a sensational tabloid story?' Anna nodded knowing there was no point in her attempting to qualify this statement. 'You are so bloody lucky they didn't find out who you are, where you work, my lady, or you would be looking for another job.'

'Can you just take the hours off my pay?' Anna said, fighting the urge to justify herself which she knew would, in this mood, only make him worse.

'We live and die by confidentiality, Anna. You know that. How can anyone trust us with their affairs if we end up starring on Crimewatch?' Ted was dangerously crimson in the face and his pale eyes were popping out like boiled sweets.

'It's hardly…'

'And it's not the first time, is it?'

Anna hung her head. If Ted was going to bring up the stuff from years before about Briony she must really be in trouble. He had hinted at it in the past just to let her know he knew, or suspected what was going on but he had never brought it out in the open. If he did, if he used his trump card, she probably would be collecting her P45 on the way out.

Ok, then, so be it. She looked him in the eye. 'I had to do it, Ted. I knew there was something terribly wrong and I couldn't just stand back and let her face it on her own.'

Ted sat on the edge of his desk, still facing her, with his arms folded. His eyes were now narrowed and glittered like chips of slate. He lowered his voice. 'Did you get Steve involved? You know what I mean.'

This was worse than she had expected. Ted had put things together more astutely than the police but then, he knew more. What could she say? That she had run from Helena directly to Steve precisely to beg that he would, with his security contacts, get involved? She could be blamed for that and would take it, but did Ted also know that instead of closing her down Steve had given her classified information? That could really hurt Steve. Ted would never sack him, he was far too valuable but he would have something on him, something that he would tuck away and use if he wanted to.

'I asked him to find out what he could about Robert Grenville Johnson for me.'

'And did he?'

'Yes.'

Ted got off the desk and went round it to sink into his chair. He seemed deflated, almost wounded and Anna had no idea which way this would now go. 'I won't ask you any more except for one question. Has this ever happened before? I mean about Steve.'

'Steve has helped me with general research like he would with any of us but has never given me confidential information before,' Anna stated firmly. 'He was worried for me, that's why he told me about that man. He would never have done it otherwise.'

'Do they know what he did?'

He didn't have to explain who 'they' were. 'No, I don't think so.'

Ted rested his chin on his hands and stared at his desk calendar which was defaced with doodles to the point of illegibility. 'You think it's the money I'm worried about, but it's not just that, Anna. It takes years to build a reputation and minutes, seconds, to destroy it. I've built Harts from nothing and now it pays the wages of twenty-five people. They depend on it. I depend on it.' He sat up, sighed and went on: 'My dad was a petty crook. He was in and out of jail most of his life and when he was at home he was useless. I made a promise to myself that I would do something with my life. We haven't had kids so this is it. This is what they call now my legacy. Can you understand that?' Anna shifted her weight on to the other foot feeling miserable. Ted was often a figure of fun to the researchers although they knew how sharp he was and how fair for the most part unless he took against someone. Anna had never seen this vulnerable side of him and it was much harder to take than his anger.

'I do understand. I'm so sorry, Ted.'

'Don't say anything to Steve, ok? I don't want him to know I know.'

Anna thought for a second and realised how difficult it would be for Steve if she did tell him. 'Ok.'

Ted flipped a hand towards the door and she turned, grateful to be dismissed. 'You can give me a list of the hours you owe me and I'll get them deducted from your pay check.'

She glanced back at him. 'Right. Thank you, Ted. I mean it.'

On her way back down the corridor Steve popped his head out of his office. 'Ok? Still in one piece?'

'He was very fair.'

'Lunch later?'

'I think I've got a bit of time to make up, actually, if that's ok with you,' she smiled, 'but if you're going out you could bring me back a bacon butty?'

She went on into the toilet and stood for a while in front of the mirror. She would never tell anyone what Ted had just told her and he would have known that. She didn't just feel relieved that she had got off lightly, she felt humbled that he had opened up to her and her respect for him had deepened. He had known exactly how far to probe and when to hold back, how much to reveal and what should be concealed. They all knew Ted had affairs; that he was vain and sometimes irascible, but none of the others knew what he had been struggling for so long to put behind him and how well he had overcome that sapping, shaming start in life. She looked herself in the eye and made a promise that if and when she could, she would do something nice for Ted.

Only Vicki was at home when Anna and Kara arrived and her face was showing the strain of the last few days. She had been expecting them because Kara had texted to say she would be picking up some things. She nodded at Anna as Kara let them both into the kitchen and then said unexpectedly to her, 'Do you want a cup of tea?'

'Do you need any help?' Anna asked Kara who was clutching bin liners.

'No, I'm ok. I won't be long.' Mother and daughter had not so much as glanced at each other.

Vicki took Anna into the sitting room and then went back to the kitchen to make the tea. Anna looked round. The floor was shining laminate and there was a black leather three-piece suite, a huge television on the wall, and a large coffee table. On shelves in the alcoves were decorator's items: a vase of twigs, a 'love' sign in white plastic and several rows of candles. There were no pictures on the walls, no magazines or books, and not a speck of dust. Vicki came back in with two mugs and two coasters which she placed on the table.

'Everywhere looks so tidy and clean compared with my house,' Anna said for something positive to say.

Vicki took this as a rebuke. 'I do my best,' she said. 'Graham's away mostly and I work full-time. I expect you have a cleaner.' Anna wished Kara had let her go upstairs to help and was wondering if it would be possible to do that anyway rather than sit here with this spiky woman who had so coldly pushed her daughter away. Vicki carefully placed her mug exactly on the coaster. 'I know you think I'm a bad mother.'

'Mrs Brandon, I hardly know you,' Anna said.

'You have perfect children, I'm sure.'

'Of course not, no-one does, but Kara is a lovely woman and you must be proud of her coming through all of this so bravely.' This was a gamble but she had to do something.

Vicki didn't reply and just stared at the floor sipping her drink. 'She's innocent, then, is she?' she said finally. 'It was self-defence?'

'Yes. She was taken advantage of by a horrible man who would have killed her if she hadn't fought back.'

'I told her not to go after him,' Vicki said, stiffening, 'I told her he was trouble.'

Anna knew that Vicki was trying to redeem herself but, important though that was, she couldn't let this pass. 'But you meant Robert Lindo Johnson when you said that, didn't you?'

Vicki's eyes slid away to the curtains and then the alcove. 'I didn't know it wasn't the same man,' she said, and risked a quick look at Anna. Anna dropped her eyes and drank her tea.

Kara appeared with four bulging black bags and Vicki stood up so quickly she almost slopped her drink. Anna was relieved, too, and grabbed two bags to lighten the load. As they got ready to leave through the back door Anna heard Vicki say the only words she'd uttered to Kara in the whole visit. 'I hope you didn't leave a mess.'

'Bye, Mum,' Kara said, adding, 'I've left you that nice coat. It would look good on you.'

On the drive back Kara was silent. Anna needed petrol and stopped at a service station in Northfield not far from Selly Oak which reminded her of where Kara had been earlier. 'What did you think of Rosa's boat?' she asked when she got back into the car and switched on the engine.

'My real dad is a murderer,' Kara said as though she had just noticed it was raining.

Anna did a U turn and pulled into the car park at Sainsbury's which was the only place nearby she could think of, her thoughts racing. How long had Kara known and who had told her? She parked away from the main entrance but kept the engine running for the heater. Kara was staring ahead, her pretty profile outlined against the orange lights. Anna fought down the temptation to ask questions, to defend Robert, to rush into it all. 'Do you want to know about him?' she asked instead.

'It's been hard for mum having to live it all down. He killed someone when I was just a baby but I never knew.' Kara was very calm. 'My aunty Elise must have known but she said he wasn't a bad man but he must have been.'

'No,' Anna said, 'he isn't a bad man.'

For a moment this passed Kara by as though she was so deep in her own thoughts that she couldn't hear anything else but then she turned her body and Anna saw that her eyes were burning black. 'How do you know? Are you just saying that?'

'I've met him and I like him,' Anna said, measuring out information in teaspoon-sized chunks.

'You've met him?'

A family returned to the car next to theirs and there was calling and instructions and doors banging until they drove off. 'Yes. He asked us, the place I work, to find you.'

'To find me?'

Kara was trembling and Anna leaned across to turn up the heat. 'I can try to answer any questions you have,' she said carefully.

Kara returned to her position looking out of the window. Her hands were clasped together tightly in her lap. 'Rosa's boat is much bigger inside than you'd think,' she said rapidly, 'I didn't think boats on the canal would have electricity but they do.'

Anna started the engine and began to back out. 'Do you fancy fish and chips for tea or would you like something else? We can pick it up on the way home. Ellis will be fine with anything.'

'Kebab and chips, please,' Kara said, 'Thank you very much. I get paid on Friday so I can pay you back.'

'You'll do no such thing,' Anna said. 'Maybe we can talk again when you're ready?' Kara gave an almost imperceptible nod and Anna pulled out on to the by-pass to go home.

Kara sat on the edge of the big bed and stared sadly at the space Anna had made for her in her wardrobe and the little row of mis-matched hangers waiting to be used. She wasn't thinking of Bob or this new Robert Johnson but she was thinking about what had happened when they got home with the takeaways.

Ellis had been in the kitchen but he looked totally different from the times she'd seen him before because he had had one of those sharp hipster haircuts. Anna had obviously been surprised but had made a joke of it. 'I see the lawnmower's been out,' she had said and got out plates.

'We've all done it,' Ellis said, moving his pile of books to one side on the table and fetching knives and forks from the drawer for the three of them. It was nice that he helped without being asked, she had never seen Gerry lift a finger.

'Even Bean?' Anna asked. 'Has he had his luscious locks shorn, too?'

'Yup. All for one and all that.'

'I thought you Posers were all about individualistic sign systems and multi-layered ironies. Seems a bit conformist.' Kara listened and watched.

Ellis had grinned at Kara as he set her glass of water down. He had a nice smile, it made his eyes go liquid like runny honey. She had been too startled to smile back. 'With the hair and the esoteric clothes it's the tension between being part of a pack and daring to stand alone, mother - we wear our coiffs with pride.'

'All that from a short back and sides?' Anna laughed, handing round plates of food.

'Cheap at twice the price, but enough of this persiflage,' said Ellis. 'I've got a job.'

'Really?' His mother had sat down but before she started to eat she had waited for Ellis to explain, to tell her about it. It seems that some parents at his tennis club had been asking for tuition for their novice children and preferred kids a little older rather than adults.

'We're cheaper,' said Ellis, 'but they pretend it's because we're less intimidating for their little Serenas and Rogers.'

'Good for you,' Anna had said. Then they had all eaten their tea together and the chat had continued but Kara had said nothing while she ate her food. When her offer to wash up had been refused she had come up here to this room.

She felt small and cold and very alone. She hadn't understood most of what they were joking about but she had felt the affection, the intimacy of their relationship. She couldn't remember the last time that she had sat down to a meal with Vicki and Graham. The dining room table in the front room was very rarely used and never for her. It had been many years since Vicki had even cooked for her. When she had been at school she would have a school dinner and then make do with a sandwich at home or something from the chip shop eaten sitting on the low brick wall outside so as not to make the house smell. Mostly she paid for the food herself since she'd been babysitting for people ever since she was fourteen. Somehow, she couldn't think how, Vicki and Graham had made it clear that they didn't want her with them in the living room in the evening so she had spent all her time in the house in her own bedroom and not really thought about it. Of course, Shell's family were different but there was so much going on in that house that they hardly ever sat down together and Shell preferred to take friends to her room.

How would it be to live in a family where people were interested enough in you to tease you? To ask you questions about your day? To praise you? Was that why she had been so stupid about Bob, so willing to believe that he cared about her and felt something for her? She shuddered – it was so weak to feel like this -

needy, like a silly girl. She understood now why Vicki would find the sight of her, her living presence, irritating but surely her resemblance to her father wasn't her fault? Shouldn't her mum have loved her despite that? A hot lump rose in her throat. That was the nub of it, the simple truth – she had not been loved even by her own mother - and as obvious to her as that now was, she had only just realised it. It made her cave in. She couldn't bear to deal with her clothes so she got out a clean pair of jeans and a fleece for the next day and left the rest.

Her new phone jingled. She had only given the new number to a few people so it made her jump but then she saw it was Helena calling and her heart lifted a little. 'Everyone at Church View is thinking of you and sending their love,' Helena said, while Kara sniffed and wiped her nose on her sleeve. 'We all think you were very brave.'

'Did Mrs Bandhal say anything about my job?'

'No. Why? Oh, you're worrying about all the publicity. No, it's fine. I will double check tomorrow but she was the main one saying how sorry they are about what you've been through. We can't wait for you to come back – only when you're ready, of course.'

'Helena?'

'Yes.'

'Did your family love you?'

There was a sound like a small cough on the other end of the phone and then Helena said, 'Not really. At least, I don't think so. I grew up in a Children's Home, Kara, I never knew them.'

Kara felt the iron band around her heart ease. 'Can I come and see you?'

'I'll pick you up tomorrow morning and we can go somewhere nice for a chat and a coffee – maybe lunch. Would that be ok?'

After she had ended the call Kara went over to the mirror and looked at herself. She had not left the red silk top behind because she couldn't bear to and now she would have a chance to wear it – she wasn't going to let Bob take that from her. She would have a shower, condition her hair and do her nails while she listened to her music. She would hold her head up despite everything.

But in the deepest part of the night she was suddenly awake, lying rigidly in her bed and staring at the ceiling, because she had remembered that when Anna had told her she had met her real father she had said that she liked him. Her heart thudded with excitement and fear and she tried to lie still but she knew that sleep or even rest was impossible. Kara was usually a considerate woman but such was her urgency that she didn't hesitate to get up, pull on the borrowed robe and slip out of the room and down the landing to where Anna was asleep. She couldn't wait a moment longer, she had to know everything.

Anna stopped on the way to work and bought a double-shot latte. She thought about buying two. It probably would have been better if she hadn't let herself go back to sleep after Kara had left her room at around five o'clock. But she had and the shock of the alarm two hours later was brutal. One thing that Kara had said last night had stayed with her – 'He's been in prison all my life.' Yes. What a terrible thing for the girl to dwell on.

Work had piled up and she tried to concentrate but the day dragged. Rosa phoned to say that she had gone round to find Kara was out but had phoned her and it seemed someone called Helena had taken her out. Was that ok? Helena called to say Kara seemed much better but nervous about meeting her father. Was that ok? Steve phoned from his office to tell her that Bob's Redditch house had been thoroughly gone over and there was plenty of evidence of people being housed there in surprisingly squalid conditions for such a respectable property. George phoned to say the van had blown a tyre on an access road to a campsite but the breakdown people had rescued them. It hadn't stopped raining since they arrived and there was currently a gale blowing. They were considering cutting the trip short or spending a bit of time in Yorkshire where things were calmer. Anna yawned again.

At around one o'clock, when Anna was propping her head on one hand and staring blearily at a 1911 census on her computer screen, Steve appeared beside her with a paper bag which was giving off a wonderful smell. 'Sausage and onion baton,' he said. 'I've just been and got us one each and another coffee.'

Anna glanced around but the office was almost empty. 'I knew there must be some reason I love you,' she said.

'Totally selfish,' Steve said, pulling across her neighbour's desk chair, 'I need to offload about Alice. You don't have to say anything, just let me rant. Here, eat this while it's hot.'

'Ok, let rip.' Anna sank her teeth into the savoury package. Little strips of golden onion dropped from her bread on to her desk and Steve picked them up and popped them into his mouth.

'It's this wedding,' he said. 'I don't know how much more I can take. There's a whole week to go and I don't know if I'll make it without having a nervous breakdown. It's that dress Briony got for her – a confection of lace and satin – you can imagine. It arrived on Saturday so it was waiting for her when she woke up on Monday and like an idiot I let her open the parcel so then she wanted to wear it to school, screamed and threw herself on the floor when I wouldn't let her, then she wanted to wear it the minute she got home and screamed again and told me I was very naughty and selfish (I bet she's heard that phrase at school a few times) and then she just sulked all bloody evening and threw her food on the floor and wouldn't speak to me. Then the whole thing started again this morning.

Anna paused before she took another bite. 'Put it away where she can't see it and tell her firmly it has to stay clean for the wedding or she won't be able to be a bridesmaid or flower girl or whatever.'

Steve took a bite of his own roll and they ate in silence for a while. 'I'll try it but I just don't like to disappoint her. I did think of getting a cheap copy, well, the same sort of thing, from the costume shop, like a princess outfit, so she could play with that and she wouldn't be so upset.'

Anna breathed evenly to avoid shouting. 'She's six years old, Steve, she's not a toddler. She has to learn to deal with waiting for good things to happen. Be firm with her.'

'I can't bear to see her cry.'

Tired as she was, Anna knew this was not the time to let her thoughts slip over her lips and be heard out loud but it took all she had not to lecture Steve any further. Alice ran rings round him and there would never be peace in the house until he took charge and stopped letting her act like a little tyrant. What would it have been like if she had been in the house that morning? She would have had to walk out and let them get on with it or risk a horrible scene. What sort of family would they be and how long before she spoke her mind and they would both hate her? There was no doubt in her mind whose side Steve would take if he was faced with a strict Anna and a plaintive, beseeching Alice. Even thinking in terms of 'sides' alarmed her. Wearily, she tried to change the subject.

'I met Kara's mum last night. She's very tightly wound. I don't think Kara's been indulged much.'

'You think I'm indulging Alice?'

She took pity on him. 'Maybe a little but you do your best. I have to decide which princess outfit *I'm* going to wear for the big event, anyway, and there may be a proper hissy fit when I look in the mirror. It's Kara's friend Shell's wedding soon, too, but she hasn't said anything about still being her bridesmaid. The big news is that she wants to meet Robert – we had a long chat last night.'

'Have you told him?'

'We're going on Saturday. I can't take any more time off and Kara wants me to be there so it has to wait till then. He's sent off the Visiting Order already.

'More high emotion then?'

'Yes, but I can't imagine Kara throwing herself on the floor and screaming, thank goodness. In fact, I can't really imagine how they'll be with each other at all to be honest. It's almost too much, isn't it?'

32

Things moved swiftly over the next three days. On Thursday Anna came home from work to find Kara's bin bags of belongings in the hall and Kara herself, looking remarkably upbeat, in the kitchen making a chilli con carne for the evening meal. She was wearing George's apron and had laid the table with paper napkins folded into a triangle and a vase full of daffodils she had bought.

'This looks lovely,' Anna said, 'and it smells great, too. Um. Are those your things in the hall?'

'It's to thank you,' Kara said, 'it's the only thing I know how to cook but Rosa's going to teach me.' She stirred and tasted and checked the pasta. 'It's not too early for you, is it? Ellis is upstairs so it'll be ready in about ten minutes.'

'Wonderful,' Anna said, 'what a nice surprise. I could get used to this.'

Kara turned to her with a serious face. 'Oh, no. It's just tonight I'm doing the dinner. I'm going to stay with Rosa on the boat. She's asked me and I'd love it. Not that I don't love it here, too, I do,' she added hastily.

Anna went over to her and gave her shoulders a hug – clearly Kara wasn't used to being teased. 'Good plan.'

'I'm going to pay rent, of course,' Kara added anxiously, 'like I did mum – it wouldn't be right not to and I want to.'

'You'll be Idle Women,' Anna smiled and then, seeing Kara's puzzled look, explained, 'that's what they called the women who worked the canal boats during World War 2 because of the initials I W for Inland Waterways. 'It was a joke, of course, they were anything but idle.' She decided to pull out a bottle to celebrate. 'How was Helena?'

'It helped to talk to her, she's so, you know, wise. I feel more sorted. She told me she's not going away now.'

'Going away?'

Ellis opened the kitchen door and nodded at the bottle Anna was opening. 'Can I have some?'

She poured him half a glass and full ones for herself and Kara. 'Pops might be home early,' she said. 'They're having atrocious weather up there.'

Kara poured the spaghetti into a colander in the sink and divided it between three plates, piling the rich, meaty sauce on top.

'Do you have any parmesan?' Ellis went to the fridge and pulled a canister out of the door compartment. Kara studied it. 'I didn't know it came like this, mum grates it off a lump.'

'We're lazy, I'm afraid,' Anna said, 'but this is delicious, you must give us the recipe.'

'I've been thinking we could castrate Big B,' Ellis said thickly through his food. Kara looked sideways at him. 'It might, you know, make him more manageable and then we could have him at home. It's what they do with stallions. They just slice open their testicle sacs and pop out their balls. They look like hard-boiled eggs.' Kara stopped eating.

'Maybe talk about it another time?' said Anna. She turned to Kara. 'Is Shell all set for the wedding?'

Kara spun a loop of pasta round her fork. 'I didn't think I'd be up for it,' she said soberly to Anna, 'but after talking to Helena I think why would I let him, you know, take it away from me? I've been looking forward to it for months – and I'm the one she chose to do her hair. Do you think that's awful?'

'I think it's the best thing you could do,' Anna said. 'Screw him.'

'*Illegitimi non carborundum*,' Ellis said. 'Don't let the bastards grind you down.'

They raised their glasses.

Later, when Kara was watching the television and chatting to Shell on her phone and Ellis had announced he was 'lucubrating' in his room (which turned out to mean studying by artificial light instead of what she had imagined) Anna rang Helena. 'You really helped Kara today,' she said, pushing back a little jealous twinge, 'she's much more herself.'

'I'm glad to hear that but she's a sensible young woman. It was her naivety that man took advantage of but she can hardly be blamed for that. I don't think her mother and Graham ever took her anywhere to broaden her horizons so she didn't know how the world works.'

'I'm a bit nervous about taking her to meet Robert Lindo. He's a lovely man but it's such a big deal after what's happened – I mean, a big deal for both of them.'

'Mm,' Helena agreed, 'but it's not about you, is it? I think it's a matter of lighting the touch paper and standing back. I think you should let them handle it any way they need to which may be very pulled back, you never know. They may be quite intimidated by the meeting and choose to be quiet and formal with each other, at least at first.' There was a brief pause. 'Actually, Anna, I was wondering if you would like to go out for a drink or something? We got off to a bad start, my fault for being over-protective of Kara which seems ironic now, but I like you and I'd appreciate a chance to talk through what's been happening.'

Anna had not expected that but it had been ages since she had gone out socially and she found Helena intriguing. The inquisitive side of her nature was piqued by the anomalies in Helena's situation and it would be satisfying to dig a bit, reprehensible though that probably was. 'I'd like that,' she said. 'How about the Queen's Head at Stoke Prior tomorrow evening? I could give Kara a lift to Shell's on the way, I know she's planning to see her on Friday night.'

'See you at eight then?'

She phoned Steve. 'All quiet on the Wedding Front?'

'Oh please, please, say you can come down, love. I did what you said and said what you said to say and she looked at me with those big eyes and I think it's worked. She thought for a bit and then told me she wanted sausages for tea. She's fast asleep in bed clutching her shoes, whoops slippers, for the big day.'

Anna ran up her stairs and checked on Ellis telling him she was going to Steve's for an hour and then had a word with Kara before putting on her warm parka and gratefully closing her front door behind her. Clouds were scudding very fast across the face of the full moon but it looked as though the moon was dashing across the sky and tree trunks were creaking around her. A tortoiseshell cat shot in front of her and nearly tripped her up. A large male figure was coming up the road from the bus stop end silhouetted against the street light and she stopped in her tracks. She had forgotten all about Len. But when the man got closer she saw it wasn't him and she tried to remember, as she walked quickly on, when the last post card from Len had come – she had been so preoccupied with Kara she'd forgotten that Rosa was expecting her to speak to him when he got home.

Steve took her into the kitchen where he was wrapping a make-up set from the Pound Shop which Alice had insisted would be the one thing Briony would really like as a present from her. Kimi seemed not to figure in Alice's dream scenario – the wedding was all about Briony and Alice walking hand in hand together down the aisle and Anna could almost see the vision the child would have, soft-edged with fleecy pink clouds.

'Oh bloody hell. I haven't even thought about wedding presents,' she said.

'Lucky I did, then.'

'You're kidding!'

'No. I called Kimi and she told me what store they have their wedding list at and I ordered something from you and me. The shop will wrap and deliver it with a note.'

'Blimey,' said Anna, 'you're a keeper, aren't you? What did you get?'

'Can't remember, a lamp or something, but you owe me thirty pounds. There was nothing on the list under fifty. The days of a nice butter dish are over.' Steve used the glue-stick to attach the label Alice had spent at least ten minutes making and pushed the package to one side. 'Glass of wine?'

'Hasn't Alice done her friend's aunt's wedding? That must have been and gone by now.' She settled down at the table with her glass as Steve tidied up bits of wrapping paper and sticky tape. 'Did she have fun?'

'Yes and no,' said Steve. 'The fun was all in the anticipation, except for the people organising it, of course, because the actual wedding fell a bit flat for Alice. I brought her home with her chin stuck out in a proper mood.'

'Why?'

'Well, I don't know really, nothing went wrong, I think it was just that she had expected to be the centre of attention and, oddly enough, the bride was.' Steve laughed and flashed one of his sparkling grins at Anna. 'Kids, eh?'

'Let's go and barricade ourselves into the living room,' Anna said, getting up, 'I can be pretty demanding, too, mister. Brace yourself.'

Helena had arrived first and was sitting in the Western-themed bar area near to a bustling log fire sipping a glass of red. 'Have you eaten?' she asked as Anna joined her.

'My son was at a friend's house for dinner so I just had beans on toast,' she said, scanning the menu. 'I might go for a pud.' It was good to have the food as a distraction because Anna had not bothered to change from work but Helena looked amazing. Her smooth silver hair was brushed to one side in a shining cap and the professional job she had done on her make-up was shown off by the soft light from the fire and the candles on the tables. Her skin glowed golden and her eyes, outlined in kohl and softened with something pale and shiny, had a hint, even at her age, of the courtesan and the demi monde. She was wearing a partly unbuttoned white silk shirt under a gorgeously patterned pashmina and, Anna glanced down, black silk trousers. Anna looked round for the waiter and noticed that people at nearby tables, men and women, were frankly staring at Helena and whispering.

A youth rushed across and asked if he could get this exotic creature anything. She nodded, smiling, at Anna. 'Hazelnut cheesecake and a house white spritzer, no ice,' Anna said, glaring at him.

Helena looked round. 'This was a good choice of yours. Do you often come here?'

'More in the summer for lunch when we've walked down the canal. There's a flight of twenty-one locks so it's fun to stroll past while people on boats sweat their way through them.' She regarded Helena mischievously, refusing to be intimidated by her glamour. 'You scrub up well.'

Helena laughed, revealing her perfect rows of whitened teeth. 'I don't have much else to do, do I?'

Anna debated with herself briefly and then launched her question. 'Why don't you? You're so fit and active and worldly – why aren't you lounging on a cruise ship or decorating the beaches of Croatia or something?'

'You're as bad as the girls at Church View – they're always asking whether I've got a toy boy on the go,' Helena said coolly, sipping at her drink.

'Sorry, I was being rude. Let's talk about Kara.'

Helena seemed eager to talk about her. 'She says you know this Rosa? She sounds a little eccentric – Kara says she has green hair. Is she trustworthy? It seems so insecure to live on a canal boat and it would be terrible if Kara made another mistake and ended up in trouble again just when she has a chance to get to know her real father.' Helena's gold and diamond rings flashed in the light from the fire as she moved her crimson-tipped hands and Anna leaped to Rosa's defence.

'We've known her well for years. She's a wonderful person and just right for Kara at the moment.'

Helena changed tack. She smiled at Anna over the rim of her glass. 'So, are you married? Children?'

Anna told her a little of her family and her recent history and Helena asked a few questions but Anna didn't like it. She reflected wryly that people must feel the same way as she felt now when she put them through one of her interrogations. Under Helena's scrutiny she felt exposed. The biter bit. 'Interviewing' was something she had to do for work sometimes but she must admit that she also enjoyed poking around in other's people's lives and feelings in just the way Helena was doing to her now. It wasn't comfortable for the subject, she now realised, although it masqueraded as showing an interest and with some people, she supposed, it was a strategy for a short-cut to intimacy. Is that what Helena was going for? Did she want to have Anna as a friend? If so, this one-way Q & A session was not going to achieve that. Finally, she'd had enough.

'So what about you?' she said, rather too abruptly, 'What's your story?' After all the questions Helena had asked, she couldn't now pull back, surely. Helena lifted a finger and the waiter was there. She ordered black coffee and a brandy and then sat for a moment in silence with her perfectly proportioned head and cameo-like profile turned towards the fire. Anna tried to read her expression but the veiled eyes revealed nothing. When the drinks came she sighed and turned away from the fire facing Anna full on.

'It's a story quickly told,' she said, 'but I would appreciate it if you didn't pass it on.'

'Of course.' Ah, the universal thrill of being told a secret!

'I'm sixty-one,' Helena said. 'A year ago I was diagnosed with Parkinson's disease in its early stages. I have no family or close friends here – my daughter has lived in Australia for the last twenty years and has no plans to return. In any case, we aren't close because I disapproved of the man she married and she never forgave me despite the fact that he turned out to be a serial adulterer. Perhaps because of that, I don't know.

'The point is, I have no-one. My professional life was all-consuming and when it stopped with that diagnosis I looked around and realised I was alone. It's not my nature to be self-pitying but I did not want to end my days among strangers with no control over my circumstances so I thought long and hard about what I would do.' She sipped her brandy and, surprisingly given her sad story, smiled merrily at Anna. 'I decided to go out in style – the way I've lived my life.'

'Church View?' Anna queried and then felt ashamed of herself but Helena only laughed.

'Church View is my perch,' she said. 'It's not too expensive, there's company and it's quite comfortable. Moving there meant that I could sell my house and all my possessions and have somewhere to stay while I planned the next part of my exit. I was never going to be there for long.'

'I'm sorry,' Anna said, genuinely sympathetic and admiring the older woman's self-possession, 'I'm sorry you're dealing with this on your own.'

'Oh, don't be. Lots of people have to and I've always been resourceful and resilient. I grew up in a Children's Home and if you're not you have a hard time of it.'

'I interrupted you,' Anna murmured to cover the shock of what Helena had just said. She had assumed Helena had had a comfortable, middle-class background. How much sheer determination and will-power she must have.

'I decided that I would find a wonderful, luxurious hotel somewhere beautiful and end my days there at my own hand. It would be unpleasant for the hotel staff to find me but I would make sure they were compensated financially and at least they wouldn't know me.' Helena was still smiling softly and Anna wondered if she was a little unhinged. 'But, as I said, I wanted to go out as happily as I possibly could. I've always been bi-sexual and in the past had a series of partners but more recently paid escorts. It's a sensible arrangement with no illusions on either side.'

Anna kept very quiet wondering what was coming next. 'So, over the last few months, since I've been at Church View, I've been researching places and people. The hotels are no problem, I've found several I would be happy to enjoy in my final days and one little self-catering cottage was ideal, but I've had less success with the people. I auditioned a new escort with each new hotel. You see, I need someone, a man or a woman, to spend those last few days with who will be fun, interesting and a good lover but most of all who will not be devastated by my death. That last condition seems hard to fulfil because in the course of spending time with people they tend to get attached even when they're professionals.'

Anna couldn't resist a sharp intake of breath and Helena reached out her hand to touch Anna's. 'Oh, please, don't misunderstand me,' she said, 'I wouldn't do it while that person was in the hotel but they may hear of it afterwards and I wouldn't want anyone to be upset or think it was their fault.' Helena swilled the remains of her brandy round the balloon glass and then downed it. 'That's it, really.'

'I don't know what to say.'

'No, of course you don't, but you see I've had a long time to think all this through.'

'So you're still searching?'

'I am, in theory, but I don't know, the urgency of it has slackened since all this business with Kara. I suppose it's made me feel needed but more than that I've felt part of the living world and there's been less time for planning to leave it. I'm wavering but not sure what that means, what other outcome might be possible. It's like that Robert Frost poem, you know, *The Road Not Taken*? I'm noticing there may be a few different tracks into my inevitable wilderness that I hadn't noticed before.'

'I hope you find one,' Anna said. 'My father would say none of us are ever really alone, that we move along surrounded by a host of companions only briefly and occasionally glimpsed in the flesh. What some people might call angels.'

Helena looked steadily at her. 'Well, that's a nice idea but I can't rely on one popping up when I'm dribbling into my nightie, can I?' She put money on the table and gathered her bag and coat. 'Time to let you go home. I haven't been at work all day. I hope you're not too shocked?'

Anna stood up, too, a rush of admiration flushing through her. This, this strategy of Helena's may be controversial ethically and she wasn't sure if she agreed with it but her attitude to her painful situation seemed to show raw courage. 'I'm honoured that you told me,' she said, 'but I have a strong feeling that this is only the first scene of what you say is the third act. I hate cliff-hangers and I think there will be much more to tell. I hope so, anyway.'

Helena leaned forward and kissed her on the cheek. 'What a kind thing to say. We'll have to see – perhaps there is a braver way than the one I was planning.'

Anna drove to Shell's to pick Kara up, listened while she talked about the wedding, dropped her off at the towpath and watched until she was safely inside Rosa's boat and then was finally free to mull over the extraordinary situation that Helena had confided to her.

'I have no-one,' Helena had said stoically and the words had fallen into Anna's heart like little grenades. How lucky Anna was and how stupid to let the internal tussle over Alice spoil her future with Steve. What was it Billy Childish had said? 'If you want to feel rich, value what you have.'

Kara lay in the middle part of the boat where Rosa had contrived a bunk for her and stared out of the porthole window at the night sky. She had watched the whole time while the moon had appeared from one side of the circle and disappeared beyond the other. She had asked Anna for a photograph of Robert Lindo and when Anna had picked her up to go to Shell's she had given one to her so she could show her friend, too. Now she didn't need to look at it because she could recall every pixel of it. Shell had borrowed her father's new copier to blow it up to life size and they had sat in front of her dressing-table mirror with the picture next to Kara's face and compared every aspect.

Obviously, the eyes caught their attention first even though Robert's brows were heavier than Kara's and there were dark shadows under his which she didn't have. Otherwise the sloping almond shape of them and the colour were the same. He had more freckles than she did but the same light skin. It was hard to see the nose shape looking straight at the face but her mouth was definitely a smaller, more feminine version of his. They had argued about the chin, Kara saying it was like hers but Shell laughing and saying Robert's was much heavier. It wasn't possible to see if he had dimples. That reminded her of Bob's lie that his mother had a dimple like hers. She felt cold and sick when he came into her mind like that, an unwelcome visitor, but she pushed him out immediately.

Anna had told her a lot about her father and she constantly reviewed the things she knew. But Anna couldn't tell her how he would behave when they met, how she would feel, whether they could ever be close. He had been in prison for twenty years – what damage had that done to him? Could she really trust him?

She shifted her position on the made-up bed and tried to think of the wedding instead. Rosa's soft snoring made her smile and relax and she liked the way the boat moved very slightly in the water with a change of wind or a passing boat which happened sometimes even during the night. She knew she couldn't stay here for ever but for now it felt so good to be wanted and to have a cheerful and encouraging companion. Rosa had told her that a large man called Len might show up but that despite his rather basic manners he was not a worry – he was a friend. If she wasn't there Kara should simply tell him so and to phone her so they could catch up.

She brought her mind back again to the wedding to chase out darker thoughts. It was only a week away now but things were going well. Mostly Shell's mum and dad had done all the booking and checking and so on, and that had left Shell free for the fun part – the last fitting for the dress, the practices with make-up and hair and the big debate about the spray tan. Kara now grinned in the darkness, relieved to have such a girly problem to think about.

Normally, Shell would not have given it a second thought. Of course she would be spray-tanned, the only question would be how deeply. But it had not escaped the girls' attention that the sun-baked look had gone out of fashion. Television presenters and pop singers and so forth now had a kind of moonbeam pallor. Shell's aunty had been on a competition show about antiques on the television and she had said that they were all made up to look very pale with some metallic powders or something. On the other hand, Shell would look much better with a bit of colour on her skin, Kara thought, as it was still a wintry greyish colour.

Also, Shell had not taken Helena's advice about minimal, naturalistic make-up and had booked a beautician. The trial run, which had happened during the horrible time when Kara was away, had resulted in Shell looking nothing like herself at all but as though eyebrows from one of the weirder reality tv girls had been pasted on to her head. Shell loved the look and wanted Kara and Lauren to have the same treatment but Kara had refused and so had Lauren which should have rung an alarm bell for the bride but hadn't.

Even so, her hair was going to be very nice and Kara hugged herself with pleasure at the thought of doing it for the actual day. Shell had wanted Kara to have her hair loose with a purple flower at the side but that wasn't going to happen. It brought back too many memories. Instead, Kara had worked on a style where she pushed the bulk of her hair to one side at the back and pinned it with a long, diamante comb topped off with the purple flower. At the front it would be sprayed flat and tucked behind her ear.

A star was now in the centre of the black circle and seemed to be winking at her. As she watched other stars which she hadn't noticed before appeared around it like timid attendants and she wondered if her father had a window so he could watch the night sky and whether he could see the same constellation she was now looking at. She closed her eyes and drifted into sleep.

33

When Kara slid into the passenger seat beside her on Saturday, Anna noticed that she was carrying a plastic tub as well as her bag. She seemed composed but there was a slight puffiness to her eyes that made Anna wonder if she had been crying or had not slept well, or both, which would be understandable. Otherwise she was as dressed as usual in her parka, jeggings and little boots.

Once they were on the main road Kara said, 'I've made some meringues for a present. Rosa showed me how to make tiny ones in the microwave and then stick them together with rose-water flavoured butter cream.'

'Mm. Lovely,' Anna said, negotiating a large island.

'I would have liked to make a cake, I never have before, but Rosa doesn't have an oven and everyone likes meringues, don't they?' She turned an anxious face to Anna. 'Will he think it's a stupid present?'

'No, it's great. But he may not have a present for you because of his circumstances – he wouldn't be able to get anything. You won't be disappointed?' Kara shook her head and stared out of the window. 'So, tell me what you're wearing for Shell's wedding – I'd love to hear about it. A friend and I are going to a wedding the same weekend and his little girl is going to be a bridesmaid, too. Of course, she's only six, but she couldn't be more excited. She takes her silver shoes to bed with her every night!'

Kara turned, smiling, and talked for the next ten minutes or so about the wedding but Anna could tell that she was merely colluding in passing the time and that she wasn't really distracted from the enormous event that was about to happen. How could she be? By the time they were on the motorway heading south Anna noticed that the young woman was trembling slightly. It was as though her whole body was suspended in an oscillator so that the tendrils of her hair were vibrating and her knees were jiggling. A service station was approaching. 'We could stop here for a few minutes,' Anna said. 'Would you like a hot drink or the loo? Anything?'

'I just want to see him,' Kara said, and the tremor was in her voice, too. 'I just want it to happen. Even if it's bad, if he doesn't like me, I want to get it over.'

Useless for Anna to protest that of course he would like her, love her, because nothing Anna could say would make any difference. It was impossible not to be reminded of the time she had met her mother and how her feelings had punched and buffeted her as though she had been thrown about by a dodgem car even though she was standing stock-still looking at a caricature of her own face. But Robert Lindo was nothing like Anna's mother.

As they turned into the approach to the prison Kara stiffened and sat up straight, her back held away from the seat. Gleams of weak sun were probing through the cloud cover but were not enough to improve the institutional blocks of cells and administration offices and the asphalt yards. Kara glanced around and lifted her chin bravely.

Anna had prepared her for the processes they would go through and she cooperated wordlessly with everything that was required. The plastic tub was opened and inspected and then closed and returned. But instead of turning down the now-familiar corridor to the visiting rooms, Anna saw that they were being led in the opposite direction. Kara walked with a straight back holding the tub out in front of her like a princess from antiquity bringing tribute to her king, Anna thought fancifully. Pictures she had seen of the friezes at Persepolis came to mind but it wasn't just the gift, it was Kara's slender beauty and upright and graceful bearing. She knew the young woman was very nervous and had herself tightly under control but she had sufficient character not to show it. Anna fell back a little so that it would be Kara who would enter first whatever room they were going to.

When the young female officer opened the door to the library and ushered Kara in, Anna, following her, saw that a table had been laid with a cloth and flowers and place settings for three people. The crockery was institutional white but there were colourful paper napkins on each plate and in the middle of the table a heaped dish of filled bread rolls and another of fancy cakes. She smiled gratefully at the officer who smiled back. But the room was empty.

Kara took a few steps inside and then halted, barely moving her head. 'Is he coming?' she whispered.

'He's here,' said the officer.

There was utter silence.

Then, from behind a tall bank of book-shelves, Robert Lindo stepped out.

Kara saw before her a tall, slim man with broad shoulders dressed in a white T shirt and jeans. He didn't move towards her and her own feet were stuck to the floor. Everything else disappeared – even feelings disappeared – and it was just the two of them in the universe. And then, it seemed without either of them moving, they were together, in each other's arms, and she was feeling the urgent beat of his heart against her body, the warmth of his arms and shoulders and the caress of his hand on her hair. After some time, how long she had no idea, they drew apart a little and he looked down at her.

'My sweet baby,' he said, choking on the words, 'my precious girl.'

'You *are* my dad - I know you are,' Kara breathed.

Then they were quiet again, standing together and fitting each other as if they had been carved from the same tree trunk. There was a feeling that Kara had never known before, a feeling that she had only heard about in songs and the whispered confessions of friends: a feeling of being home at last. Belonging.

Robert whispered in her ear, 'Better eat something, my dear, or we'll be shouted at after all their trouble. Come now.' But she knew he was smiling and she let him lead her to the table and seat her as though she was a great lady. 'A little bird told me that you like hot chocolate – it's all set up – but have something else if you wish, sweetheart, just say the word.'

'I have something for you. I made them.' Kara took the lid off the container and showed him the little meringues clustered together like balls of cotton wool.

He clapped his hands in delight and looked round for Anna who had melted away to the side wall. 'Look! Look what my daughter has brought me! Fair-weather clouds, yes?' He beckoned to her. 'Come, come and sit with us.'

It was so easy, Kara thought, when she had feared it would be so hard. They talked a little about whatever came up and laughed at whatever was said not because it was funny but because they were too full of joy not to let it out. But after a while he grew serious and Kara knew why. 'Are you ok?' he asked, his brows drawing together just like hers did, making a little tent of creases in the middle. 'I can't believe all those hard things you've been through on your own. I wanted to come to you, Kara, I tried to.'

'I know.' She took his large hand in her two small ones and squeezed it.

'You're a very brave woman. I'm sorry you had to go through it but I'm so proud of you standing up to him.' Then he dropped his eyes.

Kara didn't hesitate. It was as though she had rehearsed this conversation ever since the revelations about him from Anna in the depths of the night although she hadn't, except that some process that had been unfolding in the recesses of her heart. She pressed his hand again. 'And I'm proud of you,' she said. 'You saved your mother's life.'

His head raised and he stared at her in disbelief. 'I killed a man,' he said.

'So did I.'

No-one moved and it was so quiet that the clacking tick of the digital wall-clock could be heard. At last he said, still staring at her, 'You forgive me?'

She was calm and steady. 'You forgave me before you even knew what he had done.'

'No, angel, it's not the same, I was a strong young man.' He shook his head, as if unable to take in what she was saying, as though the scalding judgement he had heard in court all those years ago was branded on his brain.

'It is the same. There is nothing to forgive, Dad.' It seemed to Anna that Kara had grown from a girl to a woman in the few minutes they had spent in the library. She wasn't just setting him free, she was releasing herself, too. She let go of his hand, turned to the table and picked up the tub of fair-weather clouds and offered them to her father. His face relaxed into smiles and he took one and popped it in his mouth.

'I have a gift for you,' he said, quickly swallowing his meringue. He leaped up and went back to the shelves and reappeared with a roll of card. 'This is just the start, Kara, this is just the introduction.' They pushed the plates aside on the table and he unrolled the thin card. It had coloured drawings round the edges of shells and palm trees and brightly coloured fish but in the middle, in perfect draughtsman's calligraphy, was a family tree. He had even drawn and painted the connections like the trunk and limbs of a real tree with leaves and blossoms. It was a work of art. Kara sat staring at it, trying to understand it.

His sinewy arm stretched across the chart and he pointed near to the bottom with one long finger. 'Here, this is you, my Kara.'

Anna was too fascinated to stay out of it. 'But Robert, there are nine generations here going back to the late 1700s, how did you find all this out?'

Robert laughed. 'I didn't! My cousins got into it, look here they are, Claudette and Michael and they went to the Cayman Islands Archives and looked it all up – I think some of the paper records are still in Jamaica. They got all the way back to when the first Johnsons settled, when the Cayman Islands still had pirates, runaways, outlaws as well as respectable people.'

'That is where we come from?' Kara asked, her eyes wide and bright.

'Yes, darling.' Robert took an envelope from his back pocket. 'This is what it looks like, your island home.' He had a stack of about a dozen photographs, not too many for Kara to take in on this first meeting, and he named the relatives he had found and the villages and bays and colour-washed houses and everywhere there was the deep blue sky overhead.

'Maybe one day I could save up enough to visit,' Kara said softly, turning the photos over and over in her hands.

'Well, you could,' Robert replied seriously, 'or you could come with me this summer!'

'What?'

'I'm sad that you won't meet my mum, but she left me some money and I can use it for us to go there. I've never been myself, man! It will be an adventure for both of us!' He burst out laughing. 'We can meet them all, our family, they're just about going crazy waiting to meet you.'

'Really?' Kara whispered incredulously, 'Really?'

For the next hour while the tea grew cold and Anna sat back and listened, they talked, their voices overlapping, interrupting, teasing, asking questions, finding that they both woke early, liked curry sauce on their chips, hated grime music, were double-jointed in one thumb, and so on and so on. Finally the prison officer stepped forward and they had to leave. 'I'm going to email you the minute I get into Anna's car,' Kara said to Robert, 'will you write to me when you can?'

'I'm doing it now,' he said. He held out his arms and she slipped into them as though she had known the way all her life.

When they parted they both had tears in their eyes. 'Soon,' he said gently, 'soon.'

Before she followed Kara out Anna took an envelope from her bag and handed it to Robert. 'It's a letter. See what you think,' she said, 'let me know.'

He caught her arm as she turned to go. 'I will be thanking you all my life,' he said, so then her vision was blurred too as she hurried away.

On the journey home the talk re-lived the meeting: remembering snippets of information, being freshly amazed at family resemblances, planning what to do on Robert's day release, and Kara had chattered happily for an hour with little need of prompting from Anna. Anna dropped her off at the moorings and drove home feeling relieved and exhausted.

George's car had been left in the drive and the space by its side, usually taken by Anna's, was now full of Faye's Micra. This was good because Faye hadn't visited for a while and Anna wanted to know how the budget was going. She parked her car on the road and locked it, hurrying in to see her daughter and wondering whether their available food, which she couldn't off the top of her head recall, might encourage her and Jack, if he was with her, to stay for dinner. As she opened the front door she heard the familiar and unwelcome sounds from upstairs of Faye and Ellis shouting at each other.

'Like you care!' Ellis was yelling, 'You didn't even phone, did you?'

'I didn't know, you cretin, because nobody told me! It's like I don't exist!'

Anna thought about going back out again and then sighed and climbed the stairs, her buoyant mood gone. 'What's going on?' she asked, 'What are you arguing about? Hi, Faye, nice to see you, darling.'

'Well, that's just what I bloody need, isn't it?' Faye shouted at her, 'Sarcasm from my own mother!' Both she and Ellis were brick-red with their exertions and Anna saw with dismay that this was no ordinary spat because Faye seemed to be on the brink of tears.

'I wasn't being sarcastic, Faye, I meant it – it's lovely to see you. Whatever this is, it obviously needs to be sorted out so I'm going downstairs to put the kettle on and I'd like you both to come down, too.'

'If you think…' Ellis began.

'Just come down,' Anna said firmly, trudging down into the hall, 'please.'

As she set out the mugs and opened a packet of biscuits she had the sinking feeling that she knew what this row was about. Since Faye had moved out she tended to contact the family on the basis of need-to-have rather than social bonding. She would text Anna to get a simple recipe (which was the only kind her mother knew) or to ask her how to get nail varnish off sheets (impossible) or request various household items if she was feeling too languid to steal them. There had been a couple of family meals but not much more contact than that because the couple were working, socialising or taken up with various beautification projects on their new home.

Chairs scraped and Faye and Ellis sat down in their usual places. Faye's chestnut hair was pulled roughly up into a pony tail and her chocolate button eyes stared out of a face bare of make-up. Ellis' fair skin was blotched with angry red patches. Anna set down mugs before them and sat down herself. 'Are you ok?' she asked Faye, hoping that her diagnosis of the reason for the row was wrong, 'Everything all right with Jack and work?'

'You've remembered you have a daughter, then?'

'You are such a mumpsimous,' Ellis snorted, 'you get everything wrong.'

'Do you know how pretentious you sound, you little prick?' Faye retorted.

'Just hush for a minute, Ell,' Anna said, 'I want to hear what's upset you, Faye. Will you tell me, love?'

'It's you,' Faye said, her eyes full of tears, 'why didn't you tell me you were nearly murdered?'

'Well, because I wasn't. What's this about?' Oh dear, Anna thought.

'You were there, weren't you? You could have been killed by that pervert and his horrible spiders and I wouldn't have even known. You were rescuing that girl weren't you?'

'Ok. Let's just cool this down. I was never in the slightest danger and Kara rescued herself, didn't she? It had nothing to do with me. All I did was wrap my coat round her when she came out into the street. What I do feel bad about is not thinking that you might get wind of me being there because I should have told you myself, not let you hear from someone else.'

'Tash's mum told her the police arrested you!'

'They didn't.' Anna explained. Faye reached out and took a biscuit, sniffing back the mucus in her nose while she considered this.

'She's nice, actually,' Ellis said, throwing dry straw on still-glowing embers, 'I didn't realise girls your age could be nice.'

Faye froze, the biscuit half way to her mouth. 'You *met* her?'

'Mm,' Ellis said casually, taking another digestive himself, 'she stayed here for a few days.'

'She – stayed – here!' Faye yelled. 'And no-one told me!'

'She needed to be quiet,' Anna said, 'she mostly just kept to herself.'

Faye leaped to her feet. 'So what are you saying? That I don't know how to be tactful and supportive? How dare you! You can all just go screw yourselves!' She grabbed her coat and Anna desperately moved to intervene so she wouldn't crash out and sulk for weeks. She had to find some reason to keep her here while she calmed down.

'Faye, please don't go, I need your help.' What could she possibly need her help for, apart from housework which would be a pointless ask?

Faye halted at the kitchen door. 'What for?'

Inspiration struck. 'I've got to go to Briony and Kimi's wedding next weekend and I have no idea what I'm going to wear – please, will you help me look through my stuff to see if there is anything half-way decent?'

Faye dropped her coat on the big chair and glared at her mother. 'You are so hopeless, Mum, you should have sorted this out weeks ago. Come on, I haven't got all day.' She stomped into the hall and thumped her way up the stairs. In the big bedroom Faye flung open the double wardrobe doors and clicked her way through the hangers like a merchant with his abacus beads. 'Nothing.'

'I thought maybe that cream shirt with a black skirt?'

'They'll be having you hand round the prosecco. Is this really all you have?' Faye barked at her.

'There's a storage tub under the bed for old things I never wear,' Anna said feebly, 'but I don't think...' Faye was already down on her knees and pulling the tub out with its top coat of dust. 'I can't think what's in there – it's probably just rubbish.'

Faye tore the lid off scattering dust bunnies all over the pale carpet and peeled back layers until she pulled out something deep blue and lacy. 'What's this?' she demanded.

'Oh,' Anna murmured, sinking down on the bed, 'that must be over twenty years old – it's older than you. It's the dress I wore to our graduation ball. Your dad rented a tux as we called it then and I wore that. I got it from the market for fifteen pounds.'

Faye was only half listening. She shook out the fabric, checked the seams and the lining and stated, 'This is perfect. Lace dresses are totally in but I'll have to take it up at least thirty centimetres - you're such a shrimp you can't wear long dresses. Will it still fit you, though? There's no spare fabric in the seams to let out and you're probably much fatter now you're middle-aged. Put it on.'

Anna draped her day clothes over the wicker chair and slipped on the blue dress thinking it should probably be treated to a dry-clean. She felt the lining slip down her body and the lace sleeves hug her arms. It went on, yes, she could get it on, but what she wouldn't tell Faye was that it used to be a loose Kaftan in the '90s. It wasn't loose now.

'That's lucky,' Faye said approvingly, 'not such a lardarse as I thought.'

Anna looked at herself in the wardrobe mirror. 'Do you think it will do?'

'Just leave it on while I pin the length,' Faye said, 'where did you put the pins?' Anna indicated her dressing table drawer. 'I'll turn it up tomorrow, I know I've got some thread that will do for this colour but Mum, you have to buy some shoes with heels to go with it. You'll look like a total frump otherwise. Navy or nude, ok? And at least seven centimetres heel, right?'

So Anna stood on her bedroom chair while Faye crouched and worked round the hem with a mouthful of pins, every now and then mumbling an instruction. Although the dress now touched her skin everywhere she had curves, Anna remembered it very well. They had all been dizzy with excitement now that their exams were a distant horror and the graduation ceremony was over, the oldies off to their hotels and a whole night of fun ahead. In retrospect it was a blur of lights and noise and laughter and far, far too much wine, but she clearly remembered taking Harry back to her tiny student room and what happened as day dawned.

'Take it off,' Faye ordered. 'I'm going to cut the extra off now. Where are my special scissors?'

'They're in the kitchen drawer, I think.' Anna's voice was muffled by the silkiness and lace of the fabric as it slipped past. 'I used them to cut Pop's hair.'

'How could you do that?' Faye yelled and rushed off.

Anna stood in her bra and panties holding the dress and letting the fabric slide between her fingers until she found the place, not far from the hem, where she knew there was a small tear. She smiled, remembering how that had happened. She would keep the piece that Faye cut off and put it back in the box to find again and remember again.

After Faye left she discovered Ellis was cooking sausages for their evening meal so she went to the larder and got out a tin of tomatoes to go with them and a jar of English mustard. 'I'm sorry Faye was upset, it's horrible to feel left out,' she said to him, 'but she's ok now. You didn't help.'

'Oh, Mum, she just hates missing out on the drama.' He flipped the sausages with the tongs. 'Rosa phoned, wants you to phone back. Shall I do fried bread and mushrooms with these?' He snapped open the bread bin and grabbed a loaf. 'You don't mind if we paint my room black, do you? The caretaker says there's gallons of blackboard paint left over from when they went to interactive whiteboards and it's a pain in the bum to get rid of, he says.'

Anna took her phone into the front room, lit the fire and settled on the couch which still had the faint, earthy stink of Bobble. Rosa had had a postcard to announce Len's return some time mid-week and was gently reminding Anna that she was supposed to be having a word with him. She sat and thought about what to say to her brother and decided that since she had the key to his flat she would go round tomorrow and cheer it up a bit for his homecoming and get some food in. That might soften the blow. It was useless to phone him as he never replied to her and she sometimes wondered if his huge square fingers couldn't operate the keys on his cheap mobile.

She leaned her head back against the cushions of the couch and wondered about Robert and how he was feeling. The meeting had gone better than she had hoped and she knew that her part in

their lives was almost over. Just one more thing, maybe, if all went
to plan.

34

Anna climbed the concrete stairs with the garden bucket full of cleaning stuff in one hand and a bag of groceries in the other. She needed a fantasy. She had been to Len's flat a few times before and she didn't want to dwell on it while she cleaned it. Len did not acknowledge the necessity for housework or house maintenance. He had zero interest in décor. When she had been on a campaign to clean him up (to woo Rosa) she had also mentioned that 70% of household dust was human skin and that was why unclean and unventilated living spaces smelled rancid. To say this comment had had no impact was like saying that icebergs don't make it to the tropics. By the time she reached the scuffed door she had decided that she and Steve would fly out to the Cayman Islands and stay in a hotel where they could hear the sound of the surf. That should keep her mind occupied for half an hour.

Only one small window could be opened and she did that immediately and then went into the bathroom and, averting her eyes as much as possible, poured bleach into the loo and sprayed the bath thickly with a strong cleaner. Leaving that do its work while she and Steve stepped on to a pristine white beach, she took the few steps into the kitchen and picked out the hob cleaner, spraying it liberally on the greasy surface. She would be wearing something floaty tucked around her waist (which would be several inches smaller) and a sophisticated black bikini. She drew the line at his oven. As she ran water into the stained kitchen bowl until it ran steaming hot, she and Steve found a little thatched cabin among the coconut palms where a smiling young man was waiting to offer them long tropical drinks. Somewhere in the background was the sound of Salsa or was it Soca? She put on her longest rubber gloves.

She had brought rags and soaked them in the frothy hot water and then worked round the kitchen surfaces, moving crusty crockery on to the draining board, while the white surf lapped at her bare, brown feet and Steve pulled her deeper into the water. She went back and scrubbed the bathroom, rinsing off the chemicals and flushing the newly sanitised toilet before she swabbed at the sticky floor. No island paradise was up to distracting her here but things did look and smell better. She closed the door and went into the living room. (She had never seen and never wanted to see Len's bedroom.) Here was enough but the dust and clutter defeated her.

She went back to the kitchen and loaded the groceries into the fridge and the cupboards. She felt she had more than done her bit. The fantasy had only worked so far. Now she was furious with her brother for living in such a state. Other people had made their flats lovely – there was just no excuse for it.

Basically, she was fond of him and felt sorry for him because their mother had been so neglectful and selfish towards him but there were times, like today, when more negative feelings rose up. She knew that despite having no disabilities or dependents Len lived on benefits and how he had wangled that she couldn't fathom. When he had been younger he had tried several jobs, mostly zero-hours rip-offs, but he had never lasted more than a few weeks even in them. She had not talked to him about it because it wasn't her business but she secretly despised him for it. Was he actually good enough for Rosa anyway? What did she see in him? She threw her cleaning materials back in the bucket and locked the door behind her, seething with resentment. Then she had to unlock the door again to put the note she had brought with her on the kitchen counter asking him to come round on Friday night if possible. She had added that he was invited for dinner which in her current mood she regretted.

But, by the time she'd turned into her own road the ugly emotions had sloughed off like the grease on Len's hob and she decided she would see if Ellis would like to go over to Safe 'n' Sound and take Bobble out for a walk down the canal. She would see if Steve and Alice were free to come, too. It was cold and damp but not actually raining and she needed the fresh air. She needed a shower.

As she stepped into the hall Ellis and three of the band appeared from the kitchen. They were carrying paintbrushes, rollers and paint pads and making for the stairs in full cry. 'Put paper down!' she yelled after them, 'Don't get it on your feet!' A surge of sound was the response so Anna had to run up and hammer on the door and shout another demand for the sake of the poor neighbours. She would have to make do with getting changed and shower later. First, she needed to put the things in the bucket away in their high cupboard in the utility room.

Len's huge bulk planted at the kitchen table greeted her. 'Sis.'

'I thought you weren't home for a few days?'

'Last gig got nixed. No-one showed up. Rosa said to come here.'

The sights and smells of his flat were still with her like burps after fatty food and not only that, her irritation with him hadn't completely swilled away either. 'I'm a bit weary, actually, Len,' she said. 'Could we do this another time?'

'I been here nearly an hour,' he said not moving.

'I've been cleaning your flat up.'

'Why?'

Really, she thought, do I really have to do this now? She couldn't imagine being in a worse frame of mind to gently and kindly tell Len that there wasn't a cat in hell's chance of his marrying Rosa. She put the kettle on. 'There's a can of Coke in the fridge if you want it.' He lumbered over and got the can pulling out a quarter pound of cheese to go with it. In the mood she was in he could make his own sandwich, she thought resentfully, so she half threw the bread on to the table and pushed a knife and plate at him. He scowled.

'What's up with you?'

'I told you, it's been a full-on week.'

'Well, don't take it out on me.'

This was pointless and stupid - she was behaving as badly as Faye and Ellis and who was she to judge Len, anyway? 'Sorry, Len. Did you have a good tour?'

But small talk wasn't on Len's agenda. He shifted on the old chair making it shriek sharply. 'S'alright. So tell me what she said.' Anna could tell he was nervous because the generous lump of cheese was still on his plate unmolested.

She took a calming drink of her tea. 'First, Len, she wants to be sure you know how much she thinks of you and likes you.'

Len blinked this away. 'But.'

'But, she says she'll never be able to be in a proper relationship, like marry anyone, ever.'

'Why not?' Every fibre of Len's being was focussed on her and she felt as though she was caught in the main beams of a juggernaut.

Anna couldn't think of any way to soften what she had been told and still give him a valid reason. 'She didn't go into details, she only said that something bad happened to her when she was a child and because of that she feels it wouldn't be fair to marry anyone.'

Len sat silently mulling this over. It was hard to describe his expression, Anna thought, somewhere between hurt and anger. 'I don't know anything else, Len. I'm sorry.'

'Does she want me to stay away?' he asked eventually.

'I don't think so, no, but she expects you will because she says she's got nothing to offer. I told you, she's very fond of you.'

Len stood up abruptly knocking the chair he had been sitting on over and not noticing. 'I'm off then,' he said. 'Tell her you told me.' He had not taken off his coat so he was gone quickly and Anna's pity-offer of the cheese was spoken to an empty room.

She sighed and let her mind drift through the options for the afternoon. She didn't want to go out now that there were four teenage boys loose in the house whooping around with gallons of black paint and she couldn't really face Alice visiting and inevitably disapproving of her, good as it would be to see Steve. The day's joyful re-union was a distant glow. She reached for her phone and texted George to ask when he was coming home.

Kara had washed and ironed her work uniform and Rosa had shown her the bus stop on the Bristol Road and given her the times of the 144 from Selly Oak to Bromsgrove and back. She was nervous to be going to Church View because she dreaded questions from everyone but it would be good to see Helena who had sent her several nice texts. Even Mrs Bandhal had sent an email to say she was looking forward to Kara coming back and she must be sure to ask for support or time off if needed which was kind of her.

Rosa had made a special meal for her to set her up for the next day and opened a bottle of her own blackberry cordial. It was paella, something she'd never eaten before, and she'd watched in fascination as Rosa chatted to her and prepared and cooked the ingredients. For pudding there were windfall apples from the towpath that had been wrapped in newspaper and kept in a biscuit tin all winter, stewed and sweetened with honey. Up to now Kara had never realised that cooking was so interesting and Rosa had said that she had a natural gift for it which was encouraging. After dinner Rosa taught her how to play rummy and she ended up winning the last three games.

So, there should have been no reason for what happened that night. She had gone to sleep thinking as always now about her dad and whispering good-night to him and kissing her fingertips to the stars. They were there whether she could see them or not, like him.

But then, in the deepest time of darkness, the nightmare had erupted. At first she'd only been aware of a scratching at her skin but then, when it became painful, she found she couldn't move. She was paralysed and helpless to stop the biting and pulling and then there was something dark and venomous inside her and it was tunnelling, whizzing and twisting and cutting until her insides were riddled with passageways running with blood and she wanted to yell for help but couldn't because no sound would come out. Then there were things scuttling, as terrified as she, things with arms and legs and howling gargoyle faces and she saw that they were children. She tried to wake up, she tried to scream herself awake but it was no good, they were everywhere, they were going to fill her up with their terror until she burst.

'Wake up! Wake up, Kara! You're safe, you're ok, I'm here.' Rosa was shaking her shoulder and she woke in a panic and burst into tears. Rosa held her and stroked her hair and murmured to her and eventually she grew quiet and was able to wipe the wetness and snot from her face with the tissues given her. Rosa left her for a few minutes to go into the galley but was soon back with a mug of sweet hot tea. 'Sip this,' she said and sat down again beside her.

Kara sat propped up on pillows against the cabin wall letting the liquid seep into her but barely noticing it. She was staring, unseeing, into the shadows. 'Everyone thinks that the worst thing was Bob, you know, that he was going to let one of those spiders sting me to death.'

'But that isn't the worst thing?' Rosa prompted when Kara stopped.

'I was terrified. I still can't believe I killed him. I think I'm still in shock. But it's not that because that's over. It's what I saw, what's going on, what I might have done, that I can't bear.' Rosa took the mug from her and set it down and then picked up Kara's slim, shivering hand and held it between her own. Kara turned to look at her, the tears spilling again down her cheeks. 'The photographs I saw,' she said, 'those poor, poor children. I would have gone out there and brought more back, made them willing to come. I would have led them into lives of torture I didn't even know existed. I would have done that and not even realised, Rosa, not even realised what I was doing!' Rosa held her hand tightly now.

'That isn't in the past, it isn't over, is it? It's really happening here, where we live, everywhere. I know it is. I know now and I can't forget.'

'He took your innocence,' Rosa said quietly. 'He took your peace of mind.'

'Why don't the police stop them?' Kara cried, 'Why doesn't someone do something? I know about the boys they found, those ones that were killed. Wasn't anybody caring about them, wondering how they'd got here, listening to what they said when they could still speak?'

'I think the police often just assume they're illegal immigrants and report them to the Border Control people instead of quickly investigating and then, by speaking out, they've become a threat so they get killed or held somewhere no-one can find them. Sometimes the dots don't get joined up fast enough by the authorities so the kids are lost.'

The two women sat together holding each other miserably thinking that there could be children close by, certainly there would be many in a city as large as Birmingham, living with cold people whose only interest in them was exploitation. Kara said, 'I'm going to try to do something to help. I can't just pretend I don't know now.'

'Yes,' said Rosa, 'that would be a good thing to do.'

The nightmare had not completely gone away. Kara felt that there were bruises and wounds within her that never would heal and that despite the good things that her future seemed now to hold, she would never again be like Shell, like Lauren, she would never be able to return to the way she had been. Things seen cannot be unseen and terrible things known cannot be forgotten. She had observed the people who did these things - Bob, Jan and the others and she knew that wicked people look just the same as everyone else and perhaps everyone has, however small and hidden, the capacity for evil.

She looked into Rosa's eyes. 'I'm different,' she said sadly, 'I'm damaged.'

Rosa eased a little away from her so Kara could look at her properly. 'How would you describe me?' she said seriously.

'You're amazing,' Kara said immediately.

'What does that mean?'

Kara was surprised at the question. Rosa had not seemed like the kind of person to ask for compliments or even to talk about herself when Kara had just admitted something so painful. 'I don't know, um, strong, independent, caring, fun, the sort of person you feel safe with.'

Rosa did not thank her. 'Ok. I'm going to tell you something that I've never told anyone else but I'm telling it you for a reason. Remember what you just said about me, ok?' Kara nodded. 'My little brother and I lived with our mum and dad on a canal boat when we were growing up. They worked it on the stretch between here and London hauling stuff before the lorries took over and they were out of jobs. They fought a lot because there was no money and that was how they dealt with their worries like a lot of people do. Sometimes my dad hit us, sometimes my mum smacked our heads. Most families we knew were the same.

'One night, when I was eleven and Dean was a few years younger, mum and dad went off to the pub and drank too much and on the way back they had a row and he hit her and she fell in the cut and drowned.' Kara's hand flew to her mouth but she said nothing. 'He was too drunk to get her out so he stumbled back to the pub to get help. Three of his mates said they would come and he stayed behind crying and feeling sorry for himself. But they weren't interested in jumping into cold water to try to save a woman who was probably dead by then. They knew that in the boat were two children on their own and that one of them was a little girl.'

'Oh God,' Kara said, wanting Rosa to stop.

'I'm not going to tell you what happened,' Rosa said, 'but I was hurt so badly that I can never have sex or have children. That's all you need to know.'

'I'm so sorry,' Kara said deeply distressed, 'I'm so sorry that happened to you.'

'I'm telling you this for a reason,' Rosa replied, cupping Kara's face in her hands. 'What's the reason I'm telling you this, sweetheart? Think. Tell me.'

Kara leaned forward and put her arms around Rosa's neck and whispered into her ear. 'I can still be a good person, too, like you are.'

'Pain like ours doesn't ever go away,' Rosa said, kissing her cheek, 'but it settles somewhere inside you and becomes part of you and you learn to live with it.'

The sky outside the porthole was lightening into a greenish-grey and Rosa twisted her neck to see her wall-clock. 'It's almost time we were getting up,' she said. 'How about I make us working women a bacon sandwich and a proper pot of tea?'

35

When Anna tottered into the kitchen on Saturday in her lacy blue dress and nude heels Ellis, looking up from his phone, said, 'Who are you and what have you done with my mother?'

'Well, thanks for that, Ell. I do look pretty good, don't I?' She twirled carefully so as not to fall over.

'Is Steve coming here for you?'

'No, he's going on ahead because Alice has to be there early. It's not far away. I'll take my flats to drive in.'

He followed her to the front door as she changed her shoes and donned her black work coat and put his hands on her shoulders. 'I really hate to tell you this,' he said sombrely looking down at her, 'but as a responsible son I have to.'

'What?' Was he serious? Had something happened?

'You've got a pink roller stuck in the back of your hair.'

It was exciting to be going out to a special occasion all dressed up (and she did look good) where there would be fun and great food and dancing and it would be lovely to see Kimi and Briony exchange their vows. She knew that she and Steve wouldn't know many people. If anyone from Kimi's family came they would surely ignore Anna and she had no desire to talk to them – well, maybe William – and Briony had no family so her friends would be lawyers and such but it was ok. She would be with Steve and they would enjoy it together.

The country hotel near Studley was an elegant early Victorian manor house brightened on the outside by tubs of carefully forced spring bulbs against evergreen shrubs. Anna parked behind in the allocated space and then cursed them as she tried to walk on the gravel in her heels. Another guest called to her and indicated a slabbed path so she stumbled on to that. How could women wear these things all day? Her toes, jammed together in the pointy bit, were already complaining. In the foyer, which was done up with dark oak panelling and bevelled mirrors, she was able to ditch her workaday coat and pop into the loo to check that she didn't have lipstick on her teeth.

People were milling around in their best clothes and it was only ten minutes to the ceremony so she needed to find Steve to get a good seat for him to video Alice's starring performance as ordered. She turned down a dim corridor that led to the restaurant and saw, striding towards her, a tall, handsome man in a kilt, black velvet jacket with silver buttons and a white stock knotted at the neck. A sporran bounced as his thighs moved and there were silver buckles flashing on his shoes. Wow. She moved slightly to one side to watch this vision pass, wishing that Joan was here to witness the thrilling sight and possibly make a politically incorrect remark. He stopped and put his arms round her and kissed her warmly.

'You look wonderful, come on, we haven't got much time,' and she was half carried on his arm into the flower-filled room with its rows of gilt chairs.

'You're wearing a kilt,' she whispered stupidly as if he didn't know after he had checked that he could get good sightlines for Alice's big moment. 'I didn't recognise you.' She didn't like to admit that she had not actually looked at his face.

'Should I worry that you let strangers kiss you?' he said severely. 'I am entitled, you know – my parents are both Scottish and mum is a MacDonald. This is our tartan.' He flirted the hem up a little so she could see the ceremonial dagger in his sock.

'Don't get me wrong,' Anna said sincerely, 'I'm not complaining. I'm blown away. The smartest thing I've ever seen you in before was your best fleece. Promise me that from now on you will wear this whole get-up at least once a week for my private viewing.'

'Hussy.'

The registrar now appeared at an ornate desk placed between two full-length windows on to the gardens and a guitarist and a violinist dressed in black and white and tucked into an alcove began playing *Jattendrai* from Grappelli and Reinhardt's Hot Club of France. It was all very classy. The stars were, of course, five minutes late as etiquette prescribes but when the double doors opened and everyone turned to look, no-one was disappointed. Kimi and Briony had no intention of anyone giving them away (which they considered barbaric) so they had elected to walk down the aisle between the chairs together, hand in hand, with Alice behind. Their dresses were made of two shades of silk, dove grey and cream, but the style of each was different to symbolise that they were being joined by the ceremony but were still their own distinctive selves. Anna had no problem figuring out which one of them had come up with that sophisticated concept.

They stood for a moment at the doorway smiling at each other and then they began their slow walk forward looking from one side to the other waving and smiling and enjoying themselves. The jazz duo played *I've Got You Under My Skin*. It was lovely and Anna sighed with pleasure while Steve twisted and turned to make sure every moment was captured. In contrast to the relaxed grace of the two women Alice was grimly concentrating on a formal slow march - toe, heel - like the changing of the guard, which she must have decided was the correct thing to do. Of course she looked very pretty in her little silver shoes and her blush pink satin dress and gold circlet in her hair but it was all Anna could do not to burst out laughing at the severe expression on her face. As she passed, holding her dandelion-clock head up high and her posy of lily of the valley out stiffly in front of her, they could hear her counting.

After the ceremony while everyone was clapping and hooting, Joan found them and compliments on outfits were exchanged. 'I could have given you a lift,' Anna said, 'if I'd thought.'

In answer Joan jerked one thumb over her shoulder. 'He wanted to come so he drove,' she said. 'I offered to pay for his meal since they don't even know him but they wouldn't let me.' Standing waving a few rows back was a stout, smiling man with a thick crust of curls and an impeccably tailored grey suit. 'Come on, I want to introduce you.'

Alice appeared breathlessly to inform Steve that he was now needed to video her being seated with the other children at their own special table and after a quick hello to Jakub he shot off. They drifted into the lobby and accepted drinks from trays until Jakub made his excuses to leave and find the facilities. Joan dug Anna in the ribs. 'Steve looks so handsome,' she said. 'Not every man can pull off a kilt.'

'I'm thinking of pulling it off myself,' murmured Anna. 'But, on to less salacious matters. Have you heard from him?'

'Yes,' said Joan, 'I think it's all going to work very well. Gets me out of a tight corner.'

'Exactly. Win-win.'

After the food and the speeches, Kimi and Briony had decreed that there would be dancing for everyone and then they would cut the cake and leave for their honeymoon and the others could continue partying into the night. The jazz duo was replaced by a small dance band and a waltz signalled the bride and bride to take the floor. Alice had been rather put out to find that she was not included in this crowd-pleaser but had been promised that Briony would dance with her alone for the second one so she was waiting impatiently on the side-lines tapping her foot. They would go home after the cake-cutting which was well past Alice's bed-time and Anna fervently hoped that other children would not be staying. If Alice kicked off they would just pick her up and leave and not even attempt to reason with her.

But Kimi and Briony had planned a little surprise for her. When the first dance ended, Briony took the microphone, brought the little girl on to the stage and introduced everyone to her, saying that she didn't know how she would have managed without her help. Everyone clapped and cooed. Anna suspected this exorbitant praise would only encourage Alice's nascent narcissism but it was a kind thing to do. When the music started again Briony led Alice out on to the floor and a spotlight followed them around until others joined them. Steve videoed every moment.

But for the next dance Steve ignored Alice's demand to see the videos and took Anna by the hand. It was a smoochy number which her feet could just about deal with and she swayed about with her face in his velvet waistcoat thinking that life could be a great deal worse, all things considered. 'Any chance of a highland fling later?' she asked, digging her chin into his chest and grinning up at him with what she hoped was an alluring leer.

'Actually,' he said, 'I'd like to talk to you about something. Not here. I'll let you know when Alice is asleep if you wouldn't mind coming down to my house.'

His serious tone surprised her so she didn't ask questions but simply agreed.

A couple of hours later Alice was extracted from the festivities wailing and beating her fists against Steve's chest and they went home in separate cars.

As she drove along the dark country roads Anna thought about Kara and wondered how Shell's wedding had gone. A disco was planned and there would be dancing all night as Shell and Maz didn't want to miss a moment and would stay at the hotel leaving for their honeymoon the next day like sensible people, Anna thought. She knew what Steve would want to talk about – it would be only natural that today's event would trigger the desire for a decision to be made about their own wedding and the subsequent move to his house. It wasn't ideal, it wasn't really what she wanted, but she couldn't think of an alternative so how could she object? Blast him, she thought, he knows I've been softened up. She decided not to keep wearing the blue dress for their tryst, if such it was, tonight – it amounted to false advertising. Besides, her feet hurt.

Ellis' room looked much smaller now it was black but he was delighted with it and chattered away about possible epigrams from rock stars and philosophers that could be scrawled across the walls in fluorescent paint of various colours.

She went into her bedroom and got changed. She hung the blue dress up carefully and put the shoes back in their box and pushed it under the bed and then sat down at her dressing table and stared at her reflection. She loved Steve and she didn't want to prevaricate if he did ask her to name a date, or a month at least, as that might seem as though she was hesitant to marry him which she wasn't. It wasn't him that was the problem; it was moving out of her own house and trying to become a mother to a little girl who didn't want her. Nevertheless, as Delia Smith said, 'Love isn't a feeling, it's an unconditional commitment.' Time would probably help, as well. Alice wasn't difficult all the time – there were whole hours when they managed to get on together. She picked up her hairbrush and worked it vigorously to get rid of the fixative spray which she never normally used.

At just past nine o'clock Steve phoned to say that Alice was fast asleep after a nightmare bath and bed-time. 'She was just over-excited and over-tired,' he said, excusing her as always, 'but she had a wonderful day and that's what she'll remember. I'll upload the videos so she can watch them on the laptop first thing tomorrow.' Anna rolled her eyes.

The air outside was fresh but had warmth in it even at this time of the evening and Anna took her time to stroll down to Steve's house. The hedges were now thickened with new leaves and in a neighbour's garden clusters of tall white narcissi glowed in the moonlight. She stopped and looked up at the three-quarter moon as wraiths of cloud coyly obscured and revealed her face as though she was a teasing seductress doing the dance of the seven veils. What was that line from The Mikado? *Oh no, we are not shy, the moon and I, we're very wide awake, the moon and I.* Anna had played

YumYum in a satirical sketch at school and it was her line. She started singing the song from the beginning as she wandered on to see how much she could remember: '*Three little girls who all unwary, come from a ladies' seminary, fresh from our duties tutelary, three little girls from school…*' but when she got to Steve's drive she realised that he had been watching her from the gate and now clapped, laughing and kissing her.

'You have no idea how much I love you, Anna Ames.' They walked in together and she found that he had laid out a bottle of prosecco and two glasses on the coffee table in the living room. So she had been right.

They chatted for a while about the wedding and then he said, 'I've been thinking about something for a few weeks now, Anna, and, to be honest, worrying about it. Of course any decision we make will be made by both of us. I just hope you understand and that you're not too disappointed.'

This was not what she had expected. 'What is it? Tell me what's worrying you?'

Steve sat back and ran his fingers through his hair. 'Well, since Alice and I moved here I've seen a lot of Ellis as you know. It started with the climbing wall at the Leisure Centre and then the climbing club, of course, but he also got into the habit of dropping in here to watch football and we'd chat, you know.'

Anna felt chilled. 'Is that a problem?'

'What? No, of course not. I like it. That's the point, really. Since Harry died he's started, well, confiding in me a bit. Nothing really serious, just stuff about girls he likes, how to behave around them, whether what's happening to his body is normal, you know, the sort of stuff it isn't cool at that age to talk about with mates. It means a lot to me that he feels able to.'

'I didn't know.'

'He's fourteen Anna. It's a difficult age for boys and sensitive ones like Ellis don't form close attachments easily. I value the friendship, too.'

'So what are you saying?'

'I'm worried that if we get married soon and you move in here Ellis will feel that not only has he lost you, so soon after losing his dad, but he will have lost me as well because it wouldn't be the same, would it? It wouldn't be just him and me pretending to watch football but really having a talk about things.'

Anna's heart lifted. 'Go on.'

Steve took her hands. 'Can we stay as we are, Anna? Just until Ellis is older and more self-confident? Would you mind very much?'

She leaned forward and kissed him on the mouth. 'You are a very kind man,' she said, 'and I couldn't be more pleased that Ellis has you to talk to. What's the rush, anyway? '

Upstairs they heard a crash and then Alice's high, piercing voice yelling, 'Steve? *Steve!* I'm *thirsty*!'

'Coming, love,' he called, getting up and going out and Anna sat forward on the couch thanking her lucky stars while she poured another large glass of sparkling wine.

36

The four of them pushed against the wind, stumbling along the gritty ridge path, the women's hair whipping across their faces and bringing tears to their eyes. 'Yes!' Robert kept shouting, 'Yes! Blow your hardest! I love it!' The others laughed, appalled at how it would be to not feel the wind on your face for years, decades. They stopped to get their breath back.

'Look,' Anna said, pointing down the slopes to a pretty tower nestling among trees, 'that's Malvern Priory and that's the road from Upton that we came across on.'

'Cows!' shouted Robert, 'Sheep!' His feet seemed to be on springs as he leaped around. He was wearing what Anna remembered was called a donkey jacket which he must have had when he was locked away and not had much use for since, and Kara had given him a Nordic-style scarf to wind round his neck with a matching beanie and fat, warm gloves.

They walked north away from the iron-age settlement of British Camp and along the bony spine of the Malvern Hills gazing across Herefordshire to the Welsh mountains on their left and looking down on the fields and woods of the Vale of Evesham on their right. It was a glorious day in early spring, sun and wind making the blood in their veins fizz with joy.

They broke into two pairs, Robert and Kara going on ahead talking constantly and sometimes pushing each other like kids, sometimes linking their arms, their slim figures bent towards each other. Sometimes Kara leaned her head on his shoulder for a few steps. Steve and Anna walked behind holding hands. It had worked out perfectly that Robert's day release was on a Saturday and a walk on the hills was just what they needed themselves, especially on such a sparkling day. Kara had planned everything. Much as she would have liked to take Robert shopping and help him buy new, fashionable clothes, she realised that big skies and fresh air were what he craved. Alice was spending the day with Mina and George was helping Ellis put a new bed together. They caught up with the others at the next summit.

'Free at last,' Robert said, grinning to split his face, 'Good God Almighty, free at last!'

Kara shouted over the wind to Anna, 'He's been accepted on the Marine Training course on the Clyde! Isn't that cool?' They patted him and hugged him and asked questions and then, exhausted by the effort of making themselves heard, moved forward, running down the slope to climb the next hill-top. Eventually they'd had enough and turned back letting the wind help drive them back to the car park and Steve's Yeti.

Kara must have researched every pub in the area, Anna thought, because the one they were booked into for lunch was so perfect. It was tucked away in a hamlet in the Golden Valley and there was a quiet eating area warmed by a huge log fire. Robert had no idea what to order until Kara recommended the Beef Wellington which he had never had. 'I think you'll like it,' she said, 'because you get a lovely flaky pastry wrapping the tenderloin. It's like the very best meat pie only better.'

Anna smiled at her, sipping her latte to warm herself. 'You're becoming quite a foodie since you've lived with Rosa,' she said. 'Come round and cook for us any time!'

Kara blushed. 'I'd love to. I can't wait to cook for you, when you're properly out, Dad.' She turned to Anna. 'Do you think that Joan might let me use her kitchen if I promise not to mess it up? The boat's great but it's hard to make something where there's lots of preparation.'

'I think that would be no problem at all,' Anna said. 'So it's all arranged?'

'I know you set it up,' Robert said to Anna, 'and I appreciate it. Joan says I can stay there until I start the course and any time after that when I visit my daughter, here.' Kara dimpled and he dimpled back. Anna was pleased it had worked out as she'd hoped - Joan didn't have to worry about pressure from Jakub to live with him but would still be free to enjoy the friendship so it worked for everyone, except, perhaps, the amorous widower.

After the food was finished, Steve said to Robert, 'Anna told me your grandfather was in the Merchant Navy in World War 2?'

Robert leaned back in his chair. 'Stanley. Yes, he was. He died in the Battle of the North Atlantic – the longest campaign of the war.'

'My grandfather was, too – in the Merchant Navy, I mean, but he was mostly in British coastal waters. Have you been able to find out what happened to Stanley's ship?'

'I've been reading about it,' Robert said. 'Stanley ended up as the navigator on the British carrier *Aldgate*. She'd sailed out of the Caribbean up to Canada to take on a cargo of Canadian maize for Britain because at that time Britain couldn't feed itself – two-thirds of its food was imported - so the Merchant Navy was vital to stop the country starving. But the U-boats had been sinking the merchant ships since the war began, sixty to seventy a month at this point. The Germans wanted to cut off supplies to bring Britain to her knees and they made their first kill only nine hours after Chamberlain declared war. It wasn't even a merchant ship, it was a passenger liner, the *Athenia*, and a hundred and twelve men, women and children were lost – passengers and crew.' Robert paused in disbelief. 'Anyway, *Aldgate* left the St. Lawrence Seaway to join a convoy off Nova Scotia to take the northern sea lane because that was thought to be safer but they had no protection at that time from the Royal Navy because it had been diverted to the Med. Italy had come into the war on Germany's side and the Admiralty thought it was a better use of the Navy but it left the supply ships unprotected.

'The convoy was slow and they had one small gun between them – an obsolete antique salvaged from a scrapped warship. No use against the 'wolf packs' of U-boats roaming about trying to sink them. To make it worse the ship's log the First Mate kept recorded that on that night in November, 1940, there were gale-force winds – it was the worst winter in living memory in the Atlantic.'

'So what happened?' Kara asked quietly.

'Stanley died in a torpedo attack that sunk the ship on the Western Approaches to Britain. My cousins told me that, but I wouldn't have been able to tell you any more until just one week ago,' Robert said, shaking his head in amazement.

'You knew he was awarded the King's Commendation of Brave Conduct,' Anna put in, 'your cousins have got the medal with the silver oak leaf emblem.'

'Dad! Tell us!'

'It's because of you, Anna. What I just found out. I asked you how to look up war-time losses at sea, do you remember? You gave me some places to research and told me that a lot of old newspapers are online now and, of course, I've had plenty of time on my hands to look. I found the crew list from Stanley's ship and where they came from even though I didn't know if they had survived or died, but I started looking for news articles in their home towns – the local papers - from that month when his ship was lost. I'd almost given up when I found an article in a Boston paper from just before Christmas, 1940. I knew there were two Americans in the crew even though the US wasn't in the war then. It was written by a young New Englander, Frank Walker, who had been in the engine room of the ship when she was holed. Look. I printed it out and brought it to show you.' He unfolded a sheet of paper from his back pocket and passed it to Anna who started to read out loud.

'"*Tribute from Local Survivor of U-Boat Attack.*" Er,' she scanned the introductory paragraph, 'this is where it really starts. "*It was bitter cold that night but hot as blazes in the engine room. The sea was up high and we pitched about badly so all we thought of was getting through without the cargo shifting or the boiler busting. We knew we'd got separated from the other ships in the convoy in the storm. Then the whistle blew from the bridge and the Chief shouted that a U-boat was sighted near us and to put on as much steam as she could take.*"'

Anna paused and Steve took the paper from her. '"*The next thing we knew we were knocked off our feet and the noise was terrible and then water started rushing in and we were scrambling for our lives up the companionway. That is the last I remember but my shipmate, Eddie, told me that Aldgate was already listing badly and Captain Owen had given the order to abandon ship and they were trying to get the starboard life-boats away but one of them turned turtle in the wind and dropped the wrong way smashing up against the hull in the high seas so we only had one for the twenty-eight of us. The May-Day klaxon was calling all the time and white distress rockets were shooting up but she was sinking too fast. The others were far away and we found later that they had been hit as well, although not all lost.*

"*Captain Owen and the Second Mate were pushing men down the scrambling nets on to the second boat as they were lowering it. The First Mate was already on it because he was needed to take command. The Master shouted to the Second Mate to get into the boat but he saw I was missing and called for me and when no-one reported seeing me he dashed back down into the engine room as the ship was filling with water and brought me up, half dead and pumping blood, and carried me down and laid me in the boat that was then up to its gunwales and could take no more weight. Then he climbed back up to join the Master. He gave me his place on the boat even though I was just an apprentice and it was touch and go I'd live.*

"Then the Master and the Mate cut us loose. The men on the boat tore their clothes to bind me up to stop the bleeding. We were picked up at dawn by a Sunderland flying boat that had come out from Wales to look for survivors."'

Steve handed the paper to Kara. *'"Eddie told me that as they rowed the lifeboat away from the sinking ship the Master and the Second Mate were standing on the fo'c'sle and the men in the boat heard them wave and shout, 'God speed!' and all the men in the boat yelled the same back to them and then there was a sound like a beast groaning and she went under. From the torpedo hitting to her sinking was eight minutes, they said. I am writing this ..."'* Kara stopped, choking, and Robert gently took the paper from her.

'"I am writing this,"' he went on, *'"to honor the steadfast Master of the Aldgate, Captain William Owen, and to express my whole-hearted and eternal gratitude for the sacrifice of the Second Mate, Mr Stanley Johnson, who gave his life for mine. No better man lived."'*

There was silence round the table.

Steve said, 'There's a memorial now, you know, in Windrush Square in Brixton, to honour black servicemen and women from Africa and the Caribbean who served and died in both World Wars. They reckon over ten thousand volunteered from the Caribbean. It was unveiled in June this year. It's taken the powers that be far too long to commemorate them, but it's there now, and it says on the memorial, *"remembering the forgotten".'*

'Shall we go to London?' Kara asked Robert, 'Would you like to go and we can thank him and lay some roses under it in his memory?'

'Yes,' Robert said, 'let's do that – that would be good.'

They dropped Robert off at the prison and drove quietly home thinking their own thoughts. By the time they had turned on to the M5 Kara was asleep in the back and Anna stared out of the side window and thought about the *Aldgate* and Frank Walker and Stanley Johnson and the men and women and children who had lost their chances of life and happiness in that tragic conflict and it seemed beyond belief that it was only one of so many bitter wars that seem to never stop happening. Some of the lost and the damaged have been remembered, many have not, but because of a young man writing his tribute from an over-flowing heart seventy-six years ago, his saviour's grand-son and great-grand-daughter now knew about his sacrifice on that desperate night and their own sore hearts could cherish his memory.

After they had dropped Kara off at the tow-path gate Steve drove back to their street but paused only a minute to let Anna out at her house as he needed to pick up Alice from her play date. George was in the kitchen banging the bottom of a cake tin. When he saw Anna he said, 'Only a bit burned, perfectly edible. I thought I'd make a Dundee in honour of our trip where we frequently had soggy bottoms but I think I overcompensated and left it in too long.'

Anna dropped her bag on the big chair and put the kettle on. 'You could make custard to moisten it and have it for pud?'

He turned a rosy face with bright eyes over misty specs to her. 'How was your trip out?' Maybe this was where the idea of tiny human woodland creatures had come from, Anna thought, little old men just like her dad. She sat down at the table with her mug and told him about it while he poked at the cake with a spatula and banged some more. But when she re-told the story of Stanley's self-sacrifice he stopped and listened, his head cocked to one side. 'That must have had a powerful effect on Robert and Kara,' he said when she'd finished.

'On all of us, Dad.'

He came over to the table and sat down beside her, polishing his glasses on the frayed hem of his cardigan. 'Yes. I can see that. It's been a bit of a roller-coaster for you, hasn't it, the last few weeks?'

'More so for Kara. But it does make you think, doesn't it? What kind of beings are we? Here's Robert – you couldn't find a gentler or more decent person – who's spent all his adult life so far in jail and Bob who, it seems, had every advantage in life and was evil incarnate.'

'Two Robert Johnsons,' George mused, 'the same age, give or take, born within miles of each other, but what different lives.' His brows knotted. 'I don't think anyone is evil incarnate though, Annie. I can't believe that.'

'Do you know that Kara was trolled, like you? After the horrors she'd been through. Well, not like you, because the insults were different but awful things were posted on Twitter. She doesn't look at any of it, she's got more sense, but what is it with people, Dad? It's so depressing.'

George got up and opened a cupboard door pulling out a tin of custard powder. 'Auden said, "Those to whom evil is done do evil in return," and there's truth in that. You know the outward trappings of Bob's life but who knows what he'd been through?'

'I wish I could think like you but I just can't believe that's true of everyone who does horrible things. I think some people who have no excuse are just selfish and arrogant and believe that they have a right to exploit everyone and everything.'

George got milk from the fridge and poured it into a pan. 'The nature of the beast,' he said. 'That's in the heart of every story whether it's fact and fiction, isn't it? What is our nature? What kind of beasts are we? Perhaps we should remember the Stanleys of this world and forgive the Bobs so that we don't lose heart.'

Anna got up and pulled down a packet of caster sugar, passing it to her father as he blended the powder with some milk. 'Cover our indigestible cake with custard,' she said, 'so we can swallow it?' George snorted.

'Ellis is doing a timeline in chalk round his walls now,' he said as he stirred, 'from the earliest finds of human bones and human artefacts, all the way through history to the present. He's going to keep adding to it as he learns things. He's a born archaeologist. It's a good idea, isn't it?'

'Better than smug epigrams,' Anna said. 'I'll be glad when this poser phase is over.'

'Oh, I forgot.' George took the milk off the heat and scurried over to the dresser. 'This came for us from Len.' It was a card with flowers on the front and 'Happy Birthday' inside which Len had crossed out. It read: *Come to the boat Sunday at 12. Dont bring anyone else.* 'He must have hand delivered it while Ellis and I were putting the bed together. I suppose he means Faye when he says anyone else - there's only our names on the envelope. Do you know what it's about?'

'No, I don't.'

Anna walked upstairs to check on Ellis and found him up the step-ladder with a packet of coloured chalks and his ear-buds in. The new bed with its pristine mattress was in the centre of the room without any bed-clothes on it so she went to the landing cupboard and came back with an armful of linens, pillows and a duvet. This, she thought, making cakes and custard and beds and writing our ancient story on walls was sometimes the best that could be done.

The fine bright weather had kept up for Sunday but the wind had dropped so Anna and George arrived at the boat to find Rosa and Kara scrubbing the outside surfaces. Kara had borrowed one of Rosa's tie-dyed T shirts as protection and was working away at the portholes with Brasso and an old tooth-brush. Rosa was in paint-spattered dungarees and was mopping the prow with soapy water. She was clearly not expecting them.

'Hello,' she said, pausing mid-swipe. 'This is a nice surprise.'

Anna and George glanced quickly at each other and Anna said, 'It's such a lovely day, we've not come to hold you up, we're just out for a stroll.' After all, Len had not specified which Sunday.

'We're ready for a break,' Rosa said, 'let me wash my hands and get some coffee on.'

Kara sat back on her haunches and smiled at Anna. 'Dad was so happy,' she said. 'It was the best day ever. It was nice of you and Steve to take us out. He's lovely.' Anna beamed back at her.

They were just climbing on to the tiny stern-deck preparing to descend to the cabin when Len appeared. He was not smiling but he was wearing the scarlet waistcoat with its embroidered treble clef that Rosa had made for him under what looked like a new coat from the Army and Navy stores. His hair blew around his head instead of being plastered to it indicating a recent shampoo and he was carrying in his meaty hands a small, pink bag.

He arranged himself, legs apart, on the tow-path and stated, 'Rosa.'

'She's making coffee,' Anna said.

'I'll wait here,' Len replied, his face as ruddy as an old brick in the sun, but Rosa had heard his voice and popped her head out of the hatch waving a mug at him. 'I'm waiting here till you're ready to hear what I have to say,' he responded grimly. Rosa's smile vanished but she came up on to the deck and stepped lightly off the boat on to the muddy bank. Kara joined George and Anna in the stern, intrigued at what was going on and ready to defend Rosa if necessary, not that she seemed to need it. Of the two large people facing each other on the tow-path it was Len who seemed the more nervous.

He glanced across at the others. 'You're witnesses,' he said, 'like in church.'

'Ok,' Anna nodded and the others murmured.

He looked at Rosa and took her hand. 'I've got a job in a warehouse - four nights a week.'

'Good,' Rosa said tentatively, 'that's good. Congratulations.'

Len shook his head. 'No, that's not it. You told my sis that you had nothing to offer but it's me that has nothing to offer you, so now I have and I can help you out.'

Rosa shrugged. 'That's nice but there's no need, Len.'

Len's stiffness suddenly left his body and he pumped her hand. 'This is coming out all wrong! I'll just say it. The truth is I was lonely all my life until I met you. I don't care about the stuff you think I care about, I only care about you, about being with you. I love you, Rosa.'

Rosa stood speechlessly holding his hand but then he dropped it and pushed the little pink bag at her. 'Open it. One's for me and one's for you but if you don't want me I'll leave you alone and never bother you.'

The three onlookers on the boat held their breath. Rosa slowly opened the bag and pulled out two tissue packages. Giving the bag back to Len, she opened the first one. It was a long silver chain on which was suspended half of a broken heart. She opened the other which was the same. The two halves fitted together to make one whole heart. They were cheap and sentimental and perfect. Without saying a word Rosa took one and put it round her neck and then kissed Len and put the other round his. George, Anna and Kara burst into applause.

'That was so romantic,' Kara whispered to Anna.

'I know, I didn't think he had it in him,' Anna whispered back, wiping her eyes.

'Well, I think this calls for a celebration,' George said. 'How about we visit the Italian in Selly Oak to toast the happy couple and have a good feed? My treat – I insist.' He climbed off the boat and reached up to shake Len's hand. 'Well done, son, well done. Shall we go on ahead and get a table while the girls get ready?'

'Just a minute!' Kara cried, 'We must have a photo.'

Later, in the din and heat of the restaurant Anna flicked through the pictures on Kara's phone working backwards past the shots of happy faces to that moment on the tow-path where a giant and an elf, storybook enemies of old, stood shaking hands and hugging each other.

Life wouldn't be happy-ever-after for any of them because it never is, but this was, for the moment, as good as it gets and Anna silently added it to her own personal rosary.

Thanks

As always, I want to thank my family and friends and other (much appreciated) readers for your encouragement in writing these stories. My particular thanks for support with *File Under Fathers* go to Catharine Stevens, Terry Quinn, and Bernard Edwards, author of *The Quiet Heroes: British Merchant Seamen at War 1939-1945* which was my principal source of factual background information for one character's fictional story. Thanks also to my sons, John and Dan, who always make me proud of the good men they are and who have the fortitude and kindness to keep on reading.

Geraldine Wall has lived and worked in the UK, the USA and the Cayman Islands and now lives in Birmingham.

Email: geraldine.wall@blueyonder.co.uk

Printed in Poland
by Amazon Fulfillment
Poland Sp. z o.o., Wrocław